SUBMERGED

SUBMERGED

Edited by

S.C. Butler
&
Joshua Palmatier

Zombies Need Brains LLC
www.zombiesneedbrains.com

Interior Design (ebook): April Steenburgh
Interior Design (print): C. Lennox Graphics, LLC
Cover Design by C. Lennox Graphics, LLC
Cover Art "Submerged" by Justin Adams

ZNB Book Collectors #8
All characters and events in this book are fictitious.
All resemblance to persons living or dead is coincidental.

Kickstarter Edition Printing, August 2017
First Printing, September 2017

Print ISBN-10: 1940709121
Print ISBN-13: 978-1940709123

Ebook ISBN-10: 194070913X
Ebook ISBN-13: 978-1940709130

Printed in the U.S.A.

Copyrights

TABLE OF CONTENTS

Introduction by S.C. Butler   1

"Rust in Peace" by Seanan McGuire   2

"Another Dream to Europa" by Michael Robertson   12

"Go With the Flow" by Esther Friesner   23

"The Deep End" by F. Brett Cox   38

"Through Milkweed and Gloom" by Wendy Nikel   49

"Son of Blob" by Marsheila Rockwell & Jeffrey J. Mariotte   58

"Under Pressure" by Jody Lynn Nye   75

"The Last of the Real Good Days" by Bill Kte'pi   87

"The Windlost" by Jenna Rhodes   99

"Tamatori" by Susan Jett   113

"High Sulfur Hot Springs and Camping Park"
by James Van Pelt   126

"The City Under the Sea" by J.C. Koch   136

"Pen's Bracer" by Misty Massey   151

"Fathoms Deep and Fathoms Cold" by A. Merc Rustad   162

"River of Stars" by David Farland   179

"The Byssus Woman" by Sara M. Harvey   196

"The Seven Nights of Squidmas" by Nicky Drayden   203

About the Authors   213

About the Editors   217

Acknowledgments   218

SIGNATURE PAGE

S.C. Butler, editor:

_____

Joshua Palmatier, editor:

_____

Seanan McGuire:

_____

Michael Robertson:

_____

Esther Friesner:

_____

F. Brett Cox:

_____

Wendy Nikel:

_____

Marsheila Rockwell & Jeffrey J. Mariotte:

_____

Jody Lynn Nye:

_____

Bill Kte'pi:

_____

Jenna Rhodes:

_____

Susan Jett:

_____

James Van Pelt:

_____

J.C. Koch:

_____

Misty Massey:

_____

A.Merc Rustad:

_____

David Farland:

_____

Sara M. Harvey:

_____

Nicky Drayden:

_____

Justin Adams, artist:

_____

INTRODUCTION
S.C. BUTLER

From Jonah to Jules Verne, the depths of the oceans have always intrigued us. Whether it's the nightmares we can't see—Kraken, Leviathan, Cthulu—or those we sometimes wish we could—Selkies, Mermen, Flipper—the unfathomable trenches and abyssal plains that lie buried beneath three-quarters of the surface of the earth are home to some of the most celebrated inhabitants of our imaginations. Fantasy and science fiction have explored the depths of space countless times, but those nearer unknowns that lie beneath the keels of our ocean liners and canoes, not so much.

Here, then, are seventeen tales of underwater mystery and adventure, from seventeen masters of horror, fantasy, and science fiction. Cringe in terror as you investigate the Lovecraftian mysteries of the tenth planet. Laugh (and groan) through the seven days of Squidmas. Savor sweet revenge from the bottom of your victim's wineglass. High-five a giant squid, battle nautiluses with underwater magic cowboys, or experience first contact in the frigid depths of Europa. These adventures, and more, await your first plunge into the deep end of...SUBMERGED.

RUST IN PEACE
Seanan McGuire

The body of the ocean liner dominated the ocean floor, a great husk of rot and rust and broken glass. The color of her hull was no longer obvious, obscured by waving strands of opportunistic sea grass and the clinging bodies of the sea stars that had come to hunt and feed. Fish swam through the gashes in the ship's side, bodies undulating with the current, untroubled by the slow approach of our submersible.

I had never seen anything more beautiful in my life.

"There she is, Dave," I whispered, unable to keep the awe and delight—and yes, relief—from my voice. "Just where we knew she'd be. There she *is*."

Dave didn't say anything. He'd always been a careful diver, more aware of his surroundings and the risks that attended them, than anyone else I've ever known. This was the man I would trust to ferry me into Hell, if that particular dive ever became necessary. He'd get me through the rivers of molten iron and lava in one piece.

He'd gotten me here.

"The *Sendale Star*," I breathed. If Dave tended toward silence, I preferred sound. It was never quiet this far below the sea. The water had weight here, and with weight came a soft but constant susurration, like we were moving through the veins of some great, living beast. I often thought that all the people who scoffed at the idea of "Mother Earth" should be sealed in a fragile metal can and dropped to the bottom of the Pacific, where they could hear the heartbeat around them, the sound of current and tide and living sea.

Of course, they'd probably demand we pave the oceans if we did that to them. Someone who doesn't want the planet to be alive certainly doesn't want it to be *bigger* than them.

I put that line of thought brusquely aside. We weren't here for the living, or for the political. We were here for the dead, and for the biggest infusion of cash our bank accounts would ever see.

"Get us in closer," I said. Dave answered with a grunt, steering the submersible slowly toward the great rusting bulk of the *Star*.

Damn, but she was beautiful. Her lines were still as clean as the day she'd been finished, emphasized rather than obscured by the alterations her time in the living sea had made. The absence of paint and polish did nothing to lessen her beauty—if anything, they enhanced it, showing that she was the kind of lady who needed no effort, no artifice, to be beautiful beyond measure.

The hole in her side was a gaping, jagged wound that would never heal. Even after we finished wandering through her bones, learning everything we could, and notified the authorities of her location—earning ourselves a fat finder's fee in the process, naturally—that hole would remain. She had historical value, not nautical. She'd go to a museum or a lab somewhere, and everything about her would be picked apart and analyzed before she was released to someone who would tear her apart for scrap.

She would sail again. Not as she was now, but reincarnated into a hundred new forms, part of the bones of a hundred new ships. If I thought of it that way, this didn't feel as much like a betrayal. More like a rebirth. We were going to raise this fallen lady from her watery grave and set her on the waves when we were done, and while she might not be grateful, she would be gracious to the end. I could see it in the proudness of her prow.

"This is as close as I can get without disturbing the ship," said Dave.

"It's close enough." I gazed longingly out the front window at the money, at the history, at the opportunity spread before us on the sea floor, and I smiled. "We come back tomorrow, ready to dive."

* * *

The *Sendale Star* was a luxury liner. Not in the same class as the *Titanic* or any of those other big, eye-catcher ships: she was smaller, faster, and equally, intensely expensive, even though she was only ever intended to make short hops along the Pacific Coast. She was beautiful, she was exclusive; everything about her screamed "class" to the status-hungry nouveau riche who had come to the golden, hardscrabble shores of California and the Pacific Northwest looking for a fortune and, upon finding it, found no path into the high society they so yearned to enter. To the East Coast, they were new money, little better than the poor.

But the *Star*...oh, the *Star* didn't care about the age of their money, only the color, only the way it glimmered with power and potential when set against the price tag of the world. Better still, the *Star* took her bookings locally, which meant that if one of those fancy Easterners wanted to go for a ride through the most beautiful waters in the world, gazing out on miles of pristine, exploitable coast, they would have to travel to Vancouver or San Francisco, at no small expense, only to risk finding themselves in a third-class cabin, or worse yet, in *steerage*. This was something the West Coast's wealthy could have that their unwilling peers could only dream of.

She sailed the coast four times, down and back, without incident. Maybe the bloom would have been off the rose before too much longer: novelty is in many ways the most expensive thing of all.

On her fifth voyage, a man—Mr. Matthew Alder, of Portland, Oregon—boarded with his family. This was, in and of itself, unremarkable: history would have forgotten him, if not for two things.

The ship was lost, with all hands, somewhere between the ports of Seattle and Vancouver. Despite being an increasingly trafficked stretch of sea, rich with cruise liners and Coast Guard vessels, the *Star*'s location would remain unknown for decades. The cruise line that had owned her and claimed her as their biggest asset went bankrupt in the aftermath of the disaster, and their records were seized by local authorities, not to be seen until an informant responded positively to the idea of bribery. That's the first. The second...

When Mr. Alder's sister came to clean out his home and claim his things, she found a note on the mantle, positioned so anyone who entered the home would be sure to see it. In her brother's hand, it read only, *I am so sorry for what is to follow. Be assured that the damage would have been greater had we not set out to sea.*

To this day, no one has known what he meant...and to this day, treasure hunters have been seeking the fallen *Star*.

Until this day. When we finally found her. Untouched by anything save for the sea that became her grave, waiting for us to come and bring all her sweet and hidden secrets home.

Ours.

* * *

The nice thing about looking for a ship as famous as the *Star* is that it's easy to know where not to look. Just go online and look up all the places people have written about going. Then dig a little deeper, and mine the social media of your competitors for references that tie them to a specific place, a specific time. While Dave had been applying his military research skills to going over maritime records and a hundred years of weather reports, I had been chewing on Facebook and Twitter and Reddit, filtering the noise, cross-referencing the "good spots" that people had been hoarding for years while they hunted for that eventual perfect payday.

Treasure hunters love to share our successes. We're not always so happy to share our failures, reasoning that if we don't tell the competition where we've already been, maybe they'll waste their time going there just like we did. But then Dave found some current maps that had been adjusted with new data, and I confirmed that no one had yet been to our most likely site, in part because it seemed unrealistic for a ship as large as the *Star* to wind up in a region defined by little islands and shallow waters, and now here we were. Here we were, on the cusp of changing our lives forever.

My dive suit was skintight and comfortably confining. Some people find them claustrophobic, but I appreciate the way a well-fitted dive suit clings, keeping me from feeling like I'm alone in the open sea. Dave was fiddling with his equipment, checking the wireless feed that would keep my cameras streaming back to our ship. By presenting an unbroken chain of events from the moment we found the *Star* until we came up with the first of our many, many prizes, we could make it more difficult to challenge our claim to be the ones who had located the *Star*. Always important, especially with a find of this size.

Salvage law stated that, since the *Star* was located within three miles of the United States coastline, everything on her belonged to the government. But the find—the prestige and importance of being the first ones to shout "tag, you're it"—was still a pearl beyond price. We could collect rewards from the surviving relatives of several of the passengers, who had been waiting for decades to know for sure what had happened. We could write our own ticket with burgeoning treasure hunters, who would suddenly see us as the best the sea had to offer.

There is more to wealth than chests of gold and jewels. Although it would have been nice to keep a few of those, if I were being honest.

"All signals strong," said Dave.

"Awesome," I replied. "I have enough air on me for an hour, counting descent and ascent, so I'm going to get moving." Once I was in the water, he would be able to speak to me, thanks to my waterproof ear bud, but I wouldn't be able to respond. There are things technology has not yet managed to achieve.

Dave frowned. "I wish you weren't going down there alone."

"Can't be helped." My girlfriend and I had had a parting of the ways six months ago, when she decided that waiting around for me to make the big score was not as useful as moving to Montana and working for an accounting firm. Prior to that, she had been my spotter on dives. Dave was right: it was dangerous for me to go down alone. But by the time Cynthia had left us, we had been so close to the *Star* that there hadn't been time to find a replacement. We couldn't trust anyone who'd want to join us.

I was good. I was accomplished. I would be fine.

Smiling at Dave, I slipped the mask down over my face and stepped off the deck, plunging into the water. A veil of bubbles accompanied me down, wrapping itself around me like a wedding gown. When it cleared, I turned on my light and began to swim.

Our small submersible was great for scouting runs: with it, we could travel miles along the bottom of the sea, recording and analyzing everything we saw. Sometimes we found things that were of clear scientific interest, and would set those aside until the meat of the dive was done and we were no longer concerned about leading the competition to our location. Most of the time, we saw lots of spectacular fish. That was enough. No one goes into a profession like ours unless they truly love the sea. Although the money, when it happens, doesn't hurt.

Despite the submersible's undeniable ad-vantages, there are some things that have to be done by a single diver, alone against the sea. So I swam, the lights attached to my shoulders illuminating the water, until there she was: the *Star,* resting rusted and lovely on the bottom. I swallowed a sigh of relief and pleasure. Part of me had believed, despite all evidence to the contrary, that the *Star* would be gone, or crawling with rival divers, when we came back. She disappeared once before, after all, without a whisper, without a trace. Even this spot...

We followed the weather reports and we followed the last known headings for her position and we followed the rumors and we followed the gossip, and the fact remains that we got here first—us, out of all the people in the world—because we were willing to take the long shot. We were five hundred miles away from where we should be. There was no logical way the *Star* should be here, so far from where her course would have seen her go down.

But she was there, and she remained there as I swam toward her, my skin trembling within the confines of my suit. She remained there as I approached the gash in her side, my cameras rolling and my floodlights on, showing me her secrets.

The first secret was enough to make my breath catch in my throat— never a good idea when depending on canned air. The hole in her side was clearly what had taken her down to the depths. Historians had always assumed she hit something, since nothing else explained the disappearance of a ship of her size and status. They'd also assumed the hit had been sudden and catastrophic, since otherwise, she would have had the time to radio for help.

This hole was large enough to qualify as catastrophic, but it wasn't a tear in her skin, and it wasn't the punched-in pit of a hard impact. It was a blooming metal flower, the edges curled outward like petals, revealing a tempting glimpse at the secrets hidden within. The *Star* hadn't hit anything.

The *Star* had died of a self-inflicted wound.

The crawling in my skin intensified as I continued forward, careful to turn and give my camera a panoramic view of the scene. The *Star* had been a suicide, whether accidental or intentional. Had this been an act of terrorism? Or had some essential system overloaded and blown, taking her down before anyone could call for help? Neither theory explained how she'd come to rest here, so far from where she should have been, but one mystery had been solved, even if the solution raised a dozen more questions.

I paused at the opening, panning my light around, revealing layers of damaged steel and devastation. My ear piece crackled.

"I don't think you should go in there," said Dave's voice. "It might not be structurally sound."

I couldn't answer him, so I held my hand up to the camera and signed, slowly but firmly, 'No.'

"Come on, Angie. It doesn't look safe. You need to get away from there. Come back, and we can start checking out the interior later."

I didn't bother signing this time. I simply pushed forward, out of the open sea and into the confines of the *Star*'s hold. The walls closed in around me as my light played across them, revealing their details for the first time in a century.

I swam forward, and all around me, the *Star* shone.

* * *

Dave met me at the rail when I returned to the ship, a scowl on his face and a towel in his hands. "When I tell you something isn't safe, you're supposed to listen," he snapped. From him, that was a soliloquy worthy of the stage, and I felt a little bad for inspiring it.

Only a little, though. I held up my bag of small treasures, items taken from the *Star* to prove that we'd been the first to get there, and more, that she really was the vessel we believed her to be. "Sorry," I said. "You know how I love to shop."

Dave managed to hold his scowl for a few more seconds before it melted away, replaced by eager greed and a childlike awe. He was here for the score as much as I was. "Show," he said.

"Aw, did you use up all your pronouns on that little speech?" I asked. I handed him the bag and took the towel. "Give me a minute to dry off, and we can go through the goodies."

Dave nodded, silent again, and walked with the spoils toward the waiting table.

There are historians who hate people like us, and for good reason: we disrupt the sites we discover in the process of proving that we were the ones who discovered them. They hate the ones like me and Dave a little less, because at least we roll cameras and don't make off with millions of dollars in gold and diamonds and other valuables, but they still hate us. I can live with that. I hold secrets and answers in my hands every time I do my job right, and that's worth a little hatred.

Dave was sitting impatiently, his eyes locked on the bag, when I came back, now wearing warm, dry clothes. He looked up at me and grunted. I grinned.

"Good things come to those who wait," I said, and sat down to begin pulling secrets out of my metaphorical treasure chest.

Historians might hate us, but we were always careful: we only removed the pieces that were unlikely to be damaged by the transitions, and we never broke into air-filled rooms if we had any choice in the matter. Because of the way big ships go down, some compartments can stay sealed for decades, even centuries, and those are the ones with the most historical relevance. I've known treasure hunters who traveled with crowbars and small explosives, who didn't care how much they destroyed in their quest for relevance and riches. We never did that.

One by one, I produced a jar of jam, a few pieces of tarnished silverware, a bottle of wine miraculously unbroken by the blast, a small jewelry box, and—most precious of all—a green glass bottle with a wax stopper jammed firmly into its neck, trapping both air and what looked like a hand-written letter inside. The sea had never been able to break through the wax.

"Why write a letter in a bottle if you know your ship is going down?" I asked philo-sophically.

"Maybe somebody who wished they'd been alive in the age of cellphones." Dave produced a knife, beginning to slowly run it around the edge of the wax seal. He was easing it open, giving the bottle time to adjust to every change of pressure and temperature.

I should probably have told him to stop, to save this last mystery for the historians who would eventually take this site from us. I did no such thing. My cameras were good enough to have picked up the bottle when I claimed it from the silt clogging the *Star*'s hall, but not good enough to have seen that it was still airtight and perfectly sealed. We'd hand over the message and the bottle, and if we chose to be the ones who read it first, who could blame us?

While Dave was distracted with the message, I reached for the jewelry box. It was locked, but time and the sea had had their way with the findings: the lock didn't give way. The hinges on the box itself did. I flipped the lip open, peering greedily inside. Some of the pieces I'd seen dredged up from the bottom of the sea had been stunning. Even if the water had been able to rot fabric and thread, people used to sail with all manner of gold and jewels draped around their necks, as if their mere presence on the deck wasn't enough to scream that they had money. This box could hold a king's ransom—

Or it could hold a small brown rock sphere with a long crack down one side, barely revealing the sparkling shapes of the crystals inside. The water had eaten the fabric around it, but left the rock untouched: I had no doubt this thing was as smooth and inexplicable as it had been on the day a rich woman decided a *rock* was a better accessory for an ocean voyage than all the pearls in Portland.

"What the hell?" I picked up the rock, and nearly dropped it as the skin on my fingertips tingled, suddenly warm despite the chill lingering in the air. I tightened my grip, holding the rock up to the light. It sparkled with microscopic motes of shimmering dust. Still nothing impressive enough to have deserved a place of pride in the jewelry box. "This is bizarre."

"This is bad."

I glanced to Dave. He was pale, holding a curled sheet of paper toward me. It was shaking. There wasn't a wind, and it was shaking.

He was shaking.

Wordlessly, I took the papers from his hand with my free one. Our fingertips brushed and that tingle was back, inexplicable and almost hot this time, more intense than it had been before. I set the rock back in its resting place, and I read.

This is my apology to the world. I would that it had been unnecessary: that G_d Almighty, in His wisdom and grace, had not seen fit to place this trial before me. But I am only a man, and I have no influence over the divine, and my time—such as it now is—grows short.

For those who have found this note, if ever it is found: flee this cursed ship. Take nothing, touch nothing, and leave our bones consigned to the deep, where perhaps they can be allowed to rest.

For those whose families set sail with me and mine: I am so very sorry. This was the only way to be sure the foul taint was cleansed from our fair land, and while each death is set upon my shoulders, I assure you that so many more would have died if we had not boarded this vessel. It is as a pebble to a mountain. This may bring you cold comfort, but they did not die in vain.

I glanced up. "What the hell is this?"

"Keep reading," said Dave, staring fixedly at his fingertips.

I kept reading.

The fallen star was found by my son, Matthew Jr., a day before we were to sail. It had come down on the beach, and he tracked its descent with the bright fierceness that is the sole domain of children. Nothing had ever shone so brightly in his eyes as that star.

I am grateful that it was found, that tragedy was hence averted for the city and country I love. But though the thought may be shameful, I wish it had been found by other hands. That this cruel sacrifice should be placed on other shoulders, and not on mine.

My son is already dead.

"What the fuck."

"Keep reading."

The first signs of illness had already appeared, in all of us, when time came to depart for the Star. I left what apologies I could; I bought an extra ticket for my wife's maid, who thought the ocean air would cure what ailed her. She does not think so any longer, but sees the necessity of what I must do. She has family in Portland. She would keep them safe. We will *keep them safe.*

The star, if such it is, carries with it more than a taste of the heavens: it carries sickness such as I have never known sickness such as mortal flesh cannot bear. I have worn gloves to write this missive, and pray only that any who find our grave will find it before they find the star, which cannot be broken, not even with the crushing pistons of our ship's engine, nor melted, nor destroyed in any earthly way. It is cracked, yes, but I believe that to be by some foul design, for the crack is where the evil escapes.

If you have already seen the star, it is too late for you. Please. I beg of you. Choose as I have chosen, and spare the ones you love by sacrificing yourself. No man is worth the world.

I only wish I could pretend we were.

Signed, in regret, your obedient servant, Matthew Alder.

I turned the letter over in my hand, looking for a postscript—some note on the back that would tell me this was all a joke played by a man on a sinking ship, looking for one last "gotcha" before the waves closed over his head.

There wasn't one. But there was a purple teardrop sketched across my knuckles, like the flesh there had been somehow terribly bruised. I dropped the letter. Trying not to let my fingers tremble, I brushed them across the damaged skin.

There was no pain. Only a soft squishing sensation as the meat of my hand collapsed inward, revealing the structured scaffolding of the bones beneath.

I made a sound.

"Yeah," said Dave bleakly. I raised my eyes. He showed me the fingertips of his left hand, where they had brushed against mine. They were the deep, blackened purple of a bruise, and the color was spreading, winding its way up his fingers like water soaking into dampened paper.

"He sank them." He blew the boiler, or maybe he somehow had access to dynamite and smuggled it aboard. Anything to make sure the ship, once it left harbor, didn't return. Anything to sink the star, and the plague it had carried, where no one would ever find it, because it was too contagious, and too terrible, and sometimes quarantine isn't enough. Sometimes quarantine could never be enough.

There was still no pain in my hand. Whatever was eating my flesh was also deadening my nerves. A small blessing, in a day that didn't contain very many.

"Yeah," said Dave.

I looked toward the water. I looked at the box that contained the…meteorite? Asteroid? Weapon from beyond the stars? In the end, it didn't really matter what it was. What mattered was that it had come here, it had fallen *here*, and now we all had to live with the consequences.

"At least we solved one last mystery," I whispered.

"Yeah," said Dave, and we sat together, and waited to remember how to breathe.

* * *

So here we are. If you're listening to this, if you're investigating the latest great maritime disaster—the disappearance of two second-tier treasure hunters and all their very expensive tech—or if you're investigating something that happened a hundred years ago, congratulations: you've found us, and with us, the *Sendale Star*.

Now go away.

We have better than letters in a bottle these days. We have anchored probes and geo-locators, we have cloud storage and the ability to suspend messages until the right conditions are met. Until someone comes too close, more than once, which either means they're looking for us, or that they've already found us. Scavengers always know our own.

Do not dive here. Do not search here. Leave it alone. Leave *us* alone. Be a hero by doing nothing, and save the world one more time from a falling star that we were never meant to catch. This is the only wish we have left, and we're making it on the star that Alder carried to condemn a ship, and we're making it on the *Star*, who tried so hard to hide.

This is Angela Madison and David Cooper, of the *Catch and Release*, signing off and going down with the ship.

End transmission.

ANOTHER DREAM
TO EUROPA
MICHAEL ROBERTSON

Do it for the money—that stopped working after the first couple of weeks. Money's almost as good in saturation diving for the oil rigs.

My butt slides around with the skinsuit's weird oily smoothness as I rock back and forth on the wooden bench.

Do it so they won't think you're scared.

That's the one I'd been relying on. And it had worked for a good long while, shame giving me enough impulse to rise up off the bench, zip the skinsuit up, and push out that door.

Today the shame doesn't bother me. Let them think I'm a coward. Maybe I am. Let them get linked up to the dive remote, see how brave they are. Let them stare down the borehole. Let them feel the alien ice crowding on all sides while the winch hums them lower, lower, lower...

I slap myself on both cheeks. Why suffer through it twice?

Do it for the mission? I try that on for size. Thinking of myself as the anchor leg of the relay. Hundreds of women and men spent decades on this. Guiding the payload to Europa. Shepherding the robots as they chewed a base below the surface. All to get the diving mech in place, above a borehole down to that new ocean.

There's a gentle knock on the door.

"Monsieur Gregory?"

I squeeze my eyes shut. I could quit. They can't make me get in the tank and uplink to the mech.

Only, I gave my word. Signed on the line. Told them I was their man.

Do it to keep my word.

I stand up. The tile floor feels dry and warm through the skinsuit.

"Coming," I say, and step out of the door.

Laurent steps back and smiles at me. "Apologies, I do not mean to rush," he says, and turns to go fiddle with his equipment.

Melanie gives me a small smile, only half-turning from the displays she's watching.

The tank is a long, low tub with a curved lid. Fluorescent light washes a gleam over the stainless steel rim and refracts through the gel inside, deep blue like the liquid they used to use in diaper commercials to show how absorbent the diaper was.

I've avoided learning how any of it works. Like how Vikings didn't like knowing how to swim. If I knew too much about how I could lie down here and then wake up in a mech on Europa, I'd spend the whole time wondering about what-ifs. What-ifs, and, of course, how-comes, like how come it feels exactly like I'm there even when I know I'm here?

They shave my head clean, slather it with that cold jelly, and fit the interface package over it like a hood. I take the breather mouthpiece in my mouth and bite down, quirk my cheeks around until it's sitting just right.

My heart speeds up when they seal the envelope around my head, locking the breather and the interface package in place. It must look like a bad fake space helmet from a fifties comic, but I don't care so long as it keeps me breathing while I float in my gelatinous coffin.

I shiver at that thought. Jeez. No need to make things even worse.

"Uplink is green," Melanie says. "You may lie down."

Laurent's watching my vitals. Maybe that's why he adds, "When you are ready."

Melanie glances at him, then back to her displays.

The skinsuit keeps everything feeling warm and dry, so sinking into the gel is like being cradled in a nest of pillows.

Laurent's blue face leans over above me. He waves his blue hand, then grasps the lid and swings it down. And then it's dark.

Dreaming is what it's most like. Once they close that lid I start to doze. A comfortable absence settles on my mind. I don't think about anything in particular.

Like always, once I'm in, I'm cool. Jitters before? Sometimes. Sometimes even regrets after. Or nightmares. One time I was leading this tour around a shipwreck—I guess every diver works that patch of tropical tourist bullshit. So there I was in Bali taking sunburned old Midwesterners down to the good old shipwreck *Liberty*, pointing out the swirling jackfish and the anemones and keeping my eyes on all their lines to make sure they didn't suffocate themselves trying to get good pictures, and this bumphead parrotfish shoots out from behind one of the rusted out sections of the hull, just coming right for my face. Who knows why. Big fish. I don't react in the moment; they're not dangerous fish, mostly. And just when it gets close to me, it turns, and I get this momentary flash of its eyeball and that weird, tall face, regarding me, snub beak mouth half open.

That was it. The fish swam off. I kept leading the tour. Surfaced, collected my tips.

But that bumphead followed me into my dreams. Can't say why. I've had sharks give me a once over. Bull shark once even. But that bumphead, well. Even now, more years later than I care to tell you, the odd night I'll wake up with a flash of that face like a cinder block and that eye peeking out.

Just like waking up: I'm in the white chamber on Europa. Smooth rounded walls like a drained pool, only here they extend over the ceiling in a shallow dome. The black transmission node looks like a turkey popup timer stuck in the ceiling.

I go through the checks: power, uplink, sensors, motors.

Everything checks out. I signal the all clear, like giving a thumbs up in my mind.

Beneath me the hatch starts to slide. A sliver of black appears and grows into a yawning hole underneath me.

The descent begins.

Miraculous. Astonishing. Whatever. I know the engineers blew through a ton of Mountain Dew getting the builder bots to bore the hole. There's a humming in my bones. It's like a waterslide, only it takes twenty minutes.

Like every time, submersion is a surprise. Water flows over the mech. Sensors recalibrate, sonar pings. Here at the top of Europa's ocean it's like staring down into a flooded cathedral, the sense of a vast roof closing you in.

The armature clunks when it releases the mech and then I'm sinking.

My mission today: scrape some samples from the designated section of the shelf, same as every other dive.

Laurent and Melanie don't brief me on how the mission is faring compared to what they hoped and I don't pry into it. Not what I'm paid to think about. But this place is pretty empty.

The ice ceiling extends in every direction, knurled like the underside of pack ice.

It fades as I descend, then I'm in that dark clear place where I know I'm falling, because the instruments are clear on that, but I couldn't show you one piece of evidence to prove it. Oh, I know the shelf's down there, it just takes a while to drop nineteen kilometers.

And that's nothing. Laurent told me parts of Europa's ocean go down to ninety or so kilometers. They chose this site for its shallow shelf, and they're still mapping it out, expecting to find an edge.

The floor starts to ghost in. The mech sees it as brown. Who knows what color it really is.

For fourteen dives, that's been Europa. A white ceiling, then a couple of hours of falling down to a brown floor, and me dutifully extending the collector scraper and gathering smears of mud.

I swipe a sample into one of the specimen trays. Smoky plumes of mud swirl in the currents I'm creating.

Something moves out there.

I go still.

I could review the mech recording to confirm what I think I saw. But I don't like the idea of taking my attention off my surroundings.

Then I see it again.

It's moving along the bottom, about a hundred meters away. Slithering and crawling all mixed together. It humps up and then swings pairs of limbs and flattens out.

On the front of its body there's a dome. Like half of a big melon.

I'm not feeling anything much as I watch this thing, not at first. I've seen a lot of creepy crawlies back on earth.

It'll be a while before Laurent and Melissa even know what I'm seeing, much less have a chance to give me any instructions. But we did cover this: I'm to leave living things alone.

So I stay still.

But this guy is walk-sliding in my direction.

As it comes closer, I make out more details. There's a loose scarf of tissue hanging under its melon. Like a humpback whale's throat, for instance. Something that can get big, for swallow-ing.

I don't relish that thought, but if it ate this mech, I'd just wake up in the pod back home, whereas swallowing this piece of hardware would probably kill the creature. Sharp edges. Plutonium core.

So I make a small, slow motion. Turn the mech just a bit. Trying to announce my pre-sence.

The creature freezes. Half a second later, it goes hazy, like the mech's sensors can't exactly see it any more.

Then it leaps up. It's blurry now. It spreads its limbs and a membrane stretches between them. The combination—the way its outline wavers and shimmers, and the way it jumped up, and the way its membrane stretches between the curve of its limbs—turns it from a fascinating natural object to a nightmare of the depths.

I get a twisting jolt of pain in my head.

Though I tried to avoid learning how any of this stuff worked, the training did include some key points. One thing that's...problematic...is when my brain gets startled and wants to execute some basic, primitive protective behavior. That jolt of pain is what they said that would feel like. My consciousness trying to get out of Dodge.

After hanging there above me for a few seconds, the creature's membranes ripple and it swims away from me.

I stay still. The creature's escape has roiled curtains of mud up from the seafloor. I wait for them to settle. Partly trying to calm my mind, partly because I'm trying to analyze what happened. And partly because I'm scared stiff.

On dozens of late-night boats, drinking beer and putting away equipment, I've bragged: I don't get scared on dives. That's a tourist thing. I've got a handful of stories I tell to impress folks about the most embarrassing thing a scared tourist has done on one of my dives. Got a lot of laughs over the years with the story of the guy who crapped himself when a rock he was examining turned out to be an octopus.

The mud has settled. Protocol is clear: get back to the base station and upload. The video and all the other readings have already been transmitted, but for redundancy's sake the mech needs to get there with its onboard recordings, too.

I check that all the sample containers are shut, and all the scrapers and other probes properly stowed. Running through the routines loosens me up. Helps the fear subside. I lift off of the bottom. A cloud of silty brown spreads out below me.

The sensor package shows the armature hanging up there as a green reticle.

I glance down, worrying that creature could have lingered, could be following.

Since I'm looking down, when the mech slows, I don't immediately know why. Then I look up and I see, and I get that tingly itchy shock that tells me my mind just tried to wake up.

I've run into a net. Some kind of fiber woven into a network of squares, and it's stretched above me, holding me down.

I flip over and burst downward, then glance behind. If I can see the extent of the net I can sprint out from under it—

I hit another net. The mech shakes. I'm surrounded by net, all around, closing at a point off to one side. Shocks of pain jolt my head in waves.

A shape appears, like one of those Star Trek ships when they turn off the cloaking device.

The sensor package paints this thing a powdery white, shading over to blue in places. Insectile body segments form a meaty chain, and from each segment limbs stick out. Toward the bottom they flatten out like spatulas, but up toward the top they get longer, finer, like a spider's legs.

It's using these long limbs to hold the net.

Six of these things float around me, watching me struggle. Some hold the net.

They've got similar membranes stretched between their limbs as the creature I ran into earlier, and they use these to stay in place, so it's like being surrounded by drapes swaying in a light breeze. The net handlers, when they need to maneuver, use their paddle-limbs as well, flicking their tails in a way that reminds me of playful dolphins.

I stop trying to get out.

I allow myself to watch, to record their graceful movements.

They cinch the net around me until I'm bound up tight.

Something birdlike about their heads. As if they were glancing at each other in quick slashes of motion.

One lets a little slack into the net, reaches in, grasps something on the head of the mech, and twists. The scene jerks.

Red indicators flash.

That thing has snapped off the antenna. Comms back to the surface are gone.

It lets the antenna go. Just a spiraling bar of priceless composite disappearing down to the bottom.

Then they start talking to each other.

Not in English, obviously. The sounds they're making register as spiky waves on the mech's display. They're gesturing like my family talking politics at Thanksgiving.

One of them, a big, bulky one like a linebacker, keeps pointing at me.

Another one, longer, keeps swaying side to side. I think of him as Scar from the Lion King, with a sinuous way of moving. I bet whatever he's saying, it's convincing.

The way they talk blends together from speaker to speaker. I guess it would have to be that way, the way water carries sound. Would every conversation be like taking your part in one of those songs, those rounds kids sing at school pageants?

They reach a decision.

I don't understand how, but they unfasten the net almost instantly.

The linebacker grabs the mech in a pair of its segmented arms. Examines me.

Then lets me go.

They fade to shadows and are gone. I don't mean they swim away. They become transparent.

Meaning, I know they're still there.

My instinct tells me to play dead. I don't know if that's the right thing to do. But my instinct is the only one with any suggestions, so I do what it says. Floating down, down, down through the water.

The mech's going through its fault-checking routines and its auto-repair procedures. This thing was built with a bunch of redundancies and backups, just like you'd expect for something that cost tens of billions of euros to get in place.

A yellow warning indicator flashes.

The backup comms link could fire off a data burst to the base station link. I'm about to get out of range. And that presents a quandary.

The seconds are counting down.

I could do what's called an emergency exit, meaning I exit the mech and commence the process of returning to Earth. Wake up from the dream. Only, if I did that, the mech would be difficult or impossible to recover. Without the ability to see the base station, it would not be able to autopilot back. Perhaps, with time, it could repair or reroute systems, or search methodically. The plutonium battery lasts a long time.

Probably it would be correct procedure to exit. But something hangs on my mind. The mech's got the recording of the conversation, and that kind of data would make the scientists go nuts.

Never in my life, I tell myself, have I bailed on a dive. But that's not strengthening my resolve.

I think of Melanie and Laurent. Think of them seeing me wake up, or else receiving a set of data on alien communication.

It surprises me to feel generosity welling up. Well, why the fuck not? I'll wake up anyway. Probably with a blank in my memory where these events should be.

I transmit the recording.

Then I stay very still. The mech descends through black, alien water.

* * *

The way those creatures disappeared, their camouflage, means they could be around right now, watching, waiting. Confirming the mech is dead.

Or they could be long gone, back to wherever they live, to discuss the encounter in more detail.

The mech can run for years. That's not the problem.

I can't stay down here for years. It's been a little less than an hour. The shocking twinges of anxiety are coming faster.

After I heroically sent the recordings, during my descent, it dawned on me that I might have made a mistake.

I have no way to leave the mech now. I'm trapped.

It's getting harder to ignore thoughts like: Who am I, now, given that they've probably woken me up already back in Brussels?

A fragment of a dream?

Another twinge sets the mech quivering. Little curls of fine silt twist up into the water, floating on gentle currents.

I've learned a lot today. I thought I never got scared on dives. Turned out, I'd just never been on a dive scary enough. Every set of shakes that jolts the mech pushes me toward an idea. I have to move. I have to get back to the base.

But those things could be there. What if they see me?

That's a diverting question. The first time, they tore off the antenna and let me go. Why the antenna? I don't know. If they did track my fall, and if they are watching, what would it reveal if I moved?

They must be making assumptions. Based on their frame of reference. What would it do to one of them, tearing off one of the antennae?

I have no idea. All the theorists and researchers who might be able to answer a question like that are back in Brussels, excitedly texting each other to come in, to look at this new data they just received. I'm just the diver.

Another jolt.

The mech's sensor package lets me see 360 degrees, all the way around, but I still have to focus my attention, so, even though the mech's head doesn't move, I am very much peering around as I draw the mech's arms up and into the chest. I roll onto my front and push the torso up.

The layer of soft silt is about two inches; beneath that is a thicker mud.

My movement tosses up particles, like swatting a carpet under bright sunlight.

I try to prevent panic from making my motions wild.

With a slow, steady kick of the mech's tail, I raise the front part out from the bottom. I bring the propellers up slowly. Begin to ascend. Look up.

The base should be a green reticle, far up there, a pinhole in the cathedral ceiling.

Scanning, left, right, up, down. No reticle. I couldn't have drifted far enough to be out of sight of the hole.

I accelerate. Ascending, I run the mech's diagnostic program.

The self-repair has been attempting to reconfigure to restore long-range antenna functions. In the midst of such repairs, the entire suite of nav functions is offline.

And could I have found out about this while I was lying on the seafloor? Absolutely. I guess that fearlessness I was so proud of also kept me from learning how to deal with the effects of being afraid. Like its impact on decision making.

Nothing for it now. I keep the props spinning and focus on getting to the ceiling. Maybe the creatures stay near the seafloor.

Minutes pass, with me staring up, waiting for the vaulted dome of ice to ghost in from the darkness up there.

Something flickers off to one side. I snap my attention to it.

One of the creatures becomes visible there, maybe twenty feet away. No, closer. Ten feet. But it's smaller than the others.

It sings a chirruping line of sounds at me. Its antennae lean together, then twitch out. The gesture looks inquisitive, like it's raising its eyebrows.

The sample collectors are flat, like butter knives. But butter knives are still knives. I extend them all.

No way I'm letting this one tell its friends about me. I don't know what they'll do, but I need to get out of here.

The creature just draws its arms back, all down its long, segmented body. Like a spider would, encountering something unexpected.

Two more shapes flicker, and then there are three creatures. All smaller than the ones I ran into earlier.

So now I'm outnumbered. The only hope is to surprise them, act fast, get one, then maybe sprint up while the other two are confused.

I hesitate. The briefings didn't go into detail about what to do if one ran into sentient life. Just get away, was the guidance. Bring back the data.

They wouldn't want me attacking one of the things, though. I'm pretty sure of that.

But I remember lying down there, waiting, unsure what was floating there in the dark. I flex out the sample collectors into claws. Or the nearest I can make them.

One of the creatures, the one on the left, springs jagged mandibles open at the top of its uppermost segment and jets toward me.

The one in the center calmly, but quickly, jets over to block its friend.

They exchange urgent sounds, the water humming and hissing with their conversation.

The center one has that habit of twitching its antennae in toward each other, then out again. So I start thinking of him as Twitchy.

Twitchy makes some sounds at me, then stops. Its friend drifts back, still focused on me, but not making any moves.

Twitchy holds out one of its limbs, a long one with three finer extensions. The same manipulators the ones with the net had used to draw their net closed and to tear out the antenna.

It extends its spiny fingers in a claw, then relaxes and curls them into a fist.

It repeats the gesture.

It waits. Twitch of antennae.

The friend who tried to rush me has plump segments and shorter limbs, so I think of him as Michelin. Michelin screeches out a string of sounds, then rushes me again.

All this time the third one has been silent and still. But it moves now, reaching out to grab hold of a couple of Michelin's arms. It turns Michelin and holds him.

Twitchy points at my two hands, slowly, and then makes the fist closing gesture.

I withdraw the sample collectors into the mech's hands.

Twitchy chirps some sounds, then points at the mech, and points up. Antennae twitch.

I point to myself, the mech's chest, then point up.

Twitchy turns to address its friends, then turns back to me, points at me, then at itself, and then, with two fingers, up.

It jets upward.

I follow.

As we swim up I keep glancing back. Michelin floats rigid, gripped by the third creature's long spine-like fingers.

The ceiling shades into being above, first like a silk scarf floating on the breeze, then more solidly. Curvaceous swells of ice curl like inverted sand dunes.

Twitchy brings me to the borehole. I grab hold of the armature.

The creature just floats there. Holding the armature releases some of the tension I've been feeling.

Twitchy is watching me.

I hold one of the mech's hands up above my head, extend two sample collectors, spread them apart, then snap them together.

Twitchy starts back, then relaxes. It reaches out two of its spine arms, one on either side, and then extends its manipulator ends out wide, then slowly closes them.

I can't say anything to it. I don't even really know what we just said. I climb into the armature, lock in, and begin the ascent.

The ice walls flow by, smooth and cylindrical, the only disturbance the vibration of sliding along the rails.

The armature stops and I'm afraid there's been a problem until the hatch slides shut beneath me.

I'm here.

I begin the post-dive checks.

I hesitate, worrying about what'll happen to me if I try to return and they've already woken "me" up and taken me out of the tank. Will I dissolve in the tank's blue gel? Will I be held in some buffer in a computer?

I don't know. I've avoided learning how any of it works.

At least they'll get the vid of me and Twitchy saluting each other. Something for the sci-entists to chew on. Maybe I'll get an honorable mention in the Nobel Prize speech.

Post-dive checks are through.

I hesitate again. Then, like flipping a switch in my mind, I leave.

GO WITH THE FLOW

ESTHER FRIESNER

"Honey, is something wrong?" Brent Crawn drew back from the lingering kiss he'd bestowed upon his fiancée, Cecilia. "Your mind's elsewhere; I can tell. Is that the welcome I deserve when I've been away so long? Don't tell me you've found someone else!"

He couldn't help chuckling *sotto voce* at that. How could "someone else" hope to compete with what *he* brought to the table...and the bed? From one to ten on the Handsome scale, Brent ranked as Wowee and Then Some in the opinion of a *lot* of discerning ladies. Meanwhile, Cecilia's appearance and mien both could be filed under Oh, Is That You? I Thought You Were a Desk. (It wasn't a completely accurate assessment: unlike Cecilia, most desks fit in *somewhere*.) The only reason she didn't have a cat was because she was so mousey, according to some of her more shrewish acquaintances.

Cecilia shook her head meekly. "Nothing's the matter, dear. It's just that—"

"Great!" Brent slipped his arm around her waist and steered her into the living room. "I need a drink. How'd you like to bring me a bourbon, rocks?" Without waiting for her to reply, he gave her an encouraging swat on the rump and slouched gracefully into his favorite chair, the lambskin upholstery bleating softly as he settled down.

She brought his drink and took her usual place, perched on the ottoman at his feet. Although the posh penthouse and everything in it belonged to her, she couldn't help looking like a barely tolerated visitor in her own home. Brent emptied his glass and rattled the ice cubes at her, the silent command for seconds, chop-chop. Only a man of his charisma could make such an imperious gesture seem like a priceless favor. Cecilia leaped up to demon-strate her gratitude. However, though she was swiftly back with his refill, she balked at handing it over. Instead she held it just out of reach as she rocked nervously from foot to foot beside his chair.

"Is something wrong?" he asked. This question was not perfunctory since it concerned bourbon; *his* bourbon.

"Dearest, do you—do you recall the girl I sponsored up until last May?"

"Of course." He frowned impatiently. "*I* was stuck telling her she'd washed out of the Crawn Institute voice studies program. I had such high hopes when she first enrolled! That's why I chose *you* to be her patron. It was *very* hard on me when I realized she was a dead end. Why are you bringing up something so upsetting?"

"I—no—I—"

"Listen, I know we had that girl—Rita-something—we had her come here a lot while she was one of my students. I know you took a real liking to her. Do you want to see her again? Forget it. It'd give her the wrong idea, make her think the Institute's giving her a second shot."

"No, no, it's not that I want to reconnect with her; it's just—" Cecilia nibbled her lower lip, unable to go on. Her hand trembled enough to set the ice cubes tinkling.

Brent shook his head. "Cecilia, I am *tired*. Why are you working my last nerve? Am I being punished for leaving you alone for a month? It wasn't a pleasure trip. I was scouting new talent for the Institute. I hear what some of your so-called friends say: 'Oh, that Brent, Cecilia's bought-and-paid-for pet! He wouldn't look at her twice if she was poor.'" He glanced up. "Is that what this is about? Have they convinced *you*? Fine. Feel free to break our engagement. I can move out tonight. Never mind that I'm about to drop; I'll do what makes you happy."

"No! Please don't talk like that! I love you!" Tears smeared Cecilia's face. The rattling of the ice cubes went from *allegro* to *prestissimo*. "It's only—oh, I don't want to say it!"

"Your choice." He sighed and let his body slump pathetically. "But if you're going to make me play Twenty Questions, at least have the courtesy to let me do it drunk." He held out one limp hand for the glass.

She passed him his drink. The ice had diluted the bourbon to an abominable degree, but before he could demand a replacement, Cecilia took a deep breath and blurted: "Rita came by to see me a week after you left and she said you slept with her and with some of the other girls and you expelled them from the Institute when you broke up with them and you paid them off with enough to go to a trade school if they kept their mouths shut and she could use the money, especially now, but she said I was always so good to her that she'd rather give me the truth than have you give her the cash and—and—and—" She paused to get her second wind. "—and she's pregnant and it's yours."

Watered-down bourbon made for a bad drink but an excellent spit-take.

The scene that ensued was epic in scope. Brent had to unleash *all* his past methods for convincing Cecilia that being a puppet was much better than becoming a Real Girl. He tried jollying her out of believing Rita's revelations—mean girls and their mean pranks! Surely Cecilia was smart enough to see that she was being played? He tried slut-shaming—so many girls out there who were no better than unpaid whores! Surely Cecilia was smart enough to see that this false accusation of paternity was the little bitch's get-rich gambit? He appealed to her sense of dedication to the future of Art. Surely Cecilia was smart enough to see that Rita was a vengeful harpy? If she couldn't become an opera star, no one would! She'd destroy the school with this fake scandal.

When these came a cropper, he tried acting hurt. Why was she treating him so shabbily? Didn't she trust him? How could she let an outrageous lie destroy a love so true, so pure, so immortal?

No dice.

Then he just tried bullying and yelling.

For once, Cecilia held her ground. She cringed and shivered and sobbed, but she did not concede. It was an exhausting battle for them both, one that Brent soon recognized as a possible Pyrrhic victory. When he'd set out on his trip—seeking starry-eyed wannabe singers who just happened to be beautiful, pliant young women—his fond parting words included making Cecilia swear she'd pay a visit to her lawyer. He sought no bequest for himself while he was merely her fiancé—that would be too blatant. Ah, but a hefty endowment for the Crawn Institute—? So charitable, so altruistic! (So discreetly to be used at the eponymous Founder's discretion.) He didn't want to risk alienating her if she hadn't finalized that arrangement yet.

First things first.

"Baby, please stop crying." He took her into his arms with premeditated tenderness. "Why don't we talk this out later? I've got a *much* better idea of how we should spend tonight."

Cecilia crumpled into a damp little ball of acquiescence. She hated conflict as much as she loved her fiancé. Brent proceeded to pull out all the stops on the mighty Wurlitzer of Romance: he cooked her a gourmet dinner with lots and *lots* of wine. He presented all the trinkets he'd bought for her while on the road. (No need to mention that he'd had some shopping help from this or that young woman who'd warmed the solitary traveler's bed.) He devastated the bouquet of red roses from the coffee table and cast their blooms over the sheets before making intense, expert love to her. Afterwards, he ran her a scented bubble bath and strewed the remaining petals atop the foam.

As he helped her out of her robe, he kissed her neck and said, "Now wasn't that nicer than fighting?"

"Nice mucher," she said in fluent Merlot. A tipsy giggle punctuated her wobbly approach to the luxuriously deep, freestanding black marble tub.

"You take a nice, long soak, darling," he said. "Call me when you're ready to come out. I'll have some brandy waiting for us. Then you can tell me the *good* things you've done since I've been gone. You know, wedding plans?" He raised one eyebrow in a roguish manner. "Honeymoon details? A little chat with your lawyer about the Institute bequest?"

"Of course, dear," she cooed. "I saw him the day after you went away. I know that's been on your mind."

"I don't suppose you got around to mentioning the pre-nup while you were there?" he asked, giving her a steadying hand as she swung one leg over the bath's massive rim. "Maybe tell them you'd like it to be a bit less ...harsh?"

"I didn't think of it." She teetered just a bit as she prepared to lift her other foot into the tub. "But I'll do that next time, when I set up the trust for Rita's baby. You know, only if the paternity test proves he's—"

"*WHAT*?!" Brent's shock was explosive. He threw his arms wide, in a dramatic gesture many a soap-opera hero might mimic for the climactic Revelation of the Week.

What happened next was even more theatric. Brent's sudden movement yanked away Cecilia's only means of balance. She plummeted backwards into the tub, hitting the base of her head sharply on the rim as she fell. Horrified, Brent reacted without thinking, diving forward to save her.

In the instant before he could plunge his hands beneath the water, he *did* think. They were not generous thoughts. No, they were quiet, calculating, deathly *practical* ones. He was still thinking them as he calmly strolled into the living room, there to pour himself a fresh drink and wait however long would sound plausible before calling 911. *I thought she was enjoying her bath. I had no idea. By the time I checked on her, she was— was—*

Add one choked sob plus one heartrending breakdown into convincing, manly grief, and *scene*!

Trying to save her would've been useless anyway, he told his half-starved conscience. *She was probably dead as soon as she hit her head.* The thread of bubbles that had broken the surface of the scented water as he left gave him the lie, but those had been lost among the rose petals.

* * *

"Roses? I love roses. Can I have some?"

Cecilia blinked. Her head felt funny, heavier than usual. The same could be said for her entire body. She wondered who'd spoken. "I—I guess so?"

"Thanks!" The wavering image of a fresh-faced girl solidified before her, like a gradually resolving reflection on a pebble-troubled pool. The apparition's slim fingers reached up to scoop a handful of crimson petals from somewhere above her head. She buried her face in them and sniffed appreciatively. "Mmm, delicious," she said with a happy sigh. "Did he give them to you?"

"He...who—?" Cecilia was woozy. Some-where behind the wall of fog now occupying her brain was a small, urgent voice trying to impart a vital message, but for the life of her, she couldn't figure out what it was.

"You know, the man who just killed you. Although if you want to get technical, I guess he's only the man who let you die. Either way, you're dead. Pleased to meet you; I'm Lara. How're you doing? Aside from being dead, that is."

When something dawned on a cartoon character, the moment called for a light bulb flashing on above his head. Cecilia's Thunderbolt Moment merited the Paris Opera House chandelier. Memories of her last minutes of life swarmed over her, including one of supreme bitterness.

"He could have saved me." Her whole body sagged. "Why didn't he even *try*?"

"Aw, don't cry," Lara said, drifting closer and offering the comfort of a gentle hug. "No one's going to notice a few more droplets. Not down here." Cecilia jerked her head up, perplexity writ large in her expression. "Down here," Lara repeated. "Under the water. In your bathtub. With your corpse." She gave her an amiable grin. "Don't mind the corpse part: they'll be taking it away soon. Once it's out of your element, you'll be free as a fluke!"

Cecilia looked all around, bewildered. "If we're in my bathtub, with my—with my—*me*, how can the three of us *fit*?"

Lara dismissed the matter with a wave of her hand. "If myths and the spirits of dead things took up actual space, you wouldn't be able to brush your teeth without jamming your elbow into a harpy and we'd all be up to our nostrils in classroom hamsters."

"I'm going to guess you're a myth."

"Well, I'm no dead hamster, sister! I'm a naiad, a water nymph."

"I thought that beings like you only lived in streams and rivers," Cecilia said, finally finding a use for her Classical education. "What are you doing in my bathtub?"

"I came for you. It's my job. I'm also a psychopomp. That means I—"

"You guide the souls of the dead to the next world. I thought that was Mercury's line of work."

Lara was taken aback. "That's...*right*. How did you know? I mean, Mercury and I *are* a couple, so it's always nice to hear someone giving him credit, but—"

"You and Mercury?"

"Oh, yes." Lara bobbed her head with enthusiasm. "I tattled to Juno about Jupiter playing Here Comes the Lightning with one of my sister nymphs, so he told Mercury to take me to the Underworld, except he— Mercury, not Jupiter—fell in love with me and now I handle all the psychopomping when the client's underwater because my sweet Merkypoo absolutely *hates* getting those adorable little ankle-wings of his wet." The naiad giggled behind a veiling hand. "You're the first of my Special Cases to know what a psychopomp is. The others all thought it meant I was insane and being snooty about it."

"Latin major," Cecilia explained. "Vassar."

"My condolen—oh hey, they're here!" The naiad was jubilant, for the bath water began to swirl violently, sending the two of them spinning wildly around the tub. When things settled down again, Lara explained: "That was the Coroner's crew removing your body. Nifty ride, right?"

A dizzied Cecilia held her head and asked, "What happened to the E.M.T.s? What about the police? Didn't *anyone* try to bring me back?"

"They've all come and gone. Time moves differently when you stand between mortality and Next. For some it stretches out, others it scrunches in, kind of like a cosmic accordion. It'll all go back to normal once you allow me to escort you over the River Styx or across the spiritual borderland of your choice."

Like every human being even mildly susceptible to catching a bad case of Philosophy, Cecilia had often thought about death and what might come thereafter. None of her musings ever included words like "allow" and "choice." When she queried Lara about this, the reply was enlightening in the extreme:

"Of *course* it's up to you! You can go Over any time you like, to whichever afterlife you prefer. Just remember, you'll have to stay put and abide by the local rules once you get there. Eternity's a strictly no backsies deal, so take your time. Any questions?"

It was like asking "Who wants chocolate?" in a crowded anywhere. Cecilia's spate of inquiry as to the Spiritual "Now What?" yielded some startling information tidbits from her naiad guide, most amazing among these being:

"—and while you're making up your mind, we can have some fun. You don't need to stay in the tub. You can go any place you like."

"Really?" Lara's confirming nod made Cecilia smile for the first time since her death. "I've always wanted to see the pyramids at Giza."

"We could do that. From a distance. In the Nile."

"But the river's so far from the site!" Cecilia protested. "I know; I researched it when I was planning—" She stopped herself before she could say: *when I was planning where we should spend our honeymoon.* It hurt too much. "You said I could go anywhere. Why not right up to the pyramids, and the Sphinx, and the—?"

"Because it's too *dry*, okay?" Lara blurted. "You're free to leave this tub, but you've got to travel someplace where you can stay submerged. I can help you puddle-jump, but there's got to be at least *this* much water waiting for you at the other end of the trip." She cupped her pale hands. "Sure, tourists carry water bottles, but they're usually the opaque kind, or tucked away. You wouldn't be able to see a thing. Hey, don't blame me for rules I never made. Just stick to them, pick a different destination, and enjoy the privileges of an Elementary death!" Seeing Cecilia's fresh confusion, she was quick to clarify that she wasn't speaking of Sherlock Holmes. "You know, death by one of the elements? I mean the back-in-the-day kind, not your periodic table hodge-podge. The Big Four: Earth, Air, Fire and—your favorite—Water."

"How is it *my* favorite? It killed me! Where's the 'privilege' in that?"

"It's a privilege because it's not for everyone. You have to be *one* person who dies by the action of *one* element and the action—in your case, the *in*action—of *one* other person. If someone breaks your skull with a rock, that's a bankable death-by-Earth. If you're caught in Pompeii on the wrong day, not so much."

"I still don't see how you can call Water my *favorite* element," Cecilia said. "I barely squeaked by on my college swimming test."

"Well, those days are over because—"

"Because I'm dead?"

"No. Uh, actually yes, but *now* it's your Best Fluid Forever because—" The naiad spread her arms. "—because here you are, in it and of it, breathing it and being it until further notice. Water's your servant. Water's your home. Water's your *self* for as long as you like. But why don't I demonstrate? One splash is worth a thousand words. Come on!"

Lara grabbed Cecilia by the wrist and dragged her deeper into the tub. The bronzed plug glimmered dimly beneath them, the faucet above was a fleeting shadow glimpsed through a haze of rose petals and foam. Cecilia felt a moment of icy dread—*Are we actually going to go down the drain? Into the* sewer? *Ew, ew, ew!*—and then she was...elsewhere.

Repeatedly.

Dappled sunlight played over her eyes as she became a wavelet lapping a Caribbean beach.

Lobsters scuttled across her body in the cold depths of the Atlantic.

A seaweed cape flowed out behind her as Lara drew her through the Sargasso.

She danced a decorous pavane with manatees in the Everglades and raced Gentoo penguins around the Falkland Islands.

Her fingertips traced the twisted length of a narwhal's tusk and she tapped her toes gently on the sleek shell of a sea turtle.

Dead as she was, she ran no risk in teasing the tentacles of a poisonous blue-ringed octopus in an Indian Ocean tidal pool or in wearing a lethal sea krait for a necklace while she explored a mangrove swamp.

Cecilia's eyes widened, hungrily devouring so much beauty, such otherworldly creatures. Then, when it seemed as if she'd seen every marvel that her new existence had to offer, she gazed in wonder as her guide brought her into the midst of a sunken city. The weirdly ruddy water felt so hot she guessed they were near some volcanic fissure in the seabed. Massive white and orange blocks could find no resting place as the currents sent them bobbing. Here and there she glimpsed a flash of bright yellow, no doubt a titanic lump of gold from the king's treasury that somehow had cheated the dulling effect of brine. Just as she was reaching out a hand to touch its smooth surface, she gasped to behold the slow, inexorable advance of monstrously fat, white, ghostly serpents. Even though she had no life left to lose, Cecilia could not help feeling primal terror when she saw that the hideous things were entirely featureless, without even the remnants of vestigial eyes. She opened her mouth to scream.

"And one for you!" Lara darted in to tear off a bit of the closest horror and pushed it into Cecilia's mouth. "Go on, you can still taste things if you concentrate. Isn't that yummy? I swear, this restaurant makes the *best* veggie-noodle soup I ever ate!"

Cecilia chewed the savory morsel slowly, processing it along with the fact that she was inhabiting a pot of soup. For the first time since her disincarnation she did not give herself over to shock or panic. She reevaluated her surroundings calmly. The bobbing blocks were chunks of carrots and potatoes, the lump of gold a stray kernel of corn, and the water in the tomato-rich broth was her new home, like all water everywhere, until she chose to say: *Enough. I'd like to go Over now.*

"Enough," she said, then went off script to add: "I'd like to go somewhere else now." She did not accept the helping hand that Lara proffered. "There's someone I need to see before I let you take me Over and—and I want to do it by myself."

"No reason why not." Lara shrugged. "As long as you're not paying a call in the middle of the Atacama Desert." She took another bite of the giant noodle "serpent" and casually asked, "It's that guy who let you die, right?"

Cecilia blushed, though it was difficult to make out, what with the reddish broth around her, then nodded humbly, afraid to meet Lara's eyes. She feared that even if the naiad helped her see Brent again, it would be done with a smirk. Dead or alive, she couldn't bear the thought of anyone's scorn. She'd spent her whole life trimming her sails to catch the approval of others in hopes it would make them like her. The result was a handful of friends who enjoyed having a pet jellyfish but who still left her feeling perpetually unworthy, always on the outside looking in. Brent was the only one who'd ever let her believe there was a place she could truly *belong*.

"Maybe—maybe he didn't really *mean* to do that," she said. "Maybe it was just an accident after all. We were going to be married. He made me feel so...special. I want to see what he's doing now, if he misses me, if he's sorry for what happened. I want to be able to forgive him. I want closure." She gave the naiad a sheepish look. "Do you think I'm being foolish?"

"Not *too* much. I get it: love isn't logic, and it does come in handy for making things better. I can wait. Call my name when you want to come back. Now for the outbound leg of your trip, just think *where* he is and think *wet*; that'll land you in the liquid closest to your target."

"But I don't know *exactly* where my targ—where Brent is right now."

"Then make *him* your *where*. Only be careful you specify—"

Lara wasted her words on soup alone. Cecilia had vanished.

She reappeared almost at once. Her expression was a ghastly conglomeration of disgust, revulsion, trauma, and nausea.

"—*not* when he's in the bathroom," Lara finished too late to do any good. She tried not to laugh as she patted her errant pupil's back. "Don't be discouraged, sweetie. Give it another try."

Cecilia made a weak gesture of acquiescence and repeated her disappearing act. Her guiding thought was: *Take me to Brent when he's not doing...that.*

It was vague directive, but it sufficed. Her luck turned good. She found herself suspended beneath the surface of a glass of water. Brent's familiar voice resounded over her head. He was trying to speak, but huge sobs garbled his words. She looked up and saw his face contorted by sorrow as he apologized for his outburst. "I'm so sorry, officer," he said. "It's just that when I think how different it could have been if I'd checked on her earlier, or if I'd insisted she bathe with the door open, or—or something, *anything* that could have prevented this—this—" He broke down again. "I'll never get over losing her. Never."

"All right, sir." The policeman who was taking his statement passed him a box of tissues. "I think we've got enough. Under the circumstances, this is just a formality. You can go now."

Brent stood and shook hands with the man. "Don't hesitate to call if you need anything else from me, officer. You've been a great help in a tragic time."

Cecilia watched him leave. When she could no longer see him from her vantage point in the water glass, she whisked herself back to Lara and reported all she'd heard. "I'm ready to go Over now," she concluded. "He's blameless. He *does* deserve the benefit of the doubt. He *does* love me. He's heartbroken."

"He's a liar." The naiad's simple rejoinder, delivered in such a matter-of-fact manner, dashed the stars from Cecilia's eyes. "From what you just said, he told the police he wasn't with you when it happened. You and I know otherwise. But hey, if you're okay with that and ready to go, who am I to stop you? I'm a psychopomp, not a therapist. Shall we?" She arose from the makeshift divan she'd assembled out of carrot chunks and imitated a maître-d's most suave *Your table is ready, follow me* motion.

Cecilia balked. "Um, if it's all right with you, can it wait just a bit longer? It might be a good idea if I saw him just one more time." Lara waved her on her way with a knowing smile.

"One more time" multiplied. Cecilia left with a mission in mind. Lara's opinion of Brent rankled her badly, past the point where she could dismiss it and move on. Eternal irritation was one heck of a way to spend the afterlife. While she did accept that Lara was right about Brent having lied to the police, she just couldn't find it in her now-stilled heart to condemn him entirely. He was her first love, the only man who'd asked—no, who'd *implored* her to marry him. Memories of sweet words, sweeter kisses, and sex loud enough to piss off the neighbors bubbled up, sending her thoughts from zero to Totally Insane Rationalization with frightening speed:

*My death was an accident. He must have been too paralyzed with horror to save me after I fell. By the time he came out of his shock, I was gone. If he told the police the real story, who knows when they would have let him go? He's the sole administrator of the Crawn Institute. If he were detained too long, what would happen to it, to the students, to their hopes and dreams? He knows how deeply I cared about those kids. Oh, and what about poor Rita? He must remember that my last words were about helping her, but how could he do that—honor my final request—if he got caught up in a drawn-out investigation? If he did twiddle with the facts a teensy bit, he did it for me! I want Lara to know that, too. I'll trail him to gather proof of how much he loves me and how miserable he is now. She might question one instance, but what if I bring her more? Three should be enough. And when I describe each example to her, I'll—I'll—*her years interred in Poughkeepsie ultimately paid off with an inspired way to make her report to the naiad unimpeachable—*I'll swear to her by the River Styx that it's so!*

Indeed, there was no stronger or more binding oath recognized among the gods of Greece and Rome. Thus prepared, Cecilia dove into her pursuit of tailor-made truth. Her bodily odyssey carried her to those liquid lookout posts whence she hoped to gather evidence of Brent's good character and best intentions. The timing of these separate occasions was linear but compressed, verifying Lara's claim that the speed of minutes and hours and days had a different flow for souls on the near side of the Styx. It didn't take Cecilia long to embrace the slightly disorienting, highly convenient phenomenon.

She was present in a cup of coffee served at the reception following her funeral, where she heard Brent pour out his grief to her only living relative, Cousin Maud. Either there was a family gene for painful timidity or the two women had developed the trait independently. Maud was even more of a mouse than her departed cousin. It was heartwarming for Cecilia to witness that dowdy, plain-faced maiden find just enough courage to reply when Brent introduced himself, then offer him a few stammered words of comfort. And wasn't it just like him to overcome his sorrow long enough to call Maud an angel of mercy and thank her with a smile whose melancholy made it all the more alluring?

Cecilia next eavesdropped from the antique inkwell on her lawyer's desk. It was one of those old-fashioned affectations of décor that charmed his conservative clients. As that trustworthy gentleman of the bar read Cecilia's will, Brent made ample use of a large handkerchief throughout the procedure, no doubt to hide his anguish. He sighed deeply when that document named Maud as the executrix, made a sound that was possibly a stifled sob when the Crawn Institute bequest was mentioned, and nodded stiffly, as one in pain, at each entry on the list of worthy causes Cecilia had chosen to support posthumously.

He was able to restrain the full measure of his woe until the lawyer reached the sentence at the end of the document that left the entire remainder of the estate to Cecilia's husband and offspring, *if any*, and to her cousin, Maud.

Brent's unbridled moans sent ripples through the ink.

Poor darling, she thought. *He's mourning how close we were to being married.* She was right.

This would have been a satisfactory place for her to return to Lara, well-supplied with evidence of Brent's faithfulness and regret. However, Cecilia's loving spirit simply could not leave it at that. The intensity of Brent's lamentations made her fear for his sanity. What if it led to the dark path of taking his own life? She could not go Over with a clear conscience until she saw him able to accept her death.

Stepping into the stream of time and water once again, she emerged in the ruby depths of a glass containing a fine Romanee-Conti Pinot Noir from her late father's costly collection. The intoxicating environment made her a bit giddy. It took her a while to center herself and search out her beloved.

There he was, one hand cupping the bowl of the wine glass where she drifted, the other entwined with the fingers of the woman across the table from him.

Cecilia's brows rose. She'd expected to be taken to visit a few more moments along the time-stream showcasing Brent's slow, reluctant return to the joys of living. Why had she landed in the midst of a scene that showed her former fiancé neck-deep in the social swim? *Has it been* that *long since I died?* she wondered. *Where did the years go?* And then, ashamed of herself: *I suppose I should be happy, knowing that he's been able to make himself a new life after—*

"—two months ago, I thought my life was over, darling," Brent said.

His voice was as suave and caressing as Cecilia remembered it, but his words made her jaw drop. *Two months? That's* it?

"I owe everything to you for saving me," he continued. "Your kindness brought me back from the brink of despair. Your generosity allowed me to keep the Institute open, to help even more young talent."

Why would the Institute be in danger of closing? I left it a huge bequest!

"I've never known a woman with the same passionate commitment to music as I. Is it any wonder that I love you? We're kindred souls, bonded hearts, our fates entwined. Can you forgive me for speaking this boldly? I know we should keep our association strictly professional, but I'm terrified that if I don't tell you how I feel, I'll lose you. I can hardly sleep, and when I do, you're my only dream. I can hardly breathe, imagining my life without you!"

Cecilia recognized those words. They were almost identical to the ones Brent had used when he pleaded a similar load of true love's aches and ouches on the evening he first took their relationship from donor-and-donee to bedroom-and-breakfast.

A shy giggle came from the other side of the table. Although she was floating easily in the sea-dark wine, Cecilia had the sinking sensation she knew the object of Brent's recycled affection. Sure enough, when she peered through the Pinot Noir, she saw her cousin caught up in the same amorous flutter she'd experienced herself.

"Oh, Brent," Maud breathed, adoration in her eyes. "I feel the same way about you. But we mustn't give in. It's too soon. People will talk. We owe it to Cecilia to wait a decent interval until—"

"Until what, Maud?" Brent switched gears, going from soft-eyed swain to steely-voiced commander. "Until you get tired of leading me on? I know I'm not good enough for you. I'm not in your *class*." He spat out the word as though it were a dung beetle. "I get it: you're rich and I'm not. You can toy with me, but respect me? Fat chance. Well, I can't take that kind of treatment again. It's what your cousin did. Did you ever see the pre-nup she put in place as a condition for us to marry? I thought you were better than her. I thought you didn't set *conditions* on love!"

I never did! Cecilia's thoughts were wild. *It was my lawyer who insisted! It was written into Daddy's will and the family trust funds! I—*

"I'm sorry!" Maud seized Brent's hand in both of hers, skinny fingers digging into the flesh. "I'd die before I'd do that if you ever wanted to— to—" she pulled back into her meek shell suddenly, and in a shaky whisper said "—marry me."

Brent took Maud in his arms then and there, kissing her with all the fire of a thousand romance novels. As she melted in his embrace, he proceeded to do things to her on the (thankfully sturdy) dining room table that upset his wine glass and forced Cecilia to take refuge in the decanter, thence to witness Brent's expertise become her cousin's ecstasy. By the time he was done, Maud was eagerly acquiescing to take Cecilia's place as his betrothed.

It was not enough. "No, Maud. You'll never be my fiancée." Brent's face was as pitiless as his words. In the decanter, Cecilia's grim expression aped his own, though for a different reason: she recognized his gambit all too well.

Give a starving heart a morsel of love, then threaten to snatch it away forever, she thought. *Make it a big, dramatic, Verdi finale when you deign to give it back. That's how you scare your prey into a lifetime of blind devotion.* She hugged herself. *It worked on me.*

She'd called it. Brent let Maud suffer for a bit, then cupped her face in his hands, placed a gentle kiss on her forehead, and said, "I won't have you for my fiancée because I want you for my *bride*."

While Cecilia's cousin wept tears of relief, Brent filled her ears with praises for the forward-thinking laws and customs of Las Vegas, where blood tests and waiting periods were pushed to one side so that loving souls could enjoy all the benefits of matrimony, stat!

"We'll leave tonight." He nuzzled her neck aggressively. "No second thoughts, no waiting."

"Don't good things come to those who wait?" Maud said, making an awkward stab at being kittenish. It didn't suit her.

Brent's barking laugh reverberated inside the crystal decanter. "The only good thing I ever got from waiting was thanks to your cousin. If she hadn't made me wait so long to marry her, *she'd* be my wife instead of you. What a god-awful mistake that would have been!" He gave Maud a second helping of delight among the dinner dishes, done to reinforce his control and her bondage. It was not so extended or elaborate as the first, but time was a-wasting and last-minute flight reservations had to be made. Nonetheless, he still broke both wine glasses and came dangerously close to sending the decanter likewise crashing to the floor.

Cecilia saw red, and it wasn't because she was sunk in wine. Rage burned away any lingering impulses to excuse what Brent had done to her. What steamed her most was that the bastard was about to repeat the noxious process, except this time he'd learned from past mistakes. He wouldn't give poor Maud the chance for doubt, or thoughts that wisely counseled caution, or the safeguard of a pre-nup, or the opportunity to inconvenience him by dying before he could burrow into her will, like a tick on a Rottweiler.

He'll make her into even more of a puppet than I was, she thought. *I know Maud. If—when!—he cheats on her, she'll blame herself and apologize. She's got all the grit of a bowl of yogurt.* She felt a rising tide of fierce protectiveness toward her hapless cousin. *He played me for a fool. There's nothing I can do about that now, but if I let him get away with doing the same thing to her, it won't matter which afterlife I choose: they'll all be hell.*

The decanter lurched, banging Cecilia against the curved, transparent wall. Her view changed radically as a triumphant Brent brandished the crystal vessel overhead. "A toast, my dearest! Sorry about the wine glasses, but this will do. To us!" He set the rim to his mouth and drank.

Oh my God, what's he doing? Cecilia braced herself against the glass, watching her liquid world guzzle away. *I've got to get out of here before—*

She stopped. The frantic need to escape dropped from her like lotus petals. An ancient memory out of elementary school days washed over her. She was back in Miss Buxton's fifth grade class, hearing her teacher convey a rather interesting fact about Our Friend, The Human Body. Cecilia's eyes widened as a sweeping vista of *possibility* opened before her.

Of course! Eureka! Whoo-hoo! With a wicked, wonderful smile, she stopped resisting and instead rode the rushing current of Pinot Noir to what was now her *desired* destination.

Splashdown in Brent's stomach was the figurative kickoff. She wasted no time spreading out from there. She sent threads of herself through every organ she fancied, invading any soft tissue that suited her intentions. When she took over his tongue, she relished his reaction of petrified surprise, but this was only the appetizer. Soon enough she was feasting with glee over his desperate struggles to cast out the alien presence making him say...*things*—horrible, incriminating, disgustingly *honest* things!

He babbled about what a gold mine the Crawn Institute was, so long as there were well-heeled, gullible women who fancied themselves patrons of the arts. He described how that half-assed excuse for a school was his own private hunting preserve for one seduction after another. His recitation of conquests fell short of the "Catalog Aria" from *Don Giovanni*, but he took pains to tell Maud that his was still a work in progress. She fled the apartment weeping, but saved. She never noticed that while his confessions came freely, his eyes held the anguish of an animal caught in a leg-hold trap. Content with her handiwork for the moment, Cecilia gave Brent's brain a strategic tweak that rendered him unconscious on the floor before she took off to rejoin Lara.

The psychopomp was still loitering in the soup pot. She greeted Cecilia's return with a cheerful, "Ready to go Over now?"

"Not quite." Cecilia recounted what she'd seen, what she'd done about it, and what she still intended to do before she was finished with Mr. Crawn. Part of her plans involved making his hands write checks to support Rita and her baby and making his libido-linked body parts unlikely to cause any further mischief. "I'll come with you eventually," she concluded. "I don't plan to play puppeteer with Brent forever; just until he's eighty or dead, whichever comes first."

"My money's on dead. Take your time," Lara said. "I'm not one of the Furies, but I do admire their work. You might want to consider choosing the Classical afterlife for your final destination and asking them for an internship when you're done with your business in this world. But tell me, where did you get the power to take control of him like that?"

"From you." Cecilia's hands traced graceful eddies through the soup. "And from this. Remember what you told me about water? How I'm in it and of it, breathing it and being it until further notice? Especially *being* it." Her self-satisfaction was worthy of a cat, than which there is no higher bar set. "Water *is* my servant, just as you said. It answers to *me*!"

The naiad nodded uncertainly. "That still doesn't explain—"

Cecilia paid tribute to Miss Buxton's memory by assuming her long-gone teacher's crisp diction when she said, "The human body is approximately sixty per cent water." She laughed. "So is his."

"How about that. I guess you're never too immortal to learn something new," Lara reflected. "I've met some smart souls in my day, but no one as brilliant as you. Sweetie, you're a genius!"

Cecilia received the nymph's praise with the tranquility of a forest pool. Her spirit was at peace. After so many years of not fitting in anywhere, she was in her element at last.

THE DEEP END

F. Brett Cox

Breathless, Charlie floated toward the light.

He rose in silence with nothing to either side. No motion but his own. He lay as still as he could, rigid, legs together, arms stiff by his sides. A comfortable coolness surrounded him. He felt it on every inch of his body except the space around his eyes that let him focus on the light.

As he got closer, he could hear muffled sounds from above. Now there were dark shapes moving at the edge of his vision, but he ignored them. His goal was the light.

Closer...closer...

Suddenly one of the dark shapes moved directly above him. Instinctively, Charlie loosened his body and tried to float past it, but he was too late. He floated directly into it. A soft bump, a violent thrashing about, a sharp blow to Charlie's chest, and the coolness and the quiet went away.

"Ow! Watch it, doofus!"

Charlie whirled on the surface of the pool, clutching his chest where the boy he had collided with had kicked him. The boy looked older, but Charlie's diving mask had fogged up and he couldn't tell for sure. He was certainly bigger. "Watch where you're going! Jeez!" The other boy slapped both his hands on the water, giving Charlie what should have been a choking splash, but his mask protected his eyes and nose, and he had been splashed often enough to know when to close his mouth. Charlie fell back below the surface, flipped over, and swam away as fast as he could, scissor-kicking like his dad had taught him, left arm still wrapped around his chest.

Charlie followed the downward slope of the pool bottom toward the deep end. At the deepest point, directly below the diving board, there was a drain cover set into the concrete bottom. Just like the pool he swam in back home in Virginia, where it was trouble if anyone saw you getting too close. *You want to get stuck if the pump comes on?* (And rumors of much worse: *I heard some guy sat in the drain when it was on and it sucked his guts out of his ass!* Charlie didn't believe that for a minute. Who would be that stupid?) But also like back home, the pump in this Kansas hotel pool was loud, and you could tell immediately if it was on. Right now it was quiet, so the pump was off.

Except the drain cover was pushed to one side, and in the space between the edge of the cover and the side of the opening, the water was swirling. Not the whirlpool of the pump in operation, but churning like the water was boiling. Like there was something thrashing around in the drain.

Charlie wanted to edge closer for a better look, but the collision had knocked out whatever breath he had stored up. He was out of air. Two kicks brought him to the surface, where he gasped, inhaled, and dove back toward the deep end.

The cover was still off, but the churning had stopped. He floated to one side of the drain and peered into the opening but could see nothing except, a couple of feet down, the beginnings of the pump hardware. Maybe it wasn't as loud as he thought.

This time, as he made his way back to the top, Charlie made sure there was nobody above him. His chest wasn't so sore now. He broke the surface and immediately began sweeping the water with both arms while pumping his legs beneath the water in the bike-riding movement his dad promised would keep him both vertical and above the surface. *Your body wants to float. Unless something's weighing you down, you don't have to sink.* Unless you want to, Charlie had thought, even back then, when he was little and first learning how to swim.

Charlie lay back in the half-tread, half-float that was his favorite way to stay on the surface. He bit down on the snorkel attached to his mask, exhaled into it sharply to clear it of water, and then took several breaths through it, not because he needed to, but because he wanted to. The mask and snorkel weren't just prize possessions—they were the true signal of summer. When he pulled them out of the box that spent most of the year on the top shelf of his bedroom closet that meant summer was here and it was time to go to the pool.

His big sister Katie made fun of him, as usual. *So you need to see the sharks coming in the pool? Or is there treasure buried in the deep end? I know—you're just waiting for a girl to lose her top underwater so you can get a good look!*

Charlie ignored her like he always did. The mask and snorkel made him feel—connected. When he floated face down, all he could hear was the sound of his own breath funneled in and out of the snorkel. Then the dive: bending the top half of his body down, throwing his legs up as straight as he could, and letting their weight push him beneath the surface. He could see clearly, even if it was just bare concrete walls, and the closest thing to treasure was an occasional hair clip or pair of sunglasses. Every once in a while, when people crashed through the water after jumping off the diving board, as they hurled toward the bottom, they did almost lose their swimsuits, female and male, kids and adults. Charlie couldn't help noticing the sudden curves of skin so much paler than the rest of their bodies—not that he would ever admit that to Katie. The mask and snorkel didn't just connect him to this underwater world— they made it his world.

Which was why when Mom had talked about packing as efficiently as possible for the trip to Kansas, he campaigned to take his mask and snorkel for the hotel pool he and Katie had been promised. The fact that he knew he couldn't take his swim fins—both heel straps had torn off— gave him some leverage, and he looked on in triumph as his mother wrapped the mask in his swimming trunks and laid them in his suitcase. He laid the snorkel by them himself.

Now, after a few more satisfying breaths, he spat out the mouthpiece, took off the mask, and clutched its strap tightly while he looked around. This pool was never as crowded as the one back home, but today there were a lot of people, both in and out of the water. He looked for his mother and saw her reclining in the glaring white lounge chair that was twice as big as any of the folding chairs they normally took poolside. She was reading a magazine and sipping through a straw from some big drink in a plastic cup. He turned a full circle in the water, looking quickly past the kiddie pool. (Ick! Might as well go swimming in a toilet.) He had never been happier than when, three years ago, when he was six, his rapid progress as a swimmer had convinced his parents to let him go in the regular pool. He saw some older girls talking with some older boys and noted that one of the girls was Katie, taking full advantage of Dad being in meetings all day. The lifeguard was sitting in a wooden chair built into the top of a narrow platform that rose above the diving board. The lifeguards back home were sometimes not much older than Katie, but this one looked almost as old as Charlie's dad. By the diving board there were three boys talking. He thought one of them might be the boy he had bumped into when he floated up from the bottom of the pool and he quickly looked past them.

There were a lot of things Charlie just didn't get about this trip, beginning with why they were supposed to think it was a vacation to travel from their home in Virginia to Kansas City just to hang out at a hotel while his father attended yet another one of the conferences he had been sent to with his new government job—*a soldier in President Johnson's War on Poverty*, his mom had said, *and this time we're going with him to the front.* Or why he had to share a room with Katie instead of having his own room (and if it was too expensive like his mom said, then why not just all of them stay in one room and save even more money? *Grow up, little boy,* Katie had snorted—her answer to pretty much everything.) The trip out had been exhausting, although the parks in the mountains were fun, and Katie and he had found it equally funny that Dad had made such a deal about their having breakfast in Paris when they stopped in Paris, Kentucky. And there was the pool. Not as big as the one back home, which was a lot nicer than either the scuzzy old club house or the tiny golf course that went along with it. But he had a pool to swim in here, and that was enough for Charlie.

People swam differently out here, though. They spent all their time on the surface. Few of the other kids back in Virginia were underwater as much as Charlie, but most of them spent at least some time beneath the surface, diving, floating from the bottom to the surface, seeing how long they could stay under, how close they could come to swimming from one side to the other while holding their breath. Some of them had their own masks, although Charlie was by far the youngest who did. Sometimes a couple of the older boys who didn't care about lifeguards or parents or rumors about losing your guts would grab the drain cover and use it to help them stay submerged.

But here in Kansas everyone was either splashing around in the shallow end or just swimming back and forth from one end of the pool to the other, stroking and kicking like they were in the Olympics. Charlie wondered if it had anything to do with being in the middle of the country instead of near the coast where he lived, but truth was he just couldn't figure it out.

That was why he'd bumped into that guy. He wasn't used to everyone being there on the surface. It wasn't his fault.

Charlie put his mask back on, left the snorkel hanging, inhaled and exhaled three times, held the last enormous breath, and dove beneath the surface. Yesterday he had gotten halfway the width of the pool underwater with no problem, so today he ought to be able to make it. He knew he was supposed to empty his lungs rather than filling them if he wanted to stay submerged, but the extra time he could stay under made up for the extra effort.

He could tell there were people passing above him and kept pushing forward, determined there would be no more collisions. Between strokes, he looked down. The drain cover was now completely off, sitting on the bottom to one side of the opening. He tried to turn and push back down toward the deep end, but his momentum had carried him farther than he realized. When he bumped against the wall, scraping his right shoulder, he forgot about the drain cover and popped to the surface.

His mother was still sipping her drink and reading her magazine. That was another thing weird about the trip—how she kept to herself. At the pool back home, she was always with a bunch of the other moms, working on their tans, talking almost nonstop, ignoring him and Katie except when, at least once each visit, she made him get out of the water and lie out on a big towel by her folding chair. *I know you're half fish, but that doesn't mean you have to look like the belly of one. Now stay put and get some sun.* So he'd lie there, dying to get back in the water, and listen to her and the other moms talking:

—*Just look at old Jerry Stallings, strutting around like he's cock of the walk with that new wife of his.* —*I know, it's just a sin, with Marla barely in the ground.* —*He sure didn't make things easy for her, did he?* —*And those trunks! What is that, French?* —*Not like he has anything the rest of them don't...*—*That boy of yours loves the water, doesn't he? ...*—*What about that boy Katie's been dating?* —*Oh, Don doesn't have much use for him.* —*Honey, Donald McGuire isn't going to have any use for any boy coming around after his daughter and you know it...*—*Sons are not one bit easier, believe you me. I swear I'd rather he went to a whorehouse every Saturday night than spend one more minute with that Creel girl...*—*The doctor said it wasn't anything to worry about, but I'm just not sure. At least I can count on him for the Valium...*—*All right, Charlie, you can go back in.*

But here, she just lay out with her magazine and kept sipping on her drink.

He threw his arms over the rounded stones that outlined the sides of the pool and took off his mask. Despite all the water splashing over them, they felt hot. "Hey, mom!"

She looked up, smiled, and said something he couldn't hear over the splashing and yelling. Someone's radio played "Summer in the City." Katie loved that song. On that, they agreed.

"What?"

He half-heard, half read on her lips, "You'd better go see your friend," and she pointed to an unknown spot behind him.

He turned around, keeping an arm on the hot stones. Gail, the girl he had met at the pool the first day they were here, sat on the edge of the other side, kicking her legs in the water and waving at him. He realized she was calling his name: "Chaaar-lie!"

He looked up at his mother, wanting to say something grown up like, "Gotta run," but she had already turned back to her magazine. So he braced his feet against the side of the pool just under the water, pushed off, and dove down at the same time. He looked down to his right and saw that the drain cover was still off. The water in the opening looked like it was churning again, but from this far away he couldn't be sure. He wanted to swim down and check it out. But he also wanted to swim to the other side completely underwater and surface right in front of Gail. Unfortunately, he didn't have enough air to do either.

When he came up he was more than halfway across. Gail was a blur through his mask, but he could tell she was still kicking her legs in the water. He went back under, and before he could decide which direction to take, he found himself on the other side, still underwater directly below her. As much as he wanted to reach out and grab her by the ankles and pull her in the water, he still remembered their conversation on their first day at the hotel and contented himself with popping up at the wall right by her.

She looked down at him accusingly. "Hey! Didn't you hear me?"

"Sorry. It's pretty loud around here." It was. As the day got hotter and more people poured into the pool, the noise level rose accordingly. There was a radio on this side, too, playing "Easier Said Than Done," which was an old one—he only ever heard it back home on the Sunday night oldies show. And here it was the middle of the week. They even did radio different around here.

"I guess," she said. Her kicking slowed but didn't stop.

He still had his mask on. The first time he had it on in front of her, Gail said that with his nose covered he sounded like he had a cold. He thought it made his voice sound deeper. Not that he would tell her that. "So are you ready to try it?"

"Try what?"

"You know." Now he did reach out as if to grab her ankle.

"No!" She pulled her foot away and then brought it back through the water, splashing him. "I told you I'm not ready."

"I thought you said you liked to swim."

"I do! But I'm not ready to put my head under."

"Sissy."

"I'm a girl. I can't be a sissy."

"Can too."

"Can't can't can't can *not!*" She splashed him again. "Besides, Mama just fixed my hair." He thought Gail's hair was probably really long, but he didn't know for sure because she always kept it wrapped around her head, held in place by a huge hair clip. "And there's nothing to see, either. It's not like it's the ocean, with fish and stuff."

He had had this same conversation with her each day since their families arrived, and it always stopped right there. Charlie's home in Virginia was less than an hour from the coast. In the summer they went to the beach at least once a month, and while Katie couldn't wait to get there, Charlie was less enthusiastic. It was kind of exciting being in water that was always moving, but in the shallows, which was as far out as his parents would let him go, the water and the sand were constantly churning into each other. Even on a sunny day the water was grey, and if there was anything interesting beneath the surface it didn't matter because you couldn't see two feet in front of you. The pool was better.

"Besides, you told me it took you a long time before you could duck your head."

"When I was *six*. Gah." He looked past her to the people sunning on the patio beyond the pool. Katie was still there, still talking to the same group of boys. She looked in his direction, smiled and waved. Smiled? Waved? Something else that never happened back home.

"So you're just going to sit there and not come in?"

"Maybe in a little bit." She kicked her legs in the water again but this time without splashing him.

"Ok," he said, and pushed off toward the deep end. He paused to let the teenager on the diving board do her cannonball into the water. When she surfaced, shrieking happily, he bent at the waist and dove. As the water covered him, he felt a sting where he had scraped his shoulder on the side wall of the pool. Halfway down, he looked back up and saw the blurred image of Gail on the other side of the water. He thought she was smiling at him, but he wasn't sure. He also saw a small dark blob suspended near him. His shoulder must be bleeding. He'd need to get a band-aid when he got out of the pool.

The water still swirled from where the girl had cannonballed in. It looked like she had almost hit bottom before she shot back up. Charlie moved through the turbulence and went deeper. He wanted to see what was up with the drain cover. He wanted not to be talking with Gail and trying to think what to say next. He wanted, he realized for the first time since they had arrived, to go home where things were as he knew them to be.

But right now he just wanted to look at the drain cover. As he pushed himself toward the bottom, the pressure started against his ears. There was no nose clip on his mask, but he pushed its lower lip hard against his nose and blew until his ears popped. He kept moving down until he reached the bottom.

The cover still lay by the drain opening. It was coated in something that looked slimy. The water around the opening was still, and there was no sound. It was safe to approach.

Charlie pulled himself along the bottom with his hands. The chlorine was making his shoulder sting even more. His breath was ok, but the air in his lungs kept pushing him up. He peered into the drain.

The water in the opening started to churn and an arm reached for him.

It had a hand and fingers, but it wasn't a regular human arm. It was something else. The wrist was too thick for the rest of it, and it was all covered in the same slimy stuff that covered the drain cover. The hand touched the front of his mask.

Thirteen feet underwater, Charlie screamed. All the air went out of his lungs and bubbled in front of him, so that he couldn't see the drain or the arm that reached out of it. He backpedaled on the bottom like he was on land and felt the concrete scrape his feet. Then he pushed and shot himself back to the surface, kicking and thrusting as hard as he could.

When he broke the surface he choked and sputtered and gasped for breath, but before he could refill his lungs an arm pushed his head back under the water. He screamed again, thinking the arm had come out of the drain after him.

But when the arm quit pushing and he came back up, gasping, he saw that it was attached to the boy he had collided with earlier. There were two other boys with him.

"Hey, squirt," the boy said. He motioned to one of the others, who reached out, ripped Charlie's mask off, and tossed it away. Charlie heard a small splash where it fell, through the noise of all the people in the pool who weren't paying any attention to what was happening to him.

The other two boys were the same size as the first one. They were all older than Charlie, maybe in junior high.

"You know what this is, little boy? This is traffic court," the first boy said. "We need to teach you the rules of the road. You can't just be running into people."

Charlie sputtered and tried to tell the boy what he had seen, but the boy splashed water in his face, which started him choking again.

"Shut up, punk! I'm doing the talking here."

"Don't be looking for the lifeguard," one of the other boys said. "He's on break."

"Taking a leak," the third boy said.

"Getting laid," the second said, and they all laughed.

Charlie hadn't even thought to look for a lifeguard. He never paid attention to the lifeguard. He didn't need a lifeguard. He was a good swimmer. He looked around frantically for his mother, for Katie, but he couldn't see them anywhere.

"What'll we do with him?" the first boy asked.

"Take him and toss him in the ladies' room!"

"Take his trunks off!"

"Take his trunks off and then toss him in the ladies' room!" They all laughed again. Charlie splashed and circled and looked for a way out, but they circled with him.

"Let's drown him for a while first and then we'll figure out what to do." The first boy moved toward him, followed by the other two. Three sets of arms moved in and pushed him back under the water.

The arms, and then their whole bodies, pressed down and kept Charlie under the water. He had been able to take a breath before they pushed him under, but not much of one. He swirled and punched and kicked and tried to get away. One of his kicks connected with something that felt like a swimsuit that had something soft and bulging beneath it. Suddenly there was an opening as one of the boys pushed away. He yelled so loud when he broke the surface Charlie could hear him under the water.

Charlie twisted, turned, and plunged through the opening. This was his chance.

But instead of getting to the surface where there was air and his mom and Katie, and his dad somewhere, he felt his body bend at the waist and push itself back toward the bottom. Toward the drain.

He knew he was out of air, but somehow he was able to keep moving. He had to keep moving. Something was pulling him down. His head knew he should be drowning, knew he should resist, but his arms and legs kept pushing him down to the bottom and his lungs amazingly did not complain. He swam out of the churning water where the boys had corralled him into the clean transparency of the bottom of the pool. It was like looking through a telescope. It was like that song where the singer said he could see for miles.

When he reached the drain, the arm was still there. Now it was attached to a shoulder, and through the telescope view Charlie thought he saw a head emerging. It had eyes and teeth. It looked like the monster they had watched in that movie about Florida, then it looked like pictures he had seen of sharks, then it didn't look like anything he had ever seen at all. The eyes didn't change. They stared at Charlie and made him want to go closer. If he could just go a couple more feet things wouldn't be strange anymore. Things would be just as they were supposed to be, and he'd never have to get out of the water again.

The creature in the drain reached out, and Charlie felt as if he could breathe normally if he wanted to. He extended his own hand.

Then he felt another hand grab his left ankle, and yet another grab his right. He tried to kick them away. He didn't understand anything that was happening, but he knew where he wanted to go.

The hands on his ankles held firm. As they pulled him away, he could see the eyes and the teeth and the head squeezing back into the drain through water that was churning and bubbling again. Then the shoulder and the arm followed, and finally the hand that, before it disappeared entirely, grabbed the drain cover and pulled it back in place with a clunk Charlie could hear as clearly as he had ever heard anything. And now the water was still. He felt his feet hit the air, and then the rest of his body, and finally his gasping, crying mouth and chlorine-burned eyes.

They laid him by the side of the pool. The sun filled his burning eyes, but he squinted and saw it was Katie. And Gail. Gail's hair was wet and hanging in tangles down beyond her shoulders. It really was long. Katie was yelling at him, and Gail may have been crying, but Charlie wasn't sure. His mother appeared, pushed the girls aside, and knelt down to see after her son.

Later Katie told him that Gail had seen the boys circling Charlie and had yelled for help. Katie heard and jumped in after him, and Gail followed her. When Charlie asked her what it was like to finally stick her head under the water, Gail said, "It was awful! It burned my eyes. I couldn't see hardly anything." Then she punched him in the shoulder, right where he had scraped it, and told him how scared she had been, using a word that Charlie had only heard other boys use.

His mother insisted that they go home. Dad wasn't too happy about missing the last day of his meetings—*He's all right, isn't he? Just keep him out of that goddamned pool*—but Mom just stood there and stared at him, and Katie, who, like Charlie, usually got as far away as she could from their parents' arguments, stood right there by her. So Dad tracked down the lifeguard who hadn't been there and yelled at him, and Mom found the parents of the boys who had gone after Charlie and yelled at them. The lifeguard just said something about boys being boys and didn't seem too concerned. Two of the boys' parents said they were sorry and would punish their boys. The third boy, the one Charlie had run into, only had his father with him, and his father just said the same thing the lifeguard had said. Katie said they ought to sue the hotel but Mom gave her the same kind of stare she had given Dad and Katie didn't say anything else.

Just before they left the hotel, Charlie's mom asked him if he had packed his mask and snorkel, and it wasn't until then that Charlie realized he had never gone back and gotten it from wherever the boys had thrown it. Katie went to look for it, but couldn't find it.

Charlie didn't say anything immediately about what he'd seen coming out of the drain. He thought about it for the whole long drive back, and when they got home he decided he wouldn't say anything. He almost wrote to Gail about it after she started sending him post-cards, but he didn't do that, either.

How could he explain to anyone that when he had moved toward the creature in the drain, he had felt safe, and when he had looked into its eyes, he had seen himself?

He couldn't tell anyone that. Ever.

When they got home Dad bought him a new mask and snorkel, and new fins that were full-foot and didn't have a strap that would break.

Charlie put them in the closet, but it took him until almost Labor Day before he could stick his head under the water again...

Even then, he didn't dare open his eyes.

THROUGH MILKWEED AND GLOOM

WENDY NIKEL

No one entered the bog unless they had to, but when Jacob Rey's daughter went missing—the third child this spring, all from our neighborhood—there wasn't much choice, was there? We all knew what had happened to them, even if the police couldn't figure it out.

We gathered at the old Templeton place, which teetered so closely to the edge of the bog that Old Mr. Templeton could sit out on his back porch and watch the eerie bog-lights flicker. Some said the proximity had done something to him, altered him somehow and that's why, at the ripe old age of ninety-two, the old man didn't look a day over sixty.

Mama—refusing to have anything to do with it—dropped me at the door, her worry lines deeper, more pronounced than usual. As I walked up the porch steps, she leaned out the driver-side window and asked if I had my cell phone. Habit, I guess, since she knew as well as I did it'd be worthless out on the bog. I waved it at her anyway, and along with it the leather pouch she'd given me, heavy with the amulet she usually wore on her own neck, the one that had been passed down from generation to generation and was supposed to grant the wearer protection.

"Whatever you do," she called out as I waited for Mr. Templeton to answer the doorbell, "stick with your partner. Don't let them separate you. And wear that amulet. You're all I've got, Hilly; I can't lose you."

"I'll be fine," I called back, but her words stuck strangely in my ears. I was used to Mama's overprotective nature—that's what comes from being the only child of a single mom—but something about her admonition went beyond the typical "call me as soon as you get there" nagging.

I must've been the last to arrive, which figures, considering how long it took to convince Mama to let me help. Everyone else was already there, gathered around Mr. Templeton's table as if waiting for Thanksgiving dinner, but, instead of a turkey and mashed potatoes and pumpkin pie, the table was filled with sharp, gleaming tools from his shed and maps Mrs. Ferris must've photocopied from the library's reference section. She stood at the head of the table, wearing bulky, red waders that looked out of place with her cardigan and bifocals.

"I've compiled a list of mysterious disappearances from this part of town, dating all the way back to its settlement in the 18th century," she said, holding up a three-ring binder, "to narrow down what specific sort of threat we're dealing with here."

I slid into an empty seat next to Gregg, who looked so pale I thought he'd pass out right there. "You okay?" I whispered, and he nodded dumbly, like one of those bobble-head figures you see at comic book conventions. The whole time, his gaze didn't stray from Mrs. Ferris's binder. "We don't have to do this, you know."

He looked at me like I'd grown fins and gills. "You think I'd turn down a chance of finding him?"

Him, of course, being Gregg's brother, who disappeared when they were kids. It'd been over a decade now since the two had been playing hide-and-seek in the forest behind their house and Lloyd, the older of the two, had simply disappeared. I bit my lip and sat back to listen to Mrs. Ferris; there was no way *I* was going to be the one to remind Gregg the chances of finding his long-lost brother were astronomically small.

"I believe what we're dealing with here is some form of supernatural water entity," Mrs. Ferris continued, opening her binder to some sketches straight out of Grimm's fairy tales. "Sprites. Nixies. Näcken."

Around the table, murmurs arose, obviously from our newer neighbors. You didn't have to live near the bog for long to realize that something about it didn't follow the natural laws of the world. In my short lifetime alone, we'd seen surveyors, land developers, and city officials attempt to drain it, to map it, to *tame* it, and all were met with failure after failure. No one who went in alone ever came out, and the most recent team wandered in one day and emerged an hour later with full beards, convinced they'd spent months trying to escape it. For the following week, if you went out after dark and held your breath, you could hear the sprites—if that's what they were—chittering with laughter at the trick.

"How do we get our children back?" In the back of the room, Jacob Rey held an honest-to-goodness pitchfork. With his wife beside him looking just as grim, they reminded me of the *American Gothic* painting I'd seen at the Art Institute on our field trip to Chicago last year.

Mrs. Ferris pursed her lips. "First and foremost, we need to protect ourselves. These beings are shape-shifters, so we'll need a safe word, a code to indicate we are who we say we are. I suggest the word *Grimm*. We'll provide steel for everyone's pockets as well; these can protect against drowning."

I nearly snorted out loud. "If steel could protect against drowning, no one on the *Titanic* would have died."

"Hilly," Gregg scolded. "This is serious."

I slouched into my seat, crossing my arms over my chest. I knew it was serious. I also knew the difference between supernatural and superstition and there was no way plain old steel would deter the bog. Still, when Mrs. Ferris passed out the stainless steel cutlery, I slipped the spoon into my pocket along with everyone else.

"You'll be paired with Louis Bartleton," she said.

"I'm going with Gregg," I said. Sure, I felt bad that the Reys' kid was missing, but at the end of the day, I was here to help him. "Neither of us are minors, and different types of water sprites target different genders. I'll help him resist any sirens with damp hems, and he can hold me back if I start fawning over some handsome young fiddler."

Her lips twitched as she thought, but finally she gestured to the pouch in my hand. "Did your mother give you that?"

"Yes."

"You'll probably be the best protected of all of us, then." She nodded curtly. "She's the only person I know of who's gotten out of that bog alone."

* * *

It was different than I expected, out there on the bog. Like most kids who'd grown up around here, I'd played on the edges, testing the limits of Mama's patience by seeing how close I could get to the bog without going *in* it. But those moments of near-disobedience didn't prepare me for the strangeness of it, the feeling of wandering in some other place, of finding oneself suddenly lost in the fog and gloom, where every step felt like a departure from the world...a departure from life itself.

"You never told me your mom went out on the bog," Gregg said as soon as we were out of sight of the others.

"I didn't know." My tone was short, and I felt bad that Gregg, of all people, had to put up with my foul mood, but the fact that Mama might know more about the bog, but refused to tell me, left a sour taste in my mouth. Was that why she'd been so opposed to this venture?

Gregg rolled a yellow cord out behind us, a bread crumb trail with one end tied tightly to Mr. Templeton's porch railing. I'd thought it was a dumb idea—it wouldn't take much for a malevolent sprite to cut through the thin wire—but now that we were out here, with water and half-submerged trees and thick fog as far as the eye could see, I was glad to have something tangible to cling to.

The others' voices cut through the mist, but they sounded distorted and strange, as if they were speaking some forgotten, ancient language. If the Reys' daughter was still out here somehow, she'd probably run *away* from us, thinking *we* were the unearthly threats. They blended with the sounds of the bog: crickets and trickling water and, beneath it all, a cadence of something barely-heard. Something *musical.* I was about to comment on this to Gregg when I realized he wasn't beside me.

"Gregg?" I swore beneath my breath. How long had he been gone? Seconds, minutes, hours meshed together in my head, disorienting me. The swamp vegetation passed through a hundred seasons, growing and blossoming, spreading seeds and wilting, all in the blink of an eye. Panicked, I imagined emerging from the mist to discover our subdivision gone, crumbled to ruin, and everyone I knew and loved long dead. I plunged my hand into Mama's pouch and pulled out her amulet which, had I been thinking straight, I ought to have been wearing all along.

As soon as it was over my head, the music faded and my mind cleared. It hadn't been hours. The cattails and milkweed hadn't changed. Gregg had only been gone a few seconds, which meant, if I doubled back on the tracks I'd made in the wet earth, I ought to meet his soon.

I counted six steps backward before my footprints rejoined his, and there I found the cord caught on the thorny branches of some plant I'd never seen before. It had tiny, blood-red blossoms on it, and its sweet scent made me lightheaded, even with the protection of Mama's amulet around my throat.

Carefully, hand over hand, I followed the cord through the mirk and gloom, not turning aside even as the others' voices faded, leaving the world in a silence so complete that it seemed to buzz in my ears. I followed it, focused entirely on what lay ahead, until I found myself on the edge of a lake so large, so deep, that there was no way it could possibly have fit on Mrs. Ferris's plot maps.

The cord, still taut, led directly into it, forming a long angle with its reflection until it disappeared beneath the glassy surface.

Maybe I should've turned around and gone for help, but something in my marrow—perhaps prompted by Mama's amulet—warned me that a place like this was unlikely to be discovered twice. So before I could think better of it, before I could convince myself of the impossibility of what I was about to do, I stepped into the icy, still water and waded out toward the lake's center.

The silt beneath my feet was so soft that I sank into it, and, with each step, it threatened to pull me under. I clutched Mama's amulet in one hand and Gregg's cord in the other, step after step, until the water rose to my neck. Only then did I begin to panic, to wonder what would happen when I got in too deep. Who knew what lurked beneath the surface?

I'd been on the swim team in middle school, I reminded myself; I could hold my breath a few minutes at least. Clinging to that rationalization, I stepped forward and allowed the water to close over my head.

If the bog was a different world than our quiet, innocuous-looking subdivision, beneath the lake was another universe entirely. As the sediment cleared, I drew in an unexpected gasp, one that—in our universe—would have drowned me. Here, however, in the green bog-water with its strange shadows of algae, bubbles floated up from my nose and mouth, and somehow my lungs functioned normally. Mama's amulet floated into my line of vision and I tucked it beneath my collar and zipped my jacket so I wouldn't lose it.

I pulled myself along the cord using short flutter-kicks to propel me. The water here was clearer than one would expect from a bog-lake, and, as I brushed aside a curtain of algae, an entire world opened around me. Obscure shadows sharpened into the shapes of crumbling ruins, their vague hints of elegance and style consumed by lichen and the unceasing passage of time.

The yellow cord cut through the center of it all, pointing like an arrow through a darkened arch. Inside, a dome spread out overhead, and silhouettes of fish passed in and out of its shattered stained glass. In the center of the cavern, directly beneath its apex, the severed end of the yellow cord hung suspended in the gloom.

I'd been tricked.

I spun around, my hair billowing around me and obscuring my vision. When I pushed it aside, they were there, shadowy figures in the alcoves of the domed room. Whether they'd been there all along or whether they'd just appeared, now that I'd noticed them, I couldn't look away. I drew in a breath, nearly choking on the stale taste of brine and decay. The figures were distinctly human—head, torso, and appendages—but their stillness was unnatural. Though their hair wavered, dancing in the subtle currents, their bodies were eerily frozen.

Gathering my courage, I pushed myself through the water to the nearest one, squinting through the silt that sparkled in the rays of greenish light extending from far above. The terrified face that looked back at me was all too familiar.

Gregg.

Sprite-laughter, like trickling water, swirled through the ruins. Shadows darted about on the edges of my vision.

I pulled myself from one alcove to the next, my heart racing in fear at what I found. Mr. Templeton. Mrs. Ferris. The Reys, frozen in place like that awful painting. Every one of my neighbors who'd joined us today. And then, the Reys' daughter. The other missing children. A man who looked familiar, like I'd seen his face in a photograph but couldn't place where. Down and down the line, around the circle of stone, until there he was—Gregg's brother, Lloyd, looking the same as he had all those years ago in his Batman t-shirt and light-up sneakers.

The sprites' babbling had reached a cacophony, but I blocked it out of my mind. What could I do? I had to get them back to the surface, out of this lake somehow, but there were dozens of people and each was frozen stiff.

"Help me out, guys," I muttered through gritted teeth as I dragged Gregg out of his alcove. Something swooped through the broken glass overhead, and its eyes—green and glowing—stared at me from the darkness. I searched my pockets, but all I had was the spoon Mrs. Ferris had given me. Hardly a worthy weapon. I had nothing else, save the cell phone I'd forgotten to take from my pocket, now water-filled and ruined beyond repair, and the amulet around my neck.

The amulet. We'd all had steel, so it must have been the amulet that had kept me from the sprites' magic paralysis. That thought gave me some hope. Mama had given it to me, after all, and Mrs. Ferris had said she'd gone out on the bog alone and returned. She wouldn't have sent me without the means to get back.

But the others? I couldn't just leave them here.

The cord floated like a serpent in front of me, planting an idea in my mind.

First, I reached into my collar and pulled out the amulet, letting it float free before my face. I looked around. Nothing had changed. Good. The stone didn't have to be physically touching me. It was a long shot, but maybe, just maybe, if I encircled everyone with the yellow cord and slipped the amulet onto that, they'd be protected as well. The tricky part, of course, would be setting it up without the sprites' interference. And without robbing myself of its protection.

Shoving all the statuesque figures into the center of the room took longer than I'd have liked. The sunlight trickling in from overhead grew dimmer and more slanted as time wore on. Had I not been underwater already, I'd have worked up a sweat, if not from the exertion itself, then out of nervousness due to all the green pinprick eyes staring at me through the murk. The whole time, I thought of Mama. She'd escaped from here, but when? And how?

Finally, the neighbors were all gathered in the center of the room. I pulled on the end of the yellow cord, winding it carefully around each person's wrist and then encircling the group as a whole. The amulet bobbed before my face. If this failed to restore their senses, I'd have no choice but to leave them. Gregg's face stared back at me, crinkled in terror, as if bracing himself for something that was to come. He'd been my best friend for years; I couldn't imagine life without him, without the others. The thought of all those dark and empty houses sent a chill through me.

I maneuvered myself inside the yellow cord's circle, my side pressed against Gregg, and fumbled with the latch on the amulet—trickier to undo underwater than I'd expected. My fingers felt soft and unskilled, wrinkled from being submerged so long. The sunlight was fading. I didn't have much time.

All around, the green-glowing eyes of the sprites blinked and shifted in the lengthening shadows. Their restlessness was palpable, cold and sharp. They ventured closer, allowing me glimpses of their ever-shifting faces, faces that stole the features of the men and women and children gathered around me. Gregg's eyes. Lloyd's childish nose. The chin of that man whom I thought I'd seen before. A chin that, seeing it like that, disembodied as such, made me recognize its similarities to my own.

I spun around, searching for that man, and when a beam of light fell on his face, I realized where I'd seen his photograph before: tucked away in the box beneath Mama's bed. Could he be...my father? My chest felt tight with the realization: she'd had to leave him here.

The sprites chittered their devious laughter, and I turned my attention back to the amulet. I had to get it free. In my haste, the clasp broke, and as soon as the circle around my neck was broken the music of the sprites flooded my ears, and the bog-water and brine filled my nose. I held my breath; I could no longer breathe.

The music was beautiful and terrible. It was more wonderful than anything, and so loud. It was precious and powerful and I longed to stay here forever. And yet...

The amulet twinkled, suspended before my face. Mama.

I snatched it out of the sparkling suspension just as another hand—thin and green, with sharp, curved claws—reached for it. The being shrieked, a sound that, even underwater, stabbed at my ears. I repeated the syllables—*Mama, Mama, Mama*—over and over, picturing her face as I held the amulet tightly. If she'd escaped, I could, too. My fingers, numb and slow with cold and the sprites' magic, tried desperately to thread the cord through the ring atop the amulet, even as the sprites laid their hands on me, digging their sharp nails into my skin and pulling me away from the circle.

Return our stolen property, the voices hummed. *Daughter of thieves. Offspring of robbers.*

Their song burned my ears. It wanted me to stop. I wanted to stop. I wanted to lay down my arms, let my fingers go limp. Rest. Rest. Rest.

The cavern dimmed, like all the light was going out of the world, and in that last moment, when everything was merely a muddy blur of desires and mirk and green-glowing eyes, when they had me in their grasp and I could feel my body stiffening, the cord slipped through the amulet's loop and my fist closed around the two pieces of cord, completing the circle as they stiffened, becoming like stone.

Then all was still.

* * *

I woke on Mr. Templeton's back porch, spewing soupy water from my lungs.

The faces surrounding me were familiar and strange, and they burst out in smiles and laughter when I blinked. Mama's arm was around the man with the familiar chin—my father, back from the dead—and the Reys clutched their little girl's hands between them.

I sat up, coughing, and someone yelled to give me space.

"How?" I asked.

Gregg was beside me, his arms wrapped around me. "We woke up down in that cavern, tangled up in that protective circle of yours. Your hand was holding it shut so tightly, we had to all work together to drag you out of the bog. It wasn't until we crossed out of it that you woke. You saved us, Hilly. All of us. Even Lloyd."

From the edge of a circle, a small boy stared with wide eyes at all these people he'd once known. How strange it must be for him, to wander into the bog one day and wander out the next, finding the rest of the world had moved on.

"It'll be tough for him," I said quietly to Gregg.

"I know. I'll have to be the big brother now." He reached down to the cord tangled at my feet. He carefully untied the amulet and handed it to me.

"Things will be different now," I said, staring at the glimmering stone.

"Different, yeah." Gregg glanced over his shoulder at the crowd gathered there, at Mama and my father and his own, now-younger brother. "But better. *Right.*"

I smiled, because I knew that's what he wanted from me, but as I clutched the amulet—cold as ice in my hands—I could almost hear their songs again. Bog-lights flickered in the distance, restless and hungry, and I knew, somehow, instinctively, that this wasn't the end. They'd keep calling, keep taking, until we returned what was theirs.

"Come on in, everyone," Mr. Templeton called. "I've got some hot chocolate on the stove for the kiddos, and some wine for the grown-ups. We have a lot to celebrate tonight!"

I stood to the side as the others wandered through the back door, until Gregg and I were the only ones left on the deck.

"You coming?" he asked.

"Just give me a minute."

As soon as he stepped inside, I turned to the bog—that strange, otherworldly place. It was terrible and beautiful and I knew if I went through with this, I'd never set foot out there again. A small price to pay to make things right. I squeezed the amulet one last time and then, with a whisper of a prayer, I launched it as far as I could into the star-studded evening sky, watching until it dropped, lost forever among the milkweed.

SON OF BLOB

MARSHEILA ROCKWELL &
JEFFREY J. MARIOTTE

I met the giant squid one week to the day after my parents disappeared.

I was standing on the dock in Sitka, Alaska. It was a warm November day for Sitka, mid-sixties, and I was wearing a t-shirt, jeans, and sneakers. In front of me was the *R/V Ed Ricketts*, the research vessel from which my parents had vanished. I heard some gentle splashing in the water and looked down, expecting to see a wet-suited swimmer or a pelican or something. Instead, a tentacle was reaching out of the water toward me. It was terra cotta-colored, like a houseplant pot that someone had spilled water on. I uttered a wordless cry.

Gayle Federici, a Stanford grad student who was working as a research assistant to my parents, came to the rail of the *Ricketts*. "Oh, that's Lucy," she said. "She's an *Architeuthis marensi*—a northern Pacific giant squid. She was a friend of your folks. She just wants to meet you."

I peered down again. I couldn't tell how long Lucy's tentacle was, but there were already eight feet or so extending out of the water, coming closer to me, and it looked like plenty more where that came from. I could only get a sense of her size through the dark water, but she appeared to be gigantic, easily as long as a city bus, if her tentacles were included.

"Is she...dangerous?" I asked.

"Hell, yes," Gayle said. "Probably not to you, though. If you were a fish, or a killer whale, or even another squid—even another *Architeuthis*; cannibalism has been recorded in the species—she might be. But as far as I know, she's never preyed on humans."

I wasn't particularly reassured. "Umm, hi, Lucy," I said, trying to sound squid-friendly. "I'm Nick."

Lucy kept reaching up, and up, and up some more. Finally, the tentacle was waving around right in front of me. "She can't see through that, can she?" I asked.

"No," Gayle said. "But the suckers are remarkably sensitive. She knows where you are. Go ahead and give her a high five."

I held out my right hand. Nervously, I admit. "I really didn't enjoy that calamari I had last month," I said. "I felt a little sick after, in fact."

How she did it, I don't know, but I held my hand still and the squid's tentacle found it, touched it, wrapped around it. I could feel her suckers, but they didn't latch onto my flesh as I had feared.

That was it, that brief, tapping contact. I felt—I don't know. Somewhere between nothing at all and a little tingle, a *frisson*, at the idea of touching a representative of the largest sentient species on Earth. Whether Lucy felt anything different, I couldn't have said. Based on what happened later, I think maybe…but I'm getting ahead of myself.

The tentacle disappeared and, moments later, so did the squid. I trundled up the gangplank and onto the boat, backpack over my shoulder. Gayle waited with a smile on her face. She was thin, compact, with dark curls and eyes that blazed with intensity. "Welcome aboard," she said.

"Thanks for making this happen," I said. "It couldn't have been easy."

"Don't thank me," Gayle replied. "Thank the NOAA. Only, you know, thank them silently, because they don't know you're going out with us."

That surprised me. She had told me it was all set up, but not that it was on the down-low. "So what am I, a stowaway? An outlaw?"

"I wouldn't go that—" she began. Then she caught herself. "—well, okay, you could look at it that way. Is that a problem?"

I thought it over for about five seconds. "No. Not at all."

"Okay, cool," she said. "Come on, I'll introduce you to the crew. Everybody loved your folks to pieces."

My folks were Dr. Betty McFall Larson, esteemed oceanographer, and Dr. Dr. Harold Larson, the double-doctor thanks to his doctorates in marine biology atmosphere and oceanic sciences. Also thanks to his twisted sense of humor—he typically introduced Mom, whom he'd married just out of college and to whom he had remained married for almost 34 years, as "my first wife, Betty."

Gayle started away from me, but I stopped her. "Wait. First, can you explain something to me? You said Lucy was a friend of my parents. I thought giant squids were, like, super-reclusive. How can one just be floating around by the dock, and how can it be friends with humans?"

To her credit, Gayle didn't just give me the first answer that popped into her head. She considered it, then said, "How, I don't know. She just was. She would hang around the ship if your parents were on board. If they weren't, but were in the waterfront lab, she was there. If they were out in a dinghy or a submersible, she was there. Wherever they were, you'd find Lucy. It was like she was watching out for them. Once they were swimming and a hammerhead came toward them. Lucy got in between them and chased the shark away."

"Really?" That sounded like anthropomorphizing of the highest order—something Mom and Dr. Dr. Dad had always warned me against.

I guess the doubt was apparent in my tone. "None of us would have believed it, either," Gayle said. "But Collum got video of the whole thing."

I couldn't do anything but shrug. My parents had spent most of their lives in and around the water. If they wanted to make friends with squids, who was I to complain? I'd made friends with the children of corn farmers and Re-publicans, which to them was every bit as strange. I had managed to get into the football program at the University of Nebraska, where I majored in English, because hey, I already knew English, so how hard could it be? It's not that I'm not smart—I don't know any college ball players who are stupid—but I think fish are for eating, not studying.

Gayle gave me a quick tour of the *Ricketts*. Most of what she showed me involved nautical words I had never heard before. The vessel was 186 feet long, and had a double-hull, like a pontoon boat or catamaran. Gayle said it was a SWATH design, or Small Waterplane Area Twin Hull. The advantages were stability in the sometimes rough waters of the northern Pacific, and a large working deck area. At the back—*aft*, Gayle said—a crane could lower and raise a three-person submersible, the *James Cook II*, into and out of the water. Something engines, something else tons, water displacement…it all ran together, meaningless to me. There were eight laboratory spaces, and lots of scientific equipment I didn't understand.

The crew comprised fourteen people; the remaining berths were for scientists, of whom there could be as many as thirty. When it was full, the cabins were crowded, but for this particular voyage we were largely empty.

Gayle asked if I wanted to bunk in the cabin my parents had used. I looked inside. There was Mom's bible, on her nightstand. Dad had been reading Graham Greene, in those old Penguin editions with the orange spines. I even recognized the sheets and pillowcases, and the Pendleton blanket they always traveled with.

"Is there anyplace else I can crash?" I asked. I didn't even want to step into that cabin; it would feel like intruding on a ghost.

"Nick, the ship's practically empty. You can sleep anywhere you want."

"Anyplace," I said. "Doesn't matter to me. But not here."

She showed me to another cabin, one with six bunks, two stacks of three, and a desk bolted to the back wall with a computer on it. No portholes. Anonymous, and probably uncomfortable. Perfect. I picked a bottom bunk and tossed my backpack onto it. "This'll do."

"You sure?"

"It's fine," I said. The trip had never been meant as a sightseeing voyage or a pleasure cruise. I wanted to keep my sights on its real purpose—finding my folks—and nothing else. "Just fine."

* * *

Chow was served in the crew mess, which had always seemed to me like an unfortunate name for a place where people ate. I sat at a long table between Gayle and a crewmember named Collum Snow, who dressed like a hipster in a plaid shirt, jeans, suspenders, a knit cap. He had a bushy red beard he could have hidden a couple of cans of Bud Light in. But his clothes were worn, his face weathered, and instead of coming across as a hipster he came across as a man used to the ocean, the kind of hard-working soul the hipsters could imitate the look of, but not the spirit.

The others were a diverse lot, some of whom looked like they'd been born to the sea, like Collum, and others—like a scrawny, tattooed longhair named Norman Draper—who looked like they had to be along for scientific expertise instead of nautical knowhow.

A guy named Panut unrolled a map on the table after we'd eaten a meal heavy on fish and kale. He jabbed a finger at a spot out in the Pacific, well off the California coastline. "This is where the original Blob was," he said, without preamble. Then he traced a much larger circle around the spot, from northern Mexico up into British Columbia. "Basically in here, anyway."

"What blob?" I asked.

"The Blob was an area of abnormally warm ocean water that showed up a few years back," a woman named Elyse Geohagen explained. She came up out of her chair and leaned over the chart. "Water temperatures were seven degrees hotter than average—in some spots, the highest temps ever recorded. Eventually it covered an area bigger than the forty-eight contiguous states."

"Sea life died off in massive numbers," Panut added, picking up the thread again. "Whales died off Alaska. Sea otters died by the hundreds. Millions of sea stars. Hundreds of thousands of seabirds. Sea lions. Krill. A toxic algae bloom essentially destroyed California's crab industry. Tropical sea life was found in the North Pacific, way outside natural ranges. The Blob stayed from early 2013 into late 2015."

"Because of climate change?" I asked.

Panut shrugged. "There are always temperature variations in the Pacific. El Niños and La Niñas flip the water from cooler to warmer all the time. But there's never been anything like this—the Blob covered a bigger area, went deeper, and with hotter temperatures than anything in recorded history. It was unique."

"Until now," Gayle said.

"Now? It's back?" I asked.

"We call it Son of Blob," she said. She put a finger down near the same spot that Panut had originally stabbed, more or less across from the California/Oregon line, but a little farther north and closer to shore. "It's smaller, so far, and mostly concentrated in shallower waters. Which is strange. Also, it's hotter."

"*Much* hotter," Panut added. "Eleven, twelve degrees. That makes a huge difference."

"It's in what we call the Ring of Fire," Gayle said. "There are lots of undersea volcanoes, making the ocean floor uneven, and there are also deep trenches, and some hot vents. It's crazy active down there."

"That's what your folks were investigating when they...disappeared," Collum said. "I love your parents, man, like they were my own, you know? We all do. I refuse to believe they're...gone. We'll find them. That's what this whole expedition is about, right? Finding them. Son of Blob isn't going anywhere, so we'll look at that later. But we need your folks to help make sense of it."

Even then, I understood the futility of what he was saying. The US Navy had sent a search submarine. The National Oceanographic and Atmospheric Administration, the government agency that was— apparently unknowingly—sponsoring this expedition, had sent a couple of submersibles of its own, one manned and the other an undersea robot they called an autonomous underwater vehicle, or AUV.

Nobody had found a trace of my parents, or the *James Cook I*, the submersible they'd been in when they vanished. The submersible's pilot, a *Ricketts* crewmember named Pauly McBride, was also missing, but so far nobody on the ship had mentioned him in my presence. They undoubtedly missed him, too—the crew seemed as close as family, which I guess made them all my brothers and sisters, if Collum was right about everyone seeing my parents as their own. But in front of me, it was all about my folks, and McBride was an afterthought. Maybe it made me an asshole, but I was okay with that.

* * *

On our second day aboard the *Ricketts*, I was standing at the rail near the front of the ship, watching the ocean, surprised at how deep it looked as the ship plowed through the waves and troughs.

"Look at that!" somebody shouted.

I looked. I saw water. Lots of it.

Then Gayle emerged onto the deck near me. "Do you see them, Nick?"

"See who?"

She grabbed my arm and thrust a finger toward the water, pointing at something maybe forty yards away. I was used to counting by yards, but estimating distance was different on the sea than in a stadium. "I'm not seeing anything," I said.

"You're not looking. Look!"

I had thought I was looking, but I guess not. I tried to shift my perception, to focus not on the water itself, but *into* the water, and then I saw it.

We were passing something, or several somethings, that were many-armed. "Is that Lucy?"

"It's not a squid," she said, adding a kind of scoffing sound at the end of it. "It's an octopus. More than one, actually. Several octopuses. Lots. And others cephs, squid, and even some cuttlefish."

"Is that rare? Do they usually travel in packs?"

"They don't usually travel so close to the surface, or in such quantities. Do you re-member seeing any yesterday?"

"No," I said.

"Exactly. How many have you seen in the wild before right now? In your life?"

"One or two, maybe. On the shore, when I was with my folks."

"Right. You see them if they're wandering around on the shore, or if you're diving. And you never see a whole...I don't know, a school? A pod? I'm not sure there is a collective name for a group of them, because they don't usually hang around in groups. They're solitary creatures. It's a 'shoal' of squid, but not for octopuses or for cephalopods in general."

She was staring across the water, a half-smile on her lips. The intensity of that gaze seemed like it could have turned the water to steam.

"This is really unusual, huh?" I said.

"It's unheard of. Literally. I mean, during the last Blob, we saw a lot of sea life far outside its normal ranges, so it's not necessarily surprising in that respect. But so many cephalopods traveling together? Different species, even? That just doesn't happen. I hope Elyse is getting video. She's our resident videographer. This is gonna make the front pages."

"Really?"

"Of the oceanographic journals, anyway."

"I thought the trip was supposed to be a secret."

"Your presence is, not the trip itself. So if you see her with a camera, make yourself scarce."

"I'll do that," I said.

"I'm gonna make sure she's on it," Gayle said.

I caught her arm as she started to turn away. "Hey," I said. "Thanks again. For setting all this up. I appreciate it."

"It's not for you," she replied. "It's for *them*. There's not a person on this ship who wouldn't do anything in the world for your parents. I mean that."

"Well, I appreciate it, anyway."

She shook her arm free and hurried off. I stayed by the rail and watched the water for flashes of tentacle.

* * *

Over the course of that day, we saw more of them. Norman told me they were all cephalopods—which meant head-feet, a name that didn't make sense to me—of the *Coleoidea* subclass. The obvious thing they had in common was their appendages, but Norman ran through more: they could change color in a heartbeat, and they had three hearts. They also had the largest brains of any invertebrates and were considered pretty smart, as nonhuman animals went. They had very complex nervous systems, allowing them to control all those arms and tentacles and the individual suckers on them. They could squirt ink. They had huge eyes and good eyesight. Norman talked about them like a car salesman trying to get me to put down money on the priciest set of wheels on his lot.

He, like everyone else, was fascinated. Most of the conversation aboard ship turned to why they were all traveling in the same direction, why there were so many of them, and why they were so close to the surface. Someone suggested they were following us, but that didn't make sense, since we kept catching up to more; they'd have to be following us from the front, which is pretty hard to do.

"Unless," Norman said, "they're all in communication with one another. Then the ones behind us could alert the others any time we changed course."

"Is that something else that cephalopods can do?" I asked.

"Not that we know of. But they're tricky, and there's a ton we still don't know about them. There are more than 800 distinct species, and we're still finding new ones all the time."

He peered out toward the water again, hoping to see more. "We're witnessing living history," he said. "You're a lucky man."

We were on our way to look for what would probably be the corpses of the people who had given birth to me, raised me, and taught me to follow my dreams, wherever they led.

A bunch of many-limbed sea creatures were kind of cool, I supposed, but I didn't feel all that lucky.

* * *

That night, we reached Son of Blob.

I didn't know it until I rolled out of my bunk in the morning and found folks in the crew mess discussing it. The chatter and the clinking of tableware were loud, raucous, like some holiday family breakfasts I'd endured. I poured coffee into a ceramic mug, took some watery scrambled eggs and sausage, and sat at the table between Panut and Elyse.

"We're there," Panut said.

"We are?"

"Yes. Haven't you noticed that we've come to a stop?"

I hadn't. The motion of the sea still rocked the boat, but now that he'd said it, I realized the rocking was gentler than it had been when we were underway, and I didn't hear the constant thrum of the engines.

"We're just at the outer edge of it," Elyse told me. "Surface temperature is seven-point-two degrees above average here."

"That sounds like a lot."

"It's a troubling deviation," Panut said. "Disastrous. Closer to the center, it's going to be much hotter than that. Sea life will be confused, if not killed. Coral reefs, gone. We might see toxic algal blooms of unheard-of size and scope."

A burly, heavy-bearded guy whose name I couldn't remember sat heavily in the chair across from me, bringing his plate down with a clatter. "Fucking humans are determined to roast the planet," he said. "One ocean at a time."

"I always thought the oceans were the most resilient part," I said.

"They are," the bearded man said. He swallowed his eggs and added, "But the world's mostly ocean, and it's all one big system. If you boiled the blood in your veins, it wouldn't matter how much brain matter you had or how strong your arms were. You fuck with the seas, you're fucking with everything."

Collum walked into the mess and fixed me with a steady gaze. "You ready to go down, man?" he asked. "It's time."

"Don't I have to wait thirty minutes after eating to go in the water?"

It wasn't much of a joke, but the bearded guy exploded in laughter, spewing bits of sausage across the table. Wiping his mouth, he said, "Shit, man, down there it ain't a cramp that'll kill you. Plenty of other things will, though."

Everyone else at the table froze, as if the tactless nature of his comment had hit them all at once. We were, after all, operating under the assumption that something "down there" had killed my parents. I felt like the others were all waiting for my reaction, so I decided to try to lighten the moment. "As long as it's not a cramp," I said, throwing in a forced chuckle for effect. "I hate those more than anything."

Bearded Guy laughed, and the rest joined in.

For me, though, the moment resonated. It felt like an omen of some kind. And not a good one.

* * *

After breakfast, I got my first real look at the *James Cook II*. Almost twenty-four feet long, half that tall, and a third that wide, it looked almost like a clunky white football, albeit one made for giants. The front end, where the passengers sat, was basically a small sphere. It had three round windows, one on each side, and one directly in the center, peepholes in the world's weirdest door. The middle one was larger, almost like a windshield on an SUV. Several cameras were mounted around the outside of the submersible and two hydraulic arms sprouted out of its front end like antennae.

"This one's just like the one my folks went down in?" I asked Gayle, who was busy rattling off the specs on the thing as if I might actually remember them.

"Yup. Basically twins."

"Then don't you have video or whatever of what happened to them?" I asked, pointing at the camera arrays. "Don't those keep trans-mitting until the mission is over?"

"Ideally, yes. But it's not that simple. Lots of things can interfere with the cameras. They can get torn off, knocked out of alignment, crushed. Their power supply can get cut, or diverted to more essential functions, like life support."

"Is that what happened with my parents?"

She gave a little helpless shrug.

"There's no way to know for sure, Nick, not till we find them. Maybe not even then. All we know is that the cameras show them going into the Blob and then the temperature readings started spiking. There was some kind of rapid motion—if they'd been on the surface, I'd have said it was an earthquake—and then the cameras all went dead at once. I can show you the footage if you want. I don't know what you'll see in it that I haven't."

I thought about that for a moment. That footage might well show me the last things my parents ever saw. Would I understand what I was seeing? Had they? Had they known what was in store for them? Had they been terrified, or resigned? Or maybe, being scientists, even a little bit curious about what might lie beyond?

No, I decided. If sleeping in their room would have been intruding on a ghost, seeing their last moments from their vantage point would be like tearing the ghost's sheet off and exposing its spectral nakedness to the world, a violation of a much more personal nature.

"That's okay," I said. "I'm sure you're right. If there was anything to be seen, you'd have seen it."

Gayle look relieved, but she just nodded.

"All right, then. You ready to go down?"

"Ready as I'll ever be."

* * *

I'd misspoken.

There was no way I could have been ready for the descent, crammed into a ball half the size of my dorm room at Husker Hall with two other people. I'd never realized I was claustrophobic until about fifteen minutes into the trip, when I tried to adjust away from the instruments that lined the interior of the sphere for about the thousandth time, only to elbow the pilot, Hans, in the side, eliciting some German that sounded like cursing. Then again, everything German sounded like cursing. Still, I'd been at the bottom of my fair share of dog piles on the field. I knew what tight quarters were like, having someone's knee in your crotch or ass in your face. But those situations only lasted for a short while before the whistle blew and your teammates were dragging people off of you. In this case, the people smothering me *were* my teammates, and that whistle was hours away from blowing. I don't know how my parents handled it.

"Just breathe," Gayle advised. "It takes some getting used to, especially for a big guy. You feel like a bull in a china shop. But nothing in here is that fragile. Except maybe Hans."

Which elicited more German, and an answering laugh from Gayle. It was that laugh, more than anything, that got me to relax a little. That, and the flash of tentacle I spied out the starboard peephole.

Lucy.

I guess she wanted to know what happened to my folks, too.

Or maybe she already did, and wanted to be there to comfort me when I found out.

Which was utterly ridiculous, of course; squid might be smart, but empathetic? Compassionate? That seemed like a reach.

Then again, dogs exhibited those qualities and people didn't bat an eye, maybe because they were warm and furry and had those soulful, sad eyes. So why couldn't a cephalopod, which was arguably smarter than a dog? Just because they lived in an environment alien enough to be another planet didn't mean they couldn't relate to human pain just as much as a warm-blooded surface-dwelling animal, did it?

I shook my head. How my parents would laugh at my questions. Still, Lucy's presence was a comfort, and I held onto it as we descended ever farther.

* * *

"Three hundred," Panut's voice said over the comm unit. We were all wearing head-phones, so we could hear each other over the noise of the submersible's systems and stay in touch with the *Ricketts*. Crammed in together like the proverbial sardines, and we could only communicate electronically. "Temperature's at seventy-three point nine. That's just crazy."

"It's hot, that's for sure," Gayle said.

She was right. I was wearing shorts and a t-shirt and I had expected—despite knowing, theoretically, that we were descending into a heated blob—to be cold. Cold, I was used to. You didn't play for Nebraska, or live there, without getting used to that.

"Three-fifty," Panut said. "Seventy-three point—no, seventy-four even. Everybody okay down there?"

"Okay here," I said.

"Are you sure we're in the North Pacific?" Hans asked. "I think Collum was drunk when he was charting our course."

I could feel Gayle tense from where I sat. "Lights," she said. "All of them."

Hans flipped a couple of switches, and suddenly the night-dark ocean was daylight-bright, at least for a hundred feet or so. Beyond that, the darkness encroached.

And at its edge, barely visible, were tentacles. Lots of them. Thousands.

"The cephalopods," Gayle said. "There they are."

I couldn't see Lucy, but guessed she was there somewhere, amidst the others of her kind.

"They are outside the Blob," Hans said. "Maybe too hot for them here?"

"Some are warm-water cephs," Gayle countered. "This should be a picnic for them."

"Well, they don't want to go inside, it seems."

"Three," Panut said. "The floor here is at ten-three and change, but you're just skirting the slope of a volcanic dome."

Gayle started to say something, but whatever it was, it was lost in a deafening crunching sound. The submersible jolted and shuddered. I might have screamed a little. Hans definitely did.

"What was that?" Panut's voice asked.

"I don't know!" Gayle replied. "It's like we were hit by something."

"By what?"

I was looking out the big windshield but I didn't see anything, much less anything big enough to have slammed into us with that much force.

Just water. Little things swimming or floating in it, but not even many of those. Not with the water this hot.

Across from me, Gayle was doing the same thing I was: scanning for whatever unknown force had hit us. Hans was busy at the controls, and he looked worried.

"What's going on, Hans?" I asked.

"The instruments are going berserk!" he said. "Panut, are you seeing this?"

"I don't know what I'm seeing," Panut shot back. "None of it makes any sense!"

Then it happened again. This time was worse. The *James Cook II* was swung sideways in the water and I heard what sounded like the squeal of tearing steel. If I hadn't been belted in, I'd have fallen onto Hans, or past him into Gayle's lap. I thought that was the worst of it, but then we started to spin in the water, surrounded by a cloud of air bubbles.

"We're ruptured!" Gayle said. "Tanks on, quick!"

Before we left, I'd been shown submarine escape immersion equipment, which were used for deep-water emergency escapes. But I'd also been told we weren't expecting to go deep enough to make them necessary, especially since warm water was less dense, therefore diminishing the pressure. I couldn't remember where the SEIEs were, but there was Scuba gear for each of us, and it was handy.

My parents had taken me diving many times, so I was used to how it worked. What I didn't know was how to get the gear on while the vessel I was in was spinning and flipping over and the most important bodily function I wanted control of at the moment was holding in the breakfast I was about to lose, because about two seconds after I puked it up, I'd be flung right into it.

Gayle unbuckled her shoulder straps, leaving the waist strap on, and tried to shrug into a buoyancy control vest with two cylinders and a regulator attached. That made sense to me, so I tried the same trick. I had it mostly on when the walls caved in.

Whatever invisible *something* was slamming us around the ocean was squeezing the *James Cook II*, like a fist pulping a lemon. The windshield shattered, and a shard of glass slammed into my face as the ocean rushed in. I batted it away with my right hand, gripping my seat with my left so I didn't fall out. I glanced over at Gayle, who'd lost her battle with her BCV—I could just see it, through the bubble storm, dropping out of sight.

Then I saw Hans, his mouth open in a soundless cry of agony. The water around him was tinged with pink. He was pinned into his seat by a jagged chunk of steel from the hull or the instrument panel. It had sliced into his abdomen, and blood from the wound mixed with the water.

The *James Cook II* whirled around like a ride from some demented undersea carnival. I was breathing, at least, but I'd have to share what air I had with Gayle. It was too late for Hans—blood flowed from his open mouth and his eyes were blank. I didn't have a mask or fins, and if they were somewhere near me, I didn't know where. My hand bumped into a dive light and I grabbed it, slipping my arm through the wrist lanyard.

I grabbed Gayle next, or she grabbed me. I pulled her close and handed her the spare mouthpiece. We shoved free of the spinning submersible and made for the surface.

As we swam away from the wreckage, I looked for whatever had crushed it. I don't know what I expected to find—a colossal squid, a kraken, a whale—but I didn't see anything. Nothing but the warm water of

Son of Blob. It was as if the thing was malevolent, using water pressure alone to murder Hans and to try to get us.

The *James Cook II's* lights were gone. I was a pretty strong swimmer, but more than that, I was a Husker. I didn't let little things slow me down.

I held Gayle's hand, so we didn't get too far apart to use the spare tube. We were both dizzy, discombobulated, and the dive light didn't do much to show the way, but we swam with everything we had.

Worried about the bends, I was about to suggest—as well as I could, using sign language—that we stop for a bit. But then I looked up, only to discover that we had been swimming in the wrong direction—right toward the slope of the undersea dome, instead of toward the surface.

That's when I saw it. A dark spot—well, darker—surrounded by rocks. And a lone cephalopod who'd braved Son of Blob motioning me toward it.

Lucy.

I didn't hesitate.

Pulling Gayle along with me, I made for that patch of blackness like it was the end zone and I was about to score the winning touchdown in the National Championship game. Or, you know, like my life depended on it. In Nebraska, which of those was more important was often debatable, especially during football season. Either way, I made it to what turned out to be an opening in record time, feeling all the while like there was something hot and hungry on my heels, but every time I glanced behind, there was nothing but ocean.

It was the wreckage of the *James Cook I*, upside down, smashed much as our submersible had been, and lodged up under the rocks in such a way as to be invisible from above. Even at the same depth as the small vessel, if sharp-eyed Lucy hadn't been there to point it out, I'd never have seen it.

I found the open hatch, pushed Gayle through, then squeezed in myself.

The interior of the *James Cook I* was only about half-full of water. Inverted, it was apparently acting like an ancient diving bell, keeping some mostly breathable air at the top. As Gayle and I pulled in great lungfuls of the stale stuff, I saw that air wasn't all the submersible still held. A battered oxygen tank, its gauge low, but seemingly still usable, caught in some of the dangling instrumentation.

And beyond that...

"Nick...my God. I'm so sorry."

I didn't answer her. I couldn't.

I'd found them. What was left of them, anyway. Pauly wasn't there, but my parents were.

They'd only been gone a week, but they appeared mummified—some trick of the air down here, that probably held very little oxygen, after all.

God knew I was suddenly finding it much harder to breathe than I had before.

I could almost convince myself it wasn't them, if not for the customized wedding bands they wore, Dr. Dr. Dad's red coral and green opal swirled around a lapis center, Mom's the inverse, with lapis and opal swirled around the coral.

And for the fact that, even in death—maybe *particularly* in death—they were entwined in each other's arms, as if daring eternity to try to separate them.

I turned away and wrapped my arms around myself, realizing suddenly how cold it was down here. I rubbed my hands rapidly up and down my biceps for warmth, but the only heat I felt was the tears that scalded my cheeks as they made their way down to join the saltier water at my waist.

A soft splash drew my attention. One of Lucy's tentacles rose out of the water, coming near me. First, it hovered around my hands questioningly, so I reached a palm and let her touch it to feel the small amount of warmth the movement had generated.

"Friction generates energy—in this case, heat. It's a way we humans use to warm ourselves up when we're too stupid to dress appropriately for the conditions."

Satisfied with my explanation, or not comprehending it, or possibly just bored, her tentacle left my hand and moved up to my face, where it gingerly wiped one tear from my cheek, then patted it softly. I felt a strange rush of emotion, not quite of comfort, but of...com-munity. As if she were trying to tell me I was not alone in my grief.

"Thanks, Lucy."

Then a shudder rippled through her tentacle and it was suddenly pulling urgently at my shoulder.

"I think she's saying it's time to go."

I looked up at Gayle. She was strapping on the other tank as she spoke.

I nodded.

"I've seen all I needed to."

Lucy's tentacle retracted back into the water and Gayle went in after it. I took one last look back at my parents' corpses—my final farewell, for I knew it was unlikely I'd ever find this place again—and then I followed suit.

Back out in the cold dark, I felt Lucy's tentacle wrap around me and could just make out Gayle's nearby form similarly enfolded in another suckered appendage. Lucy drew me close enough to see her basketball-sized eyes, and the sharp beak at the center of her buccal mass. Then we were shooting toward the surface so fast I knew decompression sickness was likely to be a real concern. But so was running out of air before we made it there, and of the two, only the latter was certain to be fatal. So I sucked in what oxygen I had left and let Lucy do her thing.

Her thing, it turned out, involved buzzing the group of cephalopods that we'd been following, only now, instead of swimming, they were arranged in some sort of gigantic, living net, their tentacles all interlocked so I couldn't tell where one squid began and another ended. We went by them so quickly, and their myriad of appendages, small and large, were moving back and forth so fast that I couldn't see what it was they were trying to hold in—it just looked like more water to me—but I could definitely feel the heat, as if someone had opened the door to an underwater sauna.

And then we were past the cage of tentacles with its invisible prisoner and going up and up and up…

I think I must have passed out at some point, because the next thing I remember is breaking the surface and coughing up about a swimming pool's worth of ocean, Gayle doing the same beside me. Lucy hung around long enough to make sure we weren't going to choke to death on seawater and spit, then started to pull away, heading back into the deep.

"Wait!" I said—or tried to, anyway; my throat was so raw, it came out as more of a grunt. But, as usual, Lucy seemed to understand me even without words. A tentacle came questing back.

I didn't bother talking this time, just reached out a hand until we were touching, palm to sucker.

Thank you.

That rush of togetherness came again and I think I understood it this time. She wasn't just telling me I wasn't alone. She was saying I never would be. That we were family.

There was something else, too. It felt like…relief? I'm not sure human concepts could even encompass cephalopod emotions, but it seemed almost like our rescue was some sort of atonement for my parents' deaths—as if she had somehow felt guilty for not having been able to save them, and that burden had now been lifted.

Then she broke contact and disappeared back beneath the water, presumably going to rejoin the rest of her—*our?*—family.

"It's the *Ricketts!*" Gayle said excitedly, pointing behind me. I turned, and sure enough, the ship was there, as if it had been waiting for us the whole time. "We're saved!"

So we were. Lucy had done for us what she could not do for my parents. As we started to swim toward the ship, I was left wishing my own atonement could come so easily.

* * *

"…weirdest thing I've ever seen," Panut said. "Son of Blob kept getting smaller and hotter—almost boiling—and then it just suddenly...*vanished.*"

"What do you mean 'vanished?'" Gayle asked. We were back on board, dressed in warm clothes, swathed in blankets, hearing what had occurred on the *Ricketts* while we'd been gone.

"As in, one minute there was a clearly definable heat signature, and the next minute there...wasn't. The temperature cooled right back down to normal temps in a matter of minutes. It was like Son of Blob never existed."

"It was Lucy and the others," I said. "That cage they made. Whatever they were doing, they somehow managed to destroy Son of Blob."

Gayle shook her head slowly.

"No, Nick. I mean, yes, it was them, but they're not the ones who destroyed SoB. *You* are."

We all looked at her.

"What?"

"When you explained to Lucy how friction worked, remember? And then when we were going past them, their tentacles were all moving up and down, almost faster than the eye could follow? Superheating the Son of Blob, compressing it, until it ultimately—I don't know—imploded? Whatever they did, they clearly got the idea from you."

I scoffed at the thought, but I could see she was serious, and the others seemed to be taking her seriously, too.

"Well, there's no way we'll ever know for sure, I suppose," I said, and everyone nodded with various degrees of enthusiasm, and that seemed to end the conversation.

Still, I couldn't stop thinking about what Gayle said, especially as I lay in my bunk later that night. If Lucy *had* gotten the idea from me, and passed it on to the rest of the cephalopods, then in a way, I'd atoned for my parents' deaths as well. Not that I could have done anything to stop what happened—unlike Lucy, I'd been thousands of miles away when it occurred—but logic seldom got in the way of guilt when it came to the loss of loved ones. And it wasn't really atonement I was looking for, I realized, so much as vengeance. A rematch. The chance to play the game again, with a different outcome this time around.

Of course, I couldn't have the outcome I really wanted—my parents back, alive—but I could have something else almost as good. The destruction of the thing that had killed them.

If Gayle was right, I'd gotten that. Son of Blob had been annihilated because of me. And if she was wrong...well, maybe the cephalopods *could* have done it on their own—but, if so, wouldn't they have taken out the Blob, making sure there never was a Son to deal with in the first place?

Did it really matter if it was due to my efforts or to Lucy and the cephalopods'? Either way, my parents had been avenged by family. Just the way they would have wanted it.

There was a knock on the door.

I got out of the bunk, walked over, and opened it to find Gayle standing there.

"Sorry to bug you. I meant to give these to you earlier. I thought you might want them." She held out her hand. In her palm were my parents' wedding rings.

I swallowed once, then reached out and took them.

"Thank you."

She nodded, turned on her heel, and went back down the hall without another word.

I stood there for a moment staring at the rings, then I went up on deck and crossed over to the railing.

"Lucy?" I called softly.

A tentacle broke the surface nearby, as if she had been there the whole time, just waiting for me. As it rose up to my level, I reached out and placed Mom's ring in one of her upraised suckers.

"She'd want you to have this, I think."

Lucy's tentacle closed around the gift. Then she brushed my cheek with it gently before retracting it carefully back into the water, and I knew in that moment I'd never see her again.

I looked down at the ring still in my hand, thinking about family—the one we are born into and the one we choose, or that chooses us. I had always been an only child, and never imagined I'd have a sister, let alone one who was a telepathic squid, or an entire ship full of unexpected siblings.

It made me wonder who else the universe might have in store for me—maybe even a woman who I'd someday raise my own family with and in whose arms I'd be content to die entwined. And suddenly, I couldn't wait to get back to shore to find her.

UNDER PRESSURE
JODY LYNN NYE

In the mirror just underneath the lens-like door to her domicile, Dr. Nadine Charter checked the little light on a spring arched in front of her round face. *Angler fish*, she thought, sticking her tongue out at her reflection and tasting the salt of the sea. After twelve years of public education and six years of graduate school, she had turned into an angler fish. It was still so new to her, but she liked living in Poseidon a whole lot better than living on land, even a land as lovely as Jamaica.

Out of the corner of one eye, Nadine kept watch on the concave video screen sealed in its watertight case. On the news channel, yet another US senator flailed his arms. The text transcript scrolling up below the image contained the usual inflammatory nonsense about Undersea and its industries being a drain on the taxpayers and polluting the waters off the coast of the United States while blaming it on other entities, like corporations and urban water treatment plants. She caught a glimpse of her own reflection in the big looking glass attached to the wall of her bubble-like domicile and shook her head. She knew it wasn't so. Undersea, and the city of Poseidon in particular, was running clean. No one here stirred up toxins from the sea bed. She worked in the ecology monitoring station and knew that it was the corporations dumping their mess into the oceans. The bad tastes that sometimes floated in the water gave them clues as to who, but so far, her department hadn't been able to produce adequate proof as to where the contaminants came from. Nadine and her team kept on the hunt, all the time knowing that the government entities wanted to cut their funding and leave them blind.

Her light summer dress floated around her like the skirt of an anemone, brushing her legs as she swam. She liked to wear something, although after the first day, she had thrown all her bras in the disposer. Never again would she have to worry about gravity pulling her 40D breasts toward the center of the earth. Fat floated, and in a sexy way, too, if she had to mention how God had blessed her, top and bottom. Only land women had to strap themselves up with micro-corsets. Instead of panties, she wore loose bloomers that fastened at the waist with Velcro, and took care of bodily functions by pulling the crotch aside behind a clump of coral. Some of her fellows didn't bother with any outer garments, and excreted as freely as fish. Those she banned from her lab. Nadine swam up out of her doorway, batting aside the school of yellow-tailed fish that hovered there every morning, waiting for her to emerge. The boldest of them ducked under her hands and mobbed her, trying to get near the forehead light. With a silent laugh that inflated her gills to their maximum, she opened out her arms and stroked back, propelling herself through the water in the direction of her lab. The fish followed her like sheep, held in thrall by the light on her forehead.

My pilot fish, she thought, filled with affection for her charges. *We are all denizens of the deep.*

Over the last few weeks, her deep brown skin had stopped puckering as her system became used to seawater, and her eyes never teared any more. Except for a few vestiges that the surgeons and geneticists had not yet been able to adapt for undersea life, she had become merfolk. Nadine couldn't go back and live on the land even if she had wanted to, but she didn't want to. She couldn't picture living dry any more. She had left pain and isolation behind.

Years ago, she had seen the merfolk who came back to the surface to visit, to see family or to attend conferences, with the tall hydration collar around their necks, pulling the tank of seawater along behind them as though it was an oxygen tank for visitors to Undersea. The change made to them was partially genetic, partially cosmetic. The alteration to her DNA pulled her partway back to the tadpole stage of embryonic development that so many species on Earth went through in gestation, when fetuses literally breathed water. The surgeons wouldn't remove her lungs, even though she didn't need to use them, because of the concentration of healthy blood vessels in them her system needed to carry oxygen, but over time her grandchildren and great-grandchildren would begin to breed true, selecting for the implanted genes.

The denizens of Undersea who had come to welcome her six weeks before had fitted her with a forehead light and introduced them-selves, all in sign. As a child, she had been diagnosed as profoundly deaf. On land, her disability hampered her. Under water, her ability to communicate with her hands and face was an advantage over those newcomers who had relied on sound. Her new friends embraced her and took her home, down to Poseidon. Nadine had fallen instantly in love with all of them, and with her new city. Even she didn't understand the fierce protectiveness she felt toward it. If she could have cradled her city and all the creatures swimming near it in her arms, she would have. Anything she could do to defend it and make it prosper, she would do.

Glowing spires, silver domes, golden bubbles and opalescent clusters, every shape except square and flat, the rooftops of Poseidon ranging from just thirty to well over a hundred meters deep spread out below her. Land cities, even their skyscrapers, were basically two dimensional. Here, cities were for those who traveled in all three dimensions. Poseidon had been built at the edge of the continental shelf of North America off South Carolina. The widely-spaced dwellings and other buildings were tethered by strong but thin cables to the cliff and to the sea bed below. Huge cables ran up tall cliffs behind the last scattering of buildings, as Poseidon shared the fruits of its clean-running, electricity-generating turbines with the land-dwellers. The water was spectacularly clear considering that thousands of people already lived there. The few that were abroad this early waved; those out of the city's lighting were careful to keep their gestures within the range of their headlamps so she could see them. People just seemed nicer Undersea. Probably because everyone who was there wanted to be there, had been through hell and literal high water, not to mention all the physical alterations. They were united in being determined to make the largest of the Atlantic's underwater cities work.

The biggest and most profound mental leap Nadine had to make was with regard to boundaries. She had grown up on a relatively peaceful street in Kingston, but gang turf lay close by. Straying into the wrong neighborhood could be fatal. Now if she avoided sharks and lionfish, or descending too fast into the dark deeps, there was nowhere she couldn't go. She lived in three dimensions, now, like space travelers, only she wasn't tethered to air tanks or fearful of freezing to death in their environment. If she took it very slow and easy so her body adjusted to the depths, she could see wonders invisible to ordinary divers. When she was a girl, she had often fantasized about being a mermaid. She'd achieved that dream, and it was as wonderful as she thought it was going to be. Freedom felt glorious.

Undersea colonies communicated with each other via technology sealed inside watertight cases that protected the components against the seawater as well as the pressure. Even the phones, exclusively used for texting and video calls, were good to almost 12,000 meters, though the people using them weren't. Poseidon, in spite of being founded sixty miles off shore from the founder's home city, was the newest of the settlements. A couple of her new friends waved to her with both hands from a hundred meters down, near the cultivated oyster beds on a shelf outcropping over which flowed a fast current. Nadine beamed and waved back. They signed to her to come down to pass the time of day. She started to swim down, but before she had descended more than fifty meters, twin pangs erupted in her chest. She gulped to drive the pain away. The lungs that would be vestigial in future generations were an actual impediment to her in the here and now. The rest of her body had been adapted to deep sea living, but it would take a while—if ever—for her old breathing apparatus to get with the program. Instead, she tipped them a cheery salute and kicked up toward her office. Later on, when she more leisure.

Mini-subs passed between the buildings here and there, containing visitors from the surface. Almost all of them represented non-governmental organizations, but several came from corporations and government departments, looking to negotiate with the city's founder, Fin Ferrar, hoping to make exceptions to the fierce environmental policies that he had established in the territory claimed for the colony. A woman with bright-red lipstick peered out of a round porthole. Nadine gave her a big smile and a wave as she swam by. As the sub passed, Nadine tasted bitter residue in the seawater and spat it out in disgust. Despite Fin's regulations, pollutants were increasing instead of decreasing.

She passed between a couple of pillars dotted with tiny pearly blue lights marking the edge of the university research campus. Her pale green lab module was the unit farthest to the south. Through the domed ceiling, she saw her lab assistant, Norbert, a tall, skinny white man with a hollow chest and a swirl of shoulder-length black hair, already hovering at the computer. The blue glow of the screen shone all around him.

She shoved her coterie of fish away from the flexible gasket that served as a door and wriggled down to join him. When Fin had taken her on a tour of Poseidon, she had laughed at the screens on the windows. Water was everywhere, right? The Undersea humans needed a fresh flow to breathe, but the fish got in the way of everything, like pigeons. If you didn't want them investigating your experiments, you needed to shut the fish outside. They bumped their noses against the walls and the roof, then swam off looking for someone else to bother.

She tapped Norbert on the shoulder. He palmed the water to turn toward her, and gave her a grin.

"How are the readings this morning?" she signed.

"Still getting that anomaly," he replied. He took her by the wrist and drew her to the console. She floated on her tummy while he brought up the graphs. "Phthalates, more than seven parts per billion. I don't know where the pollutants are leaching from, but every factory and waste system within twenty miles of the shore has pled not guilty."

Nadine peered at the readings, her brow wrinkling with dismay. There was nowhere left on the crowded continents to dump dangerous wastes. The cost of disposing of toxic materials had rocketed higher over the last few decades, eating deeply into the profits, and executive salaries, of many of the largest corporations.

The ecology monitoring office had been one of Fin's pet projects when Poseidon was designed. With the population of Undersea growing every day, he was determined not to let the oceans get as polluted as the overcrowded continents. Nadine was proud to be a part of it. Their major problem was that over the millennia, human beings had gotten used to throwing all their garbage into the ocean. Out of sight, out of mind, right? But the traces were nine times higher than they should have been, endangering the Poseidon region as well as anyone who swam or ate seafood from this part of the ocean.

She expelled a jet of water from her mouth and set both hands moving in a vigorous retort. "I call BS. I'll send Lukas with the microsub to get readings from the corporations' output conduits to measure against those trace elements."

"Lukas is topside," Norbert gestured. "His niece is getting married."

Nadine mimed slapping herself in the forehead. "I forgot. I'll go. I haven't got any meetings until tomorrow."

"Can't it wait until he gets back?"

Nadine dithered a moment. "Let me call Fin."

"No!" The videophone screen filled with the sight of the CEO's hands when she asked the question. "It can't wait. *National Geographic* and the networks are sending teams of interviewers to tour Poseidon for an Earth Day documentary. "

Norbert opened his mouth and lifted his hands to protest, but a wave from Fin cut him off.

"I know that sounds petty to the extreme," the CEO signed, pointing off into the far distance, "but we could use good press. I don't know about you, but I'm getting tired of being accused of perpetrating a boondoggle on the treasury. We're still a decade from being profitable. We've got the assistant under-secretary paying us a visit day after tomorrow. He can cut off a significant amount of our funding, money we need to continue working on infrastructure. And where the US attacks, Cuba and Mexico aren't far behind. I'm sorry you're short-handed, but we need proof that the spill isn't coming from one of our factories." The hands receded, and the founder's handsome, angular face appeared, looking resigned and sheepish.

"I hate it," Nadine said, feeling her face get hot in spite of the cool water flowing over it. "They're wrong. No one down here is using phthalates in anything. They're too damned toxic."

"Then, who is?" Fin asked.

Norbert dragged a split screen onto the scope and filled it with short data files.

"Technically," he said, "they were outlawed in US manufacture six years ago, but a number of foreign corps probably still use them. Close to the east coast, I've got nine. Two of them are Chinese-owned. One, Nin Suliao, makes reusable grocery bags. Sounds ecologically friendly, but their pliability gave away the fact that they were using phthalates as a softener. They built a concrete storage unit about thirty nautical miles north, then got the hell fined out of them for using toxic chemicals a couple years ago."

Nadine tapped herself on the nose.

"I bet they sprang a leak."

"Go check it out," Fin said, his forehead wrinkling. "Bring me back proof. We can be heroes for pointing out an ecological crisis, and get brownie points from the US government at the same time."

* * *

Nadine signed out the hand-sub that her team shared with three other departments, hung a boom-stick and an underwater pistol crosswise over her shoulders in case of sharks, packed a lunch, and set out. It shouldn't take her more than three hours to find the supposedly abandoned storage unit.

As a newcomer, Nadine was eager for a chance to swim out into the far reaches of her underwater community and take a look around. The center of the city had the highest concentration of round-edged dwellings, but it was on the outskirts where things got really interesting. Experimental farms had been sprouting up almost every week. One of her new friends, Mehit from Indonesia, had been working on breeding a high-protein sea fruit hybrid. The purplish bulbs looked pretty unappetizing, but tasted like a cross between mangoes and breadfruit. Nadine had a chunk of sea fruit in her lunch, along with slabs of fresh fish and a kind of hardtack. Mehit kept inviting Nadine to come out and see it, but Nadine's workload so far had prevented her taking a day to wander. To have an assignment to go sightseeing along the north track was a blessing.

She grasped the curved bars on either side of the hand-sub, switched it on, and let the bullet-shaped engine pull her out toward the north of Poseidon. The bubbles that flowed back from it along her body tickled.

As she left the last of the dwellings behind, ghostly-colored coral reefs loomed up out of the gloom. Along with her headlamp, she carried a hundred-megawatt spotlight and a digital video camera to capture evidence, if she found any, of the source of the pollution. In her experience, and that of the techs that had come before her, no corporation was willing to put out money for repairs or adjustments without ample proof. Sample jars in a sack bumped against her back, exciting the curiosity of her fish friends. Brilliant-colored sea creatures appeared for a split second in the light of her headlamp, then whisked away into the dimness.

Outside of Poseidon proper, the ocean was almost dark. It took a few minutes before the wary urban child inside Nadine got past the idea that something scary was waiting out there to eat her. A GPS/sonar feature in the hand-sub warned her away from the rippling, jagged continental rock wall that loomed up on her left hand. She veered right, into a bank of sea ferns waving in the strong current. They tickled. Shadows of fish and eels nipped in and out of crevices deceptive in size. Some of those openings were small enough that only a clownfish could hide in there, but others were big enough for a four-bedroom house with a two-car garage.

The water on her lips now tasted distinctly different than it did in her home or her lab: bad, like chemistry-set explosion bad. The rush of the continental current along the sea wall carried a higher concentration of the pollutants than she had detected in town. She stopped the sub to tie a microfiber filter over her mouth and gills. That would slow her own breathing a little, but it would protect her from the leaking particulates. She couldn't do anything to protect her coterie of fish. She turned and waved wildly at the school of yellow-stripes.

"Go home! Get out of here! It's dangerous!"

They paid her no attention at all. They were fish. With a deep sigh that dragged the cloth against her neck, she continued north.

Although she was in deep water far off shore, she still saw schools of shallow-water fish casting swirling patterns overhead. A huge shadow blotted out the thin, blue light from the sun. She stopped to admire the whale shark, its vast spotted belly and plankton-catching maw the size of an automobile, swimming just a few meters above her. How could land-based humans ever understand the beauty of the sea? To them it was just something to fly over, to dump in, to dip in the shallows, but never to examine its depths. Poseidon was under constant pressure to prevent efforts in Congress and other world governments to defund their operations. She hated to be so cynical, but too much lobbying money found its way into politicians' pockets from unregulated corporations. Some companies threatened to take their businesses to countries without Undersea colonies off their coasts. Nadine shook her head, making her hair dance in the waves. Didn't they understand that Undersea was vital to the future of humanity? A healthy ocean made for a healthy planet.

Something in the water stung her eyes. Nadine blinked hard, the underused tear ducts kicking in to try and clear them. According to the GPS, she had to be within a couple of kilometers of the storage facility. She reached for one of the sample jars and scooped up a deciliter of seawater and videoed it with the date and location visible on the screen. Even her gills felt as though they were burning. A quick check on her portable screen confirmed that those were symptoms associated with exposure to phthalates. Nin Suliao was going to be embarrassed if it turned out to be coming from their facility, so she would have to be careful about obtaining proof.

She shone her spotlight ahead, scanning for the tank. According to the images in the company's EPA filing, it was a water-tower-sized cylinder of reinforced concrete with pipes feeding down into it along the continental shelf. Turning off the GPS's flashing warning signal, she aimed toward the high stone shelf and increased the hand-sub's moveable spotlight to full.

Most of her escort had peeled off and fled toward cleaner water. Her skin began to feel dirty, an odd sensation considering she had the entire ocean washing her. Though she must have been almost on top of the site, her spotlight had so far failed to illuminate anything that looked like a tank resting on the abyssal plain itself. The drift of sediment accumulating at the base of the continental rise could conceivably have buried most of the bulk, but at least the pipes ought to be visible. She swam in and out of the massive fissures and crevices, flashing her light up toward the surface. Perhaps the pipes had been laid into one of them, giving them additional stability. With a flick of a switch on the hand-sub, Nadine began filming.

The few fish that still dogged her suddenly darted away, toward the cliff. She looked up to see what had attracted them. Almost concealed by seaweed and ferns, a small red LED, no bigger than the palm of her hand, had been fastened into the stone wall. She swam close to investigate it, and her eyes stung as if acid had been thrown into them. Swinging the light down, she saw a steady outflow of white liquid that spread out into the current. Her attendant fish dipped down into the flow to examine it. To Nadine's horror, one of them began to twitch and jackknife in pain. Another simply stopped moving and turned belly up. It floated upward before her face, eyes dulled, dead.

On instinct, Nadine propelled herself upward, moving away from the flow. She swam a kilometer out and back beyond the outflow, down along the cliff-face, searching far beyond the GPS setting, and back again, puzzled. Her practical brain told her that a whole tank the size of a large building could not have floated away or been stolen by divers. Nin Suliao must never have built one in the first place!

Immediately, she sent a message to Norbert in the home office. His astonished expression agreed with hers.

"Could you be looking in the wrong place?" he signed.

"I don't think so, but I'll gather samples and keep looking," she replied. "Tell Fin. I'll be back with proof. Tell…"

She stopped gesturing as a shadow from above attracted her attention. Directly overhead, in a tunnel of pale blue boring through the midnight darkness, she saw the unmistakable splashing of scuba divers penetrating the depths, surrounded by a wash of bubbles.

That was timely, she thought. Fin must have sent Nin Suliao a memo that there might be a leak coming from their containment tank after she left and they were sending someone out to look into it. The facility was only about twenty kilometers from the shore.

Oh.

But there *was* no tank.

They weren't responding to a potential ecological problem. The red light must have been attached to a motion detector set to a particular density in the water. Only a body of a particular size would set it off, like a shark…or a human being.

She turned the spotlight up toward the divers. She counted three, all wearing deep-diving gear with clear faceplates and double-sized tanks. In their hands, she spotted long, slender objects.

Before she had time to guess what they were, one of them turned his object toward her. Her spotlight picked up the rush of bubbles heading toward her. Underwater rifles!

Suddenly, the light on the hand-sub shattered and went out. Horrified, she nearly dropped the handlebars. They were *shooting* at her! Nadine steered away from the divers, desperate to find shelter. Such guns had been used in military operations. Intellectually, she knew they weren't accurate over twenty-five meters, but she didn't want to be hit by accident, either.

Another bullet winged past her, drilling a green tube through the water not two meters from her head. Suddenly, she was back in her old neighborhood, trying to avoid becoming a casualty.

Where could she hide? At fifty meters, the only cover was the thin vegetation clinging to the sheer underwater cliff. The nearest crevasse was filled with the toxic chemical stream. She switched on the hand-sub and clung to it, glancing back over her shoulder again and again.

The men had hand-subs, too. They hooked their arms through the bars, set the rifle butts on top of the body, and focused their spotlights on her. More slugs drilled through the current. Nadine dodged back and forth, hoping she wouldn't inadvertently put herself into the path of a bullet. These men were good shots. Too good. They were firing at her even when she was not in the beam of their lights. She realized that the light shining right on her face gave them an easy target.

With her left hand, she snatched off the glowing headband, cut to the right, and tossed it away. Three bullets pierced through the waves, following the lamp as it sank into the depths. It took them each two shots before they figured out she wasn't wearing it any longer. The delay had allowed her to race ahead forty meters.

It wasn't enough of a head start. The beams hit her again from behind, growing larger with every moment. Their subs were much faster than hers. The three men spread out to catch her. She maneuvered, weaving between them. Was the gap between them wide enough that she could escape before they closed in on her? She decided to hug the wall, hoping the next fissure would give her a hiding place. Another bullet ripped by just above her body, coming close enough to ruffle her dress. She didn't have very much time.

She had been a scuba diver from her teenage years, trading working in a local dive shop for tank fills. At forty meters, leisure divers had twelve minutes on a standard tank. With the oversized tanks on their shoulders, they might have another ten minutes' worth of air. If she could keep ahead of them for twenty minutes, they would have to surface, and slowly, so as not to get the bends. Nadine flailed at the sea cliff, poking blindly at coral and rock, feeling for a gap. With neither headlamp or a spotlight, she was nearly blind. She did not want to die.

She felt the vibration through the water of the enemy's three engines. Once her eyes adapted to the lack of light, she saw their shadows converging on her.

The hand-subs meant they weren't burning much in exertion, but every atmosphere of pressure caused their lungs to gasp for more and more oxygen. She no longer needed a breather and a regulator. And she had a direction that they didn't have: straight down.

As the men triangulated in on her, she turned upside down and kicked the hand-sub into its highest gear.

A hundred meters, a hundred fifty meters down, more. Her lungs shrank from the pressure to two hard, little masses, jerking her diaphragm up into her chest cavity. The stabbing pain made her vision swim with blackness. She would have given anything to stop, to drift up toward the surface, but her life was at stake.

The men's spotlights painted the sea wall with brilliant white light that was swallowed up in shadows cast by waving ferns. She spotted an irregularly shaped blackness, a seam that must have been ten meters top to bottom. Nadine turned her sub into it, trusting that it was large enough for her to fit. The sub banged against stone, setting off the emergency flash again and again, but the red light gave her enough illumination to figure out where to steer it next.

Over her shoulder, sharp white lights proved that the divers had found her hiding place. The land dwellers had to be pushing the limits of their air. She slowed the hand-sub to a crawl. With one hand, she shoved her bang-stick business-end up into a clump of coral, then deliberately hit a rock with the sub so it flashed its warning.

One of the divers motored toward her. She dived down behind the coral, and had the satisfaction of seeing the man strike the tip of the bang-stick. The percussive charge did exactly what it would have done to a shark, sending him tumbling in the opposite direction. The other two divers came to his assistance, giving her a respite. She turned her toes up and aimed for the bottom.

Ignoring the pain in her chest, she felt for the nearest opening. A dozen small fish zipped out of her way as she backed into the small gap, feeling her way with her webbed toes. She hoped to God that there were no needle-toothed eels behind her, and that her bulky body would fit into the cave. At last, her feet touched smooth, cold, slimy rock. She shut off the sub, and waited.

All of her instincts told her to go back to the surface and get help. With this much rock between her and Poseidon, she couldn't get a signal out. She had to outwait her attackers.

Her gills worked frantically on her neck, tickling her throat. Her lungs had shrunk to angry fists of tissue, pounding on her heart from either side.

Wave after wave of water sloshed into the opening of her hidey-hole as the men kicked past it, searching for her. She ducked her head, hoping they would mistake her mass of floating black hair for coral. She couldn't last there forever. The intense pain she was suffering could bring on a heart attack. Perhaps she could last twenty minutes more at this depth. She had to survive. She had to.

All the sacrifices that she had made to live in the ocean, all the surgery and genetic alterations, all the social rejection that she had undergone as a deaf child, and now a freak of nature, had been worth it to find an accepting, loving society where differences were embraced. Her new life was worth defending, and for that, she had to get the evidence of the corporate crime back to Poseidon. Nadine forced her mind to construct the home of her dreams, one room at a time. Big windows, with double-strong screens. Five bedrooms—no, ten! The kind that could be evacuated and dried, so her family could come and visit. A video room with soft hammocks to watch from. She clutched her chest, emitting soundless screams. A kitchen with a sous-vide station. An atrium filled with clusters of bubble lights, just because she could.

The searching outside became more frantic. They had maybe ten more minutes, then they had to rise toward the surface. They would come back with an army. Nadine had to get away. Common sense kept her immobile. She forced herself to ignore the pain and waited.

At last, the lights were gone, leaving her in utter darkness. Nadine pushed her agony to the back of her mind and cupped her hand around her pocket screen. Ten minutes more, then another ten minutes. They couldn't possibly have lasted that long.

But she had.

She took in a deep gush of fresh water through her gills, feeling the filter cloth suck tight against her throat. She was alive!

Nadine didn't dare turn on her hand-sub at first, in case the divers could hear the distant thrum. Instead, she dragged it with one hand as she felt her way out of the pocket of stone, then along the sea wall toward the rush of the continental current. The rapid flow swept her along with it, dragging her toward the south.

She was so relieved she nearly let it carry her along, but she needed evidence. The men would be back soon, but Fin would have her head if she didn't do it properly.

The loss of her spotlight and headlamp hampered her somewhat but she used the light from her communication handset and the emergency beacon on the hand-sub to illuminate the flow of white particles from the fissure in the rock, and filled every jar in her pack with damning evidence. She took ten solid minutes of video, then kicked the hand-sub into high gear to take her back to Poseidon.

Nadine ran for her life, hoping that the men had not had a good enough look at her to identify her. She had no wish to be hunted down.

* * *

Back at the lab, Fin hovered with her, then watched her explanation and video with narrowed eyes. He played the footage twice more, then patted her on the back. Norbert, hovering like a mother hen, fed her green grapes and pieces of fresh fish as though she hadn't eaten in nine years. Nadine allowed herself to relax at last, but only a little.

"We're going to put you in a safe place for a while," the CEO said, turning a jar of milky-white water upside down and watching the particles settle. "You'll have to testify. It's too bad you didn't get any video of your attackers." As Nadine opened her mouth to protest, he grinned. "Just kidding. You did more than anyone could have dreamed to help make our case for environmental protection. Now we know what kinds of nonsense landsiders have been pulling on the ocean all these years. It's one of the reasons they haven't fully accepted us as a nation. And you got out of there in one piece. Well done. You're one of the best things that has happened to Poseidon in a long time. Don't quit us. We need you."

Nadine smiled. With a feeling of satisfaction, she looked out at the city's pearly lights through the translucent walls. Her fish bumped at the screens as if trying to get at her replacement headlamp. Then she signed, "As long as I'm down here, I'll do anything the city needs. It turns out that I work well under pressure."

THE LAST OF THE REAL GOOD DAYS
BILL KJE'PI

By the time the first shortboards showed up at Echo Beach, life had taken a poor turn for Mickey Lyric. The familiar faces in the lineup diminished, and so in like proportion did the offers of places to crash, pizzas to share, beers to drain. He hated the march of strangers. Not just the gremmies and hodads everyone loved to hate, but the peopleness of the crowd itself, more so with every year, as the things he did that kept him on that beach wore him down. Mickey was thirty, and his old friends and enemies had moved on. Now when people looked him over, in his old-fashioned blue swim trunks and the gold necklace with the ruby so big they assumed it was fake, it was with a smirk at the old guy. His reputation used to be like a shield that insulated him from people. Now he was going to need a place to live. He was going to need a job.

He mulled it all over the morning after Zinger showed him the door, paddling out on Argo with the dawn patrol, those surfers who caught their waves as soon as the sun hit them. There would be benefits to having a place of his own. He wouldn't have to keep his records or his boards in his woodie anymore. Argo was his favorite, nine and a half feet long, vivid green with black blobby dots and burst lines. It wasn't made of fiberglass, wasn't made at all so much as conjured. He had carried it at his side for so long his right arm felt Popeyed.

When you're paddling out, your mind can wander and worry, but once you're clambering to get on the wave, it becomes your focus. It was one of the best things about what he did. Mickey's whole being centered around the board under him and the wave approaching him from behind as he paddled beachward, just enough for the wave to catch up to him at just the right moment. He popped up with a gasp, a thrill running down his bare back as the water lifted him and Argo up. Suddenly there he was, on top of the wave in the deep water, feet gripping the board. He slid down the face of the wave, the spray of his board's wake nothing compared to the white crest that curled up and towered over him. He was suspended in space, at once aware of gravity grasping at him and his full-body denial of it.

And then before he knew it, the crest had fallen, the wave was gone, and he was pulling Argo along as he trudged out of the water into the sand. It was like he'd been on a mountain that left no evidence of itself behind.

He got a Bala Club grape soda and tacos in a paper boat from the place across the parking lot, and was fueling up when Jane found him. Mickey didn't know much about Jane, who was old enough to have been one of the first surfers at Echo, long before it was cool for girls to do that kind of thing. These days she was gray-haired, but still hit the waves when the crowd thinned.

"Listen, Mickey," she said. "I heard you need a place to stay."

"Where'd you hear that?"

"Well, the Trip's in lockup again and I know Zinger kicked you off his sofa." It was true. He'd overstayed his welcome at Zinger's hoping the Trip would be out in time to drive the woodie over there. Jimmy the Trip was Mickey's closest thing to a pal, a photographer who sold just enough drugs to get by, or maybe the other way around, but his old lady would never let Mickey stay there just the two of them. Or maybe the Trip was the one who drew that line, if he was the grudge-holding type.

"I'll work it out. Must be a surf shop needs a cashier."

"The reason I mention it, man, I thought I could help."

"You need a cashier?"

"I don't have a surf shop. But hey, I do have a house I'm not using." She nodded down the beach. "I was renting it to my daughter's old man, but he took off."

"Too many memories."

"I'm sure that must have been part of it."

Jane was watching him like she was looking for something.

"Thing of it is, Jane, till I do find somebody needs a cashier, I'd be a little short putting down any kind of deposit, or even the first month's rent or anything."

She shielded her eyes from the sun. "I thought we could work something out."

Ah, this. He had heard about this kind of thing. Usually with men younger than him, but surfing kept him in good shape.

"I need your skills, Mickey," she said, before he could make up his mind. "Your magic, whatever it is you do, whatever you call it."

"I'm not sure I know what you mean."

"Hey, I don't know the whole story but I've been on this beach since before you got here, and I know not everything's quite right out there. Not since the end of the war." World War II, she meant. It was something few people had noticed. Experiments in New Mexico for the war effort had gone all wrong. Parts of the state were unlivable now, at least by anything human. And in the rest of the world … the locks had come off of some very old doors. Sediment had been churned up. "I know sometimes when bad things happen, you're there to help. That day the bones washed up on the beach. The thing with the Wilson girl. I know you surf Echo every morning no matter the weather, and that sometimes you paddle out so far you don't come back for days." She put a cigarette in her mouth, passed him one, and he lit them both, not bothering about a lighter. "I know these might be the last of the real good days."

"Not if I can help it."

"I know. And so I need your help with this. You can keep the house. But you have to get rid of her."

"Wait, get rid of who?"

"Pamela. My daughter."

"Another daughter?"

She sighed like he was supposed to have figured this all out already. "My daughter died over in Vietnam. Red Cross, you know, the doughnut dollies?" He shook his head. "Recreational Overseas program, some such thing, they go from hospital to hospital to entertain the boys. She heard Jack Kennedy's speech and signed right up. Met a soldier, fell in love, came home with him, went back over when it didn't work out." The lines in her face deepened. "Might still be with us if not for that. Not for him."

"If she's not, eh, 'with us,' who am I getting rid of?"

She tapped the pillar of ash off her cigarette and nodded.

* * *

The house was a boxy midcentury with sky-blue paint flaking off and a deck that hadn't been cleaned in so long the butts in the ashtray were still floating in a pool from whenever it last rained. He parked the woodie in the carport. May as well get right to it.

It wasn't uncommon for the ghost of some dead person to snap back to somewhere they'd lived, even if they hadn't died there. What exactly a ghost was, that was harder to say for sure. Maybe it really was the spirit of a once-living person, or at least some kind of psychic residue. Maybe it was something conjured up unconsciously by the bereaved. Either way it wasn't usually hard to deal with. He might not be able to get rid of the ghost right away, but he could deal with cohabitation for a while, if it came to that.

He set his box of records down on a sideboard in the living room-cum-dining room. The rusty orange carpet squidged under his huarache. The place smelled and it was too cold. It was at least fifteen degrees colder than outside, but with no air conditioner that he could see.   With the windows all shut up, it should've been a heat trap. It was a murky wet cold, like when you swim through a sudden chilly current; a snotty cold, like putting your bare foot down in the worm-brown muck of a lake.

Whatever they were, ghosts could do things like that, or maybe it'd be better to say that they happened where things like that also happened. You can't assume every spider you see built that particular web it's on, you dig? Some haunted places, you couldn't keep milk from going bad, couldn't keep books from falling off the shelves while you were sleeping. Other places, everybody who hung out too long would kill somebody or themselves. This wasn't that bad, and Mickey had enough wards accumulated that, even if it was, it'd probably just make him really blue.

He chewed on a candy, rolling it around the roof of his mouth. He could make this work. Plenty of room and no rent. So it was a little squidgy. So it didn't smell great. You were expecting Versailles at this price?

Then Pamela came into the room.

He heard her first, squiidge-squidge, squiidge-squidge, like a rocking chair wringing out sponges. She walked stiffly, not moving anything but her legs, and even those moved like somebody else was moving them for her. Like the way a little kid moves a doll's legs. He would swear there were moments when she missed a step but came forward anyway, like something was just pushing or pulling her, and she only moved her feet because it was expected. He'd taken a girl to see Peter Pan on Broadway once and that's what it reminded him of: Mary Martin on wires.

"Hey," he said.

She opened her mouth and closed it again. The family resemblance to Jane was there even in death, a wide mouth and narrow eyes, prominent eyebrows. Her clothes stuck to her in places like she'd worked up a sweat and fallen asleep in them. You couldn't tell she was dead right away. She wasn't decayed or pale or any of those things. It wasn't that kind of deal. There was some drool on her chin. Her forehead had a small but definite dent with fine ridges, like wet clay somebody'd run a dime across. "Good morning, gentleman," she said, but it wasn't really in sync with her mouth any more than her legs were in sync with her walking. So that was awful.

"Hey, hi," he said, wishing he had his board in his hands. Argo was lashed to the top of the woodie in the carport. "So I'm Mickey, I'm the new tenant. Jane's renting the place to me. So. I'm just going to get moving my stuff in."

She stiff-legged toward him with an arm out and stroked his cheek with the back of her hand. Cold. Colder than the room. Her touch left a trail of something snail-gross on his skin. For a hot second he was actually drawn to her, and that was awfuller.

He hurried back out the door, got in the woodie, and drove up the street to Jane's.

* * *

"Jane, did your daughter die near the water?"

She'd answered the door as soon as he got there, obviously expecting him, probably expecting him to throw the key down and say hey the hell with this free house and whatever. "What? What's that got to do with anything?"

"Depends on the answer."

"She drowned. She was drowned. By a—by this asshole she met over there. He shot himself but he drowned her first."

"Traumatized spirit," Mickey mumbled to himself. "All that emotion in the water, overheard by God knows what, God knows how far away. Like sharks scenting blood." He was going to have to go back in, back in Deep.

"What are you saying? What are you talking about?"

He shook his head. "Listen, I don't know what you thought it was, what you believe in, the whole Heaven trip and like that? But this isn't your daughter. It's just wearing a Pamela mask. And not even that, because it's not on its face, not it, but her, but not her face, but like a—" He held up his hands in front of her face, wiggled his fingers. "Right? You know?"

"What?"

"Those little rubber monster faces, Jane. Like little kids put on their fingers." He tried making a face to get the point across. Tongue out, bug eyes.

She turned away from him. His bedside manner, it wasn't the best.

"Fuck!" he said, mostly to himself. "Anyway, don't worry about it."

"Don't worry about it? What does that even mean, Mickey?"

But he was already gone, stomping back to the woodie in his huaraches, trying to look decisive. Maybe, if he caught a glimpse of his reflection, he'd even convince himself.

* * *

The Pamela thing was sitting at the table in the breakfast nook, an upside-down coffee cup in front of her, her hands cupping the air to either side of it. What Mickey should have seen the first time was impossible to miss now, the faint trace of shadow leading away from her foot on the blue and white checkered tile. It lined up perfectly with the grout lines on the tile, and happened to continue on the other side of the floor—a jagged little twist of shadow that curled toward and beyond the front door. It was something like a siren, he figured. Something like a mermaid. Not either of those things, but some ancient half-remembered thing that gave birth to those myths. Something wet and womanly that lured you to the water.

"Uhhh," Mickey said.

"Mickeylyric," the woman said.

"Yep," he said, and left again, grabbing Argo from the rack on the woodie. She shouldn't know his last name. That wasn't great. From touching him? From being in the room with him? Or worstest, from just wanting to?

A crack in the driveway picked up where the shadow on the carpet had left off, and just happened to continue all the way across the street. When street became sand, the crack continued—a thinner, fainter version of the cracks that appeared when wet sand dried. On and on it went like that, Mickey following along. A crack would lead perfectly up to what looked like a stray piece of kelp, which happened to touch an inexplicable but almost invisible shadow, and so on, forming an unbroken line from the woman's foot to the sea. It wove a path right through crowds who instinctively stepped over it without seeing it, kids who somehow never put their board down on it, somehow never covered it up with their bingo beach blankets. Maybe it was some bullshit like this that started the whole "step on a crack" business. Just because superstitions didn't work didn't mean they never meant anything. They all meant something.

The line wouldn't end at the water, of course. It just came from there, because this was Echo Beach, where the walls were thin.

"Goddammit, Argo," he said. Argo didn't respond but surely empathized.

Mickey paddled out from the north end of the beach, ignoring the chatter from the surfers. He was trying to get into the right groove. For the routine stuff, a little grass never hurt, but he only had a vague idea what to expect here, and not much clue of the scale. This might be a dive that would be improved by a button of peyote or some tabs of acid, but if it wasn't, who knows how badly things might go, or where a bad trip could wind him up. So he went in sober, doing what he thought of as *entering the Deep*, the same way he always did. He found a good seven footer to ride, used Argo's fin to carve the sigils in the wave's face, and then let it knock him down, down, down into the water. He used to paddle out further to do this, but these days the kids on the beach didn't really know him and wouldn't be shocked to see him wipe out. Probably figured him for some guy in from the suburbs on his day off. Some kind of *dad*.

But he didn't wipe out. The sigils swam silver in the churn as the wave crashed down, most of them surrounding him in protective bands, while two of them crawled up his nose and mouth and made him breathe. The ruby in his necklace warmed up now, glowing enough to let him see in front of and below him. The line from Pamela glowed brightly in its light, leading far off into the sea. It was probably supposed to look like seaweed, and probably would, if not for the ruby.

Go deep enough into the woods and, where it gets darkest and deepest, all forests are the same. You might get lost in Big Bear and walk out in the Black Forest. Mickey didn't think it had always been like that, but it was these days. It was the same with the ocean. You can't swim from the coast to the deep ocean. The continental shelf extends too far. And yet. And yet there are certain currents you can catch. There are certain depths you can find yourself in. And suddenly, there you are, far from the worlds of men.

That was the nature of Mickey's work and what kept him tethered to Echo Beach. Something had happened during the war. Things washed up from the Deep now. Sometimes by accident, sometimes by design. Mickey kept the beach clean.

The light from above disappeared and the waters ran cold when he passed over some threshold from the shore to the deeps, still following that line attached to Pamela. It looked like a crack in the world, like the finest hairline crack.

With his board in his hands in front of him, and the silver sigils protecting him, Mickey followed the tendril to one of the deepest parts of the ocean. The water tasted different here. Thicker and saltier. At the bottom of the sea the saltiest currents of water have sunk to the bottom and slowed in the cold. On his bare skin, which the sigils protected from the crushing weight of the world above him, it felt like liquid metal.

The tendril led to a brine pool ahead of him, a place where the saltiest, heaviest water settled in a sea floor valley, and now he understood what he was dealing with, more or less. Here it stopped pretending to be a crack, or seaweed, or the space between tiles. Here it didn't camouflage and he saw it for the thin and slender tentacle it was, impossibly long, a lure tossed out from brutal depths in search of something. Something male, something to mate with. Mating magic wasn't hard to spot, it was common enough. It just didn't usually go this badly. He turned Argo around, closed his eyes, and let the world drag him back to its shores.

* * *

As soon as he was out of the water he got back in the woodie and drove straight to the Thoroughbred Club, his watering hole in times of crisis. It meant putting a shirt on for the first time in weeks, and they wouldn't let him into the dining room without a tie and probably pants, but he sat at the bar with an Old Fashioned and got the bartender to bring him a baked potato with sour cream and chives and a dish of bright orange sherbet. He sat, drank, smelled the steaks cooking in the kitchen and being carried out to the dining room, and ate his baked potato like he was just picking at it after a big meal of T-bone bordelaise or whatever.

"You're supposed to have something wise to say to me," he told the bartender. "Something that puts it all in perspective."

"Lunch is winding down," the bartender said. "It's usually pretty quiet until the early bird dinner. I didn't have anything prepared."

"You're no good to me, Jonesey." He was three Old Fashioneds down at this point, maybe four or something. The bartender's name wasn't Jonesey, that's how many Old Fashioneds down he was.

"There's always more fish in the sea, fella," the bartender said. "How about that one?"

"Jesus," Mickey said. "That'll sober me up."

But not all the way. He smoked half a joint of the Trip's grass, but it made him jittery, considered a lude from the unmarked pill bottle in his glove compartment, but put it back after a long, long time of staring at it on the dashboard, and finally decided if he sobered up any more, the only cure for it was going to be drinking again, and at that point you'd cut away to calendar pages flying off, which wouldn't get anything done.

You're thirty years old, Mickey Lyric. You're too old to learn a trade, you don't like people enough to teach them how to surf, and nobody's hiring cashiers. There's only one thing you're good at, and it's a bummer, but if you don't get it done you're sleeping in a parking lot until the Trip gets out.

The Pamela thing was sitting on the living room floor, cross-legged, staring at the ceiling. The back of its blouse was sticky.

"So hey," he said. "Hey there, Pamela."

"Miiickeylyric," the thing said.

"I had to take care of some errands, you know. Let's do this thing."

"Mickeylyric you want to make love to me," it said, or asked, or whatever that inflection was.

"I'm hot for it, babe. Come on."

It swept him up in its arms and that tendril tugged hard. Like they were walking at first, but her legs still weren't moving right. She just held him and waggled her legs, and that tendril pulled them both across the street, across the beach, and down down down into the salty thick sea. Did anyone see them getting dragged across the beach? Time got thick and salty with magic like this, too. Maybe they moved too fast or too slow to be seen, maybe nobody noticed them the same way nobody stepped on the tendril. When they hit the water, sigils unfurled from his necklace and the tattoos on his hips, letting him breathe, letting him survive this. Pamela's ex probably hadn't vamoosed on his own. He'd probably drowned when he got dragged in. Did Mickey have to tell Jane that? He didn't want to be the one, but it wasn't like there was anyone else who knew. Just Mickey and the Pamela thing.

Being dragged through the Deep is worse than swimming through it. It's a charleyhorse kind of hurt, swirled up with an ice cream headache that covers you head to toe. The sigils let him breathe, but they didn't make it nice, so his lungs stung and felt too heavy, like every breath was leaning on an old tube of toothpaste to get the last sludge out. He wished he had Argo with him, but what if he didn't survive this any better than the other guy did? What if the Pamela-thing was able to crack Argo open and slurp up its power? Jesus, what awful questions, stop it.

It was close to freezing at the bottom of the sea, the salinity keeping ice from forming. The things that lived down here, even the normaller things that weren't horrible fucking monsters, ate mostly dead whales that fell like manna from far above. There was little here that was recognizable as what you thought of as fish. Most were long and brittle-looking, with hinged jaws and recurved teeth. Some were gelatinous and globby. Those with eyes had huge ones, but the ones that never left the seafloor lived blind.

Even that weird sea life thinned out as they reached the end of the line in a pitch-black brine pool. The tattoos on his hips started pulsing a warning, and the very, very old metals alloyed with the gold in his necklace did likewise, and it was like, what could he say? Thanks for the warning, charms and amulets, but this is the thing we're here to do, so just get on board and do your part, right? Board. He should have brought Argo. So what if the thing might crack Argo open if he died, he'd be dead then, and having his board with him could be the only thing to prevent that. He should have brought him.

There was no sky above him, no silvery sheen like in the shallows. Sunlight ended ten thousand feet away. By all rights he shouldn't have been able to see what the Pamela thing was dragging him toward, and God knows he wished he could close his eyes and take it back. In the strictest terms, you could say it looked like a funhouse mirror's memory of an anglerfish, all mouth and teeth, two stories high with room for an attic, round and squashed like a balloon sneaking through the cat door. The biggest teeth were tall as surfboards and something had broken the points off a few of them. This thing had fed plenty, though. The Pamela thing wasn't bringing Mickey to its mouth. That wasn't how it fed. Whatever it had evolved to prey on had probably died off eons or worlds ago and now it sat on the sea bottom with its mouth wide open, fat and greasy. Its skin was the color of cold lard, covered in slow wiggling parasites that probably wished they'd parasited something else. Its cheeks bulged so much its dead eyes had been buried in a squint. It needed to put its calories to use. It had fed and fed and fed and now it was full of eggs and good times, and it needed to be fertilized. It had sent the Pamela thing up, like maybe a siren, like maybe a mermaid, looking for something it could squeeze just right and turn those eggs into babies.

The tendril this whole time was retracting into the base of its root on the thing's head, a protruding ridge above those fatty-fatty-two-by-four eyes.

The thing was never going to mate successfully left to its own devices, that wasn't the problem. The problem was, it was going to keep dragging men down into the ocean in the attempt, and if the lures kept not working, it might be smart enough to find a different tactic. It might start coming closer to shore. It was more than Mickey could do to rid the world of this kind of thing, but patrolling the shore and keeping it from coming to the beach, he could do that much. So far anyway.

The tendril now was furling back up into the base so fast that Mickey was starting to spin in the water. But it didn't pull him toward the head or that horrible toothy gob, but instead smacked him against its side. He was skin to skin with the thing, his warm fragile pink against its toadbumpy pulsating white.

I change my mind, Mickey thought.

I don't want to do this. This was a mistake. I'm not the guy. I should have just gone surfing. I don't want to do this again. I don't want to have to be the one who does this. I don't want to be here. It isn't worth it, just for a place to live. I could just sleep in my car, I can just get the biggest bag of cheeseburgers you can even think of and just eat them and sleep in my car and get up in the morning and surf, and that's all I ever need to do. Haven't I done enough yet? Isn't there anybody else?

Pink and white began to come together, forgetting they were separate. It was trying to absorb him and make him fertilize its eggs. It was trying to burn him to fuel its species. It didn't even have a choice in the business, but that didn't make it any better.

"I hate this so much," he said when the thing had pulled him into its flesh deep enough that he could poke around. Even with the sigils, it just came out as gibberish, but he doubted the thing would have understood English anyway. It didn't need to. The Pamela thing lifting his last name from his mind showed that it had the usual mild telepathy of Deep-dwelling horrors, and it probably even knew that it had grabbed the wrong guy, a really toxic mate who'd be all wrong for it. It knew that and maybe it couldn't do anything about it, but maybe it was okay with the way this was going to go down. Maybe it would rather die here at the bottom of everything than keep getting fatter and juicier in a world where it could never find a mate.

The cat's eye ruby in his necklace had traversed the Silk Road once, in early days, when routes carved across the earth formed sigils that warded off the remnants of those things that used to dwell here before the before. It held a lot of power, but like any other battery, the only way to know how much of a charge it carried was to turn it on and see if it worked. One of these days it wouldn't.

This time it did. He wrapped the necklace around his hand like brass knuckles and burned through the fish-thing's fleshy wall like a hot rock dropped into a bucket of butter. He pushed through it and down under the cavity of the gaping mouth to the egg sacs. There's always more fish in the sea, the bartender had said. *Wiser than you realized, Jonesey. Wiser, but pretty gross.*

This is when time gets thick again, when the coldest and saltiest things sink to the bottom. The Pamela thing was going to sit here forever, dragging hapless male after hapless male to it trying to fertilize these eggs in vain. If there was a male of her species, she would have found it by now. But this ruby of Mickey's, it could do some things even Argo couldn't do. The ruby was how he conjured fire, how he navigated the Deep, and now it was how he reached through time to another moment, another sea. It was like helping Zinger splice tape. Pasting pieces of moments together. One moment was the one Mickey was in, surrounded by the Pamela-thing's unfertilized eggs. The other moment ... involved a male of her species. Fertilizing some other somebody-thing's eggs, some eon ago. It was a foul thing to witness, but when it came to an end, those eggs were fertilized and wiggling. Popping and crackling like Rice Krispies.

He didn't think he could kill this thing himself, even with the ruby, even with Argo. But he knew he could kill the babies. And he knew the babies needed to eat.

The Pamela thing dried up and broke off the tendril; it would probably wash up somewhere someday and make some money for a tabloid photographer. It floated off and left Mickey alone to watch the gobbling chomping little toothbeasts eat away at all the good lardy flesh their mother had stored up over the ages, each of them the size of a grasping hand. When they'd eaten enough of the mother her body started to collapse, draping over him and them and all the awful business like a tent that's lost its poles, and that's when he had to scoop them up one by one and burn them with the ruby. Truth is, maybe he missed one, maybe two, and maybe that'd turn out bad someday down the line, but he got enough, and it'd be nobody's problem for a long time.

Without Argo it was a long paddle back out of the Deep and onto the shore, a long cold silence with nothing for company but memories of the thing's dying flesh around him and the other things' brand new bodies dying in his hands even as their teeth nipped at his fingers. He could still hear the sound of the Pamela thing's voice and the way it hadn't synced up with her mouth. He figured the fish-thing had known what he was doing maybe even before he'd known it himself.

* * *

When he got back to Echo Beach, Mickey's heart was pounding so hard it was hard to breathe. He made fists in the sand, grinding the wet sand against his palms the way his grandmother used to rub lard into biscuit flour. Somehow he kept forgetting how to breathe, and his throat hitched like a hiccup, his chest filling up staccato and exhaling in exhausted sobs. His eyes were hot and his back hurt and he wanted to run away, not from the beach but, yes, from the beach, too, not from the world but, yes, from the world, too, but mostly from his own body. He wanted to wrench free of it and sail off into somebodyelseness someother-wherewards.

He pulled his knees toward his chest, face down on the beach, tried to feel small, and instead felt like a rocket trembling with the anticipation of escape velocity. He was going to need that lude as soon as he could get to the car. He was going to need to remember to tell the Trip to get more for him from that doctor in the city.

"Okay," he said. "All right. Okay. All right."

He wasn't sure how long he was like that before Jane found him. Maybe she'd been watching for him, maybe somebody told the old lady that this old dude was freaking out on the beach. Maybe somebody thought he'd got jellyfish stung. But her hand was on his back and she had a cold can of Bala Club black cherry soda, and soon enough he turned around, sat next to her in the sand, and drank the soda while they passed a joint back and forth.

"I'm sorry about your daughter, Jane," he said. "I should've said it before."

"Thank you. What are you, Mickey?"

"Just doing my best. Just doing the work. Are we square?"

"We're more than square. The place is yours."

And for the next eleven-twelve years, until Jane died, Mickey Lyric always had a place at Echo Beach.

THE WINDLOST

JENNA RHODES

The airship came ka-pock-pock-eting over the island, blocking out the sun and sky with its bronze bulk. Island winds shredded pure white clouds into streamers like fine silk about its wings, stretched out like the fins of a great sea-going fish. Their scalloped edges vibrated while turbines noisily moved propellers at the fore and rear, steadily thrusting the airship forward. Bevan ran to the sea cliffs to shake his fist and curse because one of them, or rather one of their officers, had taken away his wife, leaving him with anger that could not fill his emptiness.

He should have guessed she'd leave him. Any escape would have been more interesting to a young society woman who married a historian and treasure hunter. He had promised her fame and prestige and what had he given her? A hole in the ground that he feared to excavate. When she'd left him, he'd told the tradesmen and busybodies in port that she'd died suddenly, as people can. They had probably known the truth, but let him pass the fantasy.

Built like a barge, the airship carried cargo stacked on open decks as it began its low pass. Those not docking for repairs soared above so high and swift that crewmen racing along their decks looked like twigs. This time, as the current dragged them down, he could almost see the expressions on their faces, the colors of their green and gold uniforms, the static discharges as they climbed the rigging, their steps marked by lightning outbursts. It all held him in thrall. So enchanted was he that he almost did not catch their scrambling to and fro, battered as the wind roared up. His island had a reputation for savage currents, in the sea and sky.

The airship rocked. He thought he could hear orders being shouted as the airship canted dangerously, one scalloped wing dipping low. Crates on the deck began to shift against securing lines that groaned with the strain. The cargo, clearly in sight now, had sigils etched into wood that made his pulse jump as he read them. Artifacts! What site had been looted? What treasures drifted overhead that he stood denied?

The ship's flag snapped open, revealing a death mask, black on red silk. Plague ship. The great, dark shapes on its deck carried not cargo but massive coffins, each designed to hold multitudes. He staggered back as the entire airship shuddered. Ropes snapped. The lid flew open on one of the coffins. He could see the small bodies wrapped in white, stacked like logs of firewood inside. Children. Once. Now they were silent, gauze-wrapped packages that shifted as the airship strained to stay aloft. The crate slid along the deck, the open coffin tilting precariously. A child fell from the sky.

It plunged downward, the many layers of gauze tearing open, trailing behind and billowing. He watched it breathlessly, as the only witness, the crewmen engaged in straightening their rigs. Arms akimbo, he yelled, "Oy! Hey there!" with no real hope of being heard. The massive lid snapped shut as the airship righted itself and then soared to gain both height and speed.

He quickly turned away to see the white bundle meet the afternoon tide. A bared arm broke the surface.

He ran.

Sand sprayed from his boots as he bolted downward, brush and salt grasses tangling his steps as his eyes focused on the white shape bobbing in the sea. Impossibly, he thought he saw struggle as the child fought to claw its way out of the waves. He dove into the icy water without a second thought.

Wrestling with both tide and child, Bevan found his way back to shore. A white face turned to him, mouth open, coughing, choking, eyes unseeing. He managed to keep the head out of the waves, as the child went limp when he hauled her onto the sand.

Her gauze trailed about them, and he saw henna marks on it fast dissolving in the salt water. She began to cough, deep rasping sounds, and he turned her on her side, letting her spew upon the sand.

Wiping her face with trembling hands, he leaned over her in both wonder and fear. "You live." How, he could not guess.

A flicker of understanding moved through her eyes as she blinked into the sun's dazzle. She covered her face with one hand and turned away.

Bevan held her while she retched again, and then he bent and hoisted her thin, small body in his arms and carried her off the shore.

* * *

He watched her for a few days, uncertain of his actions except to feed her soup and water, amazing over her while she slept in one of his old shirts, soft and warm. How was it she lived at all? He'd heard no rumors of a deadly sickness raging, and yet the flag had flown boldly. The crates could be mistaken as nothing other than coffins. In his scholarship, he'd read innumerable accounts of plague. Soldiers' journals. Traders. Even missionaries. He watched for fever. Pustules. Blistering stripes. Vomiting. Bleeding from the eyes and nose. Hoarse coughing that would not stop. All the signs of disease that he could remember, and saw none.

He examined the burial wrapping, but only a few of the henna designs remained, blurred and damaged by the water. He could make little sense of them and tapped his fingers irritably on his desk. He'd been out of touch too long, abandoning his own research when Rozany scorned him. Now he only used his education to translate and scrape out a living. Where had the hunters gone and what stupidity inspired them to bring plague infected to the great continent? What was he not seeing? And when would they come looking for her when they accounted for their cargo? They might remember the upheaval over Windlost Island. They might recall hearing a shout. They might have seen, in the corners of their eyes as they scurried to right the airship, a white star falling from their deck.

Or they might remember nothing.

* * *

Convinced she merely rested, he returned to translating a technical manual for the port blacksmith Bartoff. He peeked in at her periodically, listening as she murmured soft words in her sleep, a few familiar to him as Trade common, though accented oddly. Still, no sign of sickness appeared. He told himself that they were both safe and set about making a supper. When he turned about, dusting his hands off, she sat at his table, bright-eyed, her chin barely clearing the table's edge. Nut-brown hair wisped about her face, small tendrils escaping from her braid. His old shirt floated about her slender form.

"Good day." He fixed her a bowl of soup. She ate cautiously, wielding the wooden spoon with delicacy. "Do you understand me?"

She put a finger up imperiously, stopping him. Her eyes narrowed and then she nodded. She pointed to an ear. "I listen. I know." Her attention dropped back to the bowl.

"Who are you?"

She eyed him a moment. "Who asks?"

His training dared him to place her diction, but knew that Trade Common evolved from people to people. His frustration grew.

She tilted her head. "What are you?"

An odd question. She watched him as if she knew it would peel him open, demanded it of him before she would give him her trust.

"I'm a historian. A treasure hunter." He cleared his throat, for such a romantic line had gained and then lost him Rozany. He'd gone to university, done his field studies, been declared a genius, and found the map. A scrap really, but it spoke to him of a fallen queen, mislaid in time, with a hint of where to find her. The promise of great achievements beckoned and then marooned him. Bevan paused in mild embarrassment. "Eat."

She tapped her spoon on her bowl. "This is good."

"Thank you." He watched as she ate slowly, cautiously, still wary. "Have you a name? A people?"

That gave her pause. "My name is Ardith."

Disappointingly, it lacked trace of a culture or lineage. "Mine is Bevan." Curiosity drove him. "What were you doing in a coffin?"

The spoon clattered from her fingers. "Sleeping. Only sleeping, until the sickness passed us by. The magicians put us away in safety." Her sea-glass colored eyes brimmed for a moment.

"What magicians? What land?"

She eyed him as if weighing his right to answers. "I cannot tell you."

"Nothing about your city, your country? How long have you slept? You must remember something."

"Only the magicians."

Scarcely breathing, he nodded.

"They laid us down in rows and touched our eyelids with their long, red-painted nails and promised they would awaken us later, when the cure arrived. They promised to come for me." Her words rang like prophecy to his uneasy hearing.

He would comb his library later for references.

"But they didn't."

"They will."

"Tell me about the sickness."

She rubbed her brow. "It starts with a stagger. Then you fall. A horrible rash covers you. You go blind. Then die. They made us drink boiled water. They shut us away from the wind. Nothing worked. A few days and then ..."

He covered her chilled hand in comfort, even as he damned himself for making her give a name. She had become a person, not a scholarly pursuit. "You're cold."

She nodded.

The present flooded back. "Come with me."

Rozany had left her trunk behind, filled with clothes she'd thought as unimportant to take as himself. He pulled it from under his bed, opening the lid, the scent of dried flowers floating upward. Ardith fell on her knees.

"Some of these might work. I think the gardening clothes may fit best. The wind blows cold here." He paused.

Ardith pulled out a pair of pants and a long shirt, embroidery upon the sleeves still bright, and stockings and leather shoes, darting into his study to change.

"Touch nothing in there! That's my work!"

Before he had the trunk shoved away, she put her head outside the curtain. "Thank you."

He could hear fussing about. Her curiosity had obviously taken advantage of his per-mission, as he also heard the shuffle of papers. "There are a lot of words here. You must have found many wonderful things!"

"Once," he answered.

Ardith came out, pant legs rolled and stockings pulled up to secure the cuffs. The buttoned shirtsleeves ballooned on her thin arms like great sails, and shoes in hand, she looked immensely happy. He began to smile back.

She helped clean up, although her help consisted mainly of wandering about, sweeping a corner here and standing over his writing table there, stirring his papers gently with that same finger she'd upheld to halt his questions. She bounded out when he growled again to leave his things alone. When he swung a pot of stew over the banked fire to simmer, he washed his hands and called her over to wash hers.

She had a smudge of dust on her nose. He wiped it off with the ball of his thumb. Her features were finely boned and definitely not of the peoples of Windlost, or the vast continent the island hugged. Searching her expression, he sought to define the treasure that might be buried within her.

He would have to decide what to do.

* * *

The paper arrived the next morning, along with cheese and fresh bread, the shepherd boy dropping his delivery on the doorstep with an unexpected thump. Only a faint noise of the herd being driven to the leeward side of the mountain greeted Bevan as opened the door. He realized that his regular delivery had come a day late. Bartoff would be anxious for his translation work, yet the boy hadn't stopped to inquire.

Unsettled, paper tucked under his arm, he found his strikers and lit the stove before sitting down. Ardith still slept, and so he set breakfast for himself.

He ate, rustling the paper in his hands between bites. He folded the paper over and one headline caught him like a blow to the stomach.

PLAGUE PROTOCOLS IN PLACE.
FORBIDDEN CITY LOOTED.
HISTORIANS CONDEMNED FOR FOOLHARDY EXPEDITION,
TREASURE ORDERED BURNED.

Torched. All those coffins. And how many of the bodies, the children, had merely been asleep? How many burned alive? No historian could be that foolish to risk contagion and plague. Someone on the continent knew what they had financed and wanted the artifacts regardless. Why disturb tombs?

A drawing of one of the coffin crates, sigils plain now, stared at him.

Bevan's hands shook. Now that he could read it plainly, he knew those symbols. The city of lost Briatha, hidden for centuries. Dead or alive, she had value. What had he done? His breakfast grew bitter at the back of his throat. Under pressure, someone was bound to remember the barge shifting wildly over Windlost. When someone realized she'd gone missing, there would be a hunt.

Ardith appeared like the delicate, light-footed child she was. "Breakfast?"

Bevan stood hastily, shoving the paper aside and making room for her. He watched her eat, thinking of the many questions he still had. He tried to ask a few of them but she merely shook her head, and concentrated on her meal.

A heavy fist rattled the door. He turned on heel to point. "Hide. Now. Back in the study! Under the desk, and quiet. And don't touch anything!"

She dove for shelter as he opened the door to not one but a handful. He knew them: Bartoff the impatient blacksmith, Canmore the baker, Saliat the mayor, and Grifan the Meditation leader. All of them, like himself, wore the characteristics of other countries on their brows and in their manners. He bowed at them. "Bartoff! Wanting that manual? I have just finished it up. I'll fetch it. What brings the rest of you?"

The Meditation leader tapped a bony finger on his temple. "Ill news on the wind. You must have seen the airship a few days past?"

"Aye, I did my dance and cursed them royally to no good. They are sky, after all, and I am earth. I read the paper and was glad they passed me by."

Saliat, his forked beard newly oiled and curled, bobbed his head. "They struck a plague flag."

"Now that I did not see."

His visitors nodded among themselves. "We asked ourselves why excavate disaster. The paper reads that the continent is now in a panic. Why transport such danger and misery? You were a digger once. Why?"

Bevan lifted a shoulder. "I did it for the knowing of things, but backers want profit. Metals. Gems. Machines. It's always for money."

Bartoff brandished a great, knuckled hand. "They'll bring us death."

"After so long? It must have been centuries, from descriptions of the ruins." He shook his head. "Stone doesn't hold sickness. Water might, but time would have cleansed it. It's not likely to touch us, at any rate, so far off. " Bevan forced a neutral expression and gazed upon the Meditator.

"Grifan, I feel certain that you will ably discern any problems. You're in tune with the vibrations of Windlost and beyond."

It worried him that they'd all accompanied Bartoff. They had come, not only for his wisdom but to gauge his reaction to the news, if he had been aware of the development, as if they thought him linked to the happenings. As if strange, harmful things might erupt here, and he still the foreigner.

He backed to his office and retrieved the translation. He could hear her muffled breathing under his desk, panicky and fitful. He returned to give the blacksmith the valise of work. "Staying to help me cut wood?"

Bartoff laughed and shrugged.

Behind his audience, he could see puffs of dirt below the ridge. These men hadn't come alone. A dog's thin howl, barely audible, reached his hearing.

She could no longer stay here.

He slammed the door in their faces and shoved the heavy bar in place. Bartoff began pounding and shouting at the door.

"What are you hiding! Open the door, Bevan! It's an island—where can you hope to hide?"

Ardith came out of his study, one arm wrapped about her ribcage, her face wet with tears.

"Run," he told her. "Out the back window. Can you do that?"

He fetched his stove strikers from the kitchen. Grabbing the delivery sack full of cheese and bread, he burst into the study and grabbed his knapsack, stuffing papers into it right and left. She sprinted for the back room, wrestling the window open and clambering through.

He slid out and joined her with a thump, strikers in his free hand, alight and burning. He'd left two glowing in his office. All those old books. Research. They would explode in flame. Throwing the last of his strikers back through the window, he grabbed her up and ran.

He could hear the shouts at the barred front door, followed by the thud of boots and then an axe. Cries as the fire exploded.

He did not slow until the forest had gobbled them up and his side ached so that he could hardly breathe, and then he let her slide down. He no longer heard the baying hounds, but over his labored breathing, he could be mistaken.

Ardith looked up at him, her eyes shadowed. "I'm sorry. It's my fault. One of them was a Seeker. I felt his touch." She trembled.

"You...did nothing. A moment, and we'll run some more."

"Where?"

"I have a place."

He put his hand on her head, her braid wispy against his palm. "Can you keep up with me?"

She gave a slow nod.

"Then we are off again."

She scampered after him as though she were part goat.

When the sun slanted lower and the forest grew even thicker, he slowed to a walk. He could hear the dogs again, far behind, but he had no help for it.

"We're almost there."

She tilted her head. "Where?"

"I have a...place. Stareye Lake. It's hard to find, and the trees hug it close. The water level has dropped so that if you were a bird in the sky, you might see it winking deep in the stone."

She scurried after, leaping fallen logs as she held onto his hand, and giggling as they both fell over a log neither of them could clear. Her laughter rang out, fresh and clean. Historians, he thought, stayed too dusty. He rolled to his feet and put his hand out to Ardith. "Not far now."

When she finally staggered to a stop, exhausted, he picked her up again.

By late afternoon they came to the rim of a great gash in the earth, cut deep into roots and stone, as though a massive arrow from the sky had struck and buried itself straight down, splitting the world open. He lowered her and bent to breathe deeply. The dogs grew louder, and he turned a plan over in his head.

He walked them around the rim until the sunlight touched their destination brightly. He shifted his knapsack on his shoulders and tied their rations to his belt. Pointing downward, he said: "Now we climb."

Ardith went to her stomach to hang her head over. Surprised, she said, "Someone has cut a path and built ladders where it's too steep to walk. Does it go all the way down to the water?"

"That someone would be me, and yes." It had taken a while and he had the calluses to show for it. He looked down now and saw that it had endured, despite the seasons passing since he'd last been there.

"I'll go down first, that way I can catch you if you slip. We'll find light at the bottom." He had torches and other items stockpiled against the day he might have to defend his find. He began to climb down, and she looked over at him, her face a pale moon. Her hesitance touched him. He pulled a stern expression. "Don't watch me! Climb!"

She took to the ladder unsteadily. He realized that the spacing had been meant for an adult and that she hung for a moment from one rung to the next, taking it on a leap of faith that her feet would find purchase. He waited, so that if she missed, he could catch her.

They inched downward inside the pit, walking when they could, and back to the ladders when they couldn't. She slipped once, and he caught her up immediately.

"I have you," he told her, although she knew that.

She nodded, her braid rubbing against the underside of his chin. "Ready."

And they began again until they reached the bottom.

The lake spread in front of them, vaster than he remembered, light turquoise at the shore and deepening to rings of blue. The surface caught a faint sparkle and Ardith answered the call, running to the edge.

"Don't touch it!"

She teetered on the shore, looking back at him.

"The water is different. It burns."

Her brows knotted. "How can it do that?"

He drew her forward. "Trust me. There are brooks that feed the lake. We can drink from those."

He led her away to the rail track he'd put down to line the small tunnel. Buckets lay about, their ropes dangling, part of a hoist and relay system he'd used to get tools and supplies to the pit floor.

Wind overhead carried the belling of hounds. "They're close." Bevan retrieved a torch and lit it after several tries. He beckoned. She followed.

"Mind the rails."

She did with a little hop.

"I didn't bring us here to be cornered, though I doubt anyone will follow us down. But we can't stay indefinitely." He talked as much to himself as to her. "Years ago, I followed a map to Windlost. It spoke of a queen, storm-driven, off course on a desperate quest, a mission, for her kingdom. Her vessel crashed and few survived. She did, and so did the mapmaker she sent out for aid. It led me to here."

"Did you buy it from the maker? Did you save her?"

"No, no. All are long gone to dust. Remember, I'm a historian."

"Oh." Her voice, quiet and small, in the chamber behind him.

"The vessel eventually plowed to a stop—here. The crash created this pit and cavern." Putting his torch in a sconce, he leaned down to the great wheel he'd built and began to crank it about. It wheezed and squealed, but it turned, drawing in the heavy chain lying along the tunnel floor. As the chain grew taut, it dragged its burden out of the lake, water cascading off it, until it reached the rails. He put his weight on the turnstile arm to ferry it and she joined to help, straining at the wooden bar.

Ardith gasped.

The conveyance, battered though it was, sat on the cavern floor like a chariot that had lost its horses, an airship too sleek and light to compare to modern monsters. It glittered golden in the torchlight, although he knew it could not have been made from that metal. It called to him now, as it had the very first day he'd made it to the bottom of the gash following his map, and like a fallen star, it had shone from under the lake. He'd paced back and forth for days, figuring out how to bring it up, building a hoist and crank and then laying the rails. When he'd first raised it, he puttered, making sketches, and then, compelled to try and right it, to fix and repair it. It consumed him until it was clear that such a working lay beyond his skills. It had eaten at him night and day, and he'd paid little heed to anything outside this pit, Rozany included, gaining little and losing much.

"Battered, but sealed, like an eggshell, carrying its secrets."

"Secrets?"

"Many! Who built it? Who piloted it? What knocked it out of the sky, where had it come from, and where was it headed? What metal is this? What wood? What purpose did it have, important enough that they sent out a map in hope help might arrive in time, though it did not. And what of the queen it carried? And who dragged it offshore to bury it in the lake?" His voice rose as he spoke and the old excitement began to rise in his chest.

Ardith crept forward and put her palm to its side. "You tried to fix it?"

"And failed."

"It knows you tried. It doesn't blame you."

A chill swept across Bevan. "You hear it?"

Ardith walked about the prow, nodding slowly. "You're afraid of it."

"It's a lock for which I can find no key."

"Did you find her body?"

He dropped his hand on her shoulder. "Gone, as we all go."

"I should find her."

Bevan dropped to one knee beside her. "Let it go, Ardith. Don't listen." He pulled back on her gently, removing her hand from the side of the vessel.

"You don't understand."

"I understand very well."

Ardith shook her head. "No, you don't." She twisted away from him and backed up, standing against it.

"Ardith, I know how it gets in your head, in your blood, until you can't think of anything else until you've accomplished what it drives you to do. But you can't repair it. I couldn't. What it is now, is ransom. We're going to pay for our lives with it if I have to take it apart piece by piece." His gut clenched at the thought, ruining whatever historic value it had, the clues it hid. He'd sketched it but that would not replace it. He'd given up on translations, finding nothing he could decipher. It had worth to many beyond him though, a tangible worth he could trade upon. He feared what they planned for Ardith. No, he would have to buy them time.

She ducked away, darting off, and he pursued. He found her inside, tracing the etchings on the bridge dashboard that he'd straightened after a fashion, half of it splintered. "Wings of Hope," she whispered.

"What?"

"It says 'Wings of Hope.'"

He stood in shock. "You can read that?"

"It spoke to me, if you call that reading." She walked about the cabin, touching more, here and there.

She put her fingers upon a cupboard, a wooden plank of rich burls and sheen despite its age, and it creaked in answer, opening enough for her to slide her hand into it and pull a lever out all the way. A cubicle opened up, with a desk sitting center, a clever bit of carpentry. Bevan thought immediately that he would salvage that from the cabin if he could, coveting it, not wanting it to be pulled out and sold piecemeal by Saliat or Bartoff or anyone else. Papers littered the desk, like his writing table, as if someone had just been interrupted and walked away for a moment. He caught her shoulder again, turning her away from the chair in the corner, soaked with old blood stains.

"She was a..." She hesitated. "She made potions. She turned..." Ardith looked to him for help.

"Alchemist?"

"Yes!"

"Show me. I've been trying to read the engravings on the outer shell. Explain a few of the symbols, and I'll see if I can catch on."

She let out a peal of laughter and stabbed her finger at the desk. "But see the drawings."

He leaned over her shoulder and next to the flowing, graceful script there were neatly sketched diagrams and portraits of the works being done. An organized mind with attention to fine detail clearly delineated the herbs, liquids and elements being used, the only messiness about the various papers he shuffled through was the occasional, rust-colored stains. They belonged to the lost queen, for an official seal stamped a sheaf of papers every now and then. He leaned down to exam the waxy image.

Bevan jerked back in surprise. He hovered close a second time, uncertain he'd seen it properly. He looked from the seal to Ardith, and she caught his actions. Narrowing her eyes, she moved in.

"What is it?"

"She looks like you."

Ardith traced the image. "She does?"

"Very much so." He gathered up the formulas carefully, worried about their brittle nature. These he would examine until he learned their secrets. He started to speak and she halted him with that imperious index finger pointing above, and he could see thoughts, like clouds, passing through her sea-glass eyes.

She took a deep breath. Traced her face with that finger. "My people are the Eriadne. The only queen I knew we called Erianna and she pledged us a cure. This ship came from us. I've been lost as long as she has been and now we're found." She exhaled, watching him.

With those words, she handed him the key to far Briatha and his desires. He clasped his knapsack close, searching for words. From above, echoing down into the pit, came the barking and howls of dogs and the shouts of the men running the pack. Bevan backed out of the compartment, hauling Ardith on his heels, and closed the hidden panel behind them.

"Bevan Historian! We know you're down there! We want the contraband!"

Bevan looked back at the golden chariot, its rudder and fins resting on the pebbled shore. Ardith trembled at his side. Their ransom. Bevan toyed with the idea of coaxing their pursuers down and shoving them into the lake, its substance hostile, but he had no stomach for killing men he'd known for years if he could help it.

"I have a proposal for you." His words undulated upwards. He waited to see if they understood.

"Give up the cargo. There is a bounty on the ashes. We only want what is right and due."

"It's not cargo, it's a child, and she is no more ill than I am."

He could hear Bartoff yelling at the dogs to shut up and get back. "Impossible. Even you are not addled enough to keep the dead." He added, "If it lives, let us witness that."

Bevan straightened his knapsack about. "No, but I have a deal to make. Treasure hunters find treasure." Dead silence followed. He could imagine the arguments above for he had lived on their charity since his wife left. What could he possibly have?

"What have you found?"

"I'll send up an item. Look at it. Make your decision. If you're all agreed it has worth, we'll discuss our deal. I have a few artifacts here that will make us all wealthy." He heard a creak and realized someone already moved down the pit. "If you decide to come down after me, like thieves, I have the ladders rigged to give way."

The creaking halted.

He unshouldered his knapsack and gave it to Ardith. "If they come down, get in the cabin and lock the door."

"It will seal."

"Indeed. And I'll push it back into the lake from which it came."

She studied his face. "I could die there, if you don't come back for me."

"They intend to burn you. If I don't come back, when the air is gone, you'll fall asleep and never wake. An easier death."

Ardith looked steadily at him. He had the sense, for a fleeting moment, of the absolute trust the magician who had put her to sleep must have seen before he condemned her to nothingness. Wordless, she nodded.

He watched as she climbed back in and the doors slammed shut. His throat tightened as he watched the ship sink back into the waters. He spun away and found a rope to haul up a broken fin that he'd never been able to repair, its structure alone worth a fortune, as well as the material constructing it. He climbed halfway up, dragging the offering behind him. Fastening it to the supply hoist, he sent it the rest of the way. He could hear the reactions as it climbed to the rim.

"Have we a deal? Two lives for a fortune?"

A significant pause. They must be arguing among themselves.

"We need ashes."

"Take a fresh corpse and burn it if you will. They know what they're looking for."

"How many more pieces do you offer?"

Bevan considered. He had a second, whole fin. They would know then that he'd found the wreckage of a fantastic airship, royalty among the skies. No. That tempted too much. He had a broken antenna and an oddment or two he'd found in the cargo hold. If he proposed too much, they wouldn't be able to stand against their temptations, plague or not. "A bit or two more. A few gems to offer for food and ignorance to let me stay to finish my writings, and forget the child."

"And if you have the sickness?"

"It stays here with our bones and dust."

More silence. Finally, he recognized Saliat's voice, as oily as his forked beard. "Deal."

He hurried back down and gathered the goods he'd promised, hitching them together in a net of rope. Warily, he tracked its progress as it bumped up the side of the gash and disappeared. After a much longer moment, the net came back down, filled with three journey sacks of the rations the hunters had brought along with them on their pursuit.

Bevan smiled as he gathered the sacks up.

He waited until all sign of them faded away, until all he could hear was the wind whistling across the gash. Bevan raced to the lake and hauled the chain up, dragging it back into place so that he could crank the wreck back onto shore. It responded reluctantly. He threw all of the weight he had on his makeshift equipment to no avail. It refused to bob to the surface or come to shore. He'd taken off the one end. Had the other snagged and come free? What trapped Ardith below?

He'd told her she'd be safe. He hadn't known for certain. He'd hoped with all that seemed left to him, with strength he'd borrowed from her.

Bevan stood hesitantly. "Hells," he muttered, kicked off his shoes, and dove in headfirst.

It stung. Hornets biting at him over and over but it didn't scorch as it had years ago when he'd first gone after the wreck. Now he wrapped the chain about his scalding hand and swam down until he bumped blindly up against the ship. He found the hook where a fin had once been attached, and re-set the chain.

He didn't trust it to hold. On what little breath he had left, Bevan wrestled the wreck. He pushed and wrenched at it until suddenly, it popped up to the surface, dragging him with it. Fresh air came with a sob. He took it once, twice, and then kicked off to the beach, where, barely standing, he wiped his eyes and worked the turnstile, watching with relief as the ship came to the shore.

He reached up, pounding on the door, and it opened, Ardith popping her head out. She looked him up and down. "You live."

"Indeed."

She took his hand to hop out. "And how do I live?"

"Like the rest of us. A day at a time. I've struck a bargain."

She watched him, as she may have watched the magician that fated morning, calm and accepting. He would learn of the Eriadne people and their secrets, if they had magic in their veins, if they had truly lived as others do. She squeezed his fingers. "One day at a time, then. For as long as it takes."

TAMATORI

SUSAN JETT

Shizuko was nearly out of breath when she saw Keiko struggling. She swam closer. Keiko's *tenugui* kerchief had come unknotted and her loose hair had tangled around the rough coral branches, trapping her. Shizuko darted forward to help, but Keiko was panicking. Almost out of breath, Shizuko pushed hard for the surface, thinking to fetch the abalone knife they'd left floating on their buoy. Keiko clutched at her feet, but Shizuko kicked away. *I'll be back, Keiko.*

Gulping air, Shizuko grabbed the knife and dove deep. She could pass the air in her lungs to Keiko while she worked. She descended as quickly as she could, ready to steel herself against Keiko's flailing arms. But her sister's arms were limp. Desperately, Shizuko tried to give Keiko a breath, but she was past needing it. Keiko's eyes opened, red with broken blood vessels and rage. She reached out, dragging Shizuko down one last time—

In her bath five thousand miles away, Shizuko bolted upright, sloshing water across the wooden floor. She was halfway out of her tub before she remembered. Keiko's death had been a lifetime ago, in a different world, back when Shizuko was a fisherman's daughter, not a courtesan. *Just a nightmare*—everyone in San Francisco was plagued by bad dreams lately. This one had been particularly horrific, but it was still just a dream.

Taking a deep breath, Shizuko reclined again in the cooling water. It had been a long night already, and she just wanted to sleep. Preferably alone. But Old Chen had paid extra to be allowed to "surprise" her in her bath. Shizuko didn't mind too much. *If only all my clients were so easy to please…*

The door snicked open, and she closed her eyes and put on her habitual half-smile. As long as she hid her thoughts behind a smile, they still belonged to her.

"Tamatori," Chen whispered hoarsely. "See what I bring you? You want this?"

Shizuko smelled ocean brine on the old man's hands; not unusual for spot prawn season. Opening her eyes, she found herself staring down the narrow neck of a ceramic *tako*-trap. Without another word Chen dropped the jar into her bath. Shrieking in surprise, Shizuko scrambled out. A tiny octopus, rosy as a peach and no bigger than her hand, billowed out of the jar.

She stared at Old Chen in disbelief, but he just shook a tattered print in her face. *So that's why he called me Tamatori.* The erotic image by Hokusai was well-known in San Francisco's pleasure houses, though Shizuko had never heard of a client who'd tried to reenact it. Her lip drew up in a grimace, but the octopus Chen had brought was so tiny it was hard not to be amused. *Ridiculous and disgusting. Rather like my life.*

Grabbing her robe, she stalked away from Chen and his pet. "Hercule," she called. "I need you up here now!" The huge strongman thudded upstairs. "Get him out of here, Hercule-*chan*. Please."

"What's going on, Chen? Augh—!" Hercule's fluent Cantonese quickly outstripped Shizuko's understanding and she stepped out of his way. Chen's cheap print fluttered to the ground as Hercule grabbed his arm.

"The *tako*, too?" Shizuko pleaded.

Holding Chen at arm's length, Hercule leaned over and scooped the octopus back into its pot with his other hand. Never a handsome man, Hercule's face looked downright fearsome when it was pinched with disgust. He dragged Chen downstairs and tossed him out the front door. Shizuko heard the sound of breaking stoneware as the *tako*-pot landed beside him. Then the door slammed shut.

"Thank you, Hercule-*chan*," she called as she came down the stairs.

"Do I want to know what that was about?"

Instead of explaining, Shizuko handed him the woodcut print of a woman being ravaged by octopuses. Sitting across the little table from him, she poured tea for them both. *With any luck, I'll be able to stay awake until dawn.* The nightmares seemed to ease during the daytime, and she didn't think she could take another encounter with her dead sister.

In the meantime, watching Hercule's eye-brows climb up his forehead as his eyes opened wide was amusing enough to let her forget her lingering unease. "It's an old story." She sipped her tea. "Tamatori was either a princess or a fisherman's daughter. To help her husband, she stole *Kanju* and *Manju*—they were pearls that stopped and started the tides. When the sea dragon pursued her, she hid in a cloud of her own blood, like a *tako* hides in its ink."

Hercule seemed rather more interested than the old story warranted. "I'm familiar with the legend," he said. "But what does that have to do with this?" He brandished the print.

Now Shizuko smiled—a true smile, not the false one she used to hide from clients who didn't know the difference. Hercule grinned back, and her heart—which ought to be dead after so many men, so much grief—turned over inside her.

"Tamatori knew she could not escape, so she pushed the pearls into her wound and managed to bring them to the surface before she died. The artist thought that maybe the sea dragon's soldiers followed her. Punished her."

"That's a terrible ending! What's wrong with 'and she lived happily ever after?'"

Carrying her teacup, Shizuko rose and went to look out at the sunrise. "Maybe it was Tamatori's best ending," she said quietly. "She did not fail those who trusted her. There are worse things than dying."

"Like Chen's octopus?"

She smiled at his teasing, but said seriously, "Men are badder now—no, worse," she corrected herself. "It's the nightmares. Bad dreams give them bad thoughts."

Hercule nodded sour agreement. "I thought the nightmares meant the devices I told you about were nearby. But I haven't found them, Shizuko-*hime*, and I've looked everywhere." *Hime* meant 'princess.' It was their private joke. She called the giant, scarred strongman, 'Little Hercule,' and he called her—stranded as she was in a brothel five thousand miles from home—'Princess.'

He'd arrived two years ago, right after the 1904 plague outbreak ended, and told Madame Stella he'd stay until he found what he was looking for. Shizuko didn't know what she'd do when he left. He was her closest friend—her brother, since what he sought didn't seem to be the love of a woman.

She was turning away from the window when two meteorites arced low across the sky, flaring so brightly that Shizuko flinched, dropping her cup and splattering tea over her bare ankles. Shizuko dove under the table, and then the earth lurched sideways.

If she hadn't already been on her hands and knees she would have fallen like her friend, who now sprawled awkwardly on the floor. Moaning, Shizuko squeezed her eyes shut, waiting for the quake to be over. It felt like a lifetime. The shrieks of earth wrenching itself apart pierced her mind like splinters.

And then the world stilled, settling into an uneasy, waiting silence. Shizuko stood carefully and glanced uneasily at the gaslights flickering on the wall. "We need to get out of here."

"Is it over?" Hercule whispered, keeping his hands on the floor as an aftershock rippled underfoot. The house groaned like a dying thing.

Shizuko shook her head. Hercule dragged himself to his feet and they joined the women who stumbled downstairs in various states of undress. One flung open the front door and they all stared, shocked, as their city crumbled. When a warehouse tottered and collapsed, replaced by a plume of dust and smoke, most of the women gasped, a few prayed. One laughed.

Then another shock jarred them all into each other. A loose brick crashed down from the arched doorway onto the abandoned *tako*-pot, shattering it further. Picking her way around the shards, Shizuko ran barefoot into the street. The moving earth wouldn't kill anyone, but crumbling walls and shattering window panes would.

Hercule followed her, but most of the women of the house stood dazed, looking around like canaries examining their broken cage. He tugged Shizuko's arm, and she followed him willingly. *Anywhere's better than here.* They stumbled to a stop as another long aftershock stole their balance, then Hercule pulled her into a trot again. Ducking his head, he lifted her hand to his mouth and kissed it affectionately.

That was surprising enough that she nearly stopped dead in the street; Hercule had never asked favors of any of the women at Madame Stella's. Shizuko had thought that perhaps he didn't like women that way. But she'd also been relieved he'd neither presumed upon their friendship, nor given her reason to be jealous. *For I would have been, even though I would have thought less of him for the asking.*

"We've got to get to the bay!"

"No—after an earthquake there are waves. Huge waves!" She shouted to be heard over the screams and tumbling of debris as her adopted city ripped itself apart.

He halted, panting, hands on his knees as he caught his breath. "How did you know it was coming? You were under that table before I felt anything."

"There were lights. They startled me." She shook her head, trying harder to remember since he was staring at her so intently. "Bright lights, like little suns. They fell into the bay."

Now he crouched to look into her eyes. "What do you—? How many? Oh, Princess," he glanced around at the destruction. "This is what I was afraid of."

Nearby, a building collapsed with a roar, and Shizuko felt the shock in her legs. The breeze picked up then, swirling her hair like ashes in the wind. Hercule reached for her hand, to tug her down the hill again, but she shook her head. "You're going the wrong way, Hercule-*chan*. We need to leave the city."

"I think you found what I've been looking for," he explained.

"The lights? They're in the bay now. And we couldn't find them now anyway—" She gestured at the chaos around them.

"Listen to me, Shizuko. What you saw. When they went in the water they awakened a—a dragon. That's what has caused all this."

Insanity followed earthquakes like death followed plagues. "Hush, my friend," she tried to soothe him. "There are no dragons, but if there were, surely that would be another reason to run the other way?" She offered him a falsely bright smile and took a step uphill.

But he would not be diverted. His eyes were bright and clear, nowhere near as mad as his words. "Shizuko-*hime*, I'm telling this all wrong. But I'm not crazy. It's not really a dragon. It's a creature from beyond the stars that's been sleeping for a millennia, waiting for these devices to return. Once it has them, the invasion will resume and this world will be lost. Everything will be lost."

Shizuko smelled smoke and tugged frantically at his hand. "We have to go."

"Please, Princess." He nodded at the crumbling city around them. "Help me find them."

Another aftershock churned the earth. Shizuko braced her legs and shouted to be heard over the deep grinding of rock colliding underground. "It's just a story, Hercule! There are no sea dragons! No pearls! No princesses!"

His big fingers stabbed accusingly at the scars wreathing his bald head. "Please," he begged. "I'd do it myself, but the dragon marked me years ago. Now when I dive, I can't breathe. I pass out. But I'm not crazy," he repeated.

A woman screamed and Shizuko spun frantically. *Keiko?* Then, remembering, she cringed away from the direction of the sound. *We're all crazy here,* she thought wearily. Columns of smoke punctuated the sky like exclamation points. "Why have you never said anything about this before? Dragons in the bay?"

"Would you have believed me?" Her thoughts must have been written on her face, for he sighed, deflating. "I should have, because you're the only diver I know, and if we can't get them back on land, we're all dead." Fires had begun to spread. Shizuko looked at the ruins of her adopted city, the ruins of another life that had ended without warning. She was tired of running, and no matter where she went, her sister was always waiting for her.

Shizuko tried to smile at Hercule. If nothing else, he was the man her heart had settled on. If this was to be the end of her life, at least she could make her ending a good one. Still, she tried one last time to rouse him from his madness. "You rescued me from Old Chen's pet, but you want me to fight dragons?"

"Not fight," he said eagerly. "Just evade it. There's only one here. And it cannot move until it has its devices in hand. Just bring the pearls to the surface and I'll do the rest. Will you do this for me, Princess? Please?"

They'd reached the waterfront—nearly deserted because everyone else had sense enough to seek high ground. Shizuko looked out at the bay. Still calm, although that might not last long. But death certainly waited for anyone foolish enough to dive during an earthquake. She looked up at Hercule. His hopeful smile was so unlovely, so beloved. *For you, Hercule-chan, I will fight dragons.*

She nodded.

He led her into a rough-shingled boathouse and as her eyes adjusted, she saw a brass railing jutting from the water, gleaming dully. Hercule stepped onto a floating wooden platform and unlocked a low hatch near his feet.

Taking his hand, Shizuko let him swing her over the water to join him. She'd heard of these diving ships, these submarines, though she'd never seen one. This felt more and more like a dream. She welcomed the sensation. She'd died in nightmares often enough, but her dreams were usually pleasant up until the end. Numbness was better than fear.

She followed Hercule, climbing hand over hand into the little craft. It was calm here, bobbing just below the surface of the water. The thick wooden hull dampened the noises of her tortured city tearing itself apart. And Hercule was here. At the end of things, there was no one she would rather be with.

Hercule strapped his feet into pedals that he would use to turn the propeller shaft. He pushed until tendons stood out in his neck. Then, slowly at first, so slowly, the craft began to inch its way toward the far wall of the boathouse and he eased them out into open water. A school of silver fish darted past the porthole and Shizuko put up her hand, marveling.

"I should have brought you here before, Princess." Hercule's crooked smile reflected in the thick glass. "I thought you hated the sea."

I do, she didn't say. *Or at least I did.* Her mind felt clearer than it had in weeks. Months. Since long before the nightmares had made every hour of darkness a torment. She heard herself ask, "What do they do? Your devices?"

Panting, he said, "The creatures are vast, vast enough that the air of our world would crush them, were they to emerge from the seas. We think the devices protect them somehow."

"And if I find them? What then?"

"Then I'll carry them far away. Far enough that it might be a generation or more before they make their way back to the sea. They can't be destroyed, or even hidden for long. We've tried..."

Panting hard, he added, "But you and I could start over, if you wanted. If you wanted to come with me." Then he suddenly stopped pedaling. Silt billowed up around them from the seafloor. "We're here," he said, breaking the silence and relieving her of the need to answer him.

The tiny craft drifted and Shizuko took a deep breath. Now that it was time to do this, she felt less certain. She stepped out of her robe. *If Hercule would just look at me, I would go away with him now. We could live happily ever after, far from the madness that haunts us both.*

But he kept his face turned away, careful not to spy on her nudity. As carefully as if she'd be returning for it, she folded her robe and set it aside. He might care for her, but he would not leave, believing that the world would perish if he did so. Even mad, he was a better man than she deserved.

She strapped the diving knife he offered around her thigh, since its leather sheath was sized for his huge arm. The water was shockingly cold, driving the breath from her lungs. Drowning might not kill her after all. Perhaps the cold would simply stop her heart. *So be it.*

Hercule lowered the brass helmet over her head and mouthed something she couldn't hear through the thick brass and glass. It looked like he said, "Good luck," but luck was for people who hadn't failed. Luck was for heroines out of a children's story, not for her.

Shizuko let the weight of the helmet carry her down. Even near the surface, the water was clouded by sand and seaweed, and the light grew dimmer as she descended. A patch of brightness caught her eye, but it was already getting harder to breathe. She tugged the air tube three times as Hercule had instructed, and pedal-driven fans whirred overhead, forcing air into her helmet. A trail of bubbles escaped to the surface. Shizuko chose not to watch them go.

Instead, she turned toward the vague brightness she'd glimpsed on the seabed. *Probably just an odd reflection from the ship.* Drawing closer, she noticed it glinted as blue as the sky at noon. The water in the bay was green and thick with life. That rich shade of azure was as out of place as starlight.

Now her feet touched the seafloor and she walked slowly, weighted down by the helmet even as the water buoyed her up. As she approached, the silt cleared slightly and she saw the tide-jewels burning white and blue in the muck, each half the size of her fist. *They're beautiful.* She reached out for them, even though she was still half a city block away.

She stared at white *Kanju. Empress Jingū used this to stop the tides from coming in so her army could invade an island. Blue Manju swept the ocean back into place afterwards, drowning their pursuers. They're real. They're here.*

But if Hercule's story was more than a delusion, then there must also be a dragon lurking unseen in this dim underwater world.

The seawater went to ice where it touched her skin and she looked around nervously. A sea turtle drifted past, placidly curious. Beyond the turtle, a school of greenlings flickered in and out of a kelp bed. On her other side, a crimson octopus came close enough to brush the jewels. It went past, then turned, pushing at them again, unusually deliberate in its motions.

*Like the soldiers in Tamatori-*hime's *story, I think this one already belongs to the Sea Dragon.* Shizuko's skin prickled.

Another octopus came forward, as big around as a man's torso. Then another and another. They surrounded the jewels, guarding them, nudging them across the seafloor.

Warily, she crept closer. Twenty *jô* away, she spied a rough outcropping of rock, barely visible through the floating silt. She wondered if a dragon laired somewhere within, though she couldn't see an opening large enough. But the outcropping was the only place big enough to conceal something as vast as what Hercule had described.

Maybe it's gone. Or still sleeping. Or dead.

Carefully keeping the distant rocks in sight through the shifting clouds of silt, Shizuko moved toward the jewels, but her mind fought her, overwhelming her with memories of the blind terror etched on her sister's face. She forgot to breathe.

And then she saw it.

The dragon wasn't lurking in some crevasse within the rocks, it *was* the rocks. Once Shizuko looked away, her peripheral vision filled in all the things her expectations had erased: an open beak crowded with jagged teeth, She'd mistaken it for a colony of anemones. On the other side of the outcropping, she glimpsed a tangle of stony protuberances growing near what must be eyes. Eyes the size of fishing boats. An entire fleet of fishing boats.

Hercule said it slept! her mind gibbered. The creature appeared immobile. *But Hercule didn't know about its army.*

She looked around wildly, then took deep, calming breaths. Panic would do her no good. *I can do this. I only have to get the jewels to the surface before the* tako *push them to the rocks. They may be willing, but their bodies are unsuited to this task, and the distance is great. It will take them many hours.*

She dragged her attention away from the rock outcropping to plan her approach to where the *tako* guarded their prize. The glowing pearls left trails like snail tracks as the *tako* inched them away from the outcropping, toward a ring of spiky rocks as high as her head.

Away from the outcropping?

Frantically, she looked between the octopuses and what she'd assumed was their destination. Then her body recoiled involuntarily, all her muscles clenching in shock when she finally grasped the immensity of the creature she faced.

The distant outcropping was the creature's head. Which meant this spiked horror was something like a hand, bristling with claws. Her mind rebelled at the creature's size. The jewels were already in its palm. If the creature closed its hand, the world would be lost, and all Hercule's confidence in her would have been misplaced.

Another failure. He shouldn't have expected more from me.

The nearest *tako* watched Shizuko with its alien, black eyes, daring her to approach. She accepted its challenge without allowing herself to think about it. If she retreated now she'd never find the courage to return.

As if sensing her terror, her weakness, the dragon turned its full attention on her. Rational thought fled as every bit of shame and rage and grief that Shizuko had ever felt was magnified, stretched, distorted, then thrust back into her mind to cripple her. *Not real,* she insisted. *Not true! I'm sorry, Keiko!*

Shizuko screamed, forcing a gurgle of bubbles from the rim of her helmet. Now the dragon swiveled enormous eye stalks toward her, slowly but inexorably. *It's already awake. Hercule was wrong!* The jewels flared brighter. Shizuko had to reach them before it managed to close its fist. But she felt the prickling on her skin that meant something stalked her—something swimming close with predatory intent.

She held herself perfectly still, unsure if this was another trick. The dragon's slow attention drifted past her. Then a hand grabbed her ankle just as Keiko once had, holding her back.

Shizuko whirled with Hercule's knife in her hand, ready to cut off Keiko's hair, ready to end this horror once and for all.

Only it wasn't her sister; of course it wasn't. A blue tentacle as thick as her calf gripped Shizuko's leg hard enough to bruise before she yanked it free. More *tako* rippled through the water, their sly threats filling her mind, and she knew, suddenly, what had inspired Hokusai. Slowly, as in a nightmare, Shizuko struggled to keep moving toward the tide-jewels. *Did the dragon's attempts to reach the pearls cause the quake? Or did the quake awaken the dragon?* It didn't really matter.

Even if she died thwarting this thing, it would be her best ending. Not to humor Hercule's delusions, nor to atone for failing her sister, but to cheat this thing of the world's pain for even a day would be something to be proud of. *And there are things worse than dying. Tamatori knew this. As do I.*

Her unwieldy helmet forced Shizuko to lumber when she needed to dart like a minnow. The nearest octopus grabbed for the umbilical-like tubing connecting her to the world above, and Shizuko made her decision. Pausing only to gulp one last series of rapid breaths, trying to flood her body with oxygen to fuel her through what must come next, Shizuko unbuckled the chinstrap and let the helmet drift free.

The clarity the helmet's glass panes had lent her vision was gone, but she could still see the brightly burning tide-jewels, could make out the blurred outlines of *tako* writhing closer with every beat of her heart. Slashing wildly now with her knife, she closed her eyes and lunged through a break in the ring of *tako* surrounding her. Ignoring the tentacles twining around one foot, she drew close to her target. *There!* She thrust her arm between the jutting claws just as the *tako* dragged her backward. Although her fingertips grazed the jewels, contact with the dragon nearly shattered her before she could remove them.

Its attack destroyed her reality as easily as the quake had destroyed her city. Blindly, she grabbed at the jewels, but now her fingers squelched, as if she'd scooped up a handful of unimaginable filth. She nearly dropped the pearls before recognizing the trick. Then she held fast, trying desperately to shore up what was left of her mind as she worked her arm free.

Gripping the jewels tight, she saw the outcropping was merely tumbled rock again. Nothing to fear now that she'd retrieved them. Yet her breath was almost gone and the surface was a tiny circle of light far above—so far that she'd never reach it in time. All around her, the *tako* clustered, waiting.

Soon she'd have to exhale her last air, and she would begin breathing water, unable to resist the impulse to fill her lungs. Shizuko kicked hard but dozens of tiny *tako* surged forward, tangling in her hair. Larger ones drew her limbs together, weighting and stilling her thrashing legs. One darted close to the jewels in her left hand and she stabbed wildly with the knife. A cloud of ink unspooled behind it, but her attacker escaped.

Shizuko knew her hands would relax soon: a shell diver's last catch was always lost, and Shizuko's hands were growing cold. She was already dead—she knew that. No one could steal from the sea-dragon and live. But if she died before expending her last breath, her corpse might float the tide-pearls to the surface where Hercule could retrieve them and take them far away. *Oh my love. I am so sorry I doubted you. So sorry I wasted the time we had. I should have told you how I felt…*

But she was out of time. Jabbing the knife beneath the heavy leather sheath, she gouged a deep hole in the muscle of her thigh. Pain was just a thing to be endured, but her body shuddered uncontrollably and the knife drifted from her limp hand as blood poured out of her, stealing her last warmth and writing her ending on the water as if with a *tako*'s ink.

Moaning despite her resolution to save all her air for its buoyancy, she pushed the jewels deep into the wound. Weakly, Shizuko cinched the sheath tighter, though the water around her ran red.

And then the blood rushing from her body ebbed and stopped. *Tides of water, tides of blood,* she thought dreamily. *Kanju stops them all.*

The pulse throbbing behind her eyelids slowed and stopped. She was happy not to drown, it was supposed to be an agonizing death, but her body was merely growing languorous, even as it floated toward the light of the world above. *Find me, Hercule-chan.* She tried to open her eyes, but her life had already ebbed away and her ending was upon her.

*　　　* * *

Hercule crouched on his little craft's tiny deck, gripping the rail with one hand while blinking tears from his good eye. She had to be out there somewhere.

When the ocean had gone unnaturally still, he knew she'd done it. Despite everything, his little Princess had bested—at least tem-porarily—the creature below. But then her air tube had gone slack. Unthinking, Hercule had leapt into the water to rescue her, only to flop helplessly as stars spun through his mind and his body convulsed like a dying fish. He'd dragged himself back onto *Ictinéo*'s deck, weeping with misery and the terror that would not release him, even now.

Then his good eye cleared, and he saw her—a curve of white against the dull gray water. Her hair moved like seaweed, as limp as her empty hands.

He let out the breath he didn't know he'd been holding. If she had found the devices, she hadn't been able to hold onto them. Which meant the alien would regain them and the world would end. His eyes slipped closed. It was over, then, but at least he could bring her poor body in to the land for whatever time was left to them. He knew she'd never liked the sea.

He moved his craft closer, then let it drift until he could lean out and grab her wrists, lifting her up as gently as he could. *Enteroctopus dofleini* tangled in her hair and even twined around the blood-stained sheath at her thigh. He ripped the vile creatures off and hurled them back into the water.

Blood-stained...

He fought back a sob. He'd told her the dragon could not fight back. She was so small, she would have bled out quickly. His good eye blurred again. Shizuko's cheeks were still pink, as if she lived, but he held her close enough to know that she did not. Somehow this was the hardest to bear, that she should look so undamaged.

But the unspeakable thoughts that had plagued him since he'd arrived in this city were gone. Shizuko's poor thigh bulged grotesquely beneath the sheath. With a start, he wondered if she might not have been trying to staunch the flow of blood after all.

"Oh, Princess." A fierce elation swept through him as he unbuckled the sheath and the blood-washed devices tumbled into his hand. Heavier than lead, the smooth spheres seemed too small to be so important—rather like Shizuko-*hime*. "I'll take these so far from the sea that they'll never make their way back," he promised. For although the tides affected everyone and everything—oceans, stars, the ebb and flow of blood in a person's veins—it was easier to be wise when the sea was far away.

"The blood in a person's veins," he whispered, staring at Shizuko's flushed cheeks. Steeling himself, he lifted the ruined flap of muscle in her leg and peered inside. The big artery was nicked, but not severed. He had a medical kit here somewhere. He rummaged in a cupboard and found it, pulling out a needle threaded with waxed black cotton. He placed a line of tiny, neat stitches in the artery itself, trying to hurry, though of course she was far beyond pain.

Setting tide-ebbing *Kanju* as far from her as he could, he muttered a quick prayer and gently pushed tide-flowing *Manju* back inside the awful wound. If *Kanju* had stilled her heart, causing the tides of her blood to ebb before she died, then maybe *Manju* could start them flowing again. He sat back on his heels, hardly daring to hope.

He didn't have to wait long. Shizuko spasmed and coughed. Blood pulsed from the gash on her leg, despite his stitches. "Too much," he muttered, and pulled *Manju* free. The awful flow of blood slowed to a steady trickle, which meant his stitches were holding, but he wasn't finished yet.

When he set the heavy needle into her flesh, she screamed. Grimly, he held her down and tied off the first stitch before placing another and another. He did not stop, even though she screamed, for her pain meant she might yet live. Finally, she fainted and he was relieved not to be causing her more pain. Still she breathed. Still she breathed.

When he finished, he examined his work. A bristly caterpillar of knotted threads inched across her leg. Blood still oozed, but didn't stream out, even when he loosened the tourniquet that had saved her twice now. Even if she lived, she'd bear a fearsome scar and might never walk easily again. He hoped she would forgive him for that.

"Though of course, I'd carry you forever if you'd let me, Princess."

At his words, her eyes opened and she shuddered, then began retching violently. He covered her with her robe and held her close, willing the warmth of his body into hers as she shook convulsively. "Shizuko?" he said gently, calling her back to herself. "Shizuko-*hime?*"

Tears streamed from her closed eyes. He didn't ask if she was relieved or grieved to find herself on board his ship once more, alive once more. He understood more of her life than she realized, maybe. She whispered, "There was a dragon."

"Yes. And a princess who saved the world. She nearly died for her trouble, but instead she married the man who loved her and lived to a very great age."

"No, Hercule-*chan*. She died. Tamatori died. It was her best ending."

"Perhaps we could write her a new ending. Perhaps instead, the princess bore many daughters and sons to her very foolish man. Perhaps they lived for a very long time, far from the sea, and were happy to the end of their days." She'd never answered him when he'd asked the first time, so now he held his breath, waiting for her response.

Her eyes remained closed, but her lips drew up in the merest ghost of a smile. At least it was a true smile. He wondered if she knew he'd always been able to tell the difference.

"Thank you for bringing me back, Hercule-*chan*. There are worse things than dying, but I was not ready to go. Although perhaps I thought I was. But it is really over? The dragon sleeps?"

He nodded. "I'll carry the devices far away. They should never have been allowed so near the sea."

Her smile faded and she whispered, "Thank you, Hercule-*chan*. I must ask something of you—"

Her words were too formal, her expression too solemn for anything but a polite refusal. His heart sank. But whatever else she was: fisherman's daughter or courtesan or the woman he'd loved for so long without ever saying anything, she had also just saved the world. He owed her any assistance he could give her, money or physical protection or even his absence if that was what she required.

Still unsmiling, she opened her eyes. "When our first daughter is born, my love, can we name her for my sister, Keiko?"

Carefully then, as carefully as if she were made of glass or silk—strong and fragile in equal parts—he gathered her up in his arms.

"And they lived happily ever after," he whispered fiercely, a promise as much as an answer.

Her eyes found his. She nodded. And then she smiled.

HIGH SULFUR HOT SPRINGS AND CAMPING PARK

JAMES VAN PELT

"Worst job in the universe," said Harris, sprawled in the lifeguard stand under an umbrella, his nose white-zinc slathered and a towel covering his legs and feet. Red-haired, freckled, tall and smooth-muscled, he didn't tan; he broiled. "I can't believe OSHA doesn't investigate the working conditions. Haven't they heard of sun exposure and carcinoma? I'll be a human-shaped skin tumor before I'm twenty-one."

"If you're solar-phobic, you picked a poor place to work." Heat waves shimmered off the desert hills and bluffs beyond the pool ground's fence. Puddles on the cement shrank and disappeared in minutes.

"It's the competitive swimming curse. Hang around a pool for years, training to swim fast, and you're doomed to work a watch tower."

At the beginning of that summer, I'd found the best lifeguarding job I ever had—the High Sulfur Hot Springs and Camping Park in north-west Nevada—but in fifteen years I'd never guarded with a guy with a crummier attitude than Harris. I know; I'm thirty-two, which sounds old for a lifeguard. It's a college kid's job. What can I do? I like the work. Pool water got into my system, I guess. Washing down the deck in the morning. Helping the swim coach roll up the lane lines after an early practice. Putting up chairs and umbrellas.

I'd watched city pools in Tahoe and Reno. I'd done beach guarding in California, too. There's nothing like climbing on top the guard stand and settling in at the beginning of a shift. You've got an area, and you're responsible for it, so after the whine-fest with Harris, I checked to make sure the other guards were in position, then inventoried what was in front of me. The family group in the water at my feet had a five-year old with cheap, plastic inflatable water wings wrapped around her upper arms. Not safe at all. A little farther out, an adolescent couple walked in the shallow end. He carried her and her head rested on his shoulder. Very sweet. I wouldn't worry about them unless the public display of affection thing got out of hand. Three boys showed off on the diving board, whooping and doing fancy flips and twists. If they dove straight off and gave each other room, probably no problem there either, although a couple days ago, a guy I wasn't worried about at all, out of nowhere, decided to do a reverse dive. That's the kind that looks like he's going to go off in a regular dive, but at the end of the board he rotates backwards. His feet fly out in front and keep going up until they're over his head. It looks awesome and unlikely, but a good diver can do full flips that way. This guy, though, did the reverse motion without moving away from the board. Straight up, straight down. Clunk. Head on the board and he's unconscious in the water with a wreath of blood around his neck and shoulders.

I pulled him out and he got a handful of stitches from the experience. It just shows you can't ignore anyone. Guarding is about watching people who *probably* won't get in trouble, but there's enough of them that someone always does.

So the job is good wherever I go, despite what Harris said. Sun. Sitting. Great people to work with, almost all at the pool to have fun. You just have to be aware. Mostly my interaction with the crowd is either "Don't run on the deck" or "Don't hang on the ropes." Sounds calm if it wasn't also life or death work. Laid back, restful, and completely vital. Besides, there's lots of skin and people who are fit, tanned, and beautiful, at least some of them.

But guarding a beach is a totally different skill set than guarding a public pool, and guarding at High Sulfur Hot Springs and Camping Park wasn't like either. It was my first natural hot springs pool. The stuff I knew about pool chemistry went out the window here. About a million gallons of sulfurous-smelling mineral water welled up from the spring a day, so we didn't worry about adding chlorine or tracking the PH. Mostly we checked for bacterial content. The water turned over completely a couple times every twenty-four hours.

We closed at ten. Harris walked the deck to stack chairs while the other guards picked up trash, gathered lost and found (flip-flops, cell phones, keys, towels, goggles, and sun glasses made up the bulk). I loaded the beer and tequila I'd bought before work into a cooler and then onto the ten-meter board lift before sending it up.

Most man-made swimming pools don't have interesting histories, while the ocean is timeless and the same from beach to beach, but High Sulfur Hot Springs is unique. The bottomless deep end, for example. Well, not really, but it's over 400 feet down to where the spring water flows from dozens of cracks in the rock, some wide enough for a diver to get through if the water wasn't 122 degrees. No one knows how deep those cracks go. Before the pool, the spring created a good-sized pond in the desert canyon, with Cactus Creek dumping in cold water at one end, then draining off in the other, with an extra million gallons of heated water from below. It all ended in the Humboldt River. Indians never used it, although they were in the area. Maybe they didn't like it. Before the High Sulphur Hot Springs group developed the site ten years ago, this wide spot in the canyon must have been quite pretty, if you didn't mind the rotten-egg smell.

The pond's surface temperature probably ranged from 90 degrees and up depending on how fast Cactus Creek ran. If the creek dried, the springs' temperature would rise to over 120 degrees. When an animal like a deer fell in, it would scald to death in minutes. I imagined the bottom was littered with bones.

Once the developers took over, though, the springs changed its look. In the pool itself, they smoothed the rock walls ten feet down and bolted in ladders every twenty feet. They dynamited a long, wide area to be the shallow end, then poured cement deck all around. Water flows were moderated to keep the surface area at eighty-eight degrees—lots of complicated plumbing. The area to be guarded was huge. It took three guards to watch the wading section, and four in the deep end. Added to the pool area were three diving boards: two one-meter and one three-meter, and a ten-meter platform that was only open for exhibitions. Three slide tubes emptied into long troughs beside the baby pool, and they installed fountain features kids could play in near the facility's entrance and by the shallow end. They built a pool-side concession stand, a restaurant, a bar, a hotel complete with casino, and the RV park. And that's how you create a tourist attraction in Nowhere, Nevada. Before long, horse outfitters offered guided trips into the dry hills, the biking community built single-track bike trails, and a traveling carnival settled in to make High Sulphur Hot Springs its permanent home.

I liked guarding best at night, for the ambience. The spring Harris joined the staff, they put colored underwater lights in the deep end to a hundred feet or so. The blue lights were best. Green made the pool look like an apple martini, yellow was just gross, of course, and red creeped me out, as if the pool was a tremendous gun shot into the desert's forehead. I think blue lights created the conditions for Harris to become a hero. They gave Harris his chance.

The head guard picked the night lights, so I always chose blue. The deep end glowed, and the spring water ran so clear that when we stood on the ten-meter platform looking down, it was as deep as space.

We'd planned a staff party for Friday, just the evening crew, seven guards and the cashier. Four women and four guys. Maggie, a twenty-one year old studying criminal justice at Great Basin College in Elko who dealt blackjack at the casino in the mornings, started the festivities. We sat in a circle on the ten-meter platform around a little pot-bellied barbecue that had just enough room for four hamburgers. She reached into the cooler, retrieved a liter-sized tequila bottle, unscrewed the lid, and threw it into the darkness. "Whoops, we'll have to drink it all now!"

Things grew increasingly spinny and weird after that. Lots of limes, salt, tequila, and beer. At some point, we all were face down on the platform's edge, looking into the pool. I dropped an empty bottle. Not a whisper of wind. The surface was still and clear as glass. The bottle fell away as if it dropped toward a black hole. Then, sploosh, it hit, sending out a perfect bulls-eye of blue-edged ripples from the center. The bottle, trailing bubbles at first, sank farther and farther away until it vanished below the last lights.

God, it was awesome.

Which, of course, meant that we had to fly ourselves. I went first. A few steps back, a quick trot to the edge, and a leap.

I'm not a diver. A jump from ten meters makes me nervous. There's that moment when the world drops away that's always a rush, but here I felt like I was suspended over a great, blue eye. It rose toward me and I couldn't even scream. When I hit, the bubbles seemed to fluoresce. Glorious! Totally glorious.

Everyone tried it. Harris, it turned out, had a diving background along with the years on a swim team. He did a handstand on the edge, leaned out, then turned two somersaults before cutting the water in a clean dive. Maggie suggested that it didn't mean a thing unless we did it naked. Lit by the pool's azure lights and a half moon that hung over the desert, she stripped off her suit with drunken dignity. "I am a god!" she announced, hands in the air, feet apart, and then she leapt, and I thought she *was* a god, and the other guards were gods, and so was I. We laughed like fools as we pulled at our suits, then, naked, flying, crashed down into that great, blue circle.

When the party ended, Maggie and I climbed down together. Harris said he wanted to spend the night on the platform, so we left him wrapped in a blanket after making him promise not to wander off an edge. I kept the pool lights on for him. I should have known better.

In my apartment that night, I couldn't sleep. Too much liquor, I suppose, but every time I closed my eyes, I saw that one eye below me, blue at the edge, black in the center, waiting to swallow me whole. I shivered. Even in the hot Nevada night, I shook.

Harris waited for me in the guard shack. He must have had a worse night than I did. Dark circles under his eyes, pale face, even for him, hair uncombed.

"Welcome to a tequila sunrise," I said. "Too much acetaldehyde in the system?"

"What's that?"

"It's what your liver turns alcohol into."

"I'm not hung over. I saw something last night."

"A god?" I laughed.

He looked confused.

"Maggie."

"No, not that. Have you ever seen anything weird in the pool?"

"I saw a ninety-four year old bald dude in a thong a couple of months ago."

"Can you stay late tonight? I got to show you something. It's driving me crazy."

My heart sank. I had an idea what he was talking about. I hoped I was wrong. It was kind of my secret. "Yeah, sure. I'll bring the beer."

Maggie came into the shack then, interrupting us. Harris grabbed his floppy hat and sunglasses before heading to the deck. Maggie truly did seem hung over and she didn't meet Harris' eyes as he left. All I got from her was a mumbled, "Good morning." Evidently she didn't always skinny dip. I'd have to talk to her about it later. It wasn't a big deal.

Busy time at the pool. Three swimming saves, which I think is a record for a regular day. (The record for a private group is five, but everyone was drunk.) I made the first one. A thirteen-year old girl wearing a Justin Bieber tee shirt slipped under the rope between the wading pool and the deep end to get a beach ball. There's no slope. You're either in four feet or you're in four-hundred feet. Some drowners flail about on the surface, and they might even get a scream out, but she slipped off the edge and didn't come up. Most drownings are quiet like that. I watch the rope closely, so I was in the water about ten seconds after she sank, towing a rescue tube. Didn't even have to dive to get her. Snagged her hand and hauled her onto the tube.

She coughed up water and said, "That's some tough tacos," which is the weirdest thing I've ever heard anyone say in such a situation. The other guards laughed when I told them later.

Maggie made save number two. A really heavy Asian guy knocked the wind out of himself when his flip off the three-meter board went one and a quarter turns, which turned it into an epic belly-flop. She swam him to the edge and bounced him onto the deck without help, where he lay on his back for about five minutes. Maggie only weighs about a hundred and ten, I'd guess. No hangover in her when it counts.

Harris made the third. We get a lot of retirees at the pool. They swim in the morning when its cooler, gamble in the afternoon, and then come back for an evening dip. The elderly have their own set of issues. A walking cane on a slippery deck, for instance. Anyways, this guy, who didn't look all that old, stroked out in the wading pool. He was by himself and just flopped over, face down. Harris saw him right off, got to him, then rolled him so he could breathe. One side of the guy's face hung there, and blood filled his eye. An EMT unit was on deck immediately and I heard that by the evening the guy was doing okay. If you get the right drugs to someone having a stroke early, they have a pretty good chance.

The pool gave a twenty-five buck bonus for a save—the only place I've ever worked that did that—so it was only natural for me to invite Maggie to late-night two to see what Harris wanted to talk to me about. Seventy-five bucks buys a nice party for three guards.

Harris caught my eye several times during the day, but didn't say anything, while Maggie brightened up by mid-shift. "Aspirin and a Dr. Pepper work wonders for me."

I ordered a pizza for closing time. The three of us sat on the admissions counter waiting for it. The deck lights flicked out and the staff went home. A quarter mile away, across the park, the only greenery within fifty miles, the casino sent cryptic neon messages into the night.

"You stay here much after hours?" asked Harris.

"It's peaceful. Sometimes you hear coyotes."

Maggie said, "I'm just here for the food." She laughed, a pleasant contralto, not one of those high-pitched squeals that get on my nerves by the time we close up. I worked an all-girls private academy party in San Diego once. Fifty thirteen-year olds. The migraine lasted for a week and I've been sensitive since.

"Ah, the pizza guy," I said.

We sent the beer and food on the lift, then climbed the steps to the platform's top.

"I like it up here," said Maggie. She stood at the rail, looking away from the pool, toward the desert hills.

"You can't get higher unless you're on the casino roof." I was trying to picture her as the god she was last night. Maybe it was the moon or the pool light, but she still had it. Lithe, athletic, strong, great smile.

Harris didn't say anything. He sat on the platform's edge, his legs swinging free. I sighed and grabbed a beer to join him. Maggie followed. I was right about why he wanted me up here.

"Do you see them?" he asked.

I did. I'd seen them before. Deep in the pool, right at the edge of the farthest lights. At first they were hard to pick out, because they were dark-skinned on a black background, but the blue highlighted them when they moved, and once you knew what to look for, they were easy to spot. Distance is a funny thing. Thirty feet, for example, isn't that far. It's a first down in football. But if you put thirty feet on edge, that's a three-story building, and even if there's water at the bottom, it's a long fall. That's how high a ten-meter platform is. Water depth is even more problematic. A common test in a lifesaving class is to put a big rubber brick at the bottom of a ten-foot deep pool and have the student do a surface dive to get it. Surprisingly, quite a few students fail that test the first time. If you're not used to it, the pressure on the ears is uncomfortable, plus the scared kitten part of you freaks out because you've got to go back up that ten feet for air. A hundred feet, then, is ten of those ten-foot challenges, each one with higher pressure, and each one that much farther away from your next breath. It's hard to believe that the world record for free diving is over five-hundred feet.

Still, with all that scariness about distance, falling, and drowning, whatever was swimming below us was only one-hundred and thirty feet away, less than half a football field. They looked like seals, sort of—same size but with rounder heads and human features. Short arms with hands that flattened against their sides when they shot around, which they could, powered by strokes from their fin-like feet.

"How hot is it at that depth?" asked Maggie.

I thought that was an interesting reaction. "That's just below where they start mixing in cold water. Maybe a hundred and fifteen degrees. You can feel it getting warmer the deeper you go."

"A better question," said Harris, "is what are they?"

I shrugged. "Something that lives deeper down. Thermophiles."

Harris looked at me.

"Heat lovers," said Maggie. "Do they ever surface?"

"I've never seen them come up much above the deepest light. My guess is that the water is too cold for them higher up, or they need the pressure." I'd seen them first a couple weeks after they installed the lights, and only when the blue lights were on. Never during the day. Too dim to photograph them, and then after a while I figured nobody needed to know. Authorities would close the pool, of course, to investigate, which would mean I'd be job hunting again, and I just liked the idea of them. They weren't bothering anyone; why should we bother them?

"What are they doing?" asked Harris.

There were eight or nine creatures. They gathered together in a clump for a minute, then spread out, leaving one in the middle. After thirty seconds they all stopped, scattered around the middle one who started swimming a wandering route. Every few seconds, all the ones not in the middle would shift a couple of feet in unison like a school of fish changing direction at the same time. It was interesting to watch. When the middle one got close to another, the other would move slowly away, as if avoiding the middle one's path, or sprint off while the other gave chase. Things would be frantic for a few seconds. When the moving one touched another, they'd group to start again.

They swam gracefully, like ballet. In the pool's blue light, the dance was surreal and beautiful.

Maggie broke the silence. "Doesn't that look familiar?"

It did look familiar. To a veteran guard like myself, I should have seen it right away. "Marco Polo."

Maggie flopped onto her stomach, head hanging over the edge like we did last night. "They probably don't have good vision, if they live in the depths. I'll bet they're sensitive to movement, so whoever is 'it' closes his eyes, says the equivalent of 'Marco,' and all of them shifting position is their version of 'Polo.' They're kids. We're watching a game."

"I thought I was hallucinating last night when I saw them," said Harris. "They went deep before dawn. So you don't think they're dangerous? I was afraid they were...water werewolves."

I laughed. "You went supernatural? Were-seals?"

Maggie said, "There's not a full moon, Harris."

He looked sheepish. "Then they're an undiscovered species."

"No doubt. Nevada has more hot springs than any state in the union. They might not be limited to here. But they've never been seen, and that may be what has saved them. Have another beer." I handed him a cold one. "We'll keep it as our secret."

We told dirty jokes for a while. Turned out that Maggie was practically an encyclopedia of them, although Harris, once he got going, knew a couple toe-clinchers himself. Meanwhile, the were-seals, or whatever they were, continued playing their game. We kept an eye on them. I think that's just what lifeguards do, from habit. You can't spend hours and hours watching out for people's safety without it ingraining in you a bit. Heck, when I'm in a mall, if a kid runs past me, I have to bite back my reflexive, "No running on the deck!"

So we saw the same thing and interpreted it the same way. The game below had gotten faster and faster. Less searching around and more flat out tag. Like kids in a pool, I'll bet that whoever was "it" was peeking a lot to see where the others were. Lots of chasing. A bigger were-seal was it and had cornered the smallest one. The small one went left, but the bigger one cut it off. It went right, and the pursuer shifted again. Unexpectedly, the little one swam hard straight up in a panic. The big one chased for twenty feet and then veered off, but the little one didn't look back. It powered toward the surface much quicker than we could swim. At fifty feet, though, it slowed, turned around, twitched its feet-fins twice, and then was still.

I'd seen drowning before. The struggle, if any, is short, and the body goes still in a horribly unique, limp way that is unmistakable.

"It's in trouble," said Harris.

What do you do in an emergency? As a guard, I'm pretty instinctive. No hesitation. But I must not have thought of this that way. Neither did Maggie. Harris, though, ripped his shirt over his head and dove.

It took just a few seconds, but it played out in slow motion: Harris falling, his hands pointed to the water, in perfect diving form; the were-seals looking up, their faces clear; and then he cut through the water, a flaming blue plume of bubbles behind him. His momentum took him only halfway there. With strong, sure strokes, he drove himself deeper. He grabbed the still form—it was less than half his size—and then continued down, slowed by the burden. Harris was a powerful swimmer. He kicked hard and pulled with his free hand.

I could feel myself pulling with him, arms aching, lungs burning. "It's too hot that deep."

Harris reached the were-seals. He pushed the limp one toward them, then started up. His motions, at first sure and rhythmic, became weaker. Bubbles trailed up from his mouth. He quit moving at about where he'd grabbed the creature, fifty feet from the surface.

My shirt flew off. I jumped, feet first, and realized Maggie was plunging down in front of me. She beat me off the platform by a tenth of a second.

Harris's hands dangled lifelessly above him while he hung suspended, unmoving. I'd never gone this deep. The water pressed cruelly, smothering, and hot, so hot. I gritted my teeth against a scream. Everything in me wanted to turn around. How had Harris gone this far? How had he continued down?

I grabbed a wrist the same time Maggie got the other. Then I kicked with all I had toward the sky. I gasped when we surfaced, still pulling Harris to the side, kicking hard. On the deck, he didn't move. His skin had turned crimson, like a lobster. I cupped my hand behind his neck, opened his mouth, and began resuscitation. Maggie held his wrist. "I can't feel a pulse."

But after a couple minutes, he coughed hard, and I turned him on his side. He moaned, and spit up water. I stayed close and patted his back.

In the pool, down in the blue light, the were-seals had clumped around the one Harris had taken back to them. Larger ones appeared from below. Their arms were paler than the small ones, and their faces more distinct, very human-like, with large, dark eyes. The little one stirred weakly. A couple of the bigger ones steadied it, then it kicked itself forward a few feet, turned to look at them, then swam purposefully down and into darkness below the lights. The rest followed, and the pool was empty and motionless once more.

Harris rolled onto his back, red as a stoplight. "That's some tough tacos."

We hustled him into the shower and ran tepid water over him to cool him down. At the hospital later, they gave him pain pills. The emergency room doc said he'd never seen a full-body scald before: a head to toe first degree burn.

That fall I moved to Elko and took a job as head guard at the Elko Swim Pool in Johnny Appleseed Park while Maggie finished her last year in Criminal Justice. Harris stayed at High Sulfur Hot Springs Pool and Camping Park where he eventually became the aquatics supervisor. We get together a couple of times a year. This year we celebrated Maggie's thirtieth by going up on the ten-meter platform after the pool closed. No tequila this time. I had set up a blanket and beanbag chairs earlier with a couple pricy bottles of wine. Harris brought cheese, crackers, and chilled shrimp.

Scaffolding covered much of the casino side that faced us. They were renovating and adding more rooms, but the desert looked exactly the same. Moonlight painted the bluffs with bone-white light and the shadows were unfathomable. Up here, above the sulfurous water, I smelled only cactus and the long, empty land. We weren't dressed to swim this time.

The three of us stood at the edge, wine glasses in hand, looking down into the great blue eye that looked back at us. "They've never come up," said Harris. "I've waited for them for years."

Maggie said, "I have dreams about this place sometimes."

I've guarded a lot of pools. There's something about the water, kids laughing, the smell of sunscreen that I can't escape. I've had dreams, too, where the water grows hotter and hotter, and were-seals surround me, wide-eyed and pale-limbed, swimming with delight in the heat. Everything is blue and I'm joyous. My friend saved someone, and Maggie and I saved him. I have the hot springs dreams too, and they're always good.

I put my arm across Maggie's shoulders. "Happy birthday, sweetheart."

She hugged me back.

THE CITY UNDER THE SEA
J.C. KOCH

"Solar Command, this is Pilot Melissa Katano of *Neptune Ten*. We are coming into range of the planet."

"Roger that, *Neptune Ten*. All systems are go. Proceed with landing and exploration."

Commander James Conason heaved a sigh. "Ready?"

Katano nodded. "As we'll ever be." The rest of the command crew agreed.

The Neptune Program was tasked with exploring the outer planets of the Solaris System. They were a long way from Neptune, let alone Earth, but they were about to do what no human had done before—visit Planet Nine. Or, as their Science Officer and Co-Pilot Kathi Schreiber insisted, Planet Ten. She was big on supporting the Plutonian viewpoint that it counted as a full and real planet.

Conason didn't have an opinion about Pluto one way or the other. So much of the Solaris System had been claimed by Earth and turned into new homes for humanity that many of the moons could lay claim to being planets by now. Planet Nine could, using that viewpoint, be called Planet Thirty-Seven as easily as Nine. But Nine it had been called since the early part of the twenty-first century and the name had stuck.

It was a huge, black orb. Sol looked like a star from this far away, not the sun that had given life to humanity. There were smaller moons, thirteen of them, each larger than Pluto, all circling Planet Nine like the old pictures showed the electrons circling the nucleus of an atom. The moons all had what looked like clouds or weather patterns. The planet, however, seemed weather-free.

"How long before we land on Yuggoth?" Flight Engineer Joshua Adams asked.

"Oh, not that again," Schreiber said good-naturedly. She was the only one who was still willing to humor Adams about his religious obsessions.

"Thirty Earth minutes before we'll be able to start the exploratory orbit of Planet Nine." Katano didn't snap at Adams because she was a professional, and calm and cool under pressure, but Conason knew she wanted to.

Katano was a great pilot, and Schreiber was right there with her, the two women the best team in the System, at least as far as Conason was concerned. He'd been working with them for at least a decade now and planned to do so until he died, they were that good. He could pilot the ship, of course, but why, when he had the two best in the System on his crew?

In the olden days of space travel, it would have taken them ninety minutes to circle the Earth. Planet Nine was at least four times Earth's size. But ships were better now—faster, more maneuverable, able to fly to a planet, explore it, and reach escape velocity regardless of the planet's pull. *Neptune Ten* was the most advanced ship ever made. Conason was proud—of his command, his ship, his crew.

"It's certainly as dark as we expected," he said.

"Yuggoth—the strange dark orb at the very rim of our solar system," Adams said. "We're so lucky. We're going to be the first who get to greet the Old Ones."

Conason bit down on all he wanted to say. The Cult of the Old Ones was strong throughout the Solaris System, and religious tolerance was something that was stressed as vital to the well-being of all the system's inhabitants. Most people in the Cult were quiet about it, going on about their lives pleasantly, willing to witness if another showed interest, but rarely trying to force their religion down others' throats.

But Adams was different. Not only was he a fervent member of the Cult, he was also a scholar of their original texts, texts that were created in the twentieth century as entertainment. But if someone mentioned that to Adams, he just pointed to other religious texts and said they were stories that had been created, too. It was hard to argue with the logic.

Adams had worked harder than anyone to be on this mission, but the six months it had taken to reach Planet Nine were some of the longest of Conason's life, and it was all due to Adams and his constant quoting of his religious texts.

"Is Josh blathering on about his religion again?" Payload Commander Janelle Rothstein asked with a laugh as she came into the command section. "You know, I could demand that we all wear kippahs when we go out there, if we need to add some other religions into the mix."

"He is," Mission Specialist George Phillips said. "And, you know, Josh, it was funny at first. Now I, personally, would appreciate it if you stopped quoting at us all the time and actually did your job. Janelle doesn't quote the Torah, I don't recite from the Quran, James isn't reading Bible passages aloud, Melissa's not quoting Buddha at you, and Kathi doesn't constantly tell you that she believes in science not gods. Could you *please* stop quoting Lovecraft to us?"

"I always do my job," Adams replied mildly. "I wouldn't complain if you all chose to share what you believe with me. The Old Ones allow us to worship as we want, because they know they are the True Gods. We all must do what we can to prepare the way for the Great Cthulhu and His Family to return."

"That's all," Conason said, before the crew lost their tempers. "Now isn't the time for bickering. We're about to visit this planet for the first time, and it's taken hundreds of years for us to get to the point where we could get here. It's at the last possible point in its orbit where we can easily reach it from the Greater Celestials. If we fail, then we lose Planet Nine for at least ten thousand years, maybe twenty. We have a platoon of ships waiting for our okay, ready to come here and learn, but we're the first. It's an honor and an obligation, the biggest step for humankind yet, and I'll be damned if petty bickering and annoyances are going to stop us."

Katano nodded; the others gave him a little applause. Adams just smiled. "It won't matter soon," he said cheerfully, as he turned back to look at the planet. "We come from the Earth to lead-grey Yuggoth, where the cities are under the warm, deep sea."

Another quote. Or, rather, an inversion of the original quote. Adams had quoted the original enough that Conason could tell the difference. Not that he cared for this knowledge. He and the rest of the crew all heaved sighs and ignored it. What else could they do?

Not that Adams was wrong. This close, Planet Nine really did look lead-grey. It might be like Europa and have water underneath its ice—they'd spent two hundred years discovering that more of the solar system was inhabitable than anyone could have suspected. That Planet Nine might be a home for humankind was possible. Unlikely, but possible. However, the real hope was that they'd discover useful ores and minerals. The Asteroid Belt wasn't going to be able to provide for the System forever.

They had more time than he'd said. But no more than a hundred years to mine what they could before the planet's orbit would take it so far away that anything gained from it would cost more in time and travel than it was worth.

"Janelle, how are all the robots?" Conason asked.

"Prepped and ready, Commander. First wave is in the airlock." Robot explorers would actually be on the planet before any of the humans in the crew. They'd determine what kind of pressure suits the crew would need to wear, verify temperatures, take water and soil samples, and so on. They'd identify if there as any life, too, since they were set to identify bacterium.

"Good. Let's get ready for what we're going to find."

Everyone was quiet for a few minutes, other than speaking as it related to their duties.

"Beginning initial orbit of Planet Nine," Katano said as the huge, grey planet loomed in front of them. Orbiting was a requirement when landing on a new celestial body—it was wise to take a look and get readings first before plunging into an unfamiliar atmosphere.

The impression from a little farther out still held—there were no clouds on this world. They circled it using several different paths and it was always the same—dark grey, almost black, nothing. No continents were visible, no water or ice, either. From outside its atmosphere, Planet Nine was just a gigantic ball bearing.

"Strap in," Katano said after they finished their last circumnavigation. "Turning off gravity force to prepare for entering the planet's atmosphere in ten…nine…"

Everyone buckled their harnesses. Katano flipped the switch and the tug of zero-gravity hit, trying to gently pull them out of their seats.

Entry was always tough, but over time the ships had been designed to handle it better, and these days it was only a little rough. They could see the flames going past the nose, but these flames were different.

"They're grey," Schreiber said. "I've never seen anything like it."

Miraculously, Adams didn't reply. Conason looked over at him. He had a rapturous expression, and his lips were moving. So he was praying. Silently, for once. Conason would take that gladly.

They were through entry far faster than anyone expected, but Katano was ready and she pulled them up from the dive position to allow the *Neptune Ten* to begin its within-atmosphere orbit. Their orbit was high enough that the only potential issue would be if Planet Nine had giant, active volcanoes.

The ship jerked. "What's going on?" Conason asked, as a feeling of being far heavier than he'd ever been weighed on his body.

"We're being pulled down," Katano said, voice tight.

"Adjusting for stronger gravitational pull," Schreiber added. "Hold on."

Conason consulted the readings. "Sensors picking up no aboveground formations or activity. Team?" Various assents—if there was something aboveground on Planet Nine, they weren't near it. Meaning, hopefully, they weren't going to smash into anything, as the *Neptune Ten* was definitely descending faster than planned.

"No readings of geological formations," Adams confirmed. "Which makes sense—Yuggoth is all water, at least from above. Its cities are underwater. So no worries, Commander—we'll be fine."

"Really?" Conason couldn't keep the sarcasm out of his tone. "And you know this how?"

"Because it's in the texts. Oh, how won-derful it's going to see the Old Ones and awaken them! They're calling us to them, that's why we're dropping so quickly."

"Uh-huh. Science, Josh. We're on a mission, a scientific one. We're being pulled down by a stronger gravitational field than expected, meaning this planet has more mass than our calculations indicated. Now, let's see what's actually below us before we hit it, shall we?"

"Stabilized," Katano said, relief clear. "We've compensated."

"Turning high beams on now, Commander," Schreiber said, as the *Neptune Ten* leveled out. The crew chuckled, mostly from relief—this was one of Schreiber's little jokes, since high beams were as archaic a thing as the original stories Adams had based his life on. But the chuckles quickly changed to gasps.

There was nothing but lead-grey as far as they could see. Lead-grey water.

* * *

They circled the planet again, several times, in a variety of directions. But it was the same in every direction—nothing but water. Water that was moving, like waves moved on the oceans of Earth.

In one sense, this presented no issues. The *Neptune Ten* was as at home deep underwater as it was in space. However, the water was opaque and sensors weren't giving them any readings. There could be anything under the surface, and that anything could include mountains and volcanoes and other geologic dangers. The *Neptune Ten* was an amazing ship, but she wasn't invincible.

"How is there water here?" Katano asked. "Water, not ice?"

"The core of this planet must be superheated in some way," Rothstein said. "I can't come up with anything else that makes sense. Kathi, what do you think?"

Schreiber shook her head. "Your scientific guess is as good as mine right now. We need to investigate to determine more."

"Janelle, let's get your first robots going," Conason said. "Hopefully they'll tell us something."

"I'll need to reprogram them for dropping into water," Rothstein said as she unbuckled herself and shoved out of her seat. "The gravity here is really hard to take, Commander."

"It will be fine once we're underwater," Adams said, before Conason could reply. "We'll all feel more buoyant. All those who live on Yuggoth do so underwater."

No one bothered to make the effort to respond to Adams now. Rothstein just rolled her eyes at Conason, then dragged herself out of the command section.

"Do we hover or continue circling?" Katano asked.

"Can we get any underwater readings at all from here?" Conason countered.

"None," Schreiber said. The rest of the crew confirmed they had nothing.

"Then one place is as good as another," Conason said with a sigh.

* * *

"Commander, robots are reprogrammed and ready to launch," Rothstein said finally. "I'm sorry it took so long—every movement takes more effort."

"Not a problem, Janelle," Conason said. "Ready when you are."

"Airlock opening in three…two…one…first wave robots are launched."

The console indicated an issue. "Janelle, why is the airlock still open?"

"The doors won't close, Commander. I'm getting into my suit, taking breathing crystals with me just in case."

"Robots are underwater," Phillips said. "Heading down fast. Faster than normal, Commander."

"Pull on the ship is increasing," Schreiber said. "We need to move higher, if we still can, or we could be pulled apart."

"We can't risk the delay," Conason said. "Let's see if Josh is right."

"Switching to submarine mode," Katano said. "Janelle, don't go into the airlock."

"Too late," Rothstein said. "I'm already in. Just give me a second to—"

Conason waited a moment. "To what? Janelle, what's going on?"

Her reply was a scream, loud and terrified, but cut off quickly.

Conason and Phillips didn't hesitate. They were both out of their harnesses and moving out of command section as fast as they could go, which wasn't nearly as fast as normal. Phillips was in the lead; Katano's voice was on the com. "Commander, we have to switch to submarine mode in thirty seconds or less."

"Call it out," he shouted as they continued towards the airlock. They should have made it in less than fifteen seconds—they were all in top physical condition and they did drills to ensure that all of them could react and arrive quickly should there be a hull breach, a problem with the airlock, and so forth. But Katano was on twenty-five by the time they got there.

"I don't see any sign of her." Phillips moved aside so Conason could take a look through the porthole.

There was nothing in the airlock, but the door was open. Conason squinted. "It looks like the door was ripped off its hinges."

"Twenty-nine," Katano said. "Going to sub-marine mode now."

"All crew into gear," Conason said as the ship's internal systems altered to protect the crew from pressurization. They wouldn't be able to open the inner airlock door now, regardless of who or what was out there.

He could only hope that Rothstein's gear had held up.

While he and Phillips got into their exploration suits, designed to protect them from all elements, be they planetary or in space, he watched through the porthole. They were underwater fast, the spotlights still on, beaming out from all around the ship. There was more visibility underwater, but not much. Unfortunately, he still didn't see Rothstein.

"No sign of Janelle," Schreiber said, voice tight. "She wasn't hooked into the ship's monitoring system when we lost contact with her."

"Keep monitoring," Conason said as he verified that the inner airlock door was sealed tightly. Then he and Phillips headed back to the command section, Adams passing them on the way to the gear. He looked grim.

"We'll find Janelle, safe and sound, I'm sure," Conason said gently.

Adams shook his head. "She'd better not get to see them first."

Phillips and Conason kept going. "He's an asshole," Phillips commented.

"He's just having a religious experience and it's affecting him. I'd confine him to quarters but I think we're going to need all hands, if only to find Janelle." He wanted to say that he didn't expect to find more than her body, but that was negative and you didn't inspire or lead well by being negative.

Conason and Phillips relieved Schreiber and Katano while they got into their gear. Conason turned the ship around slowly, he and Phillips searching for Rothstein. Nothing.

Adams came back before the two women. "We need to dive down deeper."

"I hate to agree, but I don't see Janelle anywhere, so it's likely she's gone deeper."

"I doubt we'll find her," Adams said. "I thought about it, and I believe that she will be seen as our first offering. This is good. The Old Ones may be pleased with us. But the pressure will be less the deeper we go."

"Why would that be?" Conason asked, trying to keep the anger he felt at Adams' cavalier attitude about Rothstein's fate from his voice. "The pressure will increase the closer we get to the planet's core."

Adams shook his head. "Things are different on Yuggoth."

The women returned before Conason could argue. Phillips' expression said he was as appalled as Conason. Katano and Schreiber's expressions said they'd heard Adams' comments, too, but they took their places silently as Conason and Phillips returned to their seats. As they did so, the four of them exchanged looks that all said the same thing—Adams might very possibly be out of his mind.

"Diving slowly," Katano said.

"Following the path of the robots," Schreiber added.

"Sensors set to search for human remains," Adams said. Several throats cleared loudly. "Or life."

"Carry on." Conason stared out the command window, hoping that they'd find Rothstein's body and that it would be intact.

* * *

Thirty long minutes passed. In that time, they saw nothing that could be construed to be Rothstein or parts of her, and they also didn't catch up to the robots. Adams was mercifully silent, for which Conason was sure the rest of the crew were grateful, though Adams was correct—the feeling of being pushed or pulled down was less as soon as they were fully underwater and lessened the deeper they got.

"Gravitational pull is now similar to Earth's," Schreiber said. "That should be impossible."

"I think I see something," Phillips said, before Adams could share again that things were different here. "Ahead of where we are."

Katano brought them out of the dive they were in and leveled off. They headed for what Phillips might have seen. They didn't have to go far for the spotlights to illuminate what he'd spotted—what looked like a giant bridge made of stone.

Katano slowed the ship to a standstill and they stared. The bridge was huge—taller than any structure Conason had ever seen. Larger than anything humanity had ever built.

"Is that...is that blacker water flowing underneath?" Katano asked finally.

Schreiber adjusted the front spotlights to aim for the black. It surely looked like it was flowing, and not with whatever current there might be. "Perhaps it's like Earth's East Australian Current?" Phillips suggested.

"'The black rivers of pitch that flow under those mysterious cyclopean bridges,'" Adams quoted reverently. "'Things built by some elder race extinct and forgotten before the beings came to Yuggoth from the ultimate voids. See them and go mad.'"

"I still feel sane," Katano snapped. "Annoyed, frightened, worried about Janelle, ready to kick your ass, Josh, but sane."

"Then maybe you're our Dante or Poe, the one who will stay sane enough to tell the tale," Adams replied calmly. "If any of us do."

"Look!" Phillips shouted. "That looks like some of the robots."

Something was coming towards them, from under the bridge, over but not on the river of pitch. Conason berated himself for thinking of it as Adams had described, but he couldn't help himself. And Phillips was right—whatever was coming did reflect the spotlights in a way that seemed metallic.

More gasps, these of horror. The thing was indeed the robots, all the robots, joined together with Rothstein.

She was naked, her protective suit and space jumpsuit gone. Her limbs were splayed out spread-eagle, and the robots had warped themselves around her in a way they hadn't been designed to do—as if they'd tried to protect her, had failed, and had been fused with her in some weird, impossible way. Her hair flowed around her head; her eyes were wide and bugged out, her mouth wide open.

"She's breathing," Phillips said. "Somehow. She must have gotten the crystals up her nostrils in time."

Sure enough, there were bubbles coming out of her mouth that indicated that the underwater breathing crystals were working. "I can't believe she's alive," Conason said.

"I don't think that, whatever that is, is Janelle anymore," Schreiber said.

Rothstein beckoned to them, then turned around and headed back the way she'd come, seemingly without swimming or even really moving her limbs.

"Captain?" Katano asked quietly.

"Follow her."

Rothstein led them under the giant bridge, then under another and another, until they were able to see more than bridges. There were buildings here, gigantic, made of stone, but designed by something clearly not human. Towers and terraces, bas-reliefs depicting things with tentacles and more limbs than any creature so far found in the Solaris System. Many things with huge claws and gaping maws filled with teeth that looked somewhat like a shark's, if that shark was ten times the size of a Great White.

"There are no windows," Phillips said. "Did you notice that?"

"We need to get out of here," Schreiber said, in the calm voice someone used to prevent themselves from panicking. "Immediately, if not sooner. This looks exactly like what Josh has quoted over and over again."

Adams didn't reply. Conason looked around to see if he was praying or as horrified as the rest of them. "Where the hell is Adams?"

"We have a breach in the airlock!" Katano said. "Water coming in!"

"Close the hatch!" Phillips shouted.

"Crystals in, helmets on, suits activated first!" Conason bellowed. "That's an order!" Everyone did what he said, their helmets locked just in time. The water came rushing in before Phillips could close the command section's hatch. The interior lights went out and they were in darkness, the exterior lights all they had.

Someone took Conason's hand. He reached out and found someone else's hand. "Testing, testing," Katano said as she squeezed his hand. "Sound off. Melissa Katano, present."

"James Conason, present." He squeezed the other hand.

"Kathi Schreiber, present."

"George Phillips, present. We're all together."

"Joshua Adams, present."

"Josh," Conason said, "where the hell are you?"

"Waiting for my audience." He sounded rapturous. "Janelle and the robots were accepted as sacrifice. I am the first to speak to the Great One."

Something more than huge, and resembling a Great White in the same way the teeth in the bas-relief did, swam slowly towards them, mouth opened wide. There were more layers of teeth than Conason could count, all looking razor-sharp and deadly.

"Is that coming to eat the ship?" Katano asked, in a tone that said she knew that it was and wanted someone to tell her she was wrong.

"Yes, and we're leaving," Phillips said urgently. Schreiber tugged on Conason's hand and he followed, pulling Katano behind him. Presumably Phillips was leading them out, which was the only choice, and possibly only chance, they had.

The only saving grace was that the water was easy to move through, less like swimming, more like walking through something viscous. They were able to move more quickly than they had while in orbit.

Conason wanted to say goodbye to his ship, but there was no time. They reached the airlock hatch, the hatch that shouldn't have opened underwater, and exited as fast as possible. "Move away from the ship," Conason said. "That thing is huge and it'll hit us if we're too close."

"The Dagon is not taking you," Adams said. "You have nothing to fear."

"But the fear of your crazy religion itself being true, you mean," Katano muttered.

Conason agreed, but now wasn't the time. "Josh, where are you?"

"The Messenger is fetching you to bring you to the Great One," Adams replied.

Apparently Rothstein was the Messenger. This close it was clear that while the body might be breathing somehow, whatever had been Rothstein was gone. She found them in the last of the *Neptune Ten*'s light, each robot at the end of her limbs grabbed each of them, then she dragged them through whatever this ocean truly was.

Conason looked over his shoulder and saw the creature engulf their only hope for escape and survival.

He turned back, ready to do his best to destroy whatever he could of this hellish world.

* * *

The Messenger that had been Rothstein dragged them along through the darkness, though, after a while, it wasn't all that dark. An odd sort of phosphorescence sprang up, allowing Conason to see where they were: in what looked like a giant city made for monsters. Which, he had to admit, was probably exactly where they were.

There were things here, most of them not moving, other than with what appeared to be breathing. They looked to be asleep, if monsters such as these slept. Tentacles, claws, blobs of gelatinous flesh, horrifying things that didn't bear description, and more. They littered the place.

After what seemed like hours, they were dragged into what Conason thought might be a temple, if the pictures of the big thing with tentacles was correct.

"I've seen Josh's texts," Schreiber said quietly. "The pictures are very accurate to what we're seeing here. I think we're going into the Temple of Cthulhu."

"He's not real," Phillips said staunchly. "This is likely a group hallucination and we're going to wake up safely inside the *Neptune Ten* and laugh about whatever it was we all ate."

They were carried along, through room after gigantic room, monsters of everyone's and anyone's nightmares slumbering here just as they did in the streets outside. Conason realized he'd accepted that they were in a city. A city whose inhabitants weren't yet conscious.

Finally, they reached what was clearly the altar room. There was a large outcropping of rock, carved all over with the tentacles, claws, and horror design that was prevalent all over. A skyscraper with no sky to scrape.

There was something wrapped around this idol, and it looked to be made of stone as well, something that looked like a cross between the worst cephalopod in existence, a dragon as conceived by the most twisted of minds, and a caricature of what a man might look like if he were the embodiment of every sin ever committed.

Adams was there as well, floating in front of the weird altar, devoid of any of his gear, though it was clear that he was using the breathing crystals. That they actually worked under this kind of water was the only pleasant surprise so far, but Conason was willing to enjoy it for a moment. The Messenger might be "breathing" but that thing wasn't a human being, not anymore.

The Messenger threw them all towards Adams. As it did so, the robots detached from Rothstein's body and swarmed over the four of them, stripping them naked, taking their helmets, leaving them completely helpless, though the breathing crystals weren't taken.

Conason was shocked that he wasn't cold and that he could open his eyes without pain. "The water's warm. Amazing."

"Isn't it?" Adams said. "You all can hear me, and each other, through the generosity of the Greatest of the Old Ones."

"Why aren't you naked?" Phillips asked.

"Would that make you feel better?"

"No," Conason said. "Why are you doing this to us, Josh?"

"Because the Great Old One must be awakened. It's time."

"Time for what?" Katano asked.

"Time to cleanse the solar system," Schreiber whispered, sounding truly terrified for the first time. "The end of humanity."

Adams nodded. "You never made fun of me, Kathi."

"What does that do for her?" Phillips asked truculently. Conason knew Phillips was terrified, too, but the other man was never one to show it. "Are you going to save her, not let her die here on this Godforsaken planet?"

"Some get to die quickly," Adams said. "And some don't."

A clawed limb snaked out from the stone creature and grabbed Schreiber. She screamed as the limb dragged her towards its tentacled maw, which opened slowly. Her scream was cut off sharply as the mouth closed on her with a thud that sent shockwaves through the water.

"So," Conason said evenly, "that's not a stone statue."

"No. The Great Old One slumbers and must be awakened fully."

"I thought you were supposed to be the first meal," Phillips snarled to Adams. "You murderous traitor."

"The Great Old One called to me. I will be joined with Him forever, but first he needs to enjoy a kill."

With that, the tentacles shot out and grabbed Phillips. They wrapped around him, shoving through his body, rending him limb from limb, weaving in and out of his head through the ears, eye sockets, nostrils, ripping him apart slowly.

As Katano reached over and clutched his hand, Conason watched the breathing crystals float out of Phillips' nose to the floor. He looked back in time to see Phillips, or what remained of him, being sucked into the tentacles somehow.

"How would you like to die, Melissa?" Adams asked rather kindly. "You weren't as nice as Kathi, but you also weren't as dismissive as Janelle."

"What did you do to Janelle?" Katano asked, voice shaking. "Was it what you did to George?"

"No. Her insides fed the Dagon and allowed it to fully awaken. She was sucked dry, then filled by the robots. As you saw."

"How did it begin to awaken?" Conason asked.

"Our arrival roused it. The Dagon has been slumbering, as the rest of the Elder Gods have been, waiting for someone to come and rouse them for their next age. The Dagon smelled us before we breached the atmosphere."

"This is why you worked so hard to be on my crew," Conason said.

"Of course. Wouldn't you have done the same to bring your God back?"

"No. My God isn't like this."

"No," Adams agreed, with a laugh that sounded worse than anything had so far. "Your God is weak. All your Gods are tiny, helpless against real might."

"But Josh," Katano said, "it's going to kill you, too."

"Yes! And that is my *honor*!"

Something moved on the monster again. An eye—bigger around than a football field—opened slowly. They stared into something so inhuman as to be almost incomprehensible. There was age there, age greater than mankind, maybe greater than the Solaris System itself. And it looked upon them and there was no pity, no disdain, no interest. They were merely things, looked at by this monster as a human would look at an ant.

The monster began to rise. As it did so, the tentacles reached out again. But this time, they grabbed Adams.

"No! Wait! I am to go last! Your final meal!"

No, a voice said in their heads. *You are to go now. The other has what I truly need.*

And with that, the tentacles ripped Adams apart in the same manner as Phillips.

Once that was over, it spat at them. Schreiber flew out, tumbling head over heels. They caught her and held on. "Kathi, are you alive?" Katano asked hopefully.

Schreiber turned to her. "I am more alive than I have ever been." Her voice said her words were lies—Schreiber sounded dead, long dead. She shoved Conason away with more strength than she'd ever had as a living human woman, wrapped her arms and legs tightly around Katano as the monster grabbed both women in its claws, ripped them in half, and shoved them into its tentacles. Katano didn't even scream, though Conason was fairly sure he'd heard a whimper as she'd been pulled in half.

Now it was only him and the monster.

I am Cthulhu, the High Priest of the Great Old Ones.

"I'm Commander James Conason of the Solaris System's Space Exploration and Protection Corps. And I offer you a choice."

Cthulhu chuckled. *What choice is that?*

"You can join with our government peacefully, or we will turn all of our weapons against you and yours."

I have a different choice to offer you, Commander.

"What's that?"

You may become my emissary to your people. I will enter your consciousness and control you. Through you I will choose who among them live or die, which are our food and which are our slaves, which will die quickly and which will suffer over an eternity.

"Why me and not Josh?"

He was a fanatic and would not be listened to. You have rank. You will be given an audience.

"Why are you offering this?"

We prefer to have slaves. We find them helpful. And while we have enslaved many against their will, it would be...entertaining...to enslave an entire race with their complete permission and eager approval.

"If I say no?"

Then I will eat you, awaken my people, and destroy your pathetic race in one day.

Conason considered this. What choice, really, did he have? Besides, he was a human, the race of ingenuity, a race that had conquered the whole solar system. They would figure out how to rise up and save themselves from this horror. All they needed was time.

* * *

Commander James Conason was returned to Neptune, some said miraculously. He said it was through the grace of the Great Cthulhu, who had saved him when the *Neptune Ten* had malfunctioned and crashed during orbit of Planet Yuggoth.

The Solaris System's government was willing to work with this new race, to achieve mutual benefits and go forward together into a brave new age. The Cult of the Old Ones was declared the one true religion. Conversions were strongly encouraged and, in some cases, demanded.

A hundred years passed and humanity was joyfully and willingly enslaved to the Elder Gods, just as Cthulhu had wanted, and Conason still lived. He was now the Commander of all the Solaris System and everyone followed his orders immediately and without argument.

The Elder Gods and Great Old Ones now inhabited every planet, while there were millions of humans who were on Yuggoth, all breathing through their crystals, serving the Gods on their home world, which was considered the highest honor. The vastness of space was the blink of an eye to the Elder Gods, so even as Yuggoth moved farther from Solaris the distance meant nothing.

Somewhere inside of his body, a tiny part of Conason remained. And that part realized that the others had been the lucky ones. They were dead.

Cthulhu was more than a monster. He'd known what would happen, and he'd allowed Conason to have the last human feeling he'd ever have again—hope. Hope that had been dashed.

He was going to live forever in this form of hell, watching his people willingly turn into slaves, the ingenuity bred out, no self-will remaining, just placid acceptance that this was how it was with their Gods.

And the worst part of all? Cthulhu wouldn't allow him to go mad or to die. Conason would watch this forever, or until the Great Ones chose to slumber again in, possibly, ten thousand years. Then they would sleep until another foolish race that thought themselves wise would venture to Yuggoth and awaken Cthulhu and start the cycle all over again. As it had been done for millennium before and would be for millennium after, until every star burned out of the heavens and existence ended.

PEN'S BRACER
Misty Massey

Aysu loved the beach at sunrise. The air tossed her black hair, and gentle waves lapped at her bare toes, the water just chilly enough to send a shiver up the backs of her legs. Tiny crabs raced along the water's edge, their shells gleaming in the half-light. Off in the distance, mere shadows against the rising light, boatmen paddled from their village around the bluff to anchor in the lagoon. Their voices echoed over the water, like the low calls of marsh birds. Soon Aysu's companions, who lingered over their breakfasts of bread and fruit, would join her, and they'd all climb into the boats to be rowed into deeper water to begin the day's diving.

She walked up the beach to where the sand was always dry and sat, the sand cool and silky under her legs as she dug her toes into it. With one finger she drew patterns, the way she had when she was a child. Twenty summers, and she hardly remembered a time when she wasn't a diver. From the moment she could walk, she'd toddled down to the water's edge chased by whatever older child had been assigned her care for the day. Other little ones cried at the splashing waves, but Aysu welcomed them with laughter. Sorab had said many times that she was more fish than girl.

As soon as he'd decided she was old enough, Sorab began training her to join his crew of divers. There were other divers working the waters around Eldraga, but Sorab's people were renowned throughout the Nine Islands for their skill at searching out hidden beds of pinkshell and catching elusive flatfish. They dove until the sun was nearly to its height, then Sorab sold their catch to local buyers and merchants on the docks. In the afternoon, the older divers helped the younger ones strengthen their lungs with breath practice. The longer a diver held her breath, the more food she'd catch. Aysu could stay underwater for a little more than ten minutes on a single breath. Combined with her long, nimble fingers, she was a master at her craft. Now and then people accused her of using magic, but she laughed at the suggestion. The real magic was the world underwater. She loved the beauty of the sunbeams streaming like glass lightning through the surface, turning the entire world blue, the only sound that of her heart beating. She loved feeling at one with the schools of darting jewelfish that rich women bought to decorate the ponds in their gardens. There was nothing magic could achieve that would rival the joy of the ocean. Not for her.

A soft rustling caught her ear and Aysu turned. Two men trudged down the sandy path, heading for Sorab's home. They were dressed in black robes, hoods over their heads, their sleeves drawn over their crossed arms. She kept very still. Every islander learned from infancy never to draw the attention of a Danisoban mage. Quick to take offense at any perceived slight, their magical torments were legendarily cruel. Sailors on the docks had told her stories of Danisobans causing mens' heads to explode merely for staring at them. Mages rarely left their enclave in the city, though. What business would they have with Sorab?

As soon as they passed behind a dune, Aysu leaped to her feet and ran to the back entrance of the house. She burst into the kitchen, startling Banu into dropping a plate of fried bread.

"I'm so sorry," Aysu said, dropping to her knees to collect the spilled bread. She rose and handed it back to Banu. "I wanted to see what the mages had come for."

"Mages? Here?" Banu frowned.

"I saw them on the path." Aysu pushed past Banu to the doorway. She pulled the rough drapery aside to peek through into the main room where Sorab did his accounting. A few other divers in the kitchen crowded against her back and she shushed them.

The mages stood next to Sorab's hearth, their arms still crossed and their hoods drawn back. Both were tall men, one slender and dark skinned, with a hungry sharpness to his bones. The other was pale, and white-haired, the skin of his face hanging heavy from his brow and jaw. Neither smiled as they spoke.

"We have need of a diver," the pale one said. "We want your best, and we're prepared to pay well." He withdrew his hand from his sleeve, holding out a full pouch. A silver band around his wrist gleamed in the morning light.

Sorab didn't take the pouch. "I can't imagine what my diver could do that you, with your magic, cannot."

Aysu's eyes widened. Sorab was no coward, but refusing a Danisoban was dangerous.

The slender man scowled.

"There's an object trapped on a shipwreck just past Treleya bluff. Underneath the water," he leaned forward on the words, "where we cannot go. I'm sure you know."

The divers crowded behind her laughed softly, and Aysu herself couldn't help a smile. Sorab did know—everyone did. Danisoban mages, for all their deadly power, were weakened by salt water. They rarely ventured to the docks and never went swimming. Rumor had it that when mages were forced to travel by ship, they accomplished it by riding in boxes of dirt, to keep from having even a bit of spray touch them. There was even a rhyme children sometimes sang while playing—"Dunk a wizard in the drink, watch him bubble, thrash, and sink." She might have felt sorry for them, being forbidden from the water, but Danisobans weren't the type of people to attract sympathy from anyone.

"I see." Sorab rose from his chair, and paced to the window. "What is this object you need us to retrieve? And do you know its approximate location? Something a little more specific than 'a shipwreck?' There are a fair number of broken vessels in those waters."

The two mages exchanged a glance. "The *Peregrino*."

"Ah, and now the truth comes out."

"We can pay another fifty."

One hundred octavos. More than Sorab earned in three days at market. What could the mages have lost that was worth so much to them?

Sorab sighed, and faced the two men again. "You want me to send one of my divers into your haunted ship to collect ... what? A bauble? Some magical trinket? How much money do you think my diver is worth, once she floats to the surface in pieces?"

Aysu gasped and pressed her hand to her mouth. Too late. All three men looked toward the doorway. The divers scrambled to get out the back door, tripping over each other. Aysu bumped her hip into the table and it slowed her just long enough for Sorab to yank the drapery aside.

"Outside with you," he snapped. She nodded, frightened at the look in his eyes. Usually Sorab was the most patient of men, but something about the mages had raised a fury in him. Aysu didn't waste a second.

Aysu followed her fellow divers down to the beach, her mind whirling. She'd been diving these waters since childhood, but she'd never heard of a haunted shipwreck off Treleya Bluff. And what kind of ghost could rip a person to bits? Most important, would the mages come up with enough money to change Sorab's mind? Everyone knew who Sorab's best diver was. She could hold a breath longer than Sorab himself, or so he'd proudly admitted more than once.

The boatmen had beached their boats, and the divers were climbing aboard with their baskets by the time Aysu reached them. She took a deep breath. Time to forget about the mages and focus on work. Half the island wouldn't eat tonight without the harvest the divers brought up from the water. And being underwater always cleared her mind of even the most unsettling thoughts. She stepped into a boat and sat down.

"Aysu!" Banu was hurrying across the sand, waving her kitchen rag at the boats. "Aysu, come here."

The others laughed and cooed as Aysu climbed out of the boat again. Banu waved a hand at the boatmen. "Take them on. Aysu isn't going with you today."

Aysu watched the boats as they rowed into the rising light, then turned to the cook. "Why am I staying behind?"

Banu was out of breath, her eyes watery. Had she been crying? "Sorab needs you, right now." The older woman grabbed Aysu's hand and pulled her along. "There's no time. Come along."

Sorab sat at the dining table in the kitchen, his head cradled in his hands. The mages stood against the far wall, as motionless as statues. The heavier one nodded at Banu. She raised Aysu's hand to her lips, kissed it, then released her and left the room. Aysu walked around the table to Sorab's side. He hadn't moved, so she laid her hand on his shoulder. "Are you well? What's wrong?"

Sorab drew a breath, but he didn't raise his head. "Against my judgment, I'm accepting the job they've offered."

Aysu straightened, staring at the two mages, who still had not moved. "How much did you finally agree was proper for me to be torn to pieces?"

"Aysu," he said, "yes, they found a price." A single drop of blood splattered on the table.

Cold rushed through her, leaving her dizzy. What had the mages done to him, once no one was there to see? He lifted his head and looked at her. His eyes were oozing blood and his skin was gray. She swallowed back a cry and reached for a cloth to wipe away the blood.

Sorab let her tend to him. As far as she could tell, there was no wound on his face. They'd somehow made him weep blood, but they hadn't ruined his eyes permanently. "We dive, or they blind all of us."

"You mean I'll dive," she said. "I'm the only one who can swim deep enough for what they want."

"Yes, you are," the mage said, his voice startling her. "Your teacher tried to sell himself as the better choice, which is why we resorted to firmer measures."

Aysu stared at him. The mage stood in her home, threatening to destroy not only Sorab's livelihood but his entire school, and his face betrayed no emotion at all, as passive as if they were talking about how fast dune grass grew. Everything she'd ever heard about Danisobans was clearly wrong. They were far worse than their legends.

"What do you want me to retrieve?" she asked.

The dark man took a step forward. Uncrossing his arms, he held out a piece of silver. It had once been a circlet like the ones he wore, but it was mashed in, as if someone had stepped on it. "This belonged to Helar Pen, first Authority. He died when the *Peregrino* sank, but because of his power, he continues to interfere with certain workings we must complete. We want you to find Helar Pen's other bracer, with which we can send him to his final rest."

"He's a ghost?" she asked. The two mages shrugged.

"Ghosts are wisps," she said. "They make noise, startle people, but they can't hurt anyone."

"This is no ordinary ghost, woman," the pale mage snapped. "When a Danisoban dies, if he is not released from his binding, he continues to haunt the world. And he can employ every bit of his magic to do it."

"Everyone who's dived near Treleya in the last twenty years has either drowned or been torn apart," Sorab said, his voice barely a murmur. "Being in the water drove the ghost mad."

"One of our number was able to pull this bracer from the wreck some weeks ago, but ever since, Pen has been able to reach over the miles to our enclave. Spells have been going dangerously wrong. Before you ask," the dark man said, raising one hand, "yes, it is just our problem. For now. But what happens when he misdirects a working of ours and the market goes up in flame? Or your docks fall into the ocean?"

He was right. The threat was real. The mages couldn't stop their ghost, being trapped on land as they were. "If everyone else has died, what makes you think I won't be killed, too?"

"We're not completely insensitive," the pale mage said. "You'll be provided a spell of protection."

"What about a spell that lets me breathe underwater?" she asked, surprised at herself for even asking. "I can stay down a long time, but since I have to hunt for this bracer, it might take longer than I can manage."

"We have no spell of that nature," the pale man said. "It's not a subject we've ever pursued. All we require of you is to lay hands on his bracer. He can't wear it, since he is incorporeal. Bring it to the surface, and we will do the rest."

For one wild moment, Aysu considered telling them to go away, that no amount of money would ever be enough to convince her to perform their bidding. Sorab's bloody face quashed the feeling. She couldn't let them destroy her home, even if she didn't live through the job. She nodded.

"We will meet you at dawn on the bluff." As one, the two mages pulled their hoods over their faces, turned, and left the house.

* * *

Aysu hadn't slept a wink all night. Some of the time she'd worried that every rustle and creak was the mages returning to set fire to the house.

When no sounds distracted her, she imagined the death that awaited her in the deep water around Treleya. What had she been thinking, to say yes? She'd been almost relieved when Sorab came to wake her. The walk to the bluff would take an hour, but at least the worrying was over, no matter which way the day turned out.

The mages were waiting on the bluff when she and Sorab arrived, standing as still as statues while the wind whipped their robes against their legs. At any other time, she'd have loved the beauty of seeing the whole ocean this way. She wondered if she'd ever want to come up here again—assuming she survived the day. The dark mage approached Aysu and tied a length of fabric around her upper arm. "The charm of protection," he said. "It should keep you from his notice until you find the bracer."

"I should point out, we are not patient," the pale man said. "If you dawdle, or choose to swim away from us, someone will pay." He looked toward Sorab. Raising his hands, he sketched a pattern in the air between them. Sorab cried out, clutching his belly and bending half-over. He retched, vomiting his breakfast onto the grass in powerful spasms. Aysu started to run to him, but the mage stepped in front of her. "Dive," he said.

Aysu glared at the mage, but said nothing. There was nothing she could do, and everyone knew it. She walked down to the edge of the bluff. It extended over the water, well clear of the rocks, so she'd be able to dive without any trouble. Gooseflesh rose on her skin. She almost imagined she could see the shipwreck from her vantage point. She took one deep breath, let it out, and repeated the sequence three times before taking one last breath. Bending her knees, she launched herself into the air, brought her hands forward and dove gracefully into the waiting ocean.

The water was warm and comforting. Her death might wait, but she couldn't feel afraid in the ocean's embrace. A school of jewelfish darted by, startled by her sudden arrival. The soft light of the rising sun sent glittering beams across the shallows and below her, the depths were blue as the evening sky. Behind her, closer to the bluff, broken rocks were piled over each other. Aysu kicked out, sending herself deeper. It didn't take long before she caught sight of the wrecked ship. It sat, turned sideways, lodged in the sand of the ocean floor. Seaweed had replaced the long-since-decayed rigging, waving gently in time with the current. The ship was covered in a layer of silken algae, making it seem like some strange furred creature. Aysu swam to the bow. In spaces between the strands of algae, she could almost make out painted letters. She pushed the growth away. P, E, R, E...the *Peregrino*. This was the ship. Somewhere aboard this wreck waited a small silver bracer. But where?

The ship was tipped on an angle, so anything loose would have slid to the lower side. She found rotted ropes and broken wood, but nothing that looked like a silver bracer. Up higher, on the quarterdeck, the ship's wheel hung loose from its mooring, tendrils of seaweed waving as she went by. A waterlogged book was trapped under the broken wheel, but she didn't attempt to move it. It would only disintegrate as soon as she touched it. She'd known the bracer wouldn't likely be lying out in the open for her to find. From what she'd heard, the mage would have been belowdecks when the ship went down, staying clear of any salt water. So that was where she'd need to search. Directly under the quarterdeck, she found the closed door to what was probably the captain's cabin. Pulling on the handle, the door swung open. She could search it quickly before returning to the surface for air. Aysu reached for the doorjamb and pulled herself into the shadowy cabin.

Suddenly she fell to the floor, banging her elbow. Water dripped from her hair and clothing onto the floor. This room was as dry as if the ship was still sailing. She turned and looked back the way she'd come. A wall of dark sea rippled at the doorway. Rising to her feet, Aysu reached a hand toward it. Her fingers sank into it, but no water rushed in.

"He doesn't like the water."

She spun. A man, dressed in the clothing of a sailor. Except that there was no color to him. Skin, hair, clothing, all shades of gray. She'd never seen anyone that looked like him. She backed away a step and he raised a hand.

"You needn't fear me. But you mustn't stay here."

"Who are you?"

"Fedder," he said, with a smile. "I was asleep when the ship went down."

She looked around. A table and chairs were overturned next to a bed. The bedding was dusty and rumpled, as if someone had risen in a hurry. "This is the captain's cabin, isn't it?" she asked.

"It was." He shrugged. "Now it's a hole in the ocean."

"Why is it dry?" she asked.

"I told you, he doesn't like water." Fedder said. "You need to leave. He doesn't like people either."

"Are you talking about the mage?" she asked.

He nodded. "He was trying to make the ship fly. I told him to stop playing with his magic on my ship, but he waited until I was asleep and ended up blowing out the bilges." He smiled at her confused expression. "The lowest part of the ship. We were sunk before anyone even knew what had happened."

"I'm sorry."

"So am I." Fedder walked to the open door and passed a hand through the water. "I wish I could feel it."

"You're a ghost," Aysu said, feeling frightened and foolish in the same instant. Of course he was a ghost—who else would be living on a sunken ship? Despite what she'd said to the Danisobans yesterday about ghosts being harmless, her heart began to pound against her ribs. She grabbed at the rag on her arm. Was it protecting her? She wished she'd asked questions about how it worked. This was a dead man. Who knew what he was capable of?

"And you're in danger of becoming one yourself," he said. "Why are you here?"

"I'm a diver," she said, easing further into the room. "The mages hired me to bring them a silver bracer that used to belong to the mage that drowned. They want to release him so he'll stop ruining their spells."

"Release him?" he asked. "So he'd be free to leave here?"

"Why does it matter to you?" she asked. "After all, what more can he do to you, now that you're all ghosts?" And what can you do to me? She kept the thought unspoken.

"He holds us here, to steal our energy. He still thinks he can make the ship fly, but Danisobans need blood, so his spells all go wrong. Now and then someone from the surface shows up, like you have. He's always happy to spill their blood for another try at the spell, but it never works. And every time the living mages try to summon him, he fights. He takes what little life energy the crew has left." He looked down at his dust-gray hands. "The second mate was used up in the last round." The ghost turned away from Aysu for a moment. "His soul. The mage consumed his soul."

She'd never given much thought to what happened after death, but she always believed there was some next step. If a soul could be destroyed, what would that mean for the person it belonged to? It wasn't a question she could work through, and she pushed it aside for the task at hand.

"The mages can send him away, but I have to find the bracer. Do you know where it is?"

He nodded. "It's on the floor of the gundeck. He didn't make it to the outside before the ship sank. Still around his wrist. He doesn't like to spend time in there with his bones."

She shuddered. Seeing her own bones was an unsettling idea, and she'd had quite enough of those for one day. "Can you help me?" she asked.

Fedder reached into his jacket and withdrew a bosun's whistle. He blew into it, making no sound that she could hear. A moment later, three more gray-skinned ghosts appeared next to him. All three were dressed much as he was, and were just as gray. He waved a hand to them. "All that's left of my crew," he said. Aysu bowed to them, and they returned the gesture.

"This woman is here to help," he said to the others. "She's going to release Pen for us. But she needs a hand."

The ghosts exchanged glances. For a long moment, Aysu feared they were going to refuse, leaving her to risk death at the ghost mage's hands. At last, they nodded.

"You'll have to swim out to the hatch amidships. Be cautious—as soon as you pass the opening, the water disappears again. He doesn't like it, so he's set wards to keep it at bay within. Descend the ladder and move along the deck. You'll see the bones. The bracer you want is among them. We'll do our best to keep his attention. Go."

"Thank you," she said. The ghosts faded from her sight. She took three long breaths, letting them out slowly, then slipped through the curtain of water onto the deck. The hatch she sought lay just behind the mast. Swimming to it, she lifted the latticed cover, let it fall slowly back. Inside the passage, she saw rungs. She straightened her body, reaching with her toes to position her feet on the highest rung, and pushed herself down through the water.

The ghost hadn't lied. Just past the edge of the hatch, all was dry and cool. She climbed down the ladder, glancing around. Cannons were secured on either side of the deck and the weight of them cast an eerie shadow in the already dark space. She held for a moment, but nothing moved. Perhaps the ghosts were distracting the mage as they'd promised, or else he'd not noticed her. There was no time to waste. She crept along the deck, watching the dark corners for any sign of the mage. As she passed the last cannon, she saw it. A bundle of rags and bones. Around one of the skeletal arms rested a circlet, covered in heavy black tarnish. The bracer; it had to be. She bent, reaching out a finger, and scratched gently at the blackness. It scraped away, revealing a bright sparkle beneath. Silver. She'd found it. Hooking her fingers under the smooth edge, she lifted. The desiccated tendons crackled and the hand fell away from the arm. The bones clattered softly to the deck, freeing the bracer.

Aysu rubbed the tarnished silver with her thumb, turned it in her hand. Such an innocent object, just a round circle of metal. Somehow she'd expected it to glow, or bear magical markings. How could something so plain be so important? She would never understand magic, and, the sooner she delivered the bracer, the happier she'd be. Now that she'd found it, she realized there were no pockets in her clothing, and she hadn't brought along a basket to carry the bracer back with her. She couldn't swim as well with something in her hand, and she didn't want to slow herself down any more than necessary. Best if she wore it back. She slid the bracer over her hand, pushing it up her arm until it stopped at her elbow.

"Well done." The voice made her jump. Fedder had returned. He smiled at her. "You've found the bracer."

"I did," she said. There was something strange about the way he was staring at her. Not at her, so much, but at the bracer itself. She crossed one arm across her body, blocking his view. "Did you manage to keep the mage busy?"

"Oh, he's quite distracted," Fedder said. He stepped forward. There was a faint glow to his skin. How had she missed it before? He reached for her and Aysu stumbled backward.

"I'm leaving now," she said. Where was the ladder? She wanted to turn and run, but she feared turning her back on the ghost. She was beginning to think she'd been fooled, and so easily.

"No," the ghost said, "You're going to help me." He pulled out the whistle again and blew a short burst. One of the gray sailors appeared, but this time, his face was twisted in fear. He seemed to be pulling back against something, something that drew him closer. Fedder waved his hand at the sailor. He swept up into a swirl of silken gray, spinning into the center of Fedder's hand and disappearing. Fedder closed the distance between himself and Aysu, bending his fingers into quick, strange shapes. The charmed rag on her arm twisted, the knot coming loose on its own. It fell away. She tried to catch it, but Fedder laughed.

"Their blood washed away as soon as you entered the water. Their little charm was useless. Not that I couldn't have broken it. The brethren should have known better. Or perhaps they did. Perhaps you were a sacrifice to appease me, to apologize for all their mistreatment while I've been locked away here."

"You're the mage," she whispered.

"Well, yes. And you're wearing my bracer. Which means I'll finally be able to make this ship fly."

He continued weaving his fingers together, apart, in and out of each other. She'd never seen anyone move their hands that way. Aysu couldn't move, but she wasn't sure she wanted to any more. She was fascinated, watching the movement of his hands. So fast, so smooth. And she could almost detect when he would start the series over, found herself waiting for it. The bracer on her arm pulsed with a quiet warmth, glowed in the shadows. Magic. He was doing magic. She smiled.

"Yes, girl, that's right," he murmured. "Let me in. Carry me to the surface within you." He was close to her, so close she thought he might step right through her.

From behind her, a whirling cloud of gray exploded, sliding between Aysu and the ghost mage. She fell back, startled, and all at once was herself again. The mage's mouth was open, screaming with no words, and the last two ghost sailors were flying at him and through him.

Aysu scrambled to her feet, and ran for the ladder. Climbing as quickly as she could, she burst forth into the cool ocean water and pushed off the hatch edge to swim to the surface. But something caught her foot. She looked back. Fedder—no, not Fedder, but Pen—had hold of her foot, and was pulling her back. Anger suffused his face, anger and madness. Through the gloom of the water, she could see the sailors still whirling around him, but he was too strong. Unless...

She grabbed a sodden bit of line that still dangled from the mainmast and pulled. He drew back. She moved one hand, pulling herself a little higher. She didn't need much, just enough to pull her foot above the level of the water. Her hands began to slip on the slimy rope and she screamed, the sound bubbling through the salty water.

And suddenly, his hold released. She was free. She swam as she never had before, rising through the water like a bubble. Her arms ached, and her chest was tight with exertion. Beams of sunlight pierced the surface. She was almost there, but she hadn't been able to take a proper breath. Her lungs burned. Darkness moved at the edges of her sight. She struggled, swimming as she never had before.

Her head broke the water and she gulped breaths as if she'd never tasted air. Above her, she saw the mages peering over the edge. She raised the bracer, to let them see she'd succeeded, then began stroking toward the rocky shore. She wasn't sure how long it would take her to walk back to the bluff from the beach, but she hoped they weren't expecting her to climb. She was a diver, not a cliff bird.

The water around her began to bubble and she righted herself. Was it Pen? A shimmering light surrounded her. It lifted her out of the water and she rode in its grasp to the top of the bluff. The light faded as she slid to the soft grass. Sorab rushed forward and embraced her. She hugged him, and noticed the bracer still tight on her arm. She wiggled it free and tossed it to the dark mage standing nearest.

"Your trinket," she said.

The mage caught it. While she was gone, they'd gathered stones and built a firepit. Flames leaped from around the edges of a black pot. Together the mages chanted some words, then dropped the bracer into the pot. Light flared, sparks soared high into the air. She glanced back at the ocean. There, on top of the waves, she saw two silken wisps rising into the sky. They seemed to bow toward her before dissipating into the morning light. Somewhere in the distance, Aysu thought she heard a bellow of rage echoing across the water like the cry of a seabird.

FATHOMS DEEP AND FATHOMS COLD

A. Merc Rustad

Tage lights a cigarette and watches the man in the scarlet fedora come nearer. Hat like that's hard to miss. This one's his contact. His heartbeat gets quick. The docks are loud, briny, thick with bodies. Storms scrape the horizon, kick up sharp winds. He can't show desperation. It'll get him killed or left stranded. Same difference.

"Afternoon." The man tips his hat. Long black duster hangs about a too-thin frame, but he don't look weak. Dual revolvers rest on his hips. "I hear tell you're looking for passage."

Tage grunts, shifts his weight for better balance. He didn't expect another wizard. The twisty, rusted aura 'round the man is too fucked to be purely one Clan. It puts his guard up, fast. "Depends whereto."

The man smiles, charming. It never reaches his faded blue eyes. "We're headed for Aldare. *Whale Fall*'s a good vessel, and we have room for a couple passengers who'll work for it." He speaks with a slow drawl. "You left a calling card with the barkeeper."

"I can work," Tage says. He don't have enough to pay even a modest fare. He ran, scarce a fortnight ago. Left everything behind. He ain't got much experience, and when word gets out he's VanDrake, a wizard from one of the most feared Clans, no crew will risk taking him on.

The Clan thinks he's dead. He keeps trying not to wish it, too.

"You ever been on a submersible?" the man asks.

"Not yet."

The man hooks his thumbs through his belt. He might've been eye-catching once. Sharp-boned face, shaved, with odd-shaped tattoos across one cheek that match his hair—black and gray. He looks Tage up and down, critical. "It's cramped. Not much space, and no deck. Can you handle living in metal and glass for long days?"

Tage ain't sure. There's nowhere to run in the sea. "What'll the work be?"

"Manual, easy enough." The man's gaze is iron-hard. "Do what you're told and no magic. Clear?"

Tage's gut turns. Something's wrong here—not just the threat. The man should be asking more questions. "Yeah."

"Good." Suddenly, the man smiles again and proffers a hand. "I'm Marcus Grey."

"Tage. VanDrake." Last test. If the other wizard balks, shows any sign he's here to grab Tage, he'll run. Or fight. Ends the same—he won't be taken back to the Clan.

Marcus Grey's expression and body language don't change. "May I welcome you aboard the *Whale Fall*, VanDrake?"

Self-exile. He don't want to see the ghost-memories of everything he's lost, the ones that won't let him rest. It's Kane's face, mostly. He got his brother killed and he can't forget. It hurts too much to stay here.

Tage takes a final drag on the cigarette, drops it, then crushes the butt under his boot heel. He takes Grey's hand, shakes it once. "Yeah."

* * *

The *Whale Fall* ain't even docked. Tage squints against the salt spray whitening the wharves. Waves shatter against piers, rock the ships at anchor. He's so close to the furthest pier edge, one step and he'd be in the sea. He leans hard against the barnacle-crusted post.

Beside him, Marcus Grey holds his fedora down with one hand, shields his eyes with the other. Wind scratches their coats, bites with ice.

Tage shivers. He's soaked through. Has to shout above the storm. "Where's your boat?"

Grey leans into the wind, teeth bared in delight. "She'll be here. Hold steady."

Water froths, peels aside, and blackened steel rises from the ocean, well away from the dock. Tage can't see more than the front of the *Whale Fall*. He almost steps back off the wood planking.

The vessel's long, arrow-shaped with a domed front made of shadow-darkened glass. Sharp fins line the top like a razored spine. Under the water, he glimpses pale light: circular windows dotting the sides. Even distanced, he feels the hum of unfamiliar power in his bones. Tage ain't sure the ship's alive, but it's close.

A skiff jumps against the waves, zips right toward them. Unmanned. It bumps against the pier, holds steady. A thin cable connects it somewhere near the middle of the submersible's bulk.

"Last chance to refuse," Grey shouts.

Wind gusts hair into Tage's face and salt-stings his eyes. Escape. He tastes it, metallic in the air, sees it in the dark frame and magic-wrapped glass.

He swings down next to Grey in the skiff. Reeled in, the tiny boat skims through the choppy waters. Tage grips the edges until his fingers numb. There's a narrow ladder curling rib-like down the *Whale Fall's* side. Grey climbs, quick, wet duster slapping his sides. Tage follows.

Inside it's too warm. They enter a small chamber, smooth walls and a ceiling higher than he expected. He can stand without hunching. The smell hits him. Dry air laced with sweat, metal. All 'round him the ship's wards brush his senses, solid and...safe. He expects hostility, pain. But the *Whale Fall* feels like a home.

Unexpected, Tage wants to run. He don't deserve to feel safe again.

"Put your weapons here." Grey touches one wall, a panel pops open. A small locker. Blue-green light rings the ceiling, thin piping he don't recognize. No flames. "No one will touch your effects."

Tage eyes the other wizard. Grey's magic still ain't distilled into something he can pinpoint. It itches his nape, constant. He notices his clothes are drying fast.

Grey grins. "We're surrounded by an ocean. I don't need wet crew dripping in the halls."

Above them, a hatch snaps closed and Grey spins the lock. Air hisses, then the hatch is sealed. Tage puts the pistols and two knives in the locker. Don't take off the charms 'round his wrists, or the boot knives.

Grey only lifts an eyebrow. "If you harm anyone on this vessel without my permission, VanDrake, I'll give you to the sea."

Tage narrows his eyes. Long as no one gives him reason to hurt 'em, he won't. He's an enforcer. He's used to threats. He nods once, shows he understands.

A narrow hallway leads them to another room, this one with windows. Tage blinks. Some mirrored trick or illusion on the glass lets him see the full length of the *Whale Fall*, prow to tail.

"I can sense everything inside and out on this ship," Grey says. "But I like to give the men a good view, too."

Tage gives Grey a sidelong glance. He shifts, can't entirely dismiss the way the wizard's damp clothes cling against his body.

Engines hum, propellers turn. They begin sinking. He grabs the wall, his stomach near his throat. The storm-tossed waters turn from slate to deeper blue, then black. Downwards. Lights snap on against the *Whale Fall's* sides, illuminate the deeps.

The turbulence eases.

Tage touches the glass. It sparks with a rust-tinged magic bite, but it don't hurt him.

"I've warded the whole ship," Grey says. "I won't say it was easy, or gets easier with each voyage, but it's what I live for." The madness ain't faded from his eyes. "To traverse the ocean deeps, where no man can live. ...It's like walking among the stars of Heaven."

More like Hell, in the dark, where there's nothing alive.

"Giving your usual poetic spiel to the unwary, Mr. Grey?"

Tage turns, sharp. He keeps his back straight, don't drop hand to his pistol. Realizes too late he's already locked it away.

"You wound me, Captain." There's a smile in Grey's voice. "I did warn Mr. VanDrake what life aboard this ship was like."

A woman in an immaculate white smoking jacket and high black boots strolls towards them, flanked by two crewmen. Big, broad, hair as white as her coat, the captain projects authority, calm. She ain't one to trifle with.

Tage nods, polite. "Captain."

Captain Norris's sharp gaze sweeps Tage head to toe. It's got none of the suggestiveness Grey's looks do. "Another wizard, Mr. Grey?"

Tage glances at Grey, who shrugs one shoulder.

"Very well. You will follow Mr. Grey's orders to earn your passage." The captain offers a hand. "Might I welcome you aboard, Mr. VanDrake?"

Tage shakes Norris's hand, still tense.

The captain turns. "We dive to fifteen fathoms, and then continue deep across the sea."

The trio leave Tage and Grey alone.

"This way," Grey says. Down the hall again, into another shallow room. Brass-rimmed circular windows dot the wall. These don't show the full vessel, just the sea's darkness. "This is the port observation pod. It's got a fine view, if you fancy."

Grey leads him through all of *Whale Fall*: the bridge, the tiny crew bunks, the engines, the galley, one observation pod that smells of tobacco smoke. "If you want to smoke, you do it here and only here," Grey says.

They arrive back at the tiny cabin Tage has been given. A narrow bunk built into the wall, a chest, nothing more. It's enough.

"We run on engine power for a while," Grey says. He leans against the door, left open. "I've a few volumes of nautical research, if you like dry reading. Savatori has cards or dice. You can always ask Alton, the ship's cabin boy, if you want anything else."

Tage nods. "So what do you do?"

Grey's teeth show. "I'll show you."

Behind the bridge there's a ladder that leads up to a small domed chamber hidden among the sharp fins atop the ship. The air smells of dried sweat and leather. Tage squints. His nape tenses. Too easy to get jumped in the dark.

"Watch," Grey says, and the darkness changes, shifts. Takes a moment before Tage realizes the walls have slid back. They're in a glass bubble, nothing but the sea above and all around them.

Tage's breath catches. The submersible is descending at a slow incline, lights wrapping the ship in faint luminescence. Sleek fish flit past, a silver band in the soft headlamp's glow. The edges of rock formations shimmer with crabs and clams, and he spots a school of multi-colored fish dancing around long strands of kelp that float like ghosts.

Grey lays a hand against the glass. "This is what makes it worth it. Our cargo manifest, the jobs we take. It's mercurial. Necessary. *This* is what reminds me there are beautiful things in the world." He rests his forehead on his arm. "It's the closest I feel to home."

Tage glances sharp at Grey. He didn't expect that—the other wizard sounds lonely. Adrift, like him.

"Where you from?" Tage asks.

"Originally? Aldare, but I've not called that home in a long time."

A manta ray glides past them. Tage cranes his neck, watches the winged fish sail through the water graceful as an angel. His throat tightens. He wishes Kane were here. His brother would've loved everything about the submersible. Would've asked all the questions Tage can't think of.

"You look like you need a drink," Grey says.

In the galley, Alton the cabin boy sets two wooden mugs on the narrow table. Can't be more than fourteen. Pale, sandy-haired, bright-eyed.

Grey catches Alton's elbow and offers a wry smile. "Get the cook's old brandy, and grab a mug for yourself. New hands need to be properly christened!"

The kid grins, scuttles off. Tage don't miss the admiring glances Alton casts at Grey over his shoulder.

Grey sobers soon as the kid is out of sight. "I won't ask who you lost."

Tage opens his mouth, the words dried in his throat. Sharp pain scrapes behind his eyes, salty. He glares and clenches his hands on his knees. Grey looks at him—Tage never did find the line between pity and sympathy. Neither will bring his brother back.

"May the one you lost rest well until the Heavens return." Grey touches his knuckles against his chest and then spreads his hand, palm up.

The gesture throws Tage. That a stranger would care don't make sense. He looks away.

Alton returns. Grey takes the bottle, pours them each a brandy. He passes one to the kid.

"To our new crewmate, Mr. Tage VanDrake. Long life and health to you—and may you always stay on the ocean's good will." Grey tosses back his drink.

Why not. Tage drains his mug.

* * *

A day passes. Tage checks for any loosened bolts along the ballast tanks. Wrench in his hand's like a club. Still, it's work and he don't have to think. Marcus Grey comes to check on him, nods in approval at the job done, Tage feels good. Ain't lost that want for appreciation.

"What Clan are you from?" he asks. The odd sensation any time he's near Grey unsettles him. He needs to know.

"Originally VanMere." A Clan renowned for its fascination with and power of illusions. As if to prove it, he twists his hands and cups the life-like image of a fire dragon, the symbol from which the VanDrake Clan took its name. The palm-sized dragon hisses at Tage; its teeth look all-too sharp. Tage is impressed.

Marcus tosses the dragon into the air and it slithers into the ballast tank and vanishes. "That was a long time ago. You know how invasive magic is."

It's in blood and seed, the whole body. The magic spreads through sex: wizards taking the uninfected and turning them. Ain't always consensual. Wizards need other wizard lovers to keep the magic strong, replenished. The magic can also be taken: pulled through skin and breath. It's agonizing, messy, deadly. Takes a skilled wizard to channel another's power and use it as their own without killing their partner. Tage's handler, Bonnie Frost, is one such woman. She did it to him rarely, but he sometimes has nightmares about the pain.

"So happens, I had a few too many partners who weren't VanMere. Including VanDrake wizards." Marcus winks. "Over the years, it changes a man." He rubs a thumb along the steel-plated wall. "I call claim to no Clan anymore."

Tage's fingers twitch. He used to hunt rogues. How's he any better, now?

Unexpected, Marcus laughs. He streaks his hair back with one hand. "Clanless doesn't mean rogue, Tage. The VanMere Clan disowned me. Not the other way around."

"Clans don't let anyone go." Kane's dead because of that. Because of him. He clenches his fists before he chokes on guilt, on tears he ain't shed.

Marcus eyes him up and down again. "Hell's saddle, you're a piece of work. I forget how hard they break you in."

He tenses, throat tight. He ain't *broken*.

No, he fought to keep Kane safe. Except he pressed too hard, and Kane ran, joined a murderous rogue to escape. A malfunctioning portal killed Kane and the rogue. Alive one moment, dead the next. Nothing Tage could do to stop it.

Tage needs air, needs it bad. He turns, stumbles into the hall. He's so alone it *hurts*. Knife-wounds and crushed bones don't bring pain like this. He wants it to stop. All around, the water presses at him. The sea is forever, massive. It'll crush him. He needs out.

A hand claps his shoulder. "Breathe, mate."

He jerks away, turns.

Marcus lifts his arms, non-threatening, and steps back. "Easy there, easy. You're pressure sick. Happens to some on first dive. Breathe slow, it'll pass."

Tage leans back against the wall, fists clenched. Focuses on what's real: his coat. It's his pride. He's been VanDrake for ten years, since he was fourteen. Heavy, supple leather presses against his shoulders and spine, grounds him. Air in his lungs is enough. The panic ebbs.

Tage sucks in a shaky breath, then another. The ocean don't feel as close, now. The submersible's shielded, safe. He won't drown. He nods once, not trusting his voice.

Marcus offers a wry, honest smile. "Good. Just rest. It gets better, one way or another."

* * *

Third day into the journey, Marcus swings by his cabin after evening mess. "How you doing?"

Tage is reading one of the books Savatori lent him—a pulp novel about pirates. He's not impressed. Pirates ain't nearly that civilized in his experience. He sets the book down. "Fine."

Marcus leans on the doorframe. His shirt's unbuttoned, and he ain't wearing his hat. Looks relaxed. "Glad to hear. We'll be in Aldare by midday tomorrow. We've just entered the Trench of Heaven."

"The what?"

Marcus grins. "Norris dubbed it. It's a rift cut deep between bedrock. Total blackness. I think she meant it as a joke. Still, it's a direct path and still waters for a dozen leagues or so. Couple hours and we'll start purging the ballast tanks and rising towards the shallows."

Tage nods. "Been wondering. What'd you do before this?" Jerks his chin at the cabin, means the submersible.

Marcus pulls off his shirt. Lean, muscular, he sports more tattoos than scars. Great black and blue whorls in intricate patterns cover his back and slip 'round his waist and dip lower. Faint scar-ridges show under the ink. A whale skeleton sinks towards a sandy seabed on one arm; the other's covered with words Tage can't read.

"I've been many things, for a lot of people. I've traveled the world and seen..." He clears his throat. "Wonders and horrors is close enough to describe it. Bet you've known the same, huh?"

Tage shrugs. He's seen horrors, yeah. Maybe some wonders, too.

Marcus smiles. "Being aboard the *Whale Fall* is the most rewarding job I've had. Besides, I meet such intriguing people." He winks.

Tage hides surprise, but it's secondary to building arousal as he looks at Marcus. It feels like forever since he's been with anyone. He swallows. The loneliness is as bad as the ache, the need to be touched. Tage has always—only—wanted partners older than him. Can't stand the idea of younger lovers. It's too easy to hurt the ones who can't fight back.

And with Marcus, he don't got to worry about hurting no one.

"What are you going to do with your life now?" Marcus takes a step closer. In the cabin, he only needs one step to be nearly touching Tage.

Tage can see the other wizard's as hard as he is. "What do you mean?"

Marcus shrugs, runs a hand through his hair. Tiny barbed tattoos trace the sides of his neck and link across his spine. "You're not going back to your Clan, are you?"

Tage tenses. "You're one to talk."

"I know the look...they hurt you, and they'll do worse again if they get you back." He grabs Tage by the shoulders, brings his face close. "You could stay on, you know." His voice turns husky. "No one can find us under the sea. On this ship, you'd never be alone again."

Tage don't want to know how Marcus can read him so well. Don't want to think about that offer, or how tempted he is.

Marcus says, "Ponder it," and kisses Tage hard on the mouth.

Tage's heartbeat pounds his ears. He snags Marcus' shaggy hair and pulls him closer. Marcus' tongue against his teeth makes his whole body tingle. Skin is hot against his.

"You consent?" Marcus asks, his hands against Tage's chest.

Tage is almost caught off guard, being asked. But it snuffs out the lingering doubt. "Fuck yes."

Marcus chuckles, knees apart Tage's legs, unbuckles his belt. Tage sucks his breath in. Marcus kisses him again. Heat, pleasure, curls up Tage's belly. He wants more. He drags Marcus closer, desperate. He shifts his weight back, lets Marcus pull his jeans down, out of the way. Marcus pauses long enough to shuck free of remaining clothes. Tage appreciates the view, leans forward, cups his hands 'round Marcus' hips and pulls him close.

The cabin lurches, throws them both against the side wall. Tage flails, catches himself before he falls. "What the hell—?"

Marcus staggers back, cursing. The *Whale Fall* keels again. He scrambles for his trousers, pulls them on, bolts for the door. "Something just slammed us starboard."

Tage fumbles for his jeans. The strain in Marcus' voice has his nerves edged. Goddamn it.

Sailors brush past him, scrambling for stations. Swearing echoes. The floor tilts again. Tage grabs at the wall, his stomach lurching opposite the ship. He pushes his way into the bridge, stops cold. Can't speak, can't even breathe.

Outside the domed glass and steel mantle, all he sees are monsters.

They float, glowing in the dark. Spiraled shells rimmed in blue-green luminescence. Big, shallow eyes rest on either side of a swarm of tentacles that curl out from the shell. The tip of each tentacle has a pinkish-white glow. There's a dozen creatures, maybe, big as draft horses.

One nudges into the *Whale Fall's* nose, tentacles sliding across the glass. Wards flare bright. The creature pokes the ship again and wiggles more appendages free of its shell. The others crowd nearer, tentacles still bunched inside.

"Nautiluses," Captain Norris says. "I was not aware they migrated this high so early in the year."

Tage wants them away from the glass. He keeps picturing those tentacles ramming through the window, letting in the sea.

Marcus laughs, leaning on the captain's chair in relief. "They're just spawn."

Norris's scarred jaw tightens. "They are big enough to damage my ship, Mr. Grey."

"But not a threat," Marcus says. A swirl of tattoos, thin teal lines, shine iridescent on his skin. "We just intersected with a passing stream. Dim the forelights and they'll lose interest. They must think we're one of them."

The headlamps on *Whale Fall* fade. The great beasts still dart and twirl around the ship, bumping into it with glowing shells and tentacles. The ship rocks, holds.

Marcus laughs again. "They're just curious children, Captain. They aren't trying to hurt us."

"Their intent matters little," Norris says. "Madam d'Flay, ready the harpoons."

The gunnery officer, a swarthy woman with thick braids hanging down her back, cranks a series of wheels. Slides her hands to a bronze lever. Outside, Tage catches sight of the edge of huge bladed harpoons swiveling towards the monsters.

"No, wait." Marcus's voice has steel in it now. "*Whale Fall* will hold. Let them be."

The captain and wizard stare at each other.

"We'll be fine, Captain," Marcus says, near a whisper.

Norris looks back at the nautiluses flitting about in the deeps. "Stand ready, d'Flay, but hold."

Marcus dips his chin, turns aside.

Soon the monsters drift farther away.

Norris stands, glances between Tage and Marcus. "Is all well, Mr. Grey?"

Marcus nods, tendons taut in his neck. The tattoos almost burn against his skin now, darker, duller. "Unexpected, that's all."

"Dismissed from the bridge, Mr. VanDrake," Norris says.

Marcus flicks a hand at him, arm trembling. "I'll meet you back in your cabin?"

Tage hesitates. He don't need light to see something's badly wrong. Both the captain and the wizard are too tense, trying not to show worry. Or pain, in Marcus' case.

Tage backs out. The bridge door snicks shut—it's a thick grille. None of the inside walls block sound too well. He leans a shoulder against the metal. Hall's empty. It digs under Tage's thoughts, the slow realization that rarely are any of the crew near Norris or Marcus. Or him.

"Assessment?" the captain asks, deceptively even-toned.

"They didn't rupture any skin. No engine damage. It's the shields that took the brunt of it." Marcus sounds out of breath. "As I said, I reckon they were just curious as to what we are."

"You're shaking." Sharp accusation. "I want a full report, Mr. Grey, and I want it now."

A pause. Tage leans closer, breathes shallow so he won't be heard.

"The wards are strained," Marcus says at last. "Well below half capacity."

"Is our hull pressure compromised?"

"Not yet, ma'am."

"Not *yet*?"

A scuff of boots on the floor. "I haven't yet re-bolstered the spells. They'll hold fast to our destination if we remain steady and don't run into any more nautiluses."

"I'm not an optimist, Mr. Grey."

"Neither am I."

"So we're at minimized defenses, and we have over fifty leagues to landfall." Norris sighs. "How soon will you be able to reinforce and repair your wards?"

"We were interrupted," Marcus says slowly. "Sea monsters kill a mood right fast."

"Then you'd best be back to your acquisition before we encounter any other unexpected elements."

Tage grits his teeth, his spine chilled.

"Begging your pardon," Marcus drawls, more bitterness than sarcasm. "It's not as if I can pin him against the bunk and fuck him."

"Make it that simple."

The captain's lucky there's a metal wall between 'em. Tage swallows a curse, shaking.

"I don't coerce my lovers," Marcus says, angry. "*Don't* spit on my honor, Captain."

Norris's tone don't change. "We're over twenty fathoms deep, Mr. Grey." There's finality in those words. "We have ten leagues before we're clear of the trench and there's no room for us to surface until we're clear. I won't risk the lives of my crew on your sense of honor."

"I reckon you should remember it's my *honor* that keeps this ship intact, Captain."

Tage holds his breath, so tense his muscles hurt.

"There's Alton," Norris says. "Or the VanDrake. Those wards *will* be repaired within the hour."

Silence leeches out, heavy in the narrow hallway. Tage's heartbeat bruises his ribs.

"We have an understanding, Mr. Grey?"

Marcus don't answer right away. Then, "Yes, Captain."

The door latch grinds. Tage lurches back-wards, wedges himself into the ladder well. Slides a knife from inside his boot into his palm. Anger chokes tight. He ain't being *used* by anyone, not again. Goddamn it. He don't know if he's more mad or hurt. Worst of it is, he still wants the other wizard. It's fucked up, he knows that. Wishes he didn't *care*.

Marcus steps from the bridge. Tage bulls from the ladder well just as Marcus passes, slams the other man into the wall. Marcus grunts. Tage has the knife under his chin too fast for the other wizard to react.

"Ain't happening," Tage snarls.

Marcus scowls, don't look surprised. "Put that away. My wards are life-linked. You kill me, the pressure will crush *Whale Fall* like a tin can." He nudges Tage hard in the belly with a knife of his own. "Put it *down*, VanDrake."

Tage is tempted to ignore the threat. But he ain't gonna sentence the whole crew to death; he's got enough blood etched in his hands. Slowly, he lowers his arm. Marcus removes the knife.

"You want a proper explanation?" Marcus' worn eyes look old. Tired and hurt, for all his expression is steel. "Eavesdropping leaves out salient details."

Tage's jaw aches, teeth clenched. "Talk fast."

Marcus scoffs, shoulders past him. "My cabin's soundproof."

Tage is torn. He don't fear a fight. He's got weight and muscle on the other man. He's been well-trained how to use it. And if Marcus' words ring true, his magic's tied into wards and spells lining the submersible. Gives Tage more of an advantage. No, he ain't afraid. He wants to hear the clanless wizard's explanation, even if it makes things worse.

Stiff-backed, he follows. Marcus' cabin is in the submersible's aft. Not much bigger than Tage's bunk, but there's ink drawings on the walls— crinkled and faded, near unrecognizable with water stains—and sea charts, maps, sketches of marine life.

There's room for one chair nudged tight against the bunk, draped with Marcus' duster and red fedora. Tage ducks through the door, stops on the threshold. Blocks the way out.

Marcus slumps on the bed. "I'm hardly in a seductive mood. Relax."

"This why you brought me aboard?" Better rage than pain. "A goddamned tool to run your fucking ship?"

"Not entirely."

Tage could beat the hell out of the other man, easy. He's done it often enough. It never fixes the dull guilt or hurt when he's done, but that don't stop him, either.

Marcus glances up, don't raise his guard. Like he wants to get hit. "It wasn't that difficult to find out who you were when you left your card at Anna's. One of Madam Frost's enforcers: her prized Tage Ranheim."

Tage freezes at that. How much else does Marcus know?

Marcus rests his elbows on his knees. "The only scuttlebutt I could find was that you'd gone missing, suspected for dead. It wasn't that hard to figure out what happened after that. You wanted to get away, and I could help. I didn't hire you to warm my goddamn bed, VanDrake."

"You did it just to *help*?"

"Oh, I had hopes for more, true. Do you blame me? Madam Frost isn't exactly shy in choosing her entourage for their looks as much as skill and size, now is she?" The corner of Marcus' mouth quirks. "I made mistakes, long ago. I've tried to make them up ever since. So yes, my friend—"

Tage punches Marcus in the jaw. The other man's head snaps back. He kicks out, catches Tage in the hip, rolls off the bunk and lands crouched, his eyes suddenly flat. Tage staggers back, widens his stance, readies himself for a brawl.

"Don't call me that," Tage snaps.

Marcus stands, licks blood from a split lip. "Don't lay hands on me like that again, unless you mean to carry through."

Tage glares, wills Marcus to attack him.

As sharp as bone snapping, Marcus' mood shifts again and the threat fades. "The wards didn't need bolstering yet, for Hell's sake. We shouldn't have dove this far. Norris is impatient. We have sensitive courier messages and some, ah, goods that port masters aren't keen to allow. Expensive spices, items for spellwork. She's pushing too fast." He twists his wrist, sleight of hand, and in his palm he holds the paper scrap Tage left for contact with Anna. "You asked for help. I reckoned I could offer that." He snaps his fingers and the paper turns to ash. "Earlier? I wanted you in bed because I *like* you, Tage, there's no other reason."

"Your captain seemed pretty fucking clear what she wanted."

"Norris is my captain, not my owner. We'll make this simple. Will you help me?"

"Fuck no."

"Then I won't touch you. You can finish your stint as a hired hand and put off at Aldare."

It ain't that easy. Never is. "What're you gonna do?"

"Find a way to channel energy reserves to fix the godforsaken wards so we aren't pulled into the lockers." He yanks his fingers through his hair, tilts his head up. "I told Alton no. I'm not using him any more than I'm using you, and I'm not taking an apprentice."

"And if you got no choice?" Tage's voice is a rasp.

Marcus stares at him flatly. "Then *Whale Fall* will be lost with all hands." There's no conviction behind the words.

Tage swallows. He ain't responsible for this crew. It ain't his old gang, or his family.

He tries not to wish they hadn't been interrupted, earlier. Tries not to wish he'd never listened in on Marcus Grey and Captain Norris. He thought, in his bunk, maybe he could have something good again.

"Go back to your cabin," Marcus says, boot toes against Tage's. "I'll tell you when your muscle's needed. We pump the ballast tanks—"

A shudder slams the length of *Whale Fall*. Marcus staggers, flinches as if kicked in the ribs. "Hell's whisky."

Tage backs out. "What's wrong?"

Sweat beads across Marcus' forehead. "We've been spotted."

"By what?"

"Only thing in this trench that's bigger than us. The nautiluses—the adults."

Tage's stomach lurches as the submersible lists again. "How do you kill 'em?"

"You don't kill the gods of the sea, partner. You pray to your own. If we can't outrun them, we're dead men." He sprints for the bridge.

Tage curses and follows.

More of the crew has gathered. Savatori. D'Flay. Alton. This time, Alton's expression is glazed, content, drugged. He leans on Savatori's arm.

Tage don't get a chance to protest. Outside, lit by the ship's lamps and its own lum-inescence, a giant nautilus hovers in the water. Massive tentacles half the *Whale Fall's* girth slowly extend from a blue-grey shell. Tage can't even see its full bulk, just one huge pearlescent eye.

"Mr. Grey," Norris says.

Marcus leans against the captain's chair. "Hour's not up, ma'am."

"Clearly."

Tage feels the tension, so thick it chokes out any panic. No one moves.

"Stations, men. Prepare to fire harpoons, Madam d'Flay." Norris's commands are obeyed in silence. They're all dead men walking, and they know it.

Savatori shoves Alton at Marcus, who catches the boy, supports him.

Tage reaches for a pistol he don't have. "Don't," he whispers.

He ain't gonna stand idle while anyone—wizard or not—rapes a kid for magic-fuel. It won't work fast enough, anyhow. Those tentacles will crush *Whale Fall* long before Marcus has the strength to boost shields.

"I need your help," Marcus says, between threat and begging. He shoves Alton to the floor.

The nautilus glows whitish-green, a hypnotizing series of lights that etch the shell and tentacles.

"Harpoons ready, Captain," d'Flay says.

Norris lifts a hand. Marcus shakes his head. Despair masks even fear. Harpoons'll do no good, and they only got two shots with the forward guns.

Tage keeps telling himself if he wanted to die, he'd have shot himself when Kane was killed. He won't be used. Even if he gave in, there's no time.

Tage can't set the nautilus on fire, can't shoot it or knife it. Frustration at his lack of options bubbles under dull terror. He don't want to drown, crushed in metal and glass as the ocean pours in.

But there's more than one way to use magic.

"Make us look like it," Tage says. "Illusion the ship."

The captain says, "Fire" just as Marcus cries, "No, wait—" and d'Flay releases the harpoons. They bounce off the nautilus's shell and it rumbles.

Tage hasn't got time. He shoves the raw, unchecked magic at Marcus. It'll either work, or it'll kill them both. Marcus said his magic is different. Adapted. Changed and strengthened and malleable. He's had VanDrake lovers before. Tage won't be used, but he can give Marcus some of the energy he needs. Power shared.

The magic burns, raw fire in his veins. It'll hurt Marcus worse. But the other wizard don't scream. A small, choked sound escapes him as he pulls the magic into him. Tage feels it being *swallowed*. He gasps, pain sparking white behind his eyes.

Startled, he realizes he's seeing what Marcus sees.

The whole ship, outside and in. It don't change, but its appearance does. Its skin ripples, shifts from metal and glass to shell and flesh. The outer lights dim, become luminescent. Eyes appear where the bridge is, and instead of *Whale Fall*, an adolescent nautilus stares back at the giant before it.

The questing tentacles pause.

Tage feels his body stretched, expanded beyond proportion. Against his skin, the weight of the sea presses, cold and solid, the world's bones. It will turn him into nothingness and he'll welcome it—

Inside the shell, heartbeats flutter. His. Marcus'?

The ship-nautilus meekly pulls in its tentacles, waits before the sea god. Humble. Harmless. *May I pass?*

Tage can't find his body. Panic touches cold inside the shell, in him. The illusion wobbles, pulled at the edges. The giant nautilus reaches again.

Hands grab his shoulder, his chin. Does he have a body still? The sea takes no notice of tiny motes, fragile bones crushed to nothing.

"Hold fast," Marcus is saying, forever away. He's pulling Tage apart; inside there is a vast expanse, never filled. The other wizard feels hollow, not-real. A shell washed clean on a beach. He'll pull everything from Tage, unmake him.

Stop, Tage wants to say. He has will, somewhere. Knows he does. He ain't...weak. Promised Kane he'd never be weak again, that he'd always protect them both. He can't lose himself. He *won't*.

Tage grasps at the things he knows are real. His coat, the scars, the memory of Kane and Bonnie and the Clan and food that ain't stolen and soot in the air and cities and ghosts and pain and another's warm, solid body against his. Not alone.

His vision blurs, shows him the ship and the not-nautilus and Marcus' face right in front of him. He clamps down on the magic, on himself. Realizes Marcus is holding him up by coat front and chin.

And he's *himself*. He ain't a ship or part of the sea. He ain't a helpless kid no more. He won't be broken, no matter how it feels inside.

He takes a breath, jerks away from Marcus. The man lets him go. Tage lands on hands and knees. The glass is blurry, or maybe it's his eyes. Outside, the giant nautilus drifts by, an endless expanse of shell and light.

Tage feels the illusion burning his skin, his senses. Marcus holds it steady, body rigid and eyes blank. Tage can't hear nothin' but his weak heartbeat. Unsteady. Then stronger. He pushes himself to his knees, sways, blinks until his eyes clear. His bones ache, feels like he burned the marrow from 'em all.

"How long until we clear the trench, Mr. Savatori?" Norris's voice comes at a distance.

"One league, ma'am."

"Damage report, Mr. Grey?"

"We're fine, Captain." Marcus sounds like he swallowed razors. "We're in the clear."

Tage coughs. His chest aches, muscles strained, lungs aflame. Pain reminds him he's alive, whole. Still himself.

Shaky laughter, relieved swearing. The crew calms. Except Norris. The captain stands, looks down at Tage.

Tage tries to brace himself. He'll still fight, somehow. Ain't gonna be put down easily. He's survived because he don't give in.

Marcus kneels, claps a hand on his shoulder, steadies him. "We're in the clear now."

Tage don't blink or look away, realizes he's already got a knife in hand.

Norris nods once. "Mr. VanDrake."

"Captain," Tage says, hoarse.

Marcus helps him to his feet, offers him an arm. Tage limps on his own until he's in the narrow hallway. Wobbly, he leans against Marcus until his breath steadies.

"Thank you," Marcus says.

Tage ain't used to being thanked. He straightens a little, thinks the scraping ache from so much lost magic don't hurt as much anymore. "Didn't know it'd work."

Marcus chuckles. "I've had worse done to me. I like how you think, though."

Tage looks away. Too much is churning in his head. He stumbles, feet heavy. Marcus keeps Tage from falling.

"Get some rest," Marcus says.

Tage stares at his bunk. His vision blurs at the edges.

"You'll be safe," Marcus adds, backing away. "You have my word on that."

Tage shuts his eyes before he admits that means more than Marcus could ever realize. Safe. He believes it, too, just this once. It lets him sleep.

* * *

He's still thinking on Marcus' words—"What will you do now?"—when *Whale Fall* reaches Aldare.

A new country, a new city. He'll be alone again, this time with no backing from the Clan, no support, nowhere to return.

"You could stay," Marcus said, the words running over and over through Tage's head. He can't ignore 'em.

Stay. Maybe not for long, but it'd hurt less not to be alone. He can't forget Kane, forgive himself for failing. It can't be so wrong to want to find a little peace, though, somewhere. Or maybe it is. He's wanted worse.

The rest of the crew has disembarked. Marcus says he's staying behind to prep *Whale Fall* and keep her ready while the crew takes a day's leave and Norris sees to business. Tage stands on the low, flat deck of the submersible, staring at the rise of forest and mountains distant.

He notices Marcus beside him. The other man offers him a cigarette. Tage accepts. The wind tugs his hair, slides under his coat. One step down, into the skiff, and he won't set foot on the submersible again.

"You still looking for a crew hand?" Tage asks at last.

Marcus grins. "I like men with previous sailing experience."

A bit of strain eases inside Tage. They finish their smokes and climb below.

Marcus leans against the wall, his hat tipped back. "Not going ashore?"

Tage shrugs. He looks Marcus in the eyes. He knows what he wants. "Earlier, we got interrupted." He kisses Marcus hard.

Heat and magic-sense tingles Tage's mouth, spreads through his belly and legs. Marcus tangles his fingers in Tage's hair, hooks an arm around Tage's waist. Tage is pleased. Gentleness scares him, makes him think he'll break the one he's with.

"You all right with this?" Tage asks.

"Fuck yes," Marcus says, and kisses him again.

Impatient with clothes, Marcus drags him towards his cabin, pulls Tage down on the bunk. Tage unbuckles Marcus' belt.

He ain't alone tonight.

RIVER OF STARS
DAVID FARLAND

Aracai rose to the surface as the fishing boat sped away, motors whining softly. The surface of the Atlantic was dimpled with waves that lapped softly, as if the sea were slightly perturbed. The stars shone so brightly they throbbed, and the moon was in its dark phase, but light from the Arab colonies there created a bright band that slashed across the moon's equator like a gathering of rogue stars.

He dove beneath the water and followed the backpack dropped by Escalas' contact twenty meters to the ocean floor. The sea here was alive with sounds—the crackling of snapping shrimp, the eerie bellow of a grouper, the chiming sounds of baitfish. Though the sea was dark, Aracai's night vision was excellent. He'd been engineered to see in infrared, so many creatures seemed to emit a soft glow.

He followed the backpack down to a place where rocks were covered in splotches of anemones and starfish, all gray shapes in the night, and began circling it, swimming on his side, watching it as if it were some strange creature that he dare not approach.

He made a soft whistle, "Here," and in moments two more mer swam up, hugging the sand. Like Aracai, they were both nude. Dulce, his young wife, had hair of amber. His mentor, an old mer named Escalas—whose streaming white hair was held back by the silver circlet of the mindlink around his head—swam near and circled the backpack. But he did not watch the pack. Instead, he swam on his side, deep-set eyes watching Aracai.

He knows what is in the pack, Aracai thought. *That's why he brought us here. And now he is waiting for me to pick it up...*

Dulce circled behind them a few meters off.

Three months back, Aracai and Dulce had been living to the south, at the tip of Brasilia, where the cold waters of the Antarctic were among the cleanest in the world and the fisheries still thrived. That's when he'd met Escalas.

He was a living legend. Not only was he very old and wise, he was the only mer to have a mindlink, so that if he wanted to know something, he could wonder about it and thus access Heavenly Host—the AIs linked in geosynchronous orbit—and learn what he wanted to know.

Upon meeting, Escalas had eyed Aracai a moment and then said, "Swim with me." Among the mer, it was an invitation to swim for a ways, to talk, or perhaps to swim for a lifetime.

Now, Aracai realized that the old man had been bringing him to this point for months. "What is in the backpack?" Aracai sang, his voice a low thrumming that ended in a higher squeal.

Escalas hesitated, as if he hoped Aracai would guess, then answered, "A bomb."

Many questions crowded Aracai's mind. What kind of bomb? Who will Escalas kill? But one burst to the forefront: "How did you get it?"

Escalas's answer was leisurely, a rumble. "I bought it...from the neogods."

The news took Aracai's breath. It did not surprise him that Escalas had *bought* the weapon. No, he felt surprised at mention of the neogods. They had been human until their genetic and mechanical upgrades had boosted their intelligence so much that they no longer wished to associate with mankind any more than Aracai would want to associate with amoebas. The neogods had left Earth decades ago, learned to bend space and time, so that now they explored the edges of the universe...

"Those creatures do not talk to men—or bargain with them," Aracai said, worried that Escalas was teasing him.

"Ah, Spirit Warrior, they bargained with *me*," Escalas affirmed. "Perhaps I made the right offer, or asked for the right weapon?" He jutted his chin toward the backpack. "Pick it up."

Spirit Warrior? He thinks I am a warrior? Aracai had never thought of himself as a warrior at all.

But he had begun to believe over the past weeks that the world needed one. There was poison coming from Rio Negro—heavy metals and acids from mining, human waste, pesticides and industrial chemicals. In some places, over the past four decades, the poisons had turned the sea floor into a wasteland that even crabs could not survive. The mer were dying. The three of them were among the last.

Old Escalas had petitioned numerous national leaders, sought to get the humans to stop the "genocidal poisoning of our people." But the governments in South America did not enforce their own laws. Those who had been charged with protecting the environment merely took bribes and turned a blind eye.

Escalas swam past Aracai, studying him. "It is time to go to war," he said. "But the notion of violence sickens you."

"Yes," Aracai said. His whole frame was shaking.

"As it should," Escalas said, swimming close. "Feral humans do not need a reason to go to war. Violence is in their nature. But when they made us mer, they took our bloodlust away. So the idea sickens you, though it is long past time for us to act." He jutted a chin toward the backpack. "The problem with us mer is that we circle our problems endlessly, when we should merely grasp at the solutions."

A bomb? War is a solution? Aracai studied Escalas. The old mer held a trace of a smile, as if he were amused. That was the problem with the old man. In the past months, Aracai had learned a lot, but Escalas always seemed to be three steps ahead.

"Do not do this thing," Aracai warned, "whatever you have planned."

"Oh, I am not going to do it," Escalas said softly. "You are!"

Aracai could not imagine himself harming another. "But—"

Escalas raised a hand. "The feral humans who are poisoning our seas hurt themselves almost as much as they do us. Their society is toxic, and what do humans do when they perceive another society to be toxic? They go to war. History is full of toxic societies that are no more."

Aracai could hardly believe what he heard. He wanted to argue, but did not know where to start.

The old mer swam lazily. "This *is* the answer. Pick it up."

Numb, Aracai pulled at the backpack and dumped out the bomb—a strange device, all metal, a heavy black disk. Soft, white lights displayed the time and the bomb's GPS coordinates on top.

He lifted it. The bomb was heavier than anything so small should be. Heavier than lead. Heavier even than gold. Uranium?

Aracai trilled a warning to the others, "Stay back!" He suspected it was a nuclear device, but it was too small to have much in the way of shielding. Being this close could expose them all to radiation.

He threw it back to the ocean floor, raising a cloud of filth, but Dulce swam near and wrenched it from the mud. There was sadness in her dark eyes. "Let me carry it," she demanded. "She was my daughter, too…"

An image flashed in Aracai's mind—their infant daughter, cold and rigid, eyes and fingers gone equally white in death. The poisons had contained some sort of mutagen, so that she was born with only a small part of her brain.

"Too many mer children have died," she said.

"We can try for another," Aracai promised.

But the gill slits along Dulce's neck flared in anger. "No, no we can't," she said. They had been trying for five years. "You know that. I want to carry my vengeance in my own hands."

With a flick of her tail, she lunged forward, upstream through the brackish water.

Old Escalas said, "It is not vengeance I seek, but change."

* * *

In the night they swam, pushing through heavy headwaters, and Escalas sang to them of the dangers of the Amazon, a chant that formed dreams in Aracai's mind. There were huge black eels ahead that could emit a killing, electric jolt of blue light, and piranhas with bright-red bellies that hung like rubies in the slow waters until they smelled blood, when they would lunge and tear chunks of flesh from bones. He sang of coral-colored dolphins, anacondas, and other dangers. The fresh water itself was poison to the mer, for in time their kidneys would fail in the reduced salinity.

So Aracai feared the river.

It became quieter as they swam. The crackle of snapping shrimp died away and only the sloshing of waves could be heard.

Aracai saw evidence of toxins. There were no snails or freshwater clams on the muddy river floor. They passed no schools of fish—only a pair of huge bull sharks swimming upstream to spawn. The sharks eyed the mer hungrily.

The waters at the mouth of the Amazon were deserted. Flecks of dark moss and white decomposing bits of dead insects and fish drifted about. The water was oxygen rich, but smelled of decay, and the toxins in it made his gills itch.

So Aracai pleaded for reason as they swam in the darkness. "We cannot bomb the humans. Innocent children will be hurt."

"I do not want to hurt innocent children," Escalas agreed. "But the humans must change their ways. I have done all that I know how in order to convince them. Now, we must go to war." The old man seemed to change subjects. "The poison that killed your daughter is called C54."

The news sent Dulce into a wail of pain. Her tail thrashed, so that she surged ahead and became invisible in the cloudy water.

Aracai had never heard of C54 and felt relieved that Escalas had put a name to the toxin.

"In Venezuela, it is used as a chemical warfare agent. That is where we are going—to set the bomb off at the factory. The poison is colorless, tasteless. It was not meant to kill anyone, though it has unforeseen effects on the mer. It was designed as a mind-control weapon. The drug causes the victim's brain to release the hormone dopamine, making victims carefree and happy, but over time the victim's prefrontal lobes shrink, limiting their ability to plan ahead. This makes the Venezuelan's enemies stupid."

The waters were dark, and Aracai's gills itched. He swam briefly to the surface and flashed his gills, shaking his head, to try to rid them of grit.

Aracai wondered long about the C54, horrified that such a weapon would be unleashed on others, crippling the minds of children.

He thought of his daughter, her tiny fingers as rubbery as the tentacles of a dead octopus, her blind eyes, the malformed brain that would not work well enough to let her breathe.

"The Venezuelans create this drug, and the other nations, they do not fight back?" Aracai wondered.

"Oh, they fight back," Escalas sang. "Humans have never discovered a stick that could not be turned into a club. Venezuela's enemies wage economic war, making their country the poorest of the world's poor, and they bribe AIs to withhold information from them. Each of Venezuela's enemies have iconic celebrities who mock the Venezuelans, weakening their spirits. They use viruses and nanobots…"

"And if we go to war," Aracai asked, "are we any better than them?" The possibility that they weren't frustrated Aracai. He did not know much about humans. He had seen the hulls of their boats above water, but had never wanted to meet one.

Truth be told, he despised them. The humans had made him poorly. His eyes did not face forward like those of a fish, which made it dangerous to swim too far, too fast, lest he crack his skull on something. He had no need for hair, and would have preferred to simply have flesh alone, or perhaps scales, instead of flowing locks that were always picking up bits of seaweed and becoming home to tiny crabs. His shoulders were too large, not sleek enough to slice through the water.

It is the right of any creature to dislike his creators, he felt. *The humans created us according to some nightmarish aesthetic in-stead of constructing something more elegant.*

"I am what they made me," Aracai said.

"Is that *all* you are?" Escalas asked. "Do you not also make yourself?"

Aracai dodged between two rocks. "We can always better ourselves."

"I think," Escalas said, "that it is almost a duty for a man to better himself, or a people to better themselves. We must swim forward, not be content to drift with the tides. That is almost a duty, don't you think?"

There it was again, that secretive tone. Aracai wondered. Was he talking of genetic manipulation? That cost a lot of money, something that a mer, living off the bounties of the ocean, did not need.

But Aracai thought, *I could make money. There are still treasures under the sea—Spanish Galleons full of emeralds, sunken Mayan ruins off the coast of Mexico, filled with artifacts. Humans pay well for such curiosities. Perhaps I could find a cure for the poisons.*

But the old mer seemed to want to send a message.

"So," Aracai said at last, "do humans actually die in these wars?"

"Some die," Escalas admitted. "But there are various theories on war. The goal is not to kill, it is to demoralize, to alter the behavior of the enemy." The old mer struggled to talk and breathe at the same time. He rose to the surface, gasped a deep breath, and continued. "To be honest though, I do not think that humans value life as much as you and I do. When I found you, Spirit Warrior, you were the first mer that I had met in two years. I felt so alone, and so I begged you, 'Swim with me.' Among the mer, we crave each other's company. But with over two hundred billion human souls on earth, there are too many. If one of them dies, the others feel relief rather than loss. Why, there are sixteen million humans living along the Amazon's banks alone. It is the largest river in the world, and holds one fifth of all the fresh water..." He droned on.

Ahead of them, Dulce was slowing. She had begun to sing in the way mer women will, a threnody whose tune was beat out in the lashing of her tail.

> *"Black River, poison river, rolling to the sea*
> *Be my road, guide the way,*
> *Avenge my daughter and me."*

The old mer glanced ahead and said, "She is a fine wife for a Spirit Warrior. I hope that at the end of this, you will be able to have the children you deserve."

"Why do you call me 'Spirit Warrior?'" Aracai asked.

The old mer slowed his swimming and did a roll, so that he could peer into Aracai's face. "Among the humans, men contend with one another. But you fight your own weaknesses, your own inner demons. That is why I brought you."

Aracai eyed Escalas. "You do not want to kill humans either, do you?"

Escalas admitted, "To take a life is...reprehensible. To even force another into a certain path...weighs on my soul. But we will not reach our destination for many days and so I have time to ponder."

Aracai thought long. He realized that he need not make a decision to go to war now. He could abandon the bomb at any moment, let it sink into the mud. Changing course would be as simple as a flick of his tail.

But he plunged ahead, through the night, wondering.

* * *

By early dawn they had traveled many kilometers upriver, reaching the old gods that guarded its mouth.

The old gods came in the form of enormous ancient busts of men and monkeys, all grimacing, each perhaps sixty feet tall. A line of them had been discovered across the river channel back in the Twenty-second Century, sunk deep into the mud, but no one knew what civilization had carved them. Aracai worried for Dulce. The bomb she carried was very heavy. She held the disk clasped against her belly as she swam, near her womb, and he knew enough to be afraid for her, for them all.

How much radiation did the bomb emit? How much could they handle?

Did it even matter? When they set the bomb off, he might not have a chance to escape the blast. Even if he got away from the fireball, the detonation would create a wall of sound, a sonic boom that would carry downriver, stunning and killing fish, including him.

And he had to wonder, is there any life left in Dulce's womb worth worrying about anyway?

He took the bomb, to give her a rest, but then determined that she would carry it no more.

The old mer, Escalas, continued to struggle in the swift water. Aracai was smart enough to wonder if the old man had brought him on this journey, planned it months or even years ago, just so that he'd have strong arms to carry the weapon. Aracai considered asking, but knew that he would not get a straight answer. Escalas was always forcing him to think for himself.

So Aracai swam, hampered by muddled thoughts, a heavy burden, and strong currents. The riverbed below him looked remarkably dead in the morning light. Escalas' warnings about ferocious fish and deadly stingrays seemed to be without merit.

At dawn Aracai rose to the surface, drew a great breath, and peered about. The bank to the north was so far away he could make out only water, but to the south he saw buildings—squat and colorful in shades of lavender and canary and pearl, sitting in tiers along the bank. Peasants with mule carts walked along the roads in bare feet.

There had to be tens of thousands of them, freakish things. There were no gleaming hovercars with wealthy passengers, like he'd once seen in Chile.

Aracai dove deep and swam near the bottom.

Then came the new gods. Aracai was flapping his tail hard, driving upstream through the sepia waters, falling behind the others. Soot and algae beat against him like a storm, and suddenly he heard a ping. A brilliant blue beam of light struck his face and he squinted to see huge metal struts ahead that seemed to be covered by seaweed. He realized that it wasn't seaweed at all, but strands of plasteet—a material used to capture energy from wave action—and he followed new movement as the barrel of a cannon swiveled his way.

His heart froze and he ceased swimming, only to hear the ping and a squelchy mechanical noise that he recognized as a droid's demand for an identification signal.

"Watch out!" Escalas called a moment too late, and Aracai heard the grinding of massive metal beams, then something heavy hit the ground, raising clouds of mud.

Suddenly Aracai put the images together. There was a war droid ahead—a giant titanium crablike droid the size of a ship, scuttling on the river bottom, menacing them.

Aracai stopped to let the muddy tide carry him back from danger, just as a single shot seared through the water. An energy beam sent a tube of bubbling super-heated water toward Escalas, striking him just once. The old mer went limp as the cloud of muddy water engulfed them all.

Aracai froze, not daring to breathe, fearing a second shot. He squinted in order to avoid being blinded. He hoped the dark waters would shield him from the droid's sensors.

No more shots followed; his heart pounded.

He heard a buzz and something whipped over his head. He squinted up to see a squid-like drone with a gelatinous body. Its infrared signature made it look like a fiery octopus.

Hunters!

Aracai recognized the tech. It was called a *squill*—an ancient assassin droid, perhaps a hundred years old.

He did not know what sensory array it might have. Motion detectors? Vision? Heat? Sound? Scent?

Could it hear his heartbeat, recognize his form?

He played dead, not daring to call out, hoping that his wife would be wise enough to do the same.

The huge war droid marched north, blocking their path, stirring up more muck, impenetrably dark.

The squill began to circle and was soon followed by dozens more.

Are they armed? he wondered. The drones often carried a sac of neurotoxin, so that their stingers could kill. He'd heard legends about squills with explosives built into them. But some, he knew, were built just for reconnaissance.

Aracai drifted downstream, and often the drones passed near in the darkness, but still he dared not move. So he floated, letting the current take him, until many kilometers later the buzzing of drones faded and he was left merely floating. As the water cleared, he peered around, but his search showed him nothing.

Suddenly he caught movement: Dulce drove toward the surface, and Aracai saw a familiar form floating there.

Aracai raced upward, met them as Dulce wrapped her arms tenderly around the old mer and tried to drag him under, to safety.

When Aracai got near, the old man was a horror. Boiling water had made his skin bubble over on half of his chest and face, and skin tore away in tatters. His hair was burned off, as was his right eye. What flesh Escalas had left was red and blistered.

"Old man," Dulce asked, "can you swim with me?"

The old man's mouth was in ruins, and yet he spoke. "I can swim." He gasped for several moments, gills flashing, and glanced down. "My flesh is burned. I cannot...last..."

"What can we do to help?" Dulce asked. The old mer shook his head. "My sight..." His mouth tried to work, but pieces of flesh tore away from the hole where his lips had been, showing teeth. He gasped and sang in broken thoughts. "You, go on. Up Rio Negro, to the town Dos Brujas, where smokestacks rise, and open sewers dump into the river from both banks. There you will find a pylon, a black tower, with a light on top like a single red eye. That is where you must detonate..."

He lost his train of thought. "Take my implant..." he said, offering his greatest possession, the silver band around his head.

Escalas sang more, but his words became a soft slur, like wind lashing the water, until it died and went silent.

Dulce cried out, a barking sound, as if she had taken a mortal wound.

"Quiet," Aracai warned, swimming up to put a hand over her mouth, but she twisted her head away and wailed in frustration.

He removed the band from off Escala's head, put it on his own. The band was a silver wire, but almost as soon as he put it on, he felt a pinch at the base of his neck as nanobots began to send out probes to establish a link with his mind, one that would take days to form.

He let go of the old mer's body and let him drift away, bouncing against the muddy bottom of the river.

Dulce made a juddering cry, more of a moan than a song, and together they clasped hands and swam toward the south bank before sneaking upriver, and thus passed the warbot unseen.

He wondered why the warbot was even posted there. It was ancient, this war crab, perhaps left by governments that had fallen a century ago, during some old war. Perhaps it was as forgotten now as Aracai and his people.

* * *

Hour after hour Aracai and Dulce pushed ahead, Dulce shaking in fear and grief. He could not get the image from his mind of Escalas floating downstream, his mouth a gaping maw. He tried to calm his wife as they swam together, her holding his shoulders so that they spooned, swimming in unison.

He drifted into a waking dream, haunted by images of squills and warbots. They swam close to shore, where water gurgled through half-submerged trees and a howler monkey hooted overhead. The sunlight piercing the mud turned the river into a golden road.

They dared not slow or stop. Aracai's gut suggested that the squills might still be hunting. He suspected that they had quickly used up their energy in the initial hunt, but that after re-charging, they would be loosed again.

A boat plied the water overhead, and Aracai rose to the surface, searched the river as he cleared gunk from his gills.

To the south, he saw houses—built so close together that they glimmered like pebbles upon a beach. Children were out playing in the rain, two girls twirling a rope so that a small brown boy could jump.

Guilt weighed in Aracai's stomach as he considered what his bomb would do to them.

He dove again, lugging his burden, and began to wonder. How many days would it take to reach the target? Did he really want to kill people—children?

Was it self-defense, or something more like revenge?

He imagined Escalas talking to him, in his old reassuring tones.

Have you considered the benefits of war? the old man asked in Aracai's mind. *It sweeps away toxic societies.*

Aracai exercised his imagination, tried to find a rebuttal. *What if the toxic society wins?* he asked, for if he started a war with the humans, he knew that he personally would surely die.

Indeed, it seemed that too often the most toxic society would win the battle and thus spread.

And yet we must try, the old mer replied. *We are not just trying to save ourselves, we are hoping to save uncounted billions of people in the future.*

Aracai recalled the children out skipping and playing jump rope in the streets beside the river and pictured what would happen to them when the bomb blew. Even if he did manage to set it off, he would lose his soul.

Our species is dying, he thought. *Soon we will all be as dead as the whales.*

Does it really matter? Extinction? Every man must face his own personal extinction.

After long hours, Dulce said, "I'm hungry." He could feel pangs in his own belly. It was empty and he felt ravenous.

But the river was dead.

Aracai had once hunted briefly in fresh-water, in crystalline streams that tumbled from the Andes. Cold as ice and clearer than rain-drops, thick with trout.

An idea struck, and he took Dulce's hand and led her along the riverbank until they found a tributary, a small river that twisted through a jungle.

They swam upstream for a mile until the river came alive. Overhead, huge ferns and trees shadowed the water. Pollywogs wiggled among rushes, while frogs whistled in the trees. Water beetles buzzed in whirligig patterns and fish began to sing.

A mile up, Aracai met schools of fish—silver perch that darted in front of him like a moving screen. Huge red-tailed catfish plied the muddy bottom, using whiskers to taste for food. A parrot bass, half as long as him, hid in the shadows of a pool, the yellows and greens around its gills muted as it emitted a sonorous snoring sound.

Here, Aracai watched freshwater crabs of deep mossy green march among some stones, then he gathered water lettuce and taro roots. Dulce offered a blessing on the meal.

As they ate, Aracai tried to speak delicately. "This will be a long journey, and hard."

Dulce peered at him with exhaustion in her dark eyes. "And you wonder if there is honor in killing humans?"

"No," he said. "I know there is no honor in it."

She knew his moods. She bit her lip and a lightning flash made her eyes glow startlingly green.

"It is not about honor," he said. "I just wonder if it even makes sense. I do not want to hurt anyone. What good can come of it? Our species...is doomed." Dulce remained pensive. Aracai continued, "We could leave the bomb, hide it in the mud."

Anger flashed in Dulce's eyes, "Don't even think of it." Her tone brooked no argument. She held his gaze, her dainty nose beguiling him. She drew close and kissed his lips, pressing hard and long. "Promise me. Promise you won't turn back."

"If we do this, the humans will hunt us down."

"Everyone dies," she said.

So they ate and for a while they slept in the forest shadows, cradled in one another's arms.

The journey stretched long after that. After their nap, Aracai felt a sharp pain in his urethra. He recognized from the rhythmic motions that it was a fish. It had swum up an inch or more into him, and so he tried to pee it out.

But the tiny fish had barbs and could not be extricated, so he suffered the pain.

For four days they continued swimming along the shore of the Amazon, sometimes stopping to rest in an estuary. He saw the promised anacondas overhead and fell afoul of an electric eel. He saw colorful birds flashing over languid pools and swam unharmed through schools of piranha. There were giant arapaima longer than he and his wife, and alligator longer than any mer. The trees overhead, dripping with bright blossoms, were a marvel.

As they swam, he grew sicker. On the third day, he could no longer pee, nor could his wife. It was not the fish that had done it. Their kidneys were failing.

His body began to ache as uric acid built inside, so that every muscle felt beaten and bruised. His scales took on a milky coating. With each passing hour, he felt more certain that this journey would kill them. Freshwater was deadly. On the fifth day, he could no longer eat. His gut had given up digesting and it felt better to starve than to take nourishment.

As sick as he felt, Dulce was worse. Dulce wept as she fought her way upstream, and each day she grew slower and slower. She held to his back often as they swam, and he pushed for both, so that sometimes he blanked out and swam blind from fatigue.

He judged that they had come a thousand kilometers when they reached the junction to Rio Negro, full of its poisons.

Wearily, they stopped and tried to get a breath in a small lagoon upstream from the Rio Negro. The place was magical, pristine, the water far cleaner than any they had encountered. It was as if they were entering a lost world, the great green jungles rising above the water, vast trees streaming epiphytes. A pair of dolphins swam along the river briskly, laughing as dolphins will, their coral-colored hides a delight.

He felt as if he had found some primal place that man had never touched and marveled that such jungles still existed.

They swam into a flooded creek. Blue crayfish scuttled among tree roots and clung to floating duckweed. The day was windy, and Aracai could hear roots groaning as the trees swayed and stretched. The waters in the lagoon were golden, and huge red-bellied pacu as long as his arm swam about.

As the trees stirred, dark round nuts fell, and the pacu would bite the nuts, crunching them with powerful teeth, so that though the fish looked like enormous piranhas, they seemed like gentle giants.

Here, Aracai gazed into Dulce's eyes and said goodbye. "I want you to go back downstream," he begged. "You won't have to fight the current, and you can swim swiftly. Once you hit the saltwater, you will begin to heal." He did not know if it were true, but hoped that it was.

To his astonishment, she did not fight him. She peered deep into his eyes, reached out and stroked his beard, and apologized. "I don't have the strength to go on."

He nodded, knowing she was right.

He glanced up at the surface of the water, which rippled with waves, and listened to the plop of falling nuts, the groan of straining roots, the crunching of pacu.

Aracai considered swimming home to the sea, giving up this sad quest. He could leave the bomb in the mud. He looked up. Swarms of dragonflies were hovering above the lagoon—electric blue, fiery red, leafy green.

Dulce grabbed his bicep and peered into his face. "Promise you will go on," she said. "Do it for your daughter, for all the mer yet to be born."

Aracai imagined their child again, that sad thing thrashing about after birth as she drowned. He imagined her growing cold and stiff, her blue eyes turning to white. She'd died without a name.

He nodded.

He did not want to kill. He had argued for and against it in his mind time and time again, until nothing made sense anymore. His wife wanted him to fight, as had Escalas. That was all that mattered.

Aracai kissed Dulce goodbye, hugged her tightly, and she swam back, as if the idea of swimming downstream invigorated her.

She rose near the surface so that the sun caught her hair. But there was a flash, a violent disturbance.

Dulce gave a blood-curdling shriek and jerked hard, swimming first to the left in a wide arc, then diving, but there was a metal rod stuck in her back, with a heavy cord tied to it. No matter how hard she swam, the cord pulled her upward.

Terror and grief coursed through Aracai. Time slowed. He realized that his wife had been struck by a spear-fisherman, and the harpoon had taken her in the back. She burst up toward the surface, becoming airborne, and he heard a man shout in delight, "Ela é uma grande!" She's a big one!

He dropped the bomb and swam toward her fast. The harpoon had hit near her right lung. He doubted she could survive long.

Blood stained the water. Aracai could taste it. The giant pacu suddenly seemed to spasm, instantly turning their interest from nuts to flesh. They sped up and swam toward Dulce, who spun onto her back and grabbed the line that held the harpoon. Desperately, she jerked. "Help!" she sang.

Aracai raced to her, realizing that this must be some mistake. He'd seen monster fish in other lagoons, and though no humans had been fishing near the poison water, up here where things were more pristine, someone must have mistaken his wife for a meal.

The spear fisherman was pulling the line, trying to drag Dulce to shore. Aracai raced up and grabbed the line, tugged violently, and felt the human go off balance. A man cried out in fear.

Aracai rose to the surface, whistled a shrill warning. He could not speak the human tongue, but he could make his anger known.

He peered up into a sandbox palm, where three young men hunted from a tree fort. One held the fishing line. Another held a spear gun. A third bore an ancient rifle.

"Há outro!" the spearman called. He raised his spear gun and fired hastily. The bolt tore past Aracai's head.

"You've made a mistake," Aracai sang in his own tongue.

But the gunman peered at him with deadly intent, an eager smile playing over his face. He raised his rifle and fired. Heat tore through Aracai's shoulder and he dove for cover, down into the inky darkness beneath the tree roots.

A second shot burst through the water and at first Aracai thought it was aimed at him, but the humans had dragged his wife close to the surface and that bullet took her in the back.

Instantly, she went limp, arms falling wide.

The pacu lunged at her and nipped her flesh.

The humans yanked her into the air. As Aracai gazed up, a pacu hit him hard in the back, testing for a response.

Dulce was hauled out of the water and he could not get to her. He could not even retrieve her body. So he turned and lunged away as fast as he could and grabbed the bomb.

He wanted to rescue his wife, worried that she was still alive, that the men were torturing her. He swam to some ferns that hung over the water and rose, using them for cover.

The three men were young, hardly more than boys. They had pulled Dulce up onto their hunting platform and were admiring her, as if she were a prize catch.

One knelt and fondled her breast while another laughed. The gunman peered into the water, still hunting.

Dulce did not move. She was as dead as their daughter.

Aracai called out in grief, an involuntary wail that echoed over the water. The young man with the spear gun called, "Get out! This is *our* river."

Feral humans. Aracai had always used the term to refer to those without genetic upgrades. Now he saw the truth.

He dove, swimming near the bottom as fast as he could. He realized that he might not have much time. His wound was not bad, but the bleeding would draw predators. So he swam to the Rio Negro and became lost in its black waters.

Now the poisons and pollution worked in his favor. He did not have to face piranhas as he swam. The river was black with soot, as if ash had mixed into the water, and the riverbed was a wasteland.

So he swam, wasting himself, surging upstream, mind numb.

Until the mindlink finally meshed with the nerves in his spinal column and suddenly he understood more than he had thought possible.

He knew the names of the trees that he had seen, the weeds and the frogs. The fish inside his penis was called a *candiru,* and if he had known of its existence, he could have tied a band around his organ to protect it.

He realized that the bomb could not be nuclear. He had been holding it close and no boils had formed from radiation. So he considered Escalas's last words. Always the old mer had spoken with double entendre, always hiding his meaning, trying to force Aracai to think.

The neogods would never have leant their efforts to killing others.

But the old mer had begged a boon from them. A bomb. A heavy bomb, heavier than gold. As he guessed at the bomb's intent, his energy redoubled, and he swam forward with excitement, brimming with wonder.

Escalas had urged him to take responsibility for his own evolution.

So he asked the Heavenly Host: *If a bomb were packed with retroviruses, how heavy would it be?*

The AIs answered: *The viruses would be pure DNA, and have no cell membranes or empty plasma around them. They would weigh more than a kilo per cubic centimeter.*

Heavier than gold.

I am carrying a viral weapon, he realized. *But what will it do?*

He knew Escalas. The old mer had not had a cruel bone in his body. He had always urged Aracai to ponder. Even his last gift had been his greatest possession, the mindlink.

But viruses could be more than weapons. A retrovirus could insert itself among a person's DNA to repair damage, or even to upgrade a person.

Viruses to make us wise, he thought. That is what Escalas would have wanted. And through his mindlink he asked the AIs of Heavenly Host if retroviruses might be used to do that. The answers amazed him. There were viruses that could quadruple the number of neural connections in the human brain, while others could increase the numbers of neurons alone. Those two viruses in and of themselves could quadruple a person's thinking power.

But there were more, the AIs showed him, viruses that could make a man live longer, eradicate diseases, love one another more. Over a hundred thousand upgrades had been developed, and dozens more were coming every day.

As Aracai studied the lists, he saw that Escalas had tagged thousands of such viruses.

Escalas would have wanted all of them. Aracai thought he understood. The bomb would rid the world of feral humans once and for all.

But how valuable would such upgrades be? Human doctors charged huge sums to administer such things. After all, any upgrade could give a man huge advantages.

To his surprise, the AIs already knew: *The bomb you carry is probably worth more than the sum total of all the earth's wealth for the next thousand years.*

Aracai gasped at the thought and wondered what the old mer could have traded for such a boon. But there was nothing in this world that he could have given.

His life, Aracai suspected.

Had the bargain amused the neogods? One amoeba trading its life to help all others?

Perhaps it had amused them. Or perhaps they had recognized the nobility behind the request.

It all made a bit of sense to Aracai now. The GPS on the bomb, its red light. It could only be set off in one location, at Dos Brujas.

But why? He asked the Heavenly Host, but it went silent. Even it did not know all of the answers.

His blood did not call predators, but as Aracai swam he grew weaker. Many times he considered turning around, heading out to sea.

But it is too late to go home, he realized. He was too weak to swim that far. The ache in his muscles multiplied.

I will die no matter what I do.

So Aracai chose to die for a cause, just as a billion other martyrs had chosen to die for their causes over the millennia.

Huzzah! Huzzah for the martyrs, he thought.

If he had lived, the old mer would have revealed his plans to Aracai, he believed. He might even have begged the younger mers to help him. But Escalas had failed.

Eventually Aracai found Dos Brujas on a night where the full moon was setting in the west, glistening on the water and tinged red from the smoke of distant fires. He spotted its dark tower rising from the black waters. A red light at its top was probably meant to warn away aircraft, but it seemed to glare out over the river like a red eye.

There, on either bank, were the factories with their sewage pipes spewing poison.

Aracai felt beyond weary, numb beyond thinking. Adrenaline seemed to carry him this far, but now it was gone and he fumbled to fulfill his mission. He lay gasping, gills flaring, and rose to the surface, floating on his stomach.

Aracai found the button, saw that it now emitted a soft green light. He pressed it for what seemed minutes.

The disk twisted in his hand, began spinning rapidly in the water, then rose above the surface, whirling faster and faster until it began to rise into the air.

He watched it ascend into the night sky. Tiny white LEDs on its bottom became a blurring ring, so that as it rose, it brightened and seemed to take its place among the blazing stars.

Aracai feared a flash of light more blinding than the midday sun and a ball of fire to end his life, but instead, at perhaps three thousand feet, the bomb suddenly exploded with a shrieking whistle, sending its contents spinning and streaming in every direction.

It looked as if a watery shield suddenly spread over the city—as if a mist raced for miles in every direction. The viruses spread wide, a plague of wisdom.

He wondered how many people they would infect, and Heavenly Host answered: *The infection will start here, among the poorest people of South America, and then the viruses will be carried by the winds across Africa and India, until the plagues encompass the earth, putting an end to stupidity and avarice, waging war against war itself.*

There was no thunder, no rumbling of the earth. In wonder Aracai faded from consciousness, now sure of what he had unleashed. *Change,* he thought. *Change for the better. A new world, where men can take responsibility for their own evolution. I am so lucky to have witnessed this. Our children will inherit the stars.*

For a while he floated downstream, gasping, floundering. His eyes dimmed, he struggled to breathe, soot and poisons choking him.

A buzz rang in his ears, and suddenly he heard old Escalas' voice one last time: *Come swim with me.*

He looked up and saw the Milky Way, stars shining like a river of light in the heavens. Escalas was swimming down toward him, with Dulce smiling at his side, and holding her hand was their tiny daughter.

He reached up and, with a firm grip around his wrist, Dulce pulled him free of his wasted flesh.

THE BYSSUS WOMAN
SARA M. HARVEY

When I was a child I knew a myth, a truth, and a secret.

It was lore in our small fishing village that if a woman lost her husband, or chose not to take one, that she had been chosen by the gods to take up spinning and weaving. She would submit herself to the village council and learn to dive, to hold her breath for long minutes at a time. For what we spun wasn't wool or flax or silk, but something far finer and far stranger.

If that woman could not pass her trials, and she lived, she and her children would be asked to leave the village. It was said that anyone who stepped beyond the border would lose their memory of this place and its treasure. When my father died, I wished desperately that my mother would pass so that we might stay. Because I wanted nothing more than to be a spinner, a *spinster*, myself. Plus, this was the only home I had ever known, a place that knew me and loved me, and I didn't think that would be as easy to come by in another village.

So that was our myth, the story of the woman chosen from grief and loneliness to serve the gods with the secret knowledge that lived here and only here, erased from the minds of any who left us.

Here was the truth: we wove a sheer cloth that looked like gold, and although it was rare, priceless, we could not take money for it. We traded it, instead, for protection and alliances and the continued existence of our village. Those that wanted the cloth were powerful: kings and bishops of the faraway church in which we did not believe, foreign men and women who traveled long miles to visit us and see this glorious fabric for themselves. Although enterprising folk had tried, many times, to set up proper mills and create an industry of making the stuff, it never worked out for them. The process was long and painstaking, the results could be inconsistent, and the resources were fickle and sensitive to seasonal change and the demands of over-harvesting.

Clams and mussels lived in the grottoes and reefs just offshore. These creatures produced a slick, milky mucous that, once collected and treated in a series of seaweed and herb baths, turned a luxurious yellow-gold that shone in the sunlight and felt as fine and smooth as silk. From antiquity, it had been named *byssus*. And while the mussels and process were well-known to us villagers, it was a secret to everyone else. They only knew that it came from the sea, somehow. They believed it was magic. And we let them. Because it allowed us to live our lives fishing and farming and spinning and never worrying about war or missionaries or famine. We lived simply, occasionally indulging in a particularly lavish tribute, but overall it was quiet and sheltered and that is all I ever wished for.

My mother, as it turned out, passed her trials with ease. All the people of my village were good swimmers, but I suspected that she maybe had dreams of being a byssus-weaver, too, because she often practiced holding her breath and diving down deep beneath the waves while she and I waited for my father to return with his catch. And she let me practice, too.

Still, when she donned her blue wool shift—with the neckline trimmed with byssus scraps that we refused to let go to waste—and stood before the council, I paced nervously, chewing my fingernails until I had bitten them to the quick. And, as we all walked down to the shore, I moved on to my cuticles and nibbled them until they bled. They stung like angry jellyfish when I hugged her as she rose from the foamy seawater, triumphantly holding out her basket of slime and seaweed.

I helped her prepare the ancient recipes to cook that slime into gold. And when she wove her first square of holy cloth, the eldest matriarch declared that it was the finest she had ever seen. And so my mother's future was secured. And so I had a chance, as fine as a byssus strand, but byssus was strong for all that it seemed impossibly delicate.

She moved in with the rest of the weavers and I was left alone. Not alone, of course, as this was a village of uncles and aunts and cousins of various degrees. I was too old for children's games, but had no interest in the tame and clumsy dalliances of my peers. Although I had spent my life alone and aloof, they invited me anyway. And more than once, I longed to take part, even if just to thank them for it, but my heart was never in it, my body never hungry for it. All I wanted was the cool embrace of the sea and the feeling of the air within my lungs pushing and pressing outward on my ribs and my throat and the sweet sensation of breaking the water's surface and letting go of that rush of breath and sucking in a new one as fast as I could while my heart hammered in my ears. That was my ecstasy.

I knew the marbling of each shell and the shape of each stone in the deep bay. I never once saw the waving strands of mucus, waiting for the cut of the knife. No matter the season, or time of day. Perhaps there was magic afoot, after all. I believed our stories as much as I believed any myth, for these were the things the village was made of, what I was made of, but I did not take them to heart as many others did. But still, the women brought the byssus to the shore and they wove the cloth and traded it for our livelihoods. That much was undeniably real.

In the absence of my mother, my aunt came to visit me. She was a stout woman, my mother's eldest sister. She had deep lines on her face from scowling, but she was always kind to me.

As my body aged into adulthood, the changes that came with it alarmed and saddened me. My voice was not my own, my face grew unrecognizable. My aunt made me broth to soothe my throat and teas to soften the wiry hairs that began to grow in increasing numbers. She showed me how she plucked her own chin free of black whiskers, a thing most of the women in our village faced. She told me that if I could catch the root when I did it, each time the hair would grow back thinner and softer until it stopped coming at all. It would take time, she told me, and would be quite painful, and when I got old they might come back anew. She was bitter that after assiduously plucking her lip and chin her whole life, she was re-growing a veritable garden of coarse, dark hairs.

"But you are different," she said to me. "I can only advise, but I cannot predict."

The broths and teas helped. But I still spent a lot of time plucking and relearning how to speak.

The day my mother returned to our home, it rained. She came in without knocking, but hesitated in the doorway, as if unsure how to proceed.

I hugged her with tears in my eyes and bade her to come in.

"I cannot stay," she said, "but I have brought you a gift."

I unwrapped the parcel she handed me and time stood still. There, folded neatly across my hands was a blue woolen shift, the very color of the sea, with the finest byssus trim I had ever seen. I stared at it, my blood rushing though my ears as if I had just crested the surface after a dive. I could not move. I could not speak. When I finally shook myself free of the spell, my mother was gone and the door was closed as if she had never come through it.

I shimmied out of my dress and put the shift on over my head, feeling the way the wool already clung to my skin, watching the firelight sparkle off the byssus. I imagined the feel of the wet fabric, shrinking to fit me like a second skin, keeping me warm in the depths of the bay as I joined the generations of women before me, collecting the precious excrement with hands I had spent my whole life keeping soft and callous-free.

When the next full moon came, it would be time to face the council.

In the short weeks to come, I made arrangements for the care of our family home. No matter what the outcome, I would not be returning to it. My cousin, newly married to another, farther removed cousin, eagerly took residence and made it her own. She had a knack for the garden, and the goats and cats seemed to really like her, so it put me at ease.

When I left there, I wore nothing but the blue shift that my mother had made for me. I wonder if the wool had scratched her fingers after working exclusively with the smooth, supple byssus.

I approached the gathering house of the village council and, willing my voice to stay steady and strong, announced myself. The men of the council excused themselves and left without meeting my eyes. The women remained, some looking patient, others pained.

Our matriarchal elder barely let me pass through the doorway before she put her hands on me. She shook me by the shoulders and railed about my mother, how stupid, how disrespectful, how bold, how dare she let me think I could do this.

The other women remained silent, although I heard their tears.

With her pocketknife, the elder slit my precious shift down the center and pulled it off of me. Her voice howled like the storm that had drowned my father. She demanded that I look down at myself, behold my own body, and ask how I could dare to come before them as a woman, when I, clearly, was not one.

Although my skin was smooth and hairless, although my shoulders had never become sturdy and square, my chest did not swell and neither did my hips; and at the juncture of my thighs that which I forever tried to hide lay exposed for all to look upon.

My secret, finally bared, battled with the myth and the truth.

That once, long ago, my mother had borne a son, I thought had been forgotten, perhaps misremembered, replaced with the reality of her somewhat odd daughter. But the elder remembered. She blazed with fury at the audacity that I assumed she had not. Here I stood before her, naked and on display, to be judged and deemed unworthy.

The elder took her blade to the long, thick braid of my hair and sheared it free of my head, nicking my scalp as she did so.

"Get out of my sight and go learn to fish. Go learn to be a man and maybe you can stay in our village."

Despite the hot tears that spilled over my cheeks, plucked and scraped until they were smoother than hers, I looked right at her. "No."

I took my shift from the floor and wrapped it around myself. I turned my back on her and walked out through the door. I did not look back as I went down to the dock and took a basket from the pile. I used a bit of rope to tie my shift closed before I dove.

The water closed over my feet and surrounded me in its cold embrace and I found peace. I glided down to the seabed and checked every mollusk. I had somewhere lost my knife so I took a piece of sharp stone to cut with. I searched and searched until my lungs ached.

But maybe, just maybe, the reason I had never seen the slime sweeping like cobwebs through the swish of the tides was because the elder was right. Perhaps my body had doomed me.

I blew out a stream of bubbles and watched them float to the surface as I settled to the silty floor, stirring up sand and scurrying shrimp.

I could not return to the surface. They would be gathered at the dock, now, waiting, ridicule on the lips of some, pity in the eyes of others, but judgment with them all. Because now they all knew.

Let them find my body, I resolved. It never suited me, anyway. Let them say what they like and do as they wish with it. Let it be consumed by the creatures of the sea or the carrion eaters of the land. Let something somewhere find fulfillment with it that I had never known.

Let me remain a part of this place, forever.

I hugged my shift tight around me and thought of my mother, who had erased the name I had been given and gave me another, who taught me to braid and to weave, who treated me like a daughter and never gave my body a second thought. She had always believed in me. She believed in me, still. She would be waiting on the shore, waiting for my success, not my failure.

I would be a disappointment to her for the first time in my life.

I shuddered out a sob and it rose in an ever-shifting blob of air. I wondered if it would carry the sound all the way to the surface, or just break liked any other bubble in the waves.

My vision sparked and shimmered, desperate for breath.

I caught sight of silky strands that looked like seaweed, but pale as moonlight. I swam towards them before even deciding to move. I came within reach of them and saw that they rose from the surface of something large, something that pulsed and lived there in the darkest hollow of the bay.

This thing before me was enormous, like a shark, but soft. Like a jellyfish, but with density and opacity. The fronds of floating mucus undulated in time with what seemed like breathing.

It shifted its great bulk to regard me with round, black eyes, larger than I could put both of my arms around.

This thing…no, this *woman*, for it undeniably thought of itself that way—no, *she* undeniably thought of *herself* this way, and who was I to argue or judge?—this woman greeted me with a gust of bubbles, then drew herself towards me to kiss my lips and breathe cool, fresh air into my lungs.

She seemed, then, almost human, much smaller in magnitude, yet still impressive, and not unlike the sturdy fishwives of our village with her broad brow and prominent nose. Yes, she seemed more like a mermaid from a story than some massive, unknowable beast.

She looked at my shift, billowing open despite the sash. I looked away and she gently drew my face back towards her. She touched the shift, lingering at the byssus trimming the neckline, the cut strands of it hanging loose and twirling in the current.

She touched my unevenly shorn hair, it, too, swaying wildly and loose when it should have been orderly and bound.

She ran her hand over my body, and although it appeared no larger than my own mother's hand, I could feel the touch of it everywhere at once.

I still held the basket, stupidly, numbly. So I showed it to her, hoping she would understand. With my other hand, I ran my fingers through my hair, pantomiming how long it used to be, all the way down to my waist. She repeated my movement and I could see the braid, drifting lazily in the salty water, as if an afterimage following a flash of lightning, before it was gone again. I touched the shift, tugging it closed and smoothing it down, trying to make it look whole and proper once more. I held up the basket again and pointed to one of the swirling masses of streamers that, at this point, seemed to be hovering in the water, attached to nothing.

Woman? she asked without speaking.

And I nodded. "Woman," I replied, in a flurry of bubbles that gleamed and shone.

She regarded me a long moment and then scooped me close to her. I felt her slick flesh, cool to the touch, but warm beneath.

Woman, she agreed and stretched out her arm to bring the shimmering fronds within my reach.

I had lost the stone, too, and despaired of being able to cut free what I needed. But she drew them into a handful with ease and placed them into the basket. With her other hand, she brought forth a bunch of seaweed, the yellow-green kind that grew in a bushy clump and was the main catalyst for the transformation of slime into gold.

I took it, gratefully.

She kissed my forehead and then my lips, filling me with another breath.

I will see you again, soon, byssus-woman.

She then turned me away and gave me a nudge, sending me gliding back in the direction of the shore. I hugged the basket to my chest and kicked my legs, not daring to look back at the creature, the *woman,* that resided there in the depths.

When my head broke the surface of the water, my breath came from me in a shimmering blast like a dolphin's jet, full of water and something that gleamed. I got my feet under me and stood, rising from the bay with my basket filled with promise. My shift hung wide open, the sash gone; I could not be bothered to care. I found my mother's face in the crowd and let her be my beacon of strength. But I did not walk towards her. Instead I came to stand before the council elder. I put the basket down at her feet and stared defiantly into her eyes.

"It isn't for you to judge," I said to her.

She kicked the basket over in her fury, but all it did was prove to the village that it was indeed full of milky strands of byssus-to-be. She screamed her anger and reached out for me, her hands clawed.

But she was stayed by the other councilwomen.

"The goddess has spoken. This young woman knows our secret. She is one of the byssus weavers, now."

My mother made her way to my side, gathered up the fallen fronds of slime and seaweed. She stood beside me, pride in her eyes.

"Welcome, daughter," she said to me and put her arms around me in the fiercest hug I had ever received.

I knew a myth, a truth, and a secret as a child. But not until I became a woman did I learn that they were all three the same thing.

THE SEVEN NIGHTS OF SQUIDMAS

Nicky Drayden

Four standard months. That's how long I've been trapped on this soggy excuse for a planet. The Southern Wades are where the humanoids normally congregate, though this time of year, the cold has driven all but the most freeze-tolerant species to the northern hemisphere. There are just a few of them now, in their thigh-high rubber boots, wading through the icy slush of this half-submerged tavern, fingers flicking to the bartender to continue the endless refills of steaming ale.

"Your play, friend," a Monodorite says to me. His thick, gray skin seems impervious to frigid temps and his legs dangle freely in the icy water below his bar stool.

I fan my circular cards in my hand and look at the last cards played, then at the stack of Ytl'ssca cubes that comprise the current pot. I try to calculate if there's enough there for me to get my tri-fracquer fixed so I can finally get my ship up and running and put this whole botched heist behind me. I raise the ante by a 50 note cube. "I'm in," I say, and play a coral flush to beat his pair of whalebones. "Ytl'ssca!" I say with a smug grin.

"I've never seen such luck," the Monodorite says begrudgingly as I pull in my haul of cubes. "Especially from a beginner. Another hand?"

A quick calculation of my new net worth leaves me slightly over my goal. "No thanks," I say, eager to cash in my winnings. "It's time I got going."

"What about if we raise the stakes? Make things a little more interesting, now that you've got the hang of the game?" The Monodorite opens his massive paw, and reveals a qua'ker's gem—millions of facets gleaming under the cold blue light of the tavern. Not just any qua'ker's gem, I realize as I look closer. The Magnus Qua'ker, the crown jewel of Queen At'Kachua's scepter—the scepter I'd come here to steal. Heh. Someone had gotten to it right before me and apparently had doled out all 85 of the gems. Pity, that. It was such a magnificent scepter, worth much more than the sum of its parts, but to leave here with one of the gems, especially such a significant one, would more than make up for the tedium of sloshing away on this planet, never able to catch a break.

"Sure," I shrug. "Luck is on my side, as you say. But I don't have much of value other than this meager cube stack. Surely that isn't enough of a wager."

"What about that tri-fracquer you were talking about?" the Monodorite asks.

"I told you it doesn't work." I shouldn't have told him anything about it at all.

"Dry tech is rare around these parts. Even a broken one will fetch a fine sum."

"Mmmm..." I say, pretending to consider the risks of the gamble. There is no risk. I look at the cards I'd played on the table. To the untrained eye, they look the same as any Ytl'ssca cards. Probably to the trained eye, too. But they are not like the others. A thin film coats them, a film comprised of my very being, sloughed away and shifted to mimic the face values I need to win. It's not a perfect match, of course. The artwork on the cards is finely detailed, difficult to replicate even for me, but even a shapeshifter's shoddiest work is good enough to fool a half-drunk Monodorite easily. "I suppose I could stick around a little longer."

"All right, Mr...." the Monodorite continues to deal the cards. "What did you say your name was?"

"I didn't," I say, looking at my hand. I keep my face blank, resisting the urge to wince at how truly awful these cards are. No matter. As soon as the game starts, I'll shift them as needed.

The Monodorite plays three wild tentacles. Statistically hard to beat, but no match for the four of a kind I'm about to shift. I will the face values of my cards to morph into four conch shells, but my cells refuse to cooperate. I try again. Nothing.

"Problem, Traleel?" the Monodorite says with a grin. He knows who I am. *What* I am. And he's got some kind of tech that's keeping me from shifting.

"No problem," I say with a puckered smile. "Just an awful hand." I lay my cards face down, as they were dealt to me. It's then that I notice it: a soft glow floating in the water beneath his bar stool. I reach for it, pull it up—a little round fist-sized device that dies the instant it hits air.

"Wet tech," the Monodorite says. "A blubberphaser. Designed to keep lush sharks and other nuisances away from underwater cities, but has the curious effect of disrupting whatever it is your kind do." The Monodorite taps his gray paws together. "Now, I believe you owe me a tri-fracquer."

* * *

I dare not confront the Monodorite, because if he's smart enough to know how to trick me, he's also smart enough to know how to kill me.

Instead, I secretly follow him and my former tri-fracquer through the slushy streets of Southern Wades all the way to a dry-tech exchange in a well-to-do area. I watch the storefront as my tri-fracquer is placed in the glass display, carefully above the waterline. It taunts me there, but tonight I will sneak in and steal it, no problems. I double-check myself, extending my fingers several inches to make sure there are no other blubberphaser devices in my proximity. I'm good.

Just before the store closes, the street water in front of the store bubbles and several conch cars emerge from the depths. Water drips over the iridescent shells. On the side of each is imprinted the seal that I've grown to despise over my time spent here: the seal of the President of Squidadelphia.

Her secret service exits the vehicles before she does, a mass of tentacles so tangled I can't make out how many of them there are. Eventually, when the all-clear is given, the President emerges, tentacles aglitter, suckerflesh perfectly puckered. A jewel of the sea. She enters the shop. Moments later, I see her glittery tentacles touching all over my tri-fracquer. Then it's gone. She leaves the store, parcel wrapped up in a waterproof bubble. She gets back into her conch car and the vehicles submerge into the depths of the underwater city.

No. No. No. This isn't happening. Not when I was so close!

I dive in after them, shifting into the form of a lush shark, the fastest thing in this underwater world that I'm half familiar with. I whip my powerful tail, trying to keep up. It's dark down here, and my senses are muted. I make out the faint light coming from their vehicles, and follow it down, down, down into the depths. Detritus floats past me—scraps of plant life, plankton, small crustaceans. The occasional fish-creature conjured from my nightmares.

Finally, I make out the highlights and shadows of a submerged city. It's beautiful and sprawling and carefully crafted—everything the Southern Wades is not. The buildings are sculpted from bricks of brightly colored coral and rise up at interesting and precarious angles. The streets are wide, but not trodden. Tentacled pedestrians swim above them with grace, others barrel along in conch cars powered by wet tech. There's something festive afoot. Groups of Squidadelphians sing carols about the spirit of the Season, the new chill in the water, the spicy taste of fish egg nog, and about some character named Jolly Saint Tentacleez, who is apparently pulled along by his five giant clams—the lead one with a giant red glowing pearl that lights his way during his undersea trip to visit all of the little squidlets to bring them gifts and joy. I laugh at this. There's no way this Jolly Saint Tentacleez really exists...who in their right mind would go around giving things away when it's much more fun to take?

Perhaps it's some kind of parental ploy, designed to get the squidlets to behave all year long.

The presidential palace is hard to miss. It is the grandest building in all of Squidadelphia. Five coral towers stretch up, the centermost one twice as tall as the rest. I am able to shift into the form of a Squidadelphian, six pair of long sleek tentacles. I've spent so long as a humanoid, it takes me a while to figure out how to maneuver with them all. Once I've got it down, I make my approach. There's a long line of Squidadelphians standing at the palace's gates. I join them, trying my best to fit in, and snag some intelligence while I'm at it.

"Long line," I say to the squid in front of me. She's half-distracted by the two squidlets she's trying to wrangle.

"Tell me about it. We were supposed to get here hours ago. I thought we finally had this one ink trained, but he got too excited and spurted all over everyone on our way here. On our clothes, under our suckerflesh. It was so bad, we all had to go home and change." She sighs a stream of bubbles from her speckled beak. "Part of me wanted to stay home, but we've been to the unveiling of the reef every year since my oldest was born. We just *had* to come back here so we could get tickets."

The squid chats along, telling me how the Presidential Squidmas Reef would soon be chosen to decorate the main foyer of the palace, and that once it was trimmed a few hundred thousand lucky visitors would be allowed inside to view it. But that won't happen for several more days, and I don't have the time or the patience to stick around that long. I can sneak in right now, but first I need a distraction.

I look at the littlest squidlet and his chubby tentacles, face calm and content. I tap his shoulder, get his attention, and start making funny squid faces at him, flailing my arms all about. He laughs and a small spurt of ink slips from him. I crank up my efforts, and finally I get the effect I want, a full release.

"Oh, no! Not again!" the squid mother says, turning around. I can barely see her through the purple fog, which means people can barely see me. I start to shift into an ocean current, invisible to everyone, but once again, my cells will not rearrange themselves.

The palace must be protected by a blubberphaser as well. I sigh as my rubbery squid skin becomes caked with a layer of purple sludge. I need to get my tri-fracquer back. In order to get my tri-fracquer back, I need to get inside, undetected. Once I'm out of the blubberphaser's proximity, I can shift into anything, but it needs to be something that will serve me as is, since, once I've shifted, there's no turning back until I'm back outside the palace. I rub my tentacles together as an idea strikes me.

"Oh, I am so, so sorry," the squid mother says to me again and again, holding her kids with two tentacles and trying to clean me off with the others.

"Tell me more about this Presidential Squidmas Reef—" I say "—and we'll call it even."

* * *

The first night of Squidmas, I sit and wait in the Squidmas Reef lot, looking dull and pitiful to every customer that swims by. Finally, when I hear the sputtering of the Presidential conch cars approaching and the surrounding hubbub, I branch out, becoming the most intricate, colorful, beautiful reef with curious buds that look almost like fingers. They are fingers in fact. I need to ensure that I have the dexterity to retrieve the tri-fracquer in this state. Though I appear to be solid coral, I have prepared my structure to allow me to unfurl myself and walk about, and have also hidden away a pouch large enough to hold the tri-fracquer as I make my speedy escape...speedy for a coral reef, at least. The plan is easy. The President will select me, move me into her home, and, while everyone is asleep, I'll find the tri-fracquer and slip out into the night, off the planet by sunrise.

"This one, this one, this one, mommy!" the President's squidlets call up to my coral branches moments later. Step one of my plan is complete.

* * *

The second night of Squidmas, I sit in the Presidential foyer, frustrated. It took me all night just to get through one wing of the palace and not one sign of the tri-fracquer. The squidlets giggle at me, touch my finger buds, sometimes gently, sometimes not. The staff scolds them, though kindness rims their voices.

"I can't wait to see what Saint Tentacleez brings me!" the little one squeals.

"There's no such thing as Saint Tentacleez," the elder one says, tentacles folded, voice gruff.

"There is, too! You don't know anything," the little one says. She tickles my branches a final time and swims off.

* * *

The third night of Squidmas and still no luck. The squidlets have hung a ridiculous red pearl from my top most branch. I thought the staff would scold them again, but apparently it is meant to be there. That night, before I get ready to shift, the whole first family gathers beneath me in their pajamas. They set a wet tech device in their hearth, and millions of bubbles sweep up through the coral tower at the palace's center. They sing carols and sip mugs of steaming fish egg nog and the scents of the season swirl all around me. The little one is full of delight, swimming all over the place, her excitement unable to be contained. The elder one mopes as he sings, as he sips fish egg nog, as he does everything. By the time they all go off to bed, there is not much time before the morn and the staff starts to stir. My departure must wait yet another day.

* * *

The fourth night of Squidmas takes me to the wing of the family's sleeping quarters. I am very silent, very careful. From down the hallway, I hear the faintest voice coming from one of the rooms. I press a branch to the door and listen.

"Dear Saint Tentacleez," the voice says, and I instantly recognize the squeak of the littlest squidlet. "If you *are* really real, I would really, really, really like a sea unicorn for Squidmas—one with a horn as curly as its little tail. And don't just try to glue a horn on a seahorse, because I *can* tell the difference."

I creep on, checking nooks, checking crannies. I find many things of value—gold, pearls, great wet works of art, but none of them stir the thief in me. My only desire is to get home, and the one thing I need to do that still eludes me.

* * *

The fifth night of Squidmas, I tip-toe through the third wing. I search high and low. The tri-fracquer has to be somewhere. Finally, I see a door, a light coming from beneath. I slip a thin needle through the gap at the bottom and peek inside. I see the president, tentacles a mess, frustration on her face...nothing like the pristine image she projects to the outside world. She's working in an air bubble, constantly splashing herself with cups of water, putting together what seems to be some sort of land vehicle. Glowing at its core is my tri-fracquer. Now functioning, to boot! What luck! The door is locked, but with a simple mechanism that a couple of my buds can crack within seconds. All I have to do is come back once the president has gone to sleep. I rub my coral branches together in anticipation.

Then I hear something. A small gasp of water. I turn.

One of the squidlets stands there, the eldest one with a mohawk of tentacles sticking up from his head, his suckerflesh primed and glittered over like he's about to embark on a hard night of partying. He looks as guilty as I do.

"What are you doing here?" we demand of each other simultaneously.

I have to think quickly. These young creatures seem susceptible to fantastical tales, so I make up one of my own. "You've never heard of a Squidmas Guardian Reef?"

The squidlet shakes his bulbous head.

"Well the Squidmas Guardian Reefs are sent down by Saint Tentacleez to deter little squidlets who sneak about during the Seven Nights of Squidmas when they should be in bed."

The squidlet looks at me like he wants to believe, but he has grown too old for such fantasies. "There's no such thing as Saint Tentacleez. It's just parents bringing the presents. I know that. I'm telling mom!"

"Go ahead. Barge right in there. Ruin the surprise."

"What surprise?"

"She's building a land vehicle for you, but I'm sure if she catches you trying to sneak out of the house this late at night, she might have a change of heart."

"A land vehicle? She really got one for me?"

I nod my reef branches, but I'm sure the gesture is lost in translation. "Go right in there, if you want, and ruin the whole of Squidmas for everyone."

The squidlet crosses several sets of arms, frustrated with me, but the gleam of childish wonder still rims his eyes. "Okay," he burbles. "I'll keep your secret, if you keep mine."

* * *

The sixth night of Squidmas, my plans get derailed. The family begins to hang ornament after ornament from my coral branches, each more gaudy and awful than the last. There are gilded seahorses, iridescent clams, and glass starfish on hooks. Long strands of purple and silver pearls go round and round me, so many times I couldn't move if I wanted.

The eldest squidlet shoots me funny looks as he strings seaweed garland, overly rough with my branches, until I swat him once on the cheek. He laughs at this, and continues to sing carols. There is a difference in his voice this time. There is real joy.

When they are done, an onslaught of visitors streams in, oooohhing and aaahhing. Even if I could shake myself loose of these adornments, I have no privacy to do so. They file in, what seems like every squid in the city, all day and all night. Posing next to me. Taking pictures with their wet tech devices. The little ones go on and on about what Saint Tentacleez is going to bring them this year, and how good they've been.

The president and her squidlets are the last to take their photo in front of me that night.

"Saint Tentacleez is going to bring me a sea unicorn for Squidmas," the little one blurts out.

"There's no such thing as—"

"We'reptph!" the president says. "Not in front of your sister!"

"I was going to say there's no such thing as *sea unicorns*, mother."

"Mommy! Tell We'reptph Saint Tentacleez is going to bring me a real sea unicorn, just like I asked him for!"

"Your brother is right about that, little Nn'astlg. Sea unicorns are just made up creatures. Saint Tentacleez can't bring you a live one, but perhaps he'll have a stuffed animal one for you in his clam net."

"That's not the same," little Nn'astlg says with a pout. "And anyway, how is he going to even get to our bubble stack? Tey'stsl's brother told me that blubberphasers keep giant clams away too, so there's no way Saint Tentacleez could even come to our palace."

The president pulls her tentacles in on themselves until she's shrunk down to little Nn'astlg's level. "What if we turn the blubberphasers off for just this night?"

Little Nn'astlg nods.

"Saint Tentacleez loves to give to little squidlets like you, freely, with all his heart. But there are some things he just can't do. Like bring animals that don't really exist. But he will do everything he can to make your Squidmas joyful. Do you understand?"

Little Nn'astlg nods again, and her mother strokes her cheek with a tentacle.

* * *

Twas the night before Squidmas and all through the palace
I'm the one creature stirring, my heart full of malice.
I tear pearls from my limbs with limitless zeal,
In hopes that a tri-fracquer soon I will steal.
Plucking the core from the vehicle's socket,
I wrap it up tight in my waterproof pocket.
Up the bubblestack I go, full of not give-a-damns
When from high up above comes the clatter of clams.
I find myself trapped in this wet bubblespace,
 The squiggle of tentacles asquirm on my face.
Saint Tentacleez, I think. What horrible timing.
A long string of curses puts an end to my rhyming…

We both tumble down and hit the bottom of the bubblestack with a graceless thud. Presents fly everywhere. Tentacles flail. The whole scene is a wreck.

Saint Tentacleez looks all around. It doesn't take him long to figure out what's going on here.

"What did you do?" he asks me. "I work so hard at bringing joy, and here you are stealing it?"

"I'm only taking what belongs to me," I say, not about to be put in my place by a figment of a child's imagination.

I hear shouts from secret service coming near. They're definitely not figments and will be here soon. There's only one thing to do. I shift. They arrive seconds later, the first family close on their heels.

"Saint Tentacleez!" little Nn'astlg says to the old jolly sack of squid jelly, her mother having to hold her back. Then her eyes meet mine. "Saint Tentacleezes?"

"He's an imposter!" Saint Tentacleez screams.

"No, he's the imposter!" I say back.

"They're both imposters," says one of the secret service squid, the one holding the large piece of wet tech that looks suspiciously like a gun. "There's no such thing as Saint Tentacleez. We'll throw them both to the sharks."

"Mama!" little Nn'astlg says. "Tell them they're wrong. Saint Tentacleez really does exist!"

"Honey, the secret service is here to protect us, and we have to let them do what they think best."

Little Nn'astlg shakes her head. "No, Mama! I can prove he's real. At least one of them. The real Saint Tentacleez will know what I asked for for Squidmas."

The secret service converges on us. Tentacles tighten around me.

"Wait!" the president says. "I'll give them a chance. Tell me what my daughter wants for Squidmas."

Saint Tentacleez smiles. "Of course." He pulls out a long list, then runs a tentacle down it. While he's busy checking it twice, I shift a few cells, and pull from behind me a baby sea unicorn that fits right in my tentacled palm.

Little Nn'astlg's shrill goes supersonic, bubbles breaking violently from her beak. Tentacles flail in every direction, until finally she calms herself enough to take the delicate creature from me. "I love it! I love it! I love it!" she says. She touches its curly horn, then strokes its prickly back. I make it curl its tail around the tip of her tentacle and coo.

Then she does something I don't expect. She slips free of her mother's stunned grip and wraps her tentacles around me in a tight hug. "Thank you, Saint Tentacleez. You've given me the best gift ever."

Her embrace continues to warm me long after she lets go. Seeing the pure joy on her little squid face has done something to me. And I'm not talking the metaphorical heart growing two sizes sort of crap. The sea unicorn. I can no longer feel it as a part of my being. I can no longer manipulate it. It swims about freely, whinnying and nuzzling Little Nn'astlg's cheek. Then the little creature looks at me and smiles like it knows my secret, too, and is more than happy to keep it.

I glance over at the land vehicle, expecting We'reptph to be there fussing over his new toy, wondering why he can't get it to start, but he's not there. Instead, he stands in the rubble of Squidmas Reef decorations I'd shed, holding the big red pearl above his head, other tentacles splayed to resemble a reef.

He begins singing a Squidmas carol, and the family and I join in.

Beyond the harmony of our voices, I hear the real Saint Tentacleez getting dragged off by the Secret Service, threatening to add us all to his naughty list if we don't let him go this instant. I tune him out and try not to think about how his Squidmas day will soon be ending.

As the first family rounds into a second verse, it is time to take my leave. It is not all I take, either. While no one is looking, two dozen gold and pearl ornaments find their way into my waterproof pocket. There's enough room for them in there now. My tri-fracquer once again sits snugly in the land vehicle's socket, ready to roll.

It's a fair trade, by my calculations. I'm sure I'll be able to find a suitable replacement when the shops reopen tomorrow morning, but until then, what's one more night of Squidmas anyway?

I slip up the bubblestack, my heart full of glee
And find five giant clams there, waiting for me.
I spring to my sleigh, and pull the reins tight.
"Merry Squidmas to all, and to all a good night!"

ABOUT THE AUTHORS

F. BRETT COX's fiction, poetry, essays, and reviews have appeared in numerous magazines and anthologies. With Andy Duncan, he co-edited the anthology Crossroads: Tales of the Southern Literary Fantastic (Tor, 2004). He is a member of the Cambridge SF Writers Workshop and serves on the Shirley Jackson Award Board of Directors. A native of North Carolina, Brett is Professor of English at Norwich University and lives in Vermont with his wife, playwright Jeanne Beckwith. Facebook: https://www.facebook.com/brett.cox.3956

NICKY DRAYDEN is a Systems Analyst who dabbles in prose when she's not buried in code. She resides in Austin, Texas, where being weird is highly encouraged, if not required. Her debut novel THE PREY OF GODS is forth-coming from Harper Voyager this summer, set in a futuristic South Africa brimming with demigods, robots, and hallucinogenic hijinks. See more of her work at http://www.nickydrayden.com or catch her on twitter @nickydrayden.

DAVID FARLAND is an award-winning, New York Times bestseller with dozens of novels to his credit. He has written for *Star Wars* and the *Mummy*, but is best know for his "Runelords" fantasy series. Dave serves as the lead judge for the world's largest science fiction and fantasy writing contest, and has helped numerous writers go on to start their own careers. You can learn more about him or contact him at www.mystorydoctor.com.

Nebula Award winner **ESTHER FRIESNER** is the author of over 40 novels and more than 200 short stories. She is also the creator/editor of the Chicks in Chainmail series (Baen Books). The sixth, Chicks and Balances, appeared in July 2015. Deception's Pawn, latest in her popular Princesses of Myth YA series (Random House), was published in April 2015. Esther is married, a mother of two, grandmother of one, harbors cats, and lives in Connecticut. There is no truth to the rumor that her family motto is "Oooooh, SHINY!"

SARA M. HARVEY lives and writes fantasy and horror in (and sometimes about) Nashville, TN. She is also a costume historian, theatrical costume designer, and art history and fashion teacher. She has three spoiled rotten dogs, one awesome daughter, and one feisty son; her husband falls somewhere in between. Sara's fiction has appeared in various anthologies such as *Steam-Powered: Lesbian Steampunk Stories*, *Upside Down: Inverted Tropes in Storytelling*, and *Dark Futures*. Her novel-length fiction includes *A Year and a Day* (available as ebook only), *Seven Times a Woman*, *Music City,* and *The Blood of Angels* trilogy. She tweets @saraphina_marie, wastes too much time on facebook.com/saramharvey, and needs to update her website saramharvey.com

SUSAN JETT lives far from San Francisco in an old farmhouse filled with books where she and her husband both write stories and try to civilize a small human. She's never woken a slumbering cephalopodic alien. Sometimes she says stuff online:
www.susanjett.com and @JettSusan

J.C. KOCH is scared by horror stories but writes them anyway. Her stories have appeared in Arkham Tales, Necrotic Tissue, and Penumbra e-zines, and a variety of excellent anthologies, including The Madness of Cthulhu Vol. 1 and Out of Tune II. J.C. also likes to do scary things like pay attention to politics, keep up with the Kardashians, and play the stock market. However, she tends to stay hidden under the bed, letting more of the terrors of the mind bleed onto the page, metaphorically and literally. Reach J.C. (aka Gini Koch) at Going Bump in the Night
(http://www.ginikoch.com/jkbookstore.htm).

BILL KTE'PI has been publishing short stories since 1991, and is the author of two novels, LOW COUNTRY and FRANKIE TEARDROP. He can be found online at ktepi.com.

JEFFREY J. MARIOTTE is the award-winning author of more than sixty novels, including thrillers *Empty Rooms* and *The Devil's Bait*, supernatural thrillers *Season of the Wolf, Missing White Girl, River Runs Red*, and *Cold Black Hearts*, horror epic *The Slab*, the *Dark Vengeance* teen horror quartet, and others. With partner and wife Marsheila Rockwell, he wrote the science fiction/horror/thriller *7 SYKOS*, and has published numerous shorter works. He also writes comics, including the long-running horror/Western series *Desperadoes* and original graphic novels *Zombie Cop* and *Fade to Black*. He has worked in virtually every aspect of the book business, and is currently the division chief of Visionary Books.

MISTY MASSEY is the author of Mad Kestrel, Kestrel's Voyages and the upcoming Kestrel's Dance, and co-edited The Weird Wild West and Lawless Lands: Tales From The Weird Frontier. Misty is a founding member of Magical Words. When she isn't writing, she studies and performs Middle Eastern dance. She's a sucker for good sushi, African coffee, and blackstrap rum (to nourish her dark heart!). Find her at mistymassey.com, Facebook, Twitter and Dreamwidth.

SEANAN MCGUIRE lives and works in the Pacific Northwest, where she attempts to keep her massive blue cats from eating people. She writes a lot of things, because otherwise she stops sleeping. Sleep is good. She is the author of quite a lot of books, and takes quite a lot of naps. Keep up with her on Twitter at @seananmcguire or at www.seananmcguire.com.

When **WENDY NIKEL** isn't traveling in time or space, she enjoys a quiet life near Utah's Wasatch Mountains. She has a degree in elementary education, a fondness for road trips, and a terrible habit of forgetting where she's left her cup of tea. Her short fiction has been published by *Fantastic Stories of the Imagination*, *Daily Science Fiction*, *Nature: Futures*, and various other anthologies and e-zines. For more info, visit wendynikel.com.

JODY LYNN NYE lists her main career activity as "spoiling cats." She lives near Chicago with her current cat, Jeremy, and her husband, Bill. She has published more than 45 books, including collaborations with Anne McCaffrey and Robert Asprin, and over 160 short stories. Her latest books are Rhythm of the Imperium (Baen), Moon Beam (with Travis S. Taylor, Baen), and Myth-Fits (Ace). She also teaches the annual DragonCon Two-Day Writers Workshop.
Visit her at www.jodylynnnye.com,
on Facebook or Twitter @JodyLynnNye.

JENNA RHODES is the fantasy writing pen name used by myself, Rhondi Vilott Salsitz. I also write in other genres and for different age groups. My books have been translated in French, Spanish, Russian and Italian. In May 2017, THE QUEEN OF STORM AND SHADOW was released by

DAW Books, completing my Elven Ways series written as Jenna Rhodes. Learn more at www.rhondiann.com.

MICHAEL ROBERTSON manages projects as his day job, and fits writing fiction around that. And then he also does other things besides just those two. Watching SNL reruns, playing Zelda, eating pizza, etc. But those aren't relevant to this situation. Born and raised in New York City, he lives in Maine now, where the lack of tall buildings leaves him constantly exposed to avian predators. Or that's how he feels, anyway. He can be found on twitter as @michaels2cents, and his web site is mrobertson.com.

Multiple Scribe and Rhysling Award nominee **MARSHEILA (MARCY) ROCKWELL** is the author of twelve books to date, the most recent being a novel based on the popular video game Mafia III (written with husband/writing partner Jeffrey J. Mariotte). Her work also includes the acclaimed H/SF novel *7 SYKOS* (w/Mariotte); a Xena: Warrior Princess trilogy (w/Mariotte); *The Shard Axe* series, the only official novels for the global MMORPG, Dungeons & Dragons Online; two collections; dozens of short stories and poems; and multiple articles on writing and the writing process. Find out more here: http://www.marsheilarockwell.com/.

A. MERC RUSTAD is a queer non-binary writer who lives in the Minnesota. Favorite things include: robots, dinosaurs, and monsters. Their stories have appeared in Lightspeed, Fireside, Apex, Uncanny, Shimmer, and other fine venues. Merc likes to play video games, watch movies, read comics, and wear awesome hats. You can find Merc on Twitter @Merc_Rustad, Patreon (https://www.patreon.com/mercrustad) or their website: http://amercrustad.com. Their debut short story collection, SO YOU WANT TO BE A ROBOT, is available from Lethe Press (May 2017).

JAMES VAN PELT is a part-time high school English teacher and full-time writer in western Colorado. He's been a finalist for a Nebula Award and been reprinted in many year's best collections. His first Young Adult novel, *Pandora's Gun,* was released from Fairwood Press in August of 2015. James blogs at http://www.jamesvanpelt.com and he can be found on Facebook.

ABOUT THE EDITORS

S.C. BUTLER is a writer living in New Hampshire with his wife and son. He is the author of the Stoneways trilogy: Reiffen's Choice, Queen Ferris, and The Magicians' Daughter, published by Tor Books; and a contributor of short stories to several anthologies and magazines. Submerged is his editorial debut.

* * *

JOSHUA PALMATIER is a fantasy author with a PhD in mathematics. He currently teaches at SUNY Oneonta in upstate New York, while writing in his "spare" time, editing anthologies, and founding the anthology-producing small press Zombies Need Brains LLC. His most recent fantasy novel *Reaping the Aurora* (August 2017) continues a new fantasy series begun in *Shattering the Ley* and *Threading the Needle*, although you can also find his "Throne of Amenkor" series and the "Well of Sorrows" series on the shelves. He is currently hard at work writing his next novel and designing the kickstarter for the next Zombies Need Brains anthology project. You can find out more at www.joshuapalmatier.com or at the small press' site www.zombiesneedbrains.com. Or follow him on Twitter as @bentateauthor or @ZNBLLC.

ACKNOWLEDGMENTS

This anthology would not have been possible without the tremendous support of those who pledged during the Kickstarter. Everyone who contributed not only helped create this anthology, they also helped solidify the foundation of the small press Zombies Need Brains LLC, which I hope will be bringing SF&F themed anthologies to the reading public for years to come...as well as perhaps some select novels by leading authors, eventually. I want to thank each and every one of them for helping to bring this small dream into reality. Thank you, my zombie horde.

The Zombie Horde: Asha Bardon, Simon Dick, Andrew Wilson, Sarah Cornell, J.R. Murdock, Kimberly Lloyd, Bruno Girin, Sharon Wood, Kari Maaren, Heidi Cykana, Nancy Lambert, Vicki Greer, Ash Marten, Diana Castillo, Brian Quirt, David A. Holden, Gabriel Sinclair, Jason M Hough, David Rippere, Kerry Ebanks, Stephanie Cranford, Stephen Goodrow, Kimba Wilson, Jakub Narębski, Gia B., Tina Black, Christina Roberts, Erin Kenny, Ryan Poindexter, Pierre Gauthier, Phil Olynyk, Scott Drummond, Patrick & Sarah Pilgrim, Alexander Gideon, Carolyn Petersen, Elizabeth Belden Handler, April Steenburgh, Aurora N., Marissa Lingen, Veronica, Millie Calistri-Yeh, Jean Marie Ward, Stephanie Cheshire, Christine Swendseid, Fred Herman, Sidney Whitaker, Teresa Carrigan, Jen Edwards, Fred and Mimi Bailey, Cyn Wise, Brenda Moon, Kristin Evenson Hirst, Juli, Jeffery Lawler, Andrew Kinstetter, Petter Wäss, Duncan and Andrea Rittschof, Nick W., Anders M. Ytterdahl, Michael Fedrowitz, Andy M., Susan Carlson, Cate Crowley, Kelly Crowell, Kerry aka Trouble, John Idlor, Claire Sims, Tibs, Steven desJardins, Sheryl R. Hayes, Anna Rudholm, Jake Woodworth, Chuck Hickson, Jill Chinchar, Andrija Popovic, David Bruns, Elyse M Grasso, RKBookman, Tamara Michelle Slaten, Miranda Floyd, Becky Allyn Johnson, dbschlosser, Samuel Kohner, Carol J. Guess, shadow cat, Patti Short, Don Larson, Zoe, Jenny Barber, Michele Hall, Jim and Darla Nault-Tait, Peter Donald, Mandy Stein, Shawna Jacques, M. E. Gibbs, Scott Raun, Chad Bowden, Mr. And Mrs. Smooth, Rachel Stuart, Sarah Brand,

Michele Fry, Lauowolf, Eleanor Russell, Elise Power, Susan Oke, Michele Dainiak, Elizabeth Inglee-Richards, Cathy Green, Debra Stewart, Douglas Park, Kerri Regan, ANDREW AHN, David Hill, Stephen Ballentine, William Hughes, Atthis Arts LLC, Dina S Willner, Ashley R. Morton, James Conason, Jennifer McGaffey, E. Smith, Katherine Malloy, Lace, Leslie Gawne, Sidsel N. Pedersen, pophyn, Elaine (Lainey) Rothman, Lark Cunningham, Helen Cameron, Sachin Suchak, Niall Gordon, Robby Thrasher, Lennhoff Family, Chris Matosky, Jules Jones, Laura Sheana Taylor, Patrick Thomas, Fen Eatough, Jennifer Berk, Jaq Greenspon, Sontaran Empire, Kevin Winter, Marty Poling Tool, Peter Hansen, Cindy Cripps-Prawak, Alan and Morva, Kyrielle, Diana Ramos, SusanB, Matthew Markland, David Quist, Stephanie Lucas, Erin M. Evans, Tony Anjo, Keith Jones, Colleen R. Cahill, Pulp Literature Press, Steven Saus, Cheri Kannarr, Catherine Sharp, Gary Phillips, Tindra Tieren, Gina & Jon Freed, Adora Hoose, Caryn Cameron, Todd V. Ehrenfels, Debbie Matsuura, Rachel Blackman, Jörg Tremmel, Pat Knuth, Simon Niklasson, Yoshio Kobayashi, Yankton Robins, Ferd Burfle, Carol Mammano, Karen Laage, Michael Bernardi, Mark Carter, Andrew Hatchell, Annie Mosity, Chris 'Warcabbit' Hare, Morgan S. Brilliant, Chrissie & Jake Palmatier, Vespry family, Harvey Brinda, Brendan Lonehawk, Sheryl Ehrlich, Tom P. Powers, E.G. Languzzi, Robert Killheffer, Andreas Gustafsson, Thea Maia, Kai Herbertz, A.K. Skelding, Mervi Mustonen, Ed Ellis, Alisha Henri, Merav Hoffman, Gavran, Chris Gerrib, Keith Bissett, Brenda Rezk, Dave Hermann, Richard P Bissmire, Jessica Reid, Jerel D Heritage, Yes, Robin Yang, Pat Hayes, Keith Setzer, Elizabeth Ann Scarborough, Deborah Fishburn, Colette Reap, Revek, Eagle Archambeault, Tory Shade, Katrina Allis, David Rowe, Ivan Donati, KixieKat, Sharon E. Altmann, Rafe Brox, Molly Elizabeth Atkins, Linden Vimislik, Catherine Gross-Colten, Henry W Schubert, Deborah Blake, Julie Hendershott Kovac, Jaime O. Mayer, Alysia Murphy, JE Chase, Karen Grennan, Peter T, Rick D, Cynthia Porter, Tahmi DeSchepper, Anne M. Rindfliesch, Holland Dougherty, David Medinnus, Clara Strzalkowski, Eduard Lukhmanov, Melme, Cheryl Preyer, Gary Clark, Rachel Sasseen, Kathryn L. Whitlock, Annette Agostini, Sarah Liberman, Svend Andersen, Kristi Chadwick, Pam Blome, Betty Law Morgan, Hisham El-Far, Kathy Holzapfel, Jen B, Sofie Bird, Mark Kiraly, Mary Alice Wuerz, Keith West, Future Potentate of the Solar System, Sally Novak Janin, Mary Jeh, Steven Mentzel, S. Worthen, Hannah Maxwell, Curtis Frye, David Drew, Paul Bulmer, Rolf Laun, Jesse Klein, Shel Kennon, Cathy Schwartz, Christina Stiles, Ross Hathaway, Tammy Greco, Christine Ethier, Bruce Shipman, Tibicina, Michelle Carlson, Missy Katano, Donna Gaudet, Danielle Ackley-McPhail, Jenn Whitworth, Jessica K. Meade, Leah Webber, Chris Barili, Tina Connell, Janka Hobbs, Ian Chung, Rissa Lyn, Jonathan S Chance, Gretchen,

Cheryl Losinger, Brenda Cooper, Corey T., Anonymous Reader, ARNSProprietor, Thomas Santilli, Heather Kelly, Nancy Barber, Selwyn, filkferengi, Ron Currens, Lily Connors, Melissa Shumake, Charlie Russel, Jason Palmatier, David Zurek, Connor Bliss, Tomas Burgos-Caez, Natasha A., John Senn, Nancy M. Tice, Andy Funk from Atlanta, Karen Dubois, Nesa Sivagnanam, Paul McNamee, Robert Early, John Green, Echo Mae, Deena Cates, nobe, Janet Oblinger, Jen Woods, Julia Haynie, Andy Miller, Dr.Deb, Julie Pitzel, John Sturkie, Michael Kahan, Jake Parrick, Ronnie J Darling, Jen1701D, Amelia Smith, Samuel Aronoff, Max Kaehn, Ron Hogan, Patricia van Ooy, Kelly J Cooper, Mollie Bowers, Alexander Smith, CGJulian, Leshia-Aimée Doucet, Andrew and Kate Barton, David Eggerschwiler, Ian Harvey, Amanda Nixon, Mark Newman, Rachel Conner-Maling, Mark Gerrits, Smashingsuns, D-Rock, Simba, Hero, and Nahla, Nathan Turner, Lauren E. Mitchell, Maria Lima, Anne Burner, Orla, Lisa Kruse, Colleen Harkins, Tina M Noe Good, Bill and Laura Pearson, Philip Barkow, Sandy, @lenoxartist, Steven Halter, Dan & Chris Brewer, Elaine Tindill-Rohr, Ty wilda, Kaitlin Thorsen, Heather Fagan, Jeremy Brett, Maureen Brooks, Cherie Livingston, Julie Benda, Tris Lawrence, Michelle Palmer, Rosanne Girton, Evergreen Lee, Kate Larking, Jaymie Larkey Maham, Margaret St. John, Kelly Melnyk, Carolyn Mackriell, Jena Marie Klees, Emily Weed Baisch, Freya Jackson, Paul Gunther, Tristan Smith, Karen H, Annastasia (medicinalink) Gallaher, Kathryn A Patterson, R.T. Bryson, Galena Ostipow, Jeremy Audet, K. Hodghead, Phillip Spencer, Jen Bishop, Hedrigall, Cathy Brown, K. McLeod, Jay Barnson, Kathy Bond, Megan Hungerford, Tony F, Amy Streifel, Noah Bast, Ellie, SwordFire, Gary Ehrlich, ChanieB, V. Hartman DiSanto, Holly Daugherty, Kimberly M. Lowe, Barbara Hasebe, RJ Seymour, Erik T Johnson, Patrick Osbaldeston, Anthony R. Cardno, Russell Martens, Jacob Carson, Andy Clayman, Shelly Jones, Elizabeth Kite, Bill Sykes, Erin Penn, Janito Vaqueiro Ferreira Filho, John/Susan Husisian, Aurelia McDonald, Keith E. Hartman, Gustaf B., Ilene Tsuruoka, Linda Pierce, Wolf SilverOak, Gnondpom, Rebecca M, Lucas Santiago, Crazy Lady Used Books & Emporium, Samuel Lubell, Theresa Glover, Annaliese Smith, Bill Emerson, Liz Wyatt, Abi Scott, Cheryl, Chris Fielding, R Kirkpatrick, Jonathan Adams, Stephen Kissinger, Iain Riley, Robert Parks, Erin Kowalski, Michael Cieslak, Mini Lizard, Kitty Likes, Krystina Harrington, R. Hunter, C.N.Rowen, Rachel "Nausicaa" Tougas, Terry D. England, Judith Mortimore, Daria Fox, Bill McGeachin, RBC, Pat Connelly, Zion Russell, Kevin Niemczyk, C. Liang, anne m gibson, David J Fortier, Justin P. Miller, C. Lennox, Pete Hollmer, Sue Shelly, Nellie, Tammy Graves, Kristy K, Aaron R, Matthew Walker, K.G. Anderson, Vancano Smith, Carina Erk, Lauren Wallace, Laura F., Melissa Burkart, Dino Hicks, J. I. Rogers, Gabe Krabbe, Judy Bemis, Dina Barron, Troy

Bucher, Margaret S. McGraw, Kathi Schreiber, Carla Hollar, Lyn Godfrey, Kimberly H., Marc D. Long, Donaithnen, Lisa Deutsch Harrigan (Auntie M), Axisor, Gai LaMarche, Cliff Winnig, Janet Armentani, Danny Neimeyer, Belkis Marcillo, Ian Monroe, Lynn Kramer, Crystal Sarakas, Pamela Lunsford, J.P. Goodwin, Wendy Kitchens, Michael Grey, Rhel ná DecVandé, Terri Oda, Judith Bienvenu, Heather & Zachary Jones, Victoria L Sullivan, Jamie FitzGerald,

www.ingramcontent.com/pod-product-compliance
Lightning Source LLC
Chambersburg PA
CBHW031223260626
47169CB00007B/2166